SPLIT TICKET

★ ★ ★

H. L. RICHARDSON

WORD PUBLISHING
Dallas·London·Vancouver·Melbourne

Published in association with the literary agency of Alive Communications, P. O. Box 49068, Colorado Springs, Colorado, 80949.

Library of Congress Cataloging-in-Publication Data:
Richardson, H. L., 1927-
    Split ticket / by H. L. Richardson.
        p.   cm.
    ISBN 0-8499-3933-X
    I. Title.
PS3568.I3175S67   1996
813'.54—dc20

95-53353
CIP

Printed in the United States of America
6 7 8 9 RRD 9 8 7 6 5 4 3 2 1

To the sixth-generation Californians
who call us "Omie" and "Poppa."

Only in California! With just a little bit of hanky-panky, all that is written in these pages could really happen, given the election laws of the Golden State. Don't laugh too loudly . . . your state could be next!

ONE

★ ★ ★

Nadine Stewart impatiently tapped several perfectly polished pink nails on the heavy glass door of the office building, trying to get the attention of the security guard. He appeared to be in deep concentration, closely watching the bank of television monitors which covered every floor in Stewart Towers. "He's either an excellent watchman or he's fast asleep," Nadine mumbled, revealing her impatience.

Nadine was justifiably nervous. Downtown Los Angeles at eleven o'clock on a Thursday night amid drizzling March rain was no place for a lady alone—especially one dressed to the nines. Shivering, she looked up and down the deserted boulevard and pulled the sable jacket tightly about her. The sequined evening dress she'd chosen to attend the Crippled Children's Benefit offered little protection from the cold. When she noticed two dark shapes weaving across the street, stumbling in her direction, she grabbed the car keys from her purse and rapped them hard on the glass.

The guard jerked to attention in a manner that told Nadine he had been dozing. Cautiously, he loosened the gun in his holster as he approached the main entrance.

His eyes widened when he recognized her and hurriedly unlocked the doors. "Mrs. Stewart! What are *you* doing out on a miserable night like this?"

Nadine quickly stepped inside, vaguely remembering the guard's face but not his name. "Thank you. Whew, it's freezing out there! I promised my husband I'd pick up some company briefs for him, on my way home." Smiling warmly at the elderly gentleman, she said, "Nice to see you again."

He blushed. Nadine Stewart was a beautiful, elegant woman and her friendly greeting pleased him a great deal.

"Would you like me to accompany you upstairs?"

"No. That won't be necessary." She lightheartedly replied, "I'll just be a minute." With a cordial wave of her hand, Nadine hastened to the elevators, entered the express lift, and pushed the button for the top floor, where Stewart and Associates executive suites were located.

Leaning back against the elevator's mirrored interior, she smiled prettily and studied her reflection. "Nadine Stewart, your husband's going to kill you—but you can handle it, can't you?"

Nadine opened her black Hermes handbag as she stepped into the reception area, and hurried across the plush carpet to the hallway. She removed the documents from her purse as she slipped into the luxurious office of the firm's chief accountant.

Struggling to calm her anxiety after fruitlessly searching through the desk and file cabinets, she caught sight of a credenza in the darkened corner of the room. Nadine held her breath as she pulled open the cabinet door, then inhaled deeply upon finding the neatly boxed stamping device—the notary's seal.

In less than a minute, she'd impressed and stamped the official document, moistened and sealed the manila envelope, and was on her way.

★　★　★

SOMETHING WAS UP; Nadine was being exceptionally sweet . . . much too agreeable for a Sunday afternoon. Doug Stewart had been stretched out on the leather sofa watching the Houston Rockets play the Boston Celtics for better than two hours. Nadine had said nothing about the noise, the crushed Coke cans, or the remnants of a bag of Fritos strewn on the coffee table. Usually, by now, she had discovered something needing instant repair about the house, which she inevitably remembered during the last half of every game.

"Douglas, have you fixed that dripping faucet in the upstairs bathroom?"

"Sweetheart, did you remember to patch the fence behind the flower bed?"

"Honey, we really have to do something about your boxes of hunting gear in the garage. I can barely park my car!"

Occasionally, it would be something even more dramatic. "Doug, come quick—there's a man-eating wasp in the kitchen!"

Her husband's answer was always the same. "All right, honey, I'll get to it right after the game."

Nadine was definitely not a sports fan. Watching any athletic event was a massive waste of precious time to his hyperactive wife. She was annoyed by basketball, bored with baseball, and especially intolerant of football—a sport reserved for her special contempt. Football season was her least favorite time of year. Nadine hated all sports with equal intensity, especially during the month of October.

During election years, October meant that November was only a month away and there were plenty of fall sports to capture Doug's attention. Baseball had its World Series, football was in full swing, and basketball pre-season games were just beginning. October Sundays were a sports bonanza, with Doug joyfully flipping from one television channel to another. To make matters worse, it was also the heart of hunting season, adding yet another distraction to what his wife believed was every American male's real autumnal responsibility . . . going door-to-door, handing out campaign literature for conservative candidates.

Nadine's anti-sports sentiments ran high. "How any red-blooded man can watch sports when they could be working at campaign

3

headquarters for a good conservative Republican is beyond me!" Her idea of enjoyable Sunday TV was watching "Meet the Press" and cursing the liberal bias of Sam Donaldson.

Doug accepted the fact that his vivacious wife was a rock-rib conservative who had little time for any endeavor that didn't relate to church, their three children, politics, or business. As past president and current membership chairman of PRISS—the Pasadena Republican Independent Study Society—she had little patience for anything that had a ball in it—round, oblong, or otherwise.

On the other hand, Douglas Wallace Stewart wouldn't think of watching anything that didn't have a ball in it. He, like his wife, believed the news media was boringly biased and that most evening television represented the warped imagination of some Hollywood thirty-five-year-old with raging hormones.

Doug liked sports; it was alive with real people, not the figment of some writer's fertile fantasy. Athletic events showcased energetic human beings giving their competitive best. Doug had been a jock in both high school and college, never attaining stardom, but always having just enough ability to make the team. "No blue ribbons on the wall or trophies on the mantle, but plenty of memorable splinters in the butt," he humorously remarked to fellow jocks.

Doug could get emotionally worked up during a well-played game, then forget about the outcome as soon as it was over, except when a Los Angeles team was involved. He was a southern California loyalist—an avid supporter of the Dodgers, the Kings, the Clippers, and the USC Trojans. Sometimes he even rooted for UCLA when its team was pitted against an out-of-state school.

Doug's penchant for Sunday sports drove Nadine nuts. But after twenty-five years of marital bliss, blessings, and blow-outs, Doug had learned the fine art of "yes-dearing" his way through the Sabbath afternoon while remaining sloppily immobile in the den. After church, Doug turned into an inert mass of mush, wasting away the afternoon, snoozing and munching his way through an assortment of junk food while flipping from one cable sporting event to another. Every weekday after work, he faithfully dropped by the L. A. Athletic Club for a workout, keeping himself in excellent shape for an almost fifty-year-old executive. But on Sunday afternoons he turned into a couch potato and spent the day watching the jocks, with Nadine interrupting every chance she could.

Today was different . . . very different. Nadine was cheerfully fussing about in the kitchen and hadn't said a word, all day, about how loud the TV was turned up or why coverage of sporting events was always so ear-splitting. Suddenly, she appeared with a full tray in her hands.

"Honey, I've fixed you a bite to eat. You must be hungry." Doug's eyes lit up at the sight of his favorite sandwich—a grilled ham and cheese, accompanied by a large helping of potato chips and another diet Coke. Placing the tray before him, she leaned over and gave him a kiss. "Love you, sweetie," she said.

"Why . . . thank you, dear." His right eyebrow raised in curiosity. Although the Celtics were ahead by just two points and only one-and-a-half minutes remained in the game, Doug could no longer concentrate on the TV screen. His wife's strange behavior had captured his attention. To make sure he wasn't imagining the situation, he increased the volume and waited for the inevitable complaint . . . none came.

He devilishly cranked up the volume once more. Same result . . . no comment, even when he increased it to the point where it hurt his own ears. By now, he had completely lost interest in the Celtics. *What's that good-lookin' blonde up to?* Doug adored his wife, and he knew her moods very well. He rose from the couch and peered out the window at their cars parked in the driveway, looking carefully for obvious dents or scraped paint. No damage there. He returned to the sofa and tried to watch the game's end, but his mind was elsewhere, on his wife's weird manner.

Doug's curiosity was killing him. The last time Nadine had displayed such behavior was when she bashed the rear end of their Mercedes into the grill of a Rolls Royce, leaving the San Gabriel

Country Club's membership dance. She was docile for a whole week after that expensive episode.

Finally, he flicked the off button and as the deafening silence filled the house, he called out, "Nadine, would you come in here, please? I want to talk to you."

"You called me, dear?" she cooed from the kitchen. "Want another sandwich?"

"No, thanks. I think we'd better have a little chat."

Nadine Stewart sauntered into the den with a nervous grin on her face. "You know something's up, don't you?" And before the next breath, stated matter of factly, "Doug, your wig's on crooked."

Doug smiled as he thought, *That's my girl . . . go on the offensive. Next comes the guilt trip she'll lay on me before we get down to what she really has up her sleeve.* He didn't have long to wait.

"Honey, did you send a note to the Crosbys thanking them for that lovely dinner invitation honoring Senator Haynes?"

"No, remember? I didn't go. You and my money did. The Clippers were playing the Sacramento Kings for the Western Division leadership. Couldn't miss that game," he replied with a laugh and a wink. Doug hated fundraising events, ranking them slightly below enemas and candidate nights. "You know I bought a block of season tickets and usually take some clients along."

"Well, you should have thanked the Crosbys anyway; it was a smashing success."

"My thank-you note consisted of four engraved portraits of Ulysses S. Grant, two Ben Franklins, and one Hamilton." Doug reached up with his right hand and removed the reddish-brown hairpiece, exposing his balding head. Very little of his own hair remained on top. He knew taking it off would end the guilt trip. Nadine was always inordinately concerned over how he looked and dressed and she was never pleased when he wasn't wearing his hairpiece. Only at bedtime did she relent. Doug couldn't care less about how he appeared to others, but it was of major importance to his wife, so he complied with her wishes.

. . . And had since they were married soon after graduation from the University of Southern California and Nadine immediately began to insist that he improve his appearance. "A successful businessman is always properly attired, especially a corporate tax attorney who intends to go places." She convincingly argued that one's clothing contributed 90 percent of how one is perceived.

"If you look sloppy, people will think you're mentally disarranged as well. That's not good when appearing in court!" Doug had to agree but he had no idea how far she would go. From the beginning, Nadine meticulously picked out and supervised the tailoring of Doug's suits. She chose his ties and shirts from the finest Pasadena and Beverly Hills haberdasheries.

Every morning as Doug showered, she would lay out his daily attire on the bed, even down to the selection of his underwear, making sure his shorts matched the rest of his outfit. He was comforted in the knowledge that were he ever in an accident and taken to the hospital, he would at least be color-coordinated. After work, when he came home, his casual evening wear would be neatly arranged on top of the dresser. Her taste was superb and Doug's tall, lanky physique was made to order for any and all clothing. He was a handsome, dignified package by the time Nadine got through with him.

The hairpiece bothered him, but Nadine was persistent. "Old and bald is one thing, but not for my young man. You can discard it after you turn forty." Forty was almost ten years ago. The full head of hair was as much a part of his appearance as his expensive suits, and could prove embarrassing were he to change now. Nadine had even slightly grayed the temples of the toupee over time, so subtly that the blending with his real hair was impossible to tell. Only their children and a few very close friends were aware the hair was not his own.

Although Doug didn't have trouble with his vision, Nadine suggested that he wear horn-rimmed glasses. The dark frames, she insisted, added a studious, serious look to the young tax attorney. These enhancements to his overall look became a part of his daily uniform and a key ingredient to the image Nadine had fashioned for her husband.

Doug prospered. Now he was sole owner of the largest and most prestigious accounting firm in Los Angeles, and for many years, money had ceased to be a problem for the Stewarts. They lived quite comfortably, rattling around in a large Spanish-style home in San Marino, tucked up against the foothills of Pasadena.

Their two daughters, Marianne and Diana, were married and living miles away and their son, Wally, was in law school at Yale. The departure of all three children was quite an adjustment for Nadine. She compensated for their absence by developing a close association with Ma Bell. Nadine called her daughters daily and even had an "800" number installed so their offspring could dial home whenever they pleased. The phone bill was staggering, but it was well worth the cost. Besides, they could afford it.

Nadine increased her political activities tenfold. She helped staff Republican headquarters during campaigns, belonged to a local unit of the California Republican Assembly, the most conservative of the party's volunteer organizations, and played a leadership roll in PRISS. The organization was comprised of the most hard-core conservative activists in the San Gabriel Valley. Their motto, "Principle before Pragmatism," was not only prominently printed on their handout material, it was fire-branded on each of their hearts. The ladies of PRISS were tough, well-educated, and uncompromising—characteristics that often set them apart from other Republican organizations. Woe to the uninformed candidate who ventured through their doors soliciting support.

Doug was fairly sure that whatever was bothering Nadine this afternoon had political implications, for only her dedication to God and country would change her predictable Sunday behavior so perceptibly.

"All right, sweetheart, tell me what's going on in that pretty blonde head of yours." Smiling, Doug extended his hand to her, then patted the seat of the couch, encouraging his hesitant wife to sit beside him. She did . . . snuggling up close.

"Oh, Doug," she moaned while wrinkling her brow. "You're just going to *kill* me!"

Still smiling, he gave her a hug. "Okay, tell me what you've done. Is it going to cost me a bundle?"

"No. Nothing like that." She nestled even closer to him. "What I did was for the best of reasons. I hope you will forgive me."

"Well . . . tell me, what did you do?" He laughed. "Rob a bank?"

"Don't be silly." She moved away, upset at his light-hearted manner. "This is very serious, nothing to laugh about. If anyone found out, I could go to prison."

"You committed a felony?" he incredulously asked.

"Yes." With great haughtiness, she launched into a disjointed diatribe against their elderly state assemblyman, Russ Newton. He had recently surprised everyone by retiring mid-term, throwing the district into a special election, coming up the following May. Assemblyman Newton had feigned ill health but political insiders knew the real reason was a new, flirtatious young wife who refused to live in Sacramento. Old Russ was worn out, commuting every other day between the state capitol and Pasadena.

"If the old fool had married someone his own age, this wouldn't have happened," complained Nadine.

Doug knew right away she wasn't as upset over Newton's jealousy as much as she was furious over who would probably replace him. The moderate Republican mayor of Pasadena, Austin Chitmour, was sure to be the odds-on favorite. Nadine's worst enemy in leadership battles among her political cohorts was Arabella Chitmour, the mayor's wife and president of the Pasadena Mary Lincoln Club, rivals of PRISS. Arabella considered herself to be "Mrs. California Republican," having been elected to the county Republican central committee and appointed to the GOP's prestigious state committee by Assemblyman Russ Newton.

Nadine thought both the Chitmours were the pits. "That woman would vote for Stalin if he were a registered Republican! She and that twit husband of hers are more interested in socially mixing with the elected elite than bothering their pea-brains over what they stand for."

Doug was well aware of Nadine's frustration, for their dinner-times would not be complete without hearing about the latest episode regarding any upcoming election. Nadine and the board of PRISS had scheduled a candidate's night in order to hear what the multitude of potential assemblymen had to say. Arabella's club scheduled one for the same night in order to keep her husband away from any penetrating questions they knew would undoubtedly come his way.

The Fifty-fourth Assembly District was solid Republican and whoever won the primary in the spring was a cinch to make it to Sacramento. So far, only a lackluster array of candidates had filed papers to be on the ballot. Austin Chitmour was, by far, the best-known of the lot and because of his broad political base, had already secured endorsements from the local press. The very thought of Austin Chitmour being her representative for years to come pushed Nadine to the edge of illness each time she thought about it.

"Did you ever shake Austin's hand? What a klutz! You would think he was priming a pump. Remember when he shook my arm so violently I spilled hot coffee down the front of my blue silk suit? And the nerve of that clown, yanking out his handkerchief and dabbing away at my bosom!" Nadine had worked herself into a lather. She was amply endowed and tended to wear dresses that displayed her charms. Doug recalled the incident clearly; his wife's roundhouse right had nearly decked the mayor. Austin's black eye was the talk of the town for months. Arabella Chitmour was not amused.

And now, Arabella had new cause to be furious—a newsletter listing the probable candidates, put out by the ladies at PRISS.

There was a glaring printing error in the spelling of Austin's last name and a large volume were distributed before the typo could be corrected and the remaining lists destroyed. Inadvertently, Chitmour was spelled with an "S," rather than the letter "C." Arabella was convinced that Nadine was secretly at fault, while Nadine simply attributed it to a happy coincidence that fortune occasionally provides.

So far, none of the other campaigners had a chance against Austin Chitmour. Every new entry into the race assured his victory all the more, by splitting up the vote among so many candidates. The deadline for filing papers for the office was last Friday. Monday morning's *Pasadena Star News* would publish the complete list of names to appear on the ballot.

Doug was getting impatient with Nadine's beating about the political bushes; he needed to know what crime she had committed. "Sweetheart, come to the point. What did you do illegally?"

Getting up from the couch, Nadine began to pace nervously about the room, unconsciously wringing her hands. "Honey, I found just the right person to be our assemblyman. He's honest, knowledgeable on the issues, moral, a fine Christian family man, and someone who would make a great leader. The trouble is, he doesn't want to run, so I forged his name on the filing document, gathered the necessary signatures from the gals at PRISS and, late Friday, submitted the papers to the county registrar of voters."

Doug was dumbstruck. He looked at his wife with his mouth agape, having difficulty finding something to say. At first, he didn't believe her, but the downcast, guilt-ridden look on her face was evidence enough that Nadine was telling the truth. Forging election documents was a serious crime—usually punished by a hefty fine and time in jail. He had a hard time believing his normally intelligent better half would do anything so stupid.

"Well, Doug, aren't you going to say anything? Please don't just sit there with your mouth open!"

"Yeah, I've got a lot to say!" Angrily, he jumped up from the couch, towering over his nervous spouse. "Who is this poor sucker you've put in this box? You better hope he's a nice guy, or you could wind up being sued."

Nadine moved in close to her husband, placed her arms about his neck, and nuzzled so near he was forced to step backward. "Oh, Douglas," she cooed, "*you* wouldn't sue me . . . *would you?*"

TWO

★ ★ ★

HEY, MR. STEWART, going to Sacramento to straighten out that mess?" Doug smiled sheepishly and nodded at the grinning receptionist. He walked hurriedly by her without stopping. The long walk down the busy corridor to his office seemed to take forever, and Doug was embarrassed by all the well-wishers commenting on his entry into the rough-and-tumble world of politics.

Smiling heads poked out of office doorways, offering both humorous condolences and campaign advice; everything from "Go get 'em, Mr. Stewart" to "Where do I send the check, Boss?" Doug was mortified by all the friendly attention. *It's gratifying to be well thought of by my staff and peers, but NOT for politics!*

He smiled politely at every grinning face while quickening his pace until he was safely inside his spacious office. *Little do they know I hate politics, politicians, and—temporarily—my lovely, duplicitous wife!*

Doug sat down heavily into his high-backed desk chair and drummed his fingers on the leather arm, thinking of what he would say to his employees about his present predicament. In fifteen minutes, their weekly Monday morning conference would begin. *What should I tell them? Dear staff, my wife is a certified nut or . . . The felonious female with whom I reside has made me a partner in a loony-tunes political conspiracy.*

Doug spun his chair around and looked out the expansive window. The forty-fourth floor offered a wide panorama of downtown

Los Angeles and a breathtaking view of the San Gabriel Mountains, curving around to the city's east basin. A Santa Ana wind was blowing, clearing the basin of auto exhaust and smog, allowing for a particularly special spring morning. The rugged mountains contrasted bright green, next to the touch of snow still clinging to the higher peaks. The last of the winter white brought back pleasant memories and temporarily caused Doug to forget his present predicament.

Doug Stewart was a one-man Chamber of Commerce for the Golden State. He loved California passionately, and he also loved L.A. As a loyal native son, he could argue a Texan into the ground on which was the best state in the Union. As a young man, he surfed from San Diego to Monterey and, in the winter, skied the mountains from Big Bear to Lake Tahoe. At Thanksgiving, he would store away his surfboard and skin-diving gear, raise the top on his fifty-five Ford convertible, and take a few of his buddies to Mammoth Mountain for the first skiing of the season.

After a hard day on the slopes, they would head for a favorite spot—the little-known natural hot springs. There, they would soak away the twilight hours, sipping wine with a bevy of ski-bunny beauties. It's where he first saw Nadine, paddling around in the sulfated stream, enjoying the steamy waters. He discovered the gorgeous, shapely blonde also attended USC, was one of the sorority row darlings, and had been selected homecoming queen. For Doug, it was love at first sight, a knot in the stomach, and a joyful pain in the heart. But for now, the pain was located a little lower and toward the rear. The thought of Nadine brought him back to the reality of the moment.

"Politics!" He wrinkled up his nose as if he'd smelled something awful. Doug shuddered at the very thought of being a candidate to the California assembly. Having labored hard and long hours to reach his present lofty position, he considered his current circumstances as near perfect. He had wealth, good health, and lots of free time to pursue his love for flying and fishing. In the summer, it was trolling for the mighty king salmon in the Hakai Straits off western Canada and in the winter months, it was marlin-fishing with good friends off the coast of Mexico. There was no place in his enviable life for associating with politicians.

Politics represented unnecessary pain. Every year, some Sacramento hot-shot legislator thought it would be a good idea to fiddle with the tax codes, creating a wealth of new problems for business in general and his clients in particular. Stewart and Associates was responsible for figuring out how to "live with" the new laws. Doug's firm was often called upon to testify before the revenue and taxation committees at the capitol and, on occasion, before the appropriate government bodies in Washington, D.C.

Doug had testified before the legislature in the early years of his business and was appalled to find so little knowledge about the free market and how it operated. He found it easier to discover ways of legally circumventing bad laws than having to deal with meddling, muddle-headed solons. In their ignorance, legislators sometimes created large enough loopholes to drive a truck through. He had been very successful in advising his clients on how to cope with every new regulation and code change, but every year, it became harder and more complicated.

Thanks to Doug's legal and accounting acumen, the business had grown to the point where the young movers and shakers in his firm handled any necessary contacts with the legislature, leaving him free from that unpleasant task. His world was schmoozing with other corporate heads at the Jonathan Club and taking them fishing on his yacht.

Doug couldn't help it; he felt like King Tut, looking out over the city of Los Angeles and reflecting on his success. Los Angeles was his big oyster, chock-full with a passel of pearls. Stewart and Associates was deemed the industry leader, the epitome of accounting excellence. Around him, Doug had gathered some of the finest minds in the field of taxation law and had the pick of the graduating crop from UCLA and USC. The firm had captured the best accounts in the western states—including much of the aircraft industry and the major west coast oils and shipping conglomerates. Stewart and Associates was synonymous with success, and the ambition of every aspiring young tax attorney was an opportunity to get a résumé past the front desk.

Doug Stewart was the executive every ambitious, up-and-coming account advisor tried to emulate. His contacts within the business community gained him valuable investment knowledge which he put to good use, enabling him to amass a sizable estate. Unlike his wife, his parents were of modest means and were it not for the GI Bill, high school would have been the end of his education. Serving in the marines in Vietnam gave him the opportunity to enter the University of Southern California.

Nadine, however, was raised in well-to-do surroundings. The Logan family were fourth-generation Californians and had prospered when oil was discovered on their Bakersfield property. Being raised around successful people, she was accustomed to wealth. Her family's close friends and acquaintances were great assets for an aspiring young tax attorney.

After all their years together, Doug still loved her deeply, but given the present circumstances, he felt like choking her lovely, graceful neck until her blue eyes bulged in fright. He was still burning-hot under the collar. *How dare she do this to me? In a few minutes I'll be in the conference room facing my top guys. What can I say?* He shrugged his shoulders. *One thing's for sure—I can't tell them the truth.*

The process of turning the firm's total management over to his senior executives was working out well, so far. Having accumulated a rather substantial fortune, Doug intended to spend more of the dividends enjoying his toys, more time on the yacht and in his plane. His beach home in Baja and the hunting cabin on the middle fork of the Salmon River in Idaho were finally going to be put to good use. The Cessna Centurion 210 was hangared at Burbank, gassed up and ready to go, and the forty-foot fishing yacht, along with her full-time skipper, was anchored in Cabo San Lucas and ready for his arrival at any time.

Still gazing out the window, he shouted, "Marlin and albacore are in—Nadine's politics are out!" while thrusting both arms up into a Nixon "V."

★ ★ ★

"EXCUSE ME, SIR," interjected a voice from behind him. His efficient executive secretary was obviously somewhat perplexed by her boss' unusual behavior. "The staff is assembled in the conference room."

Startled, Doug turned at the sound of her voice, his arms still above his head. "Miss Keppel," he blushed, "I look rather ridiculous, don't I?"

She smiled. "I've seen you look . . . more dignified."

Doug lowered his arms, "Well, let's venture into the lion's den."

Begrudgingly, Doug marched to the conference room doors adjoining his office, pausing just before he grabbed the doorknob, dreading what could be in store for him. His close associates knew of his aversion to politics and the questions over his entry into the assembly race would surely come thick and fast . . . if he let them. He had to shut them off quickly.

Doug swung open the double oak doors, shocked to be greeted by the raucous cheers of his colleagues and a face full of multicolored confetti. Before he could say a word, his associates broke into strains of "Happy Days Are Here Again," the theme song of Franklin D. Roosevelt and the Democratic Party. Handpainted campaign signs adorned the walls, "Elect Doug the Dauntless!" "Stewart the Stalwart for Assembly!" and "A Leader Who Listens." Added to the political motif were entwined red, white, and blue crepe paper streamers draped from the chandelier to the doorways, over the chairs, and across the conference table.

When at last the laughter quieted down, Doug motioned for

everyone to sit down and said, in mock seriousness, "Lucky for all of you Nadine isn't here. She'd insist I fire the lot of you for singing THAT song."

"Aw, Doug, it's the only one we all know," joked Ben Bently, his chief accountant.

"Yeah," commented one of the others, "and besides—it's the thought that counts."

"Well, get the campaigning out of your systems right now, because this will be the end of it. I'm not a serious candidate for the office," Doug stated.

"What do you mean by that?" asked Bently, echoing everyone's startled confusion.

"I agreed to be a protest candidate in our district's special election for Nadine and a few of her friends. They weren't satisfied with the bunch who've already thrown their hats into the ring. Anyway, they wanted an alternative to vote for. I agreed to let my name be filed with the understanding that I wouldn't have to do a thing. In fact, in two days time, I intend to be a hundred miles off Cabo San Lucas fishing for marlin and albacore. And that's all there is to it."

Clearly, his associates were disappointed by his answer. Finally, Clyde Brown, a senior financial advisor, spoke up. "Darn it, Doug, we're sorry to hear that. We all agree you would make a great assemblyman."

"Yeah!" dittoed the rest, "and one day—governor."

"We've been discussing what a novelty it would be to have someone in Sacramento who understood tax matters," added Ben Bently.

"You bet!" piped in Bob Dornant, the chief of research. "Maybe with you up there, they might get an angle on getting a budget out on time."

"I appreciate your confidence, but the only angle I'm interested in right now deals with fishing." Doug took his seat at the head of the table and smiled affectionately at them all. "Shall we get down to business?"

SPLIT TICKET

★ ★ ★

NADINE STOOD BY THE DOOR of Tiger Air as Doug readied the Cessna Centurion before taxiing toward the appointed runway. She watched him go through the necessary pre-flight procedures for takeoff. *What was that routine he went through? What did he call it? C-I-G-A-R? Yes, that was it. Controls, Instruments, Gas, Attitude, and Run-up.*

Nadine wasn't too enamored with flying in a single-engine aircraft. Although she knew Doug was a good pilot and the Cessna was fully instrumented, she still felt much more comfortable traveling in the corporation's Lear jet.

She watched the pressurized Centurion roar down the runway, waving to Doug as he climbed skyward. Even though he undoubtedly couldn't see her, she blew him a kiss anyway, since she wouldn't be seeing him for over a month—a fact he was totally unaware of. The Stewarts' fabulous, rambling Spanish-style home on the Gulf side of the Baja Peninsula included a long private beach, boat dock, and landing strip. Doug, at her subtle suggestion, had invited a series of good friends and clients to join him there for some serious fishing and relaxation in the sun.

Nadine intimated she would fly down in a couple of weeks, knowing full well her intentions were otherwise. While Doug and his pals caught albacore, she had *political* fish to fry. Hurriedly, she left the Tiger Air terminal and slipped into the driver's seat of her Mercedes. Picking up the cellular phone, she called her best friend and closest political ally, Kathleen Rowe—the current president of PRISS. The phone rang twice before Kathleen answered.

"Kathleen? He's gone!" Nadine gleefully exclaimed. "Is the meeting set up?" She paused. "Okay, I'll hold."

Kathleen was on the other line while Nadine impatiently waited . . . and waited. Finally she said, "Nadine, sorry I took so long. I was on the other line with Carlos Saracino. It took forever to run him down. He seems to be very busy and much in demand.

I had to work hard to keep him from hanging up on me. He wasn't too interested in our project."

"Oh, that's terrible. We've got to get him. Tell me, is he coming to the meeting or not?" eagerly inquired Nadine.

"Yes . . . he said he'd be there."

"Oh, this is terribly exciting. We can't do it without him if he's half as good as you claim he is. What did you have to say to get him to come? Did you tell him about our conservative ideals?"

"No, that wasn't it," answered Kathleen.

"Was it the challenge we presented?"

"No . . . not quite. He actually giggled and then yawned when I brought up both of those subjects. In fact, only one thing seemed to peak his interest at all."

"What was that?" asked Nadine.

"When I told him you were richer than King Farouk's wife and willing to spend every dime of it to get your husband elected."

THREE

★ ★ ★

Don't you think you're playing a massively dirty trick on that sweet husband of yours?" asked Kathleen. Nadine nervously paced about the living room, ignoring Kathleen's pithy comment, her mind on other matters. Nadine angrily sputtered, "Where are they? They're already fifteen minutes late. I'll be a basket case if they don't show up."

"Don't worry, Saracino and crowd will be here," Kathleen promised, and yawned. "Political folks are notoriously unpunctual except when showing up for a free meal or picking up a paycheck from their candidate's diminishing campaign funds. Now . . . back to my original question. Won't Doug kill you when he finds out what you're up to?"

Nadine continued to ignore her. "Is this Carlos fellow really as good as you say he is?"

"Carlos Saracino is the best Republican campaign manager in the entire West," answered Kathleen. "Last election, most of his candidates won. Some were real surprise winners, knocking off a few incumbents. You said you wanted the best, so I got 'im for you."

Nadine stared at her sophisticated friend, then walked to the living room window and looked out at the quiet San Marino street. Kathleen Rowe, my good pal and political mentor, you'd better be right! The check she had written to secure the services of Saracino and Associates was astronomical.

★ ★ ★

FIVE DAYS OF APPREHENSION had passed since Nadine and Kathleen had flown to Sacramento for the brief meeting in Saracino's office. He strongly recommended a professional poll be taken to survey the philosophical landscape in the fifty-fourth district and, since Kathleen thought it was a good idea, Nadine agreed. Kathleen's practical political experience was extensive compared to Nadine's, having participated in many a California race. At one time, she served as a district aide to a conservative state senator. Three times, Kathleen was president of PRISS and was the recognized grand dame of San Marino's Right Wing. Her conservative credentials were impeccable and Nadine trusted her implicitly.

Personally, Nadine didn't think a survey was necessary. To her, the issues were abundantly clear based upon conversations with the gals at PRISS. Saracino, however, had been insistent. Saracino's acidic comment clarified the issue when he said, "If I were trying to ascertain the popularity of sauerkraut, I wouldn't do so at a German picnic."

"Who's this pollster, Arnie Kleinberg?" asked Nadine, continuing to peer out the window.

"Arnie served as the top aide for a U.S. congressman for a number of years, then went out on his own to set up his survey business," responded Kathleen. "He has clients all over the country and they are usually conservative. He's an excellent pollster, but I'll warn you—his social graces leave a lot to be desired. He's highly temperamental, super-bright, and nervous as a pregnant nun."

"What do you mean by that?"

"He's like spilled gun powder; it doesn't take much to set him off," Kathleen answered dryly. "Speaking of the like, I'll ask once more. Won't Doug want to throttle you for this wild plan of yours?"

"Oh, maybe . . . but when it works, it'll be worth it. I'm firmly convinced Doug would make a wonderful legislator and someday, maybe even governor. Lord knows he has the time, the knowledge, and the prestige to serve."

"And the wife!" added Kathleen. "Be honest with your old buddy and with yourself. You'd love to be the spouse of an assemblyman, delving into all those juicy issues." She smiled knowingly. "I know you all too well, Nadine Logan Stewart! You would be in a constant state of political euphoria, joyful in the middle of all the intrigue that abounds in Sacramento. You would have a blast . . . now, wouldn't you?"

Kathleen waved a finger at her friend and devilishly winked. "Besides, you'd come unhinged, be ready for a padded cell, if Arabella's husband won the election. I can tell . . . that jaw muscle of yours twitches overtime whenever the mayor's name is mentioned."

Nadine's impish grin confirmed her friend's remarks hit close to home, but she replied contritely, "That's not the main reason, Kathleen. You know as well as I do that my husband would be a great representative. With my help, of course."

To Nadine, Doug Stewart was a paradox—a mix of strange contradictions. He handled tax laws daily, understanding their complexities better than anyone and was vociferously aghast over the glaring inequities and loopholes saturating the California tax codes. Doug seemed to have little interest, however, in the election of those who made the laws. Years ago when they had changed residences, Nadine noticed that Doug hadn't even taken the time to re-register to vote. He was off hunting caribou on the Alaskan Peninsula, forgetting all about an upcoming election. Understanding her husband's lackadaisical civic posture, she took advantage of the ultraliberal election laws and registered for him, by mail. In California, that's all it took; request a registration form, sign it, and mail it in to the county.

Piece of cake! She forged his name and who would ever know—or care, for that matter? Since Doug was always preoccupied with hunting each early November, she merely requested absentee ballots in his name and voted for him. The signatures matched, for she had signed both the voter registration form and the absentee ballots. Nadine had been doing this for years and Doug certainly didn't seem to mind. When he returned from hunting, or wherever else he may have gone in November, she always showed him how he had voted. He never appeared to disagree with how she had cast his ballot, so how could he get too upset now if she ran him for office?

Doug's regard for politicians was clear. "They're all the pits, but Democrats are the pittiest." He often stated that his job was like the keeper of commodes—to clean up the messes legislators made for his clients and to make the best out of the compost they created.

Nadine knew her chances for success were minimal but before she was through, Arabella Chitmour and her wimpy husband, Austin, would feel political pain that a good jolt of morphine wouldn't cure. That fact alone gave Nadine a sense of fiendish satisfaction.

★ ★ ★

THE DOORBELL RANG. "Well, it's about time!" Nadine exclaimed as she rushed to open the door. Much as a grubby insect changes into a beautiful butterfly, her demeanor changed from harried to happy as she welcomed the three people standing on the doorstep—Carlos Saracino; Laurie Noble, his research assistant; and pollster Arnie Kleinberg.

"Sorry we're late," apologized Carlos. "The computer printer only works so fast. We had to get copies of the survey for everyone."

"Oh, are you late?" Nadine inquired with a smile, as she graciously showed her guests into the spacious family room. She directed them to the semi-circular leather sofa and matching chairs surrounding the huge mahogany coffee table before seating herself on the large butter-leather ottoman. Wasting no time, she asked, "Arnie, what do the poll data tell us? Can my husband win?"

Arnie Kleinberg had just barely lowered his thin frame into the deep soft leather and was nervously fidgeting with his briefcase, as her question came barreling his way. He rolled his eyes toward the ceiling, lowered his head, and looked askance at the naive client sitting across from him. He had been commissioned to do the survey just four days ago—a task that normally took weeks to properly complete. The results had to be tabulated, digested, and pondered before he could answer that question with any degree of accuracy. Whenever pressured, Arnie would twitch nervously and stutter a caustic reply.

Carlos Saracino, having worked many years with Arnie Kleinberg, sensed the impending explosion and interrupted before the irate pollster could voice his opinion.

"Mrs. Stewart, that's why we are here. We can go over the numbers together and discern what chance your husband may have of winning." Carlos looked around the room. "By the way, where *is* the candidate?"

"Oh, Doug couldn't make it today. We'll have to proceed without him," coyly answered Nadine.

Kathleen shot daggers at her friend, then pointedly stated, "Nadine . . . tell 'em the truth. They'll be working under enough of a handicap as it is."

"Wha . . . what truth?" Arnie asked nervously. "Is there something we don't know?"

"Well . . . there *are* a few minor details we should cover," answered Nadine.

Laurie Noble, Saracino's sophisticated research whiz, leaned forward in her chair and seriously inquired, "Any black sheep in the closet that we should know about?"

"No, nothing like that," interjected Kathleen. "Doug's as solid as a woodpecker's pecker and honest to a fault." Smiling devilishly and nodding toward Nadine, she continued, "The only problem he has is seated over there."

Carlos, squinting from under one eyebrow while arching the other, inquired in rapid succession. "What then are the difficulties? Does he present himself poorly? Will he be a problem with the press? Is there some troublesome issue we could face due to an outlandish statement he has made? Tell us, please. We need to be informed."

"It's really none of those things," said Nadine.

"Well, then, what is it?" asked Saracino impatiently.

"Doug's not here right now," she answered meekly.

"We're all bright enough to see that," sarcastically intoned Kleinberg.

"What I mean is . . . he won't be here for . . . awhile."

"What she means is, her husband won't be available for *any part* of the campaign. He's off fishing in Mexico until the day before the election," stated Kathleen.

"You're joking," Carlos stated, looking straight at Nadine. "You can't have a campaign without a candidate."

"Does it look like she's joking?" responded Kathleen seriously. "Look at her; notice the set of her jaw. You don't understand the fire that burns in that gal."

"Kathleen's right. When I signed your contract and gave you my check, there was no mention of my husband having to be present."

"Mrs. Stewart, you are asking the impossible," offered an exasperated Arnie Kleinberg. "Good, we are—Houdinis, we ain't. Who will attend the candidate forums, the Chamber of Commerce bashes, the service clubs? Someone's got to be there!"

"I'll go in his stead," replied their determined hostess.

"I'll help too," offered Kathleen.

"It won't work," said Carlos. "We can't run a campaign without him. We . . . "

"Oh, yes, you can and yes, you will," Nadine firmly interrupted.

Condescendingly, Saracino said, "Mrs. Stewart, I really can't do that . . . may I call you Nadine?" He continued politely. "I'll refund your money . . . minus expenses, of course." He rose from the couch and started to close his briefcase.

"Where do you think you are going?" Nadine was instantly on her feet. "Call me anything you like, but sit your posteriors back down and let's get on with electing my husband. I have a written contract with you and, candidate or not, you're going to earn your keep or we'll spend the next few months in court. My husband's firm is loaded with young lawyers eager to fulfill my slightest whim. Taking your scalp would be all in a day's work."

Saracino didn't know whether she was bluffing or not, but was visibly intimidated. Though campaign consultants made very good money during election years, they often scraped bottom during the off times. Special elections, such as the fifty-fourth, was unexpected gravy. The last thing Carlos wanted to do was hire a lawyer in an attempt to renege on his own contract. The Stewarts' business and legal empire was well-known to him, having had Laurie Noble check into their financial status previous to meeting with Nadine in his Sacramento office. Laurie's investigation confirmed Kathleen's commentary that King Farouk's wealth paled next to the Stewart-Logan holdings.

Carlos sank heavily back into the couch and met Nadine's stern gaze, beaming laser-like from her sparkling eyes. With an air of resignation, he said, "Okay, but it will cost you a bundle. It's tough enough electing a candidate who's in the flesh, much less someone who's off fishing." Turning to Kleinberg, he asked, "What're the numbers, Arnie?"

The diminutive pollster perched his reading glasses on the end of his pointed nose and quickly thumbed through the thick computer printout. After a few minutes of mumbling and hurriedly jotting down statistics, Arnie looked up and said in pointed nasal tones, "Mrs. Stewart, the way it stands now, your husband's got about as much chance of winning this assembly seat as I do of being mistaken for Arnold Schwartzenegar."

"That bad, Arnie?" asked Carlos.

"Well, listen to this: it's one of the key questions. If the election were held tomorrow, who would you select from the following list of candidates? Austin Chitmour got thirty-three percent, and the other eight candidates combined got only twenty-five percent. Chitmour has an obvious lock on the election; his favorable comments were very high. Those who know him think he's done a good job as Pasadena's mayor."

"Bullpuckey!" spat Nadine. "He's been a lousy mayor. What did you do, poll the winos on skid row?"

Carlos slowly shook his head. "Alas, Mrs. Stewart, we did a comprehensive sampling of more than eight hundred voters—ample numbers to give us a factor of four-percent accuracy."

"Are you absolutely sure?"

"I'm sure."

Nadine was quiet for a moment, then asked, "What were Doug's favorable comments?"

"The few who knew of him rated him very highly," offered Arnie. "However several had him confused with Stewart, the actor."

"Jimmy Stewart?" asked Kathleen incredulously.

"None other."

"How discouraging!" moaned Nadine.

"Welcome to the real world of politics," remarked Carlos. "In California, candidates have dropped dead, their demise well-publicized, and they were still elected. There is nothing new under this tainted political sun that would surprise me, especially in the Golden State."

Dejectedly, Nadine turned to Laurie. "You haven't said a word. You've been doing research on the mayor and the district. Is there any hope? What do you think?"

The astute, attractive brunette shrugged her shoulders. "I agree with Arnie. Though winning is highly improbable, it is not totally out of the question."

Nadine brightened at the small ray of hope. "Tell me more."

Laurie continued. "Austin Chitmour voted for some pretty silly boondoggles and he headed a move to raise taxes on garbage collection. It failed and everyone forgot about it. He subsequently received a contribution from the waste disposal business. Also, one summer, his son worked for the city. We could hit him on the charge of nepotism. It's all pretty thin stuff. A lot depends on what kind of race he runs and how he takes the heat. So far, he seems confident and isn't working hard collecting funds. He's undoubt-edly taken a poll and has come up with the same results we have. It would take a pile of cash to expose the mayor's few weaknesses . . . but, who knows? A few slick hit pieces might loosen his politi-cal girdle and cause him to panic. He's never been in a tough race and it's anybody's guess how he might react. If someone could get him in a dogfight, he just might make a horse's butt out of himself."

"Count on it!" emphatically stated Nadine.

"We sure couldn't take him head on. We would have to run a stealth campaign," added Arnie.

"What's a stealth campaign?" Nadine's eyes were snapping bright.

"If we have enough bucks, we try to sneak up on 'em, lull our opponents into complacency," answered Saracino. "We try not to show up on the political radar until the very last minute."

"How do we do that?" inquired Nadine.

"There are a variety of ways. For instance, we already have computer tapes on high-propensity voters. We mail to them in the last couple of weeks."

"What's a high-propensity voter?" asked a befuddled Nadine.

"Someone who's shown a propensity to vote in every election. In special elections such as this, only a small percentage of voters bother to cast their ballots. High-propensity voters are ones who will actually take the time to vote. We have computerized the names of those who fit that description and we concentrate our efforts on them."

"Also," added Arnie, "by phone, we poll precincts and identify high-velocity issues, then mail them special-interest brochures that light their candles on our candidate."

Carlos said, "And don't forget the absentee ballot. Few candi-dates are wise enough to use it to their full advantage."

Arnie piped in. "Remember, in this liberal state, they've made it so easy, even the dead can vote; that is, of course, if someone does it for them. Voting absentee is now extremely easy, a lazy but popular way to pick your favorite politician. Just mark your ballot and drop it in the mail."

"That's right," Carlos added, grinning. "The outcome of an election can often be predicted by the size of the absentee vote. We can wage a sizable campaign to secure this group by mailing an absentee ballot request form to the high-propensity voter, encouraging them to vote at home. We make sure Doug Stewart's literature arrives at the same time as their ballot. We're lucky this election is late spring, when people are busy gardening and planning their summer vacations. A lot of them will vote absentee, given the chance."

"Unfortunately, that way of voting is subject to abuse," stated Kathleen.

"Of course!" added Carlos. "But, when handed lemons, we must make lemonade."

"On election day, we work hard to turn out those voters who didn't vote absentee—the ones we have identified as favorable to your husband," Laurie Noble explained. She smiled.

"Yeah!" agreed Carlos, and grinned. "We will unload on the mayor and catch him with his political pants around his toenails. We hit 'em with targeted direct mail, phone banks, door-to-door literature drops, and media blitzes."

"What do you think the issues will be?" asked an awed Nadine.

"Who cares!" responded Carlos. "The voter survey will tell us what to say and what not to say. We could hit him with charges of being a big spender or not spending enough." Turning to Arnie, Carlos asked, "How do taxes play in this district?"

"It's Mother Dow Jones," glibly replied the pollster. "The area is so conservative, they think Ronald Reagan is a moderate. The district voted seventy-eight percent for Reagan anyway, and about as much for what's-his-name."

"Bush?"

"Yeah, Bush. It's a yellow-dog district," added Noble.

"What's a yellow-dog district?" asked their thoroughly confused and slightly irritated hostess.

"The Republicans in this area would rather vote for a yellow dog than a Democrat," answered Carlos. "Every district has them . . . in both parties. A Democrat would have a better chance of levitating than winning in this gerrymandered GOP district."

Kathleen exclaimed, "I'd rather think of my fellow Republicans as discerning."

"Think of them anyway you want, but let's identify which of these canary-colored bowsers can be swayed to vote for Stewart," Laurie Noble stated emphatically.

Nadine's jaw was working overtime. "We're not going to lie to the voters. We're going to run a clean campaign."

"Of course, we are," Carlos replied soothingly, while casting a sly wink at Arnie. They had both heard that song before. During the intense heat generated in close campaigns, they had too often witnessed what they called "the V's." Charges and counter-charges became so vicious, vituperative, and volatile that whatever honesty and reason that existed was replaced by vain, vomitous vindictiveness—ugly pragmatism borne out of the fear of defeat and slighted vanity. Many a gutterball attack had flowed from a candidate's lips who, in the beginning, emoted pristinely, "I *insist* on running a clean campaign!" Not only candidates, but their devoted followers, reacted like Pavlov's dogs when attacked in the waning moments of a hard-fought political battle. Badly bruised egos begot bountiful buffoonery.

"You may be assured, Mrs. Stewart," schmoozed Carlos, "we won't do anything which has not first been submitted for your approval."

Nadine left the room and quickly returned with her checkbook. She immediately scribbled out a draft on the First Security Bank. "Here's a hundred thousand. Will that do for a start?"

Carlos smiled sweetly as he reached for the check, retrieving it delicately between his thumb and forefinger. "Yes, my dear . . . *as a start*, it will do quite nicely."

FOUR

★ ★ ★

Doug DIDN'T SAY A WORD as he got into Nadine's Mercedes. He kissed her perfunctorily on the cheek and slumped down into the leather seat.

"Fishing lousy?" she asked.

"Could've been *worse*," yawned her husband as he stared out the window.

"Well then, what's bugging you? That was less than a cousin-kiss you just gave me." Nadine was curious; such a weak peck was an announcement that a problem was bubbling. Panic suddenly gripped her. *Could he know what I've been up to?* Now was definitely not the time to bring it up. She had to get him home and in a mellow mood before she broached the subject of politics.

"If you want to know," Doug answered curtly, "you, being a no-show in Mexico, caused me a great deal of grief. Everybody we invited showed up . . . except the cook and the housekeeper. I was left with a hacienda full of guests with absolutely no help, not even my devoted wife. I had to handle all the entertainment, most of the cooking, and of course, the cleanup." Doug looked more than irritated. "I'm not into changing sheets and washing bath towels."

Nadine let out a huge sigh of relief at his response. *He still doesn't know . . . so far so good.* However, Doug's comments about the servants surprised her. The Lopezes had promised to be there. "Doug . . . where was Mrs. Lopez? Maria assured me that she and Manuel would take care of everything, as always."

"Well, Maria was there for two days. Then she got word that her mother was pretty sick. Without notice, she and that no-account husband of hers took off for Guadalupe." Doug slumped deeper into the comfortable seat as Nadine accelerated the engine, sliding the sleek sports car into the jammed traffic on the Glendale Freeway.

"Where were you, sweetheart?" he asked. "You said you were going to join me and, no matter the absence of Maria and Manuel, I missed you like crazy."

"I got too involved with the girls at PRISS and the bevy of candidates to interview for Newton's replacement. Somehow, there was no time to get away."

"Find a candidate you like?"

She smiled impishly and purred, "We think so."

"That's good," Doug said, smiling. "I'm happy you gals picked out some poor soul you could all agree on. Now, back to Baja. Better than half of the guests were clients and not one of them knew beans about fishing. One brought along his three kids and two of them got seasick, making a mess of the boat. Guess who cleaned it up? You'd have been proud of me."

Nadine glanced sorrowfully at her husband. "I'm sorry, hon, but I became so engrossed in the campaign that time just flew by."

Doug looked at her and let out a long sigh. "I wish I could say the same." He reached over and squeezed her knee, affectionately. "I missed ya, babe. I could have stood all the hassle and maybe even enjoyed it . . . if you had been there."

Nadine took one hand from the wheel and gently patted Doug's hand on her knee. "It's good to have you home, sweetheart, . . . oh, no!" Suddenly, she jerked the wheel and recklessly swerved over two lanes to the shoulder, then moved back into traffic as swiftly as she had left it, weaving dangerously between honking cars. Her erratic lane-changes threw Doug roughly against the door.

"What the . . . ! Nadine! Watch what you're doing!"

"I'm sorry, Doug. Didn't you see that car swerve our way? I had no choice." He settled back down again, closing his eyes.

She lied. The Ford Bronco immediately in front of them had a STEWART FOR ASSEMBLY sticker on the back window. She panicked; it was the last thing she wanted her husband to see. She had carefully planned when and where Doug was to find out . . . now was not the time. She glanced over at him as he relaxed, so tired, he was falling asleep.

The campaign to elect Doug Stewart had been going extremely well. It was costing her a fortune, but it was worth it. The latest tracking information showed that the Stewart campaign was rapidly closing the gap. Saracino had insisted they keep up-to-date on their progress, a polling technique designed to follow any change in voter attitudes. The recent returns were evidence that their negative campaign against Mayor Chitmour was paying off.

They had mailed some fairly heavy hit pieces exposing some unpopular city council votes. The material caught Chitmour completely off-guard. Reacting in anger, Chitmour called a press conference in order to put a better "spin" on the charges made against him. He handled himself very poorly, sputtering and fuming, responding to the media's pointed inquiries. All he did was elevate the controversial charges made against him, allowing the press to have a field day, at his expense.

Austin Chitmour's record as mayor wasn't all that bad, but almost any incumbent would make a few mistakes over the years. A good campaign consultant could artfully take a minor error and elevate it into a national tragedy. One of Chitmour's mistakes was getting the city to hire his son.

We really rattled his cage on the nepotism issue, Nadine thought, smiling with satisfaction.

Although Chitmour's son was employed for just the summer months, the Stewart campaign staff had made a very big deal out of it. Saracino turned out a clever brochure which read, "Does nepotism begin at home? Ask the mayor!" The thought of it made Nadine giggle, as did a clever cartoon showing the mayor taking money from the city treasury and stuffing it into his son's pockets.

The mayor had called, "Foul!" and accused Doug of dirty, skuzzball tactics. Chitmour's campaign struck back, calling Doug the "No-Show" challenger and the candidate of the rich. The Stewart campaign team then hit hard again, this time with a leaflet which showed the mayor admitting his son had worked for the city. The headline shouted, "Mayor Admits Guilt!"

Nadine was concerned and spoke to Carlos about it. "That's a little nasty, don't you think? Aren't we making too big of a deal over a low-paying, dirty job repairing city streets?"

"It was nepotism nonetheless and, big issue or not, you must remember, Nadine—the mayor has a high name identity; your husband does not. Every time Chitmour responds to our attacks, he repeats our charge and elevates the Stewart name. He also makes it a two-man race by singling out Doug as his only opponent."

"What would you do if you were Chitmour?"

"Ignore us. Treat us as just another one of the desperate, yapping candidates who's trailing behind. A wise counsel once advised, 'Never respond to an attack until it reaches such a magnitude that you can take advantage of it.' Chitmour's never been given that advice, nor has he been in a difficult campaign before . . . and it shows. Now that he's good and nervous, we'll assail him with a new issue, keep him off balance. The polling survey shows that taxes ignite the public's interest. We can call him Mayor Taxmour."

Laurie Noble, while digging into his past record, found only one issue to hang a hat on. A number of years ago, Chitmour had lent his name to ballot Proposition 313, a state tax initiative that barely failed passage. The issue was promoted by the Association of California Cities in an attempt to increase state revenues to local governments. Austin Chitmour was an officer in the association at the time and it was difficult for the mayor not to support it.

So, Saracino and the campaign staff produced a large fold-out brochure containing a montage of press clippings, each one mentioning the mayor's support for the tax measure. It created the impression that he supported every tax increase in the last century.

In her heart, Nadine didn't approve of the tactic. She and Doug both believed Austin Chitmour was a pompous nerd, but a fiscal conservative, nonetheless—the proof being that the residents of Pasadena hadn't experienced a tax increase in years.

The San Gabriel off-ramp was just ahead and Nadine had smoothly guided the car to a stop at Huntington Drive when Doug began to stir. Like a bolt before the light turned green, she screeched into a rubber-burning right, throwing his head back, waking him with a jolt. Perched on top of the building across the way was a huge billboard announcing her husband's candidacy. Had she not immediately turned right, he couldn't have missed his handsome face announcing, "I'll clean up the tax mess in Sacramento!"

Once more, Doug readjusted himself in the front seat. "Nadine! I've never seen you drive like this. Maybe a little music will calm you down."

As Doug reached forward and turned on the radio, Nadine's hand darted out and shut it off. "Music makes me nervous. All they have on at this hour is that rap-talk junk." Again, she fibbed. The campaign had purchased every available spot on L.A. radio. There was little doubt one of their ads would air before they reached home.

She desperately hoped they could avoid an ugly scene and put off the inevitable confrontation until that evening, when she led him into campaign headquarters. The place would be packed with people and Doug was too much of a gentleman to argue or create trouble in public. Anyway, if they lost, it would all be over and she could be remorsefully sorry, telling him she would never do anything to displease him again. And if he won? Well, Nadine would cross that bridge when it came into view.

Driving through residential Pasadena, she couldn't help but notice the sizable number of people distributing literature, door-to-door. Mayor Chitmour had his workers out en masse, as were the Stewart forces. The conservative California Republican Assembly had endorsed her husband, as had all the anti-tax groups. The College Young Republicans were going house-to-house, dropping flyers, while all of the ladies of PRISS were handling the get-out-the-vote drive, calling favorably inclined voters and encouraging them to get to their polling places. Volunteers were even lined up to drive the handicapped. Phone banks were humming at Stewart headquarters and Nadine had gone so far as to install callers at the main offices of Stewart and Associates.

She had spent more than four hundred thousand dollars, but she could easily afford it . . . a cheap price to pay for an assembly-man who would be voting responsibly on billions of dollars worth of appropriation bills. The surveys showed the race had narrowed down between Doug and the mayor. The other seven candidates had neither the prestige, money nor management to make a real show of it. The county registrar expected a low turnout; no better than 15 percent of the registered voters were likely to exercise their franchise. Carlos figured that if they took 30 percent of those who voted, Douglas Stewart would win by a landslide.

Nadine was approaching the San Marino city limits and was in a quandary as to which streets to steer clear of. STEWART FOR ASSEMBLY residential lawn signs were all over town. The blaze-orange and blue signs were visible just ahead. She had to distract him before he noticed any of them.

"Honey," she sweetly purred, "remember the last time we were alone together in Baja?"

Doug grinned. "You mean the day the guests flew back to the states and we finally had that quiet evening together? You bet I remember."

"Let's do that again soon," she giggled.

"How about tomorrow? In fact, let's turn around and go back to the airport right now. I can have a flight plan filed, the Centurion gassed up, and we'll be airborne in an hour."

She smiled and glanced his way. "How about this afternoon?" Now that she had her husband's full attention, he didn't notice at

all when she darted down a side street to avoid a number of plac-
ards instead of following the regular route to their home. She
pulled into the driveway without a mishap. Only a few hours more
and the polls would be closed. About nine o'clock, they would
make their appearance at headquarters. She was sure she could
keep him occupied until then. *Love still conquers all,* she thought
triumphantly, as she gave her husband her brightest smile.

★ ★ ★

EXPERTLY, NADINE EASED the car into a slot at Pasadena's Lake
Towers basement parking garage. Before Doug could say a word,
she quickly got out of the car and hurried for the elevators. The jet-
black spangles on her designer cocktail dress sent sparks of light
flying as she half-walked, half-ran. She hugged her black mink
stole tight with the hand that still held the keys to the Mercedes.
"The headquarters is on the seventh floor," she shouted over her
shoulder.

Doug ran to catch up. "Nadine, you still haven't told me much
about your candidate. What did you say his name is?"

"In about ten seconds, you'll be meeting him. He's a handsome
devil and he has a wonderful disposition."

"Do I have reason to be jealous?"

"Not in the least," she answered, punching the elevator button.
"He's just a nice family man, devoted to his wife."

Doug reached out and hugged her. "Just like me?"

She stood on her toes and gave him a kiss. "Yes, sweetheart, just
like you."

As the elevator door opened, a crowd of young people suddenly
arrived behind them and pushed their way in, shoving Nadine and
Doug to the back. They were laughing and jabbering excitedly
among themselves. One of them turned and recognized Mrs.
Stewart. He curiously stared at her companion, then at a campaign
brochure he pulled from his pocket. Wide-eyed and deferential, he

thrust out his hand to Doug. "I'm so-o-o-o honored to meet you, sir. Gang, look who we have here—the next assemblyman from the fifty-fourth district, fightin' Doug Stewart!"

All the young people turned in awe, crowding around him, patting him on the shoulder, and trying to grasp his hand. Just then, the elevator stopped and the doors opened on the seventh floor, exposing a giant ballroom overflowing with supporters.

Someone shouted, "Our candidate's here!" as all bedlam broke loose. They began cheering and stamping their feet, whistling, shouting, "Hi Doug . . . hello Nadine!" Arms outstretched with eager hands offered greetings to their hero.

A red, white, and blue-bedecked four-piece band was tucked in a corner and upon the Stewarts' appearance, immediately struck up the political refrain, "He's a Jolly Good Fellow." The well-wishers began to sing as TV sets blared out election results; the noise was deafening. Doug felt like he was staring into a thousand mirrors; his picture was plastered all over the walls, grinning back at him.

A large chalkboard was stretched across one end of the room, where several people were jotting down the early precinct returns. A packed bar was set up in another corner, alongside a huge table brimming with beverages and platters of food. The entire array looked like a Fourth of July carnival. Colorful streamers draped from the ceiling to the overhead lights down to each campaign poster. STEWART FOR ASSEMBLY was everywhere—on coffee cups, matchbooks, banners, sashes, stickpins, and campaign buttons.

Doug was stunned and speechless, his mouth agape. He was completely overwhelmed by the adulation and good cheer showered upon him. Friends, clients, and business acquaintances gathered around, patting his back, shaking his hand, offering him their best wishes.

"Congratulations, Doug, you've put on a great race!"

"First time I've actually enjoyed contributing money to a candidate."

A cute, sparkle-eyed young lady offered him a plastic glass filled with iced white wine. Doug wasn't much of a drinker but he accepted it gladly and gulped it down. His throat was so dry, he still could not speak.

Crowding around him were Herbert Dawkins, president of Dawkins Realty; Clay Crowe, his stockbroker; Barry Stone, insurance magnate and president of USC's Alumni; and several prestigious members of his athletic club.

"Herb! Barry! What are you guys doing here?"

"Why wouldn't we be? We're members of your finance committee," answered Barry.

"Yeah!" cracked Herb Dawkins, "Nadine hit us up for a bundle."

They all laughed hilariously—everyone but Doug, who was turning to look for his wife; she was edging away. Doug grabbed her by the back of her dress and pulled her close before she could escape into the crowd. "Not so fast, sweetheart."

Carlos Saracino pushed his way through the throng, then grabbing Doug's hand tightly in his own large one, asked Nadine, "Isn't it about time I met the man?"

Relieved, Nadine smiled and faced her husband. "Doug, this is Carlos Saracino, the man I hired to manage our campaign."

Doug's cheeks were flushed and his jaw thrust menacingly forward as he murmured through clenched teeth, "Nadine, is there someplace around here where we can meet in private? We have a few things to discuss."

Before she could answer, Arnie Kleinberg came bursting through, grinning fiendishly. Flashing several papers under Carlos' nose, he stuttered, "I-I go-I got 'em!" All eyes transfixed on the material in Arnie's hand.

Completely ignoring her husband, Nadine blurted out, "Arnie, do you have the absentee vote count?" She knew that soon after the polling stations closed, the county registrar would release the extremely important results of the ballots turned in by mail. Arnie said nothing. He was waving the pages over his head, rolling his eyes and doing a little jig in front of them.

Suddenly, he stopped the gyrations and turned to Doug. "So, *this* is our new assemblyman!"

★ ★ ★

THE REPORTER FROM THE *Pasadena Star News* was persistent. "Mr. Stewart, when did you realize you had the election in the bag?"

"Uh, just two minutes ago," answered a perplexed and angry Doug Stewart.

"At what exact period in the campaign did you feel you actually might have a chance of winning?" asked the man from the *Los Angeles Times*.

Eyes flashing, Doug said, "Uh, just a few minutes ago."

"When did you become aware of the effectiveness of your stealth strategy?" probed the ABC cameraman.

Doug's jaw muscles were working overtime. "Uh, just a few minutes ago."

Nadine, watching from behind the media people, saw that the Stewart volcano was about to erupt. She waved desperately for Saracino to intercede.

Carlos expertly stepped forward and smoothly interrupted the interview. "Gentlemen, Mr. Stewart has had a hard campaign and it has been a very tiring evening for him. Let's give him a moment's rest. In the meantime, why don't you talk to his inspiration, the lovely woman who stood faithfully by his side." Motioning for Nadine to come forward, he continued, "This little lady was the driving force in the success of this campaign, second only to her husband." He smiled graciously as he presented an effervescent, triumphant Nadine Stewart to the California media.

Nadine was in her glory. Those nearby crowded to catch the impending interview and broke into loud applause when Nadine was introduced. And when she kissed Doug on the cheek and raised his right arm in victory, the crowd went wild.

Amid the raucous cheering and unrestrained adoration being heaped upon them both, Doug could see it was no time for dissent.

He leaned close to his wife's ear and whispered firmly, "Nadine, now's not the time or place to get into this. Let's go home, quick."

"Sweetheart, I can't right now. You have been asked by CBS to go downtown to their main studio for a live interview. Carlos said you couldn't make it, so they requested me instead." A wistful hopefulness spread over her face as she asked, "Do you mind?"

Doug looked into her pleading blue eyes and could see the joy and excitement pulsating through her body. She was on top of the world, the queen of the hill, oblivious to the chaos she had created for him. Doug realized he had given her too much leeway in his affairs. Out of his love for her or unwillingness to argue, he had conceded too often, at least politically. He should have put his foot down years ago, but most certainly, when she first mentioned forging his name to the nomination papers.

But he hadn't. Now was no time to make a scene . . . tomorrow would be soon enough. Let her have her night of honor and praise. "How will you get to the TV station?" he asked. "I'm bushed and really need to get home."

"I'll take the car. I've arranged for Kathleen to drive you. Wait up, sweetheart. I'll be there just as soon as I can." The cheering had subsided as Nadine began to skillfully handle further questions from the reporters.

Doug watched for a moment, then motioned to Kathleen to meet him by the exit. Quietly, they slipped away and headed for the elevator. On his way out, he overheard one of the campaign volunteers comment on Nadine's competent handling of the press. "Boy, that Mrs. Stewart is terrific with the media. She'd make a great candidate one day."

Doug thought, *Someday? She already has.*

FIVE

Tʜᴇʏ ᴅʀᴏᴠᴇ ᴀʟᴏɴɢ Huntington Drive in silence. Not a word was said until Kathleen turned her blue Honda Civic into the Stewart driveway and pulled to a stop. Doug pushed the door open and struggled to get out of the small car, his exit complicated by the piles of books, posters, lawn signs, and campaign brochures crammed into the tiny vehicle. Some of the material fell out with him.

Doug reached down and picked up one of the red, white, and blue flyers; there it was again, his smiling face on the front. He tossed the flyer onto the empty seat, as one might discard a burning match. "Thanks for the ride, Kathleen. The evening was memorable." He turned abruptly and walked toward the door.

Kathleen slid over from the driver's seat and hollered out the window, "Don't be too hard on her, Doug. She honestly thinks she's done the right thing." She hesitated, then added, "and I think so too."

Doug stopped short, looked back, and stared woefully at Kathleen. "I think both of you are candidates for the Screwloose Resort." Raising his arms wide in exasperation, he called to her, "Come on inside, Kathleen. I need some advice on how to get out of this mess."

Kathleen looked surprised. "What do you mean . . . get out of? You're not thinking of undoing all the work we've done . . . are you?"

Doug flashed a determined smile. He suspected that neither she nor Nadine had ever contemplated his refusing to serve if elected.

"That's exactly what I have in mind. Let's see how we can make it as painless as possible." He continued up the flower-bordered pathway to the house, then glanced back. "Kathleen, aren't you coming?"

Still startled, she quickly climbed out of the car, hurried after her newly-elected candidate, and followed him into the house. "Now, Doug, let's not be hasty."

This was a totally unexpected twist, a political curve ball he had tossed out, a strike that left Kathleen flustered. Even though he was uncooperative, a candidate who refused to campaign after all the money and effort spent on his behalf, they never dreamed Doug Stewart would refuse to take the oath of office.

"Doug, tell me that you're kidding. You filed to run for the seat; you can't back out now."

Doug flicked on the den lamps and stared at the startled politico. "Oh, so Nadine didn't tell you?"

"Tell me what?"

He folded his arms and shook his head in mock disbelief. "I thought you were the best of friends and told each other everything."

"We do," said Kathleen. "Everything political, that is."

"I'm afraid not, my dear Mrs. Rowe. She obviously withheld some rather vital information. Are you aware that I never filed any papers for any office? That was the felonious brainchild of my deceitful bride, your bosom buddy, the incorrigible Nadine Logan Stewart."

Kathleen, tired, dropped heavily into the chair, in shocked disbelief. "She wouldn't. That's illegal."

"She did and you're right . . . it is. Prime time in the Crowbar Motel." Doug headed for the kitchen, changing the subject. "Where did you get that screw-top wine you were serving at the headquarters? It made an acid vat out of my insides. I'm going to have some milk and soda crackers, a surefire cure. Want some?"

"No, thank you," she responded. "But, if you have something a little stronger, like some coffee?"

"No problem . . . I'll make a pot." Doug began to rummage through the cabinets, as Kathleen joined him in the kitchen.

She watched his fumbling about in all the wrong places. "I know where she keeps the coffee; I'll do it. Go on back to the den and turn on channel two. We don't know, as yet, if there'll have to be a run-off with a Democrat. If we don't take at least fifty-one percent of the vote, there will be a final election sometime in the early fall."

Doug closed the refrigerator, poured himself a large glass of nonfat milk, and grabbed a box of crackers. He returned to the den with a joyful smile across his suntanned face. "What's that you say? There has to be another election?"

Kathleen didn't get the significance of his cheerful tone of voice. "Oh, don't worry. There's not a ghost of a chance a Democrat can win in this district."

"Wanta bet?" Doug did a bit of tap dancing as he whistled, "Happy Days are Here Again."

In bewilderment, she frowned, then let out a gasp. "Doug . . . you wouldn't!"

"Oh, wouldn't I!" He stopped his antics and flopped down on the couch, completely ignoring the milk he'd spilled on the deep piled rug. "How much did Nadine spend getting me this silly nomination, two hundred thousand dollars . . . three hundred thousand?"

"Ha! You're not even close," answered Kathleen. "What are you thinking of doing, financing your Democrat opponent?"

"What's wrong with that? He wants the job; I don't." Doug was really enjoying this train of thought. "I can see it all now, headlines in the *Star News*: 'Stewart Admits Opponent Is Better Qualified to Be in Office!'"

"You're being ridiculous!"

"Am I? How about this newsy item coming over the TV evening news? 'Republican Stewart makes a fool of himself in every debate with his opponent!'"

"There will be no need for debates," Kathleen declared.

"Oh, yes there will!" Doug was savoring the conversation even more. "I'll demand them . . . one a week! During each debate, I'll be weaker than weak! I'll mess up on schedule. I'll do so poorly that it will soon be evident that my defeat was preordained." Doug rubbed his hands together gleefully, thoroughly delighting in the verbal torturing of the political Kathleen Rowe. "Now, tell me, how do I go about getting some money to my opponent?"

Kathleen, flipping from one TV channel to another, rolled her eyes and said in disgust, "Oh, brother! Doug . . . we don't know yet who your opponent will be. Two Democrats filed for the seat. Probably, for no other reason than to win a spot on their party's central committee. One's named Agatha Watson; she's a student radical from Pasadena City College who thinks Angela Davis is too conservative. The other is a political asparagus named Elmo Smythe who wants to socialize socialism."

"What's a political asparagus?"

"A perennial candidate. They emerge from the political soil every election year and run for office, any office."

"I hope Elmo wins," offered Stewart. "Perseverance should be rewarded. But then again, you and Nadine deserve a radical feminist as payback for the dirty deal you handed me."

Their conversation was interrupted by the sonorous tones of the commentator. "And now, for the final results of the special election in San Gabriel Valley's fifty-fourth district, the seat vacated by Russ Newton. The Republican victor is Doug Stewart and, with all the late returns now coming in, it looks as though his stealth campaign has been successful. Mr. Stewart, one of the leading businessmen in Los Angeles County but a political unknown, has captured the majority of the votes." Through a toothy smile, the announcer added, "There will be no need for a run-off election. Congratulations, Assemblyman Stewart."

Anguish, then dread spread across Doug's face. "Kathleen, did I hear that right; there will be no run-off?"

Kathleen couldn't stifle a smirk. "That's right, Doug . . . or should I say, Assemblyman Stewart? It looks like you will have to resign from the legislature before you're even sworn in and cause the governor to call another expensive special election to replace you."

Doug was fuming; never could he have imagined being placed in such an intolerable position, or a more embarrassing set of contradictory circumstances. Unconsciously, he pulverized the remaining crackers between his hands, dusting the rug with a coat of pale powder.

"Kathleen, I'm too tired to think. Tomorrow, I'll talk to my counsel, John Rogers. He's an expert on the election laws. There has to be an angle." Suddenly, in frustration, he rose quickly. "No, I can't wait 'til tomorrow."

Doug picked up the portable phone from the coffee table and dialed. A sleepy voice answered, "Hello . . . who is it?"

"Sorry to call you at this hour, John, but it's important."

"Who is this?" the befuddled voice asked.

"It's me, John, Doug Stewart."

"Hey, congratulations, Doug. I just heard the great news, right before I went to—"

"Wait a second John—someone's trying to reach me. I insisted Nadine install call waiting. She was always talking to someone when I needed to reach her. Hold a second; I'll see who it is. Probably an inebriated well-wisher."

He pushed the button and said curtly, "Hello?"

"Mr. Stewart?" Doug didn't recognize the somber voice.

"Yes."

"This is Officer Morlock with the California Highway Patrol. I am terribly sorry, sir, to have to tell you that your wife has been in a horrible accident."

★ ★ ★

THE MEMORIAL SERVICE at the Lutheran Church in San Gabriel was overflowing with friends and acquaintances. Relatives from all over the country, business leaders, and state legislators were present to honor Nadine Stewart and offer their condolences to the bereaved husband and children. She was loved by many and admired by scores.

At the close of the service, it took better than an hour for the last guests to pay their respects and Doug was in a state of numbed shock, mumbling his thanks. The ugly reality hadn't really set in as yet; he expected someone to shake his shoulder and jar him awake, dispelling the nightmare he was experiencing. Hopefully, it would be Nadine, so he could wake up and kiss her . . . hold her tight.

When the last mourner had departed and only his son and daughters remained, Doug roamed about the old church, taking in the stained glass of Christ in the Garden of Gethsemane, the side room where he had taught fifth-grade Sunday school and where they had attended Bible classes. Memories flooded his mind—treasured moments, baptisms, communion with the family, and weddings. *Now, Nadine is with God.* That comforted him somewhat. Upon reflection, twenty-five years, seven months, and three days. . . . it suddenly seemed like such a short moment they had together.

"Dad, it's time we go home. Wally and the boys are getting the car." Diana grabbed his right arm and Marianne the other, both hanging on tightly to their father, while quietly weeping.

★ ★ ★

"WHAT ARE YOU GOING to do, Pop?" asked Wally as he sat down beside his father on the sofa. "You going to give politics a try? Everyone I've talked to thinks you'll be great."

"Yes, Dad, what about it?" Diana spoke for both girls.

"Frankly, I don't know. I haven't had much time to think it over." He hadn't informed them as to felonious facts regarding his campaign and nomination. The last thing he intended to talk about now was the foolhardiness of their mother and his deep desire to be rid of the political obligation.

"Mom was very proud of you, Dad," offered Diana. "She called us that night from the car phone to tell us about your big victory." She dabbed at her eyes as she realized that phone call may have been the last one her mother ever made.

"Me, too," added Marianne. "We were just as pleased as she was."

"When do you expect to be sworn in?" asked Wally.

Doug collected his thoughts and shook his head, trying to clear his brain of missing Nadine. "Today is Tuesday, isn't it? It's been a week now, let me think. Oh, yeah, the ceremony was scheduled for tomorrow, but the assembly Speaker's office called to say it could be delayed because of my present circumstances."

"That's too soon," said Marianne. "You should take some time."

"Maybe not," interrupted Diana. "Dad needs to think about other things, not sticking around here, fraught with memories. We're all scheduled to go home tomorrow and Dad will be alone."

"Yeah!" Wally agreed. "I think you're right; it would be good for Dad to head straight for Sacramento. It might help ease the pain."

"Mom would like that," softly added Marianne. "Don't you think so, Father?"

Doug smiled for the first time in a week. He looked at each one of his children before he answered. "Yes, my beloved daughter, she most certainly would." *I guess I can stand to serve one term in office . . . for her.*

SIX

Brad Clark thumbed through the stack of press clippings on his desk, then leaned back in his plush leather chair, hoisted his feet on top of his immense antique desk, and reflected on the news stories. "Maybe I've got a new political hot-shot on my hands!" he muttered. He pulled the phone forward and dialed his chief administrative assistant. "Mike, would you come in here, please?"

Within seconds, the door to the staff offices swung open and a slender, immaculately tailored young man came hustling into the spacious old capitol room reserved for the Republican minority leader. Brad Clark got up from behind his desk as Mike Buffington entered and waved him over to the old-time upholstered couch in the corner. The Republican leader dropped his huge frame into one of the Victorian armchairs, causing it to groan under his weight. Bending forward with difficulty, he slid the press clippings across the massive coffee table separating the two men. "Mike, what do you think? Looks like we might have a real pro on our hands—and a wealthy one, to boot."

The young man picked up one newspaper and read aloud from the feature article in the *San Francisco Times*.

> Douglas Stewart, the newest member of the assembly, is considered the master of political dirty tricks. His recent overwhelming victory can be attributed to a last-minute smear campaign. Even

members of his own party have complained about the vicious-ness of the attacks. Rob Gouty, a member of the Los Angeles central committee, stated that the assault on the respected mayor of Pasadena, the Honorable Austin Chitmour, was "a slimy gutterball tactic, unequaled in the recent annals of California politics."

Mike pointed to the name in the article. "Rob Gouty; that's a laugh. He managed Chitmour's try for the office." He continued reading:

The Stewart campaign has been referred to as the ultimate in stealth, the art of sneaking up on an opponent and blindsiding him at the last moment with half-truths and innuendoes. Some respected consultants are saying Stewart is the dirtiest cam-paigner to emerge in the last fifty years. A highly placed Democrat official said he fears what may occur, statewide, if more men like Stewart are elected and manage to control the Republican purse strings. When asked if the Democrats have anything to worry about, our source, who asked not to be identi-fied, quipped, "Does a deer doodoo in the woods?"

Mike looked up and snickered. "Doodoo in the woods? What a dumb response."

"Didn't everybody around here think Austin Chitmour was a shoo-in?" dryly inquired the minority leader. "I sent him a thousand bucks out of my campaign fund."

"You and a bunch of others. Stewart made mincemeat out of 'im. He completely stunned everyone by taking fifty-one percent of the vote." Buffington then added, "I recently saw some of those hit pieces; they were really top quality. Chitmour squeaked like a rusty door when they flooded the district, calling our office daily, demanding an ethics investigation."

"Did Stewart tell outright lies about the mayor?" asked Clark.

"Nah, from what I can tell," Buffington responded, laughing. "He committed the unpardonable political sin of revealing the truth, coloring it up a little to make it more interesting. By the way, Boss, I just examined Stewart's reports to the secretary of state's office. Guess who ran his campaign?"

"Carlos Saracino . . . and that's not all. Arnie Kleinberg did the polling and Laurie Noble did his research." Mike crossed his arms and leaned back into the uncomfortable antique chair. "How about those political apples?"

Brad Clark let out a low whistle. "So Saracino, Kleinberg, and Noble were involved."

"That's right. Stewart hired the best money can buy and from what we can tell by the early financial reports, he spent more than half a million in the last two weeks."

"Looks like we have a real heavy hitter in our midst," commented the Republican leader. "Is there anything else you can tell me about this guy?"

Buffington smiled knowingly. "Well, Stewart used the most significant strategy I have ever encountered—a brilliant ploy that completely caught the Chitmour forces off guard. What's more, it's a technique absolutely unheard of in contemporary American politics but practiced quite often before the nineteen hundreds."

"What was it?" eagerly asked Clark.

"In the eighteen hundreds, it was considered beneath the candidate's dignity to openly campaign and ask for votes. His friends and supporters did all the work. Speeches were permissible, but asking for votes was considered demeaning to the office and to the man."

"What are you trying to tell me . . . . Stewart didn't campaign?"

"He went fishing."

"What's so brilliant about that? Even I go fishing once in awhile."

"For the whole campaign?" smirked Buffington. "He even took a whole slew of people along on his yacht. His guests came back talking about what a great time they had and how accomplished

Stewart was at grilling albacore, but not a word was said about his politics. Neither Chitmour nor Gouty—nor anybody else, for that matter—had a clue about what he was up to."

"He never came back to campaign at all?"

"Not once did he leave Baja, California. He returned election night, just in time to celebrate his victory." Mike grew serious. "Of course, you know what happened that night after the celebration."

"Yes, that was tragic." Clark frowned, then added, "I hear they were a devoted couple, that he took it very hard. Do you know if she shared her husband's political ambitions?"

"I'm not really sure, but from what I hear, she wasn't a typical candidate's wife—standing in the background, pretending to glory in her husband's every word. As you know, spouses of the bright ones are usually rather apolitical . . . not this one. By the way, she was one of the Logan family. You know, the oil people out of Bakersfield."

"Yeah, I've heard of them. Bakersfield's answer to the Rockefellers."

"Yeah, they're the ones I mean. Stewart's wife was an only child and the sole beneficiary when her parents passed away. Upon her death, Stewart inherited it all. The combined wealth of Stewart and Associates and her estate make him one of the richest men in California, if not the country. It would be a good idea for you to talk him into helping with fundraising. Our assembly political action committee is practically broke. Stewart's business contacts are as good as you can get. We could use his assistance."

"That's a thought," said Brad. "Our caucus chairman, good ol' Lon Schmitz, has been doing a lousy job raising funds. I doubt if he could raise a sweat in a steam room, much less get contributions from a willing and able business community. He needs a helping hand or, should I say, a boot in the right direction."

"Or we'll all be getting the boot," wisecracked Mike.

Brad couldn't help but laugh. Buffington was right again. Brad Clark's leadership team was in question. He'd better protect his incumbents and gain new seats or be moved out for someone else to take over. Lon Schmitz had been a poor choice for the caucus chairmanship, enjoying the perks that came with a leadership job but not the work. Brad had supported Lon for the position because he'd been a key vote in attaining his own title of minority leader. At the time, Lon was an asset; now, he was a burden and threatened his jurisdiction. Mike was accurate; they all could get the boot.

Brad Clark was often amazed at the wealth of knowledge that was packed into his assistant's head. He was the minority leader's political eyes and ears—nicknamed "the Electrician," due to all the intrigue and legislative shenanigans he was wired into. Rarely did anything happen which affected the assembly's politics that wasn't picked up by Buffington's well-tuned antenna. His contacts were legion.

Mike's concern over the fiscal well-being of the party's pocketbook was well-founded. Schmitz's poor performance in helping their incumbents' reelection campaigns was becoming more apparent and they were grumbling. Although the caucus chairmanship crown rested precariously on Lon's head, no one else wanted the responsibility of being the chief fundraiser, especially not this late in the legislative session.

"Yeah, Mike, getting Stewart involved is a good idea. As soon as the opportunity presents itself, I'll try to finagle him into helping Lon."

"Boss, don't you think you might be building future competition for your own leadership position?"

"Probably, but so what? He can join the crowd. You know as well as I, there's a move afoot to topple me right now. Several of my dear colleagues salivate at the very thought of being minority leader." Brad shrugged his shoulders. "If we can't raise some bucks pretty soon and maintain our incumbents, I'll be history anyway."

★ ★ ★

SURPRISINGLY, THE FIRST month went by swiftly for Doug. The bombast, budget, and buffoonery were at least entertaining, dulling the heartache that still gnawed in his chest. Providentially, the special election had put him in the capitol at a propitious time. The most controversial budget in the state's history was being dissected, discussed, and cussed by both sides of the aisle. Revenues were down and the governor's budget was up 10 percent, creating a two-billion-dollar deficit. Doug had a front row seat on the floor of the Assembly chamber, watching the megabuck drama unfold.

The conservatives wanted cuts, the liberals wanted more spending. The liberals of both parties wanted an increase in taxes to pay for the expanding programs they had implemented. The conservatives, on the other hand, were ready to slash, cut, and burn. On both sides, the pompous pontificating abounded. The Democrats called their opponents hardhearted and the Republicans shouted about their fiscal irresponsibility.

Doug Stewart kept his own counsel; he had no intention of raising his microphone to enter the debate. Since he hadn't campaigned on any issues, there was no point in voicing an opinion. Quietly, without fanfare, he voted with the conservative Young Turks. *Nadine would be pleased,* he thought with a twinge of sadness. However, the tune the conservatives were singing wasn't new. The rabid oratory reminded him of the old melody, "It seems to me I've heard that song before."

The assembly committee on rules allocated sufficient funds for Doug to staff both his Sacramento and district offices. Each was equipped with state-of-the-art computer capabilities, modems, and laser printers. All were purportedly for state business but, in reality, Doug soon grasped the fact that every incumbent actually had a year-round campaign force at taxpayer expense.

The two parties each had their own caucuses, heavily staffed with partisan employees, available to fulfill almost any request. They provided the legislators with speech writing, press releases, research, radio and television opportunities, and much, much more. The state coffers even supplied twice-a-year district-wide newsletters, enabling all those elected to extol their own virtues to every constituent.

"Hey," Doug exclaimed, "no wonder these guys are reelected year after year!"

Doug interviewed a number of experienced women for his lead secretary and settled on petite, dark-haired Lorraine Menta. She was all-business, knew her way around the capitol, and Doug wisely allowed her to hire the other office personnel.

For the job of chief administrative assistant, he interviewed a dozen or so who had plenty of political experience in Sacramento, but found few had the productive work habits he required. In business, Doug had developed a formula for evaluating people; he called it his "P to BS factor." "P" stood for Productivity and "BS" was short for Bull Stuff. Doug realized that everyone had some of each—but to what degree?

If their "BS factor" exceeded 50 percent, Doug wouldn't think of hiring them or keeping them employed. He was an equal-opportunity employer—firing the unproductive no matter their race, sex, or color. However, if he judged their "P factor" was high, he gave them every opportunity for advancement. In his evaluation of those he interviewed for the administrative assistant position, he found much more BS than P. Doug thought he'd better reach into Stewart and Associates and bring Sean MacGruder to Sacramento. Sean was one of the bright young tax attorneys whose "P factor" was over 80 percent.

In short order, Assemblyman Stewart put together an excellent capitol crew, then sat back and enjoyed the shenanigans. Unlike his conservative colleagues, he was in no hurry to save the state. He quietly cast his votes, faithfully attended the caucus meetings, and served on the committees to which he was assigned. The first month, he just took it all in. He was surprised by the deferential treatment he received from other legislators and state employees, and by all of the political questions he was being asked. Although he kept repeating that he was new at this political stuff, his colleagues just raised their eyebrows and winked at him.

Eventually, whenever he was asked his opinion about something he knew little or nothing about, he learned how to respond: he said he'd delve into it and get back to them later. In time, when someone looked at him expectantly, he refined his response even further—into a knowing smile and a wink. It seemed to work. Doug saw that with his quiet, unpretentious manner and good nature, he was becoming quite acceptable in Sacramento's political circles.

The conservatives liked his votes, the liberals liked his silence, and the veterans were impressed with his respect to their seniority— particularly when he listened attentively and compliantly to their unsolicited advice. Personally, he found much of it contradictory, though entertaining. One of the older rural county members even took him aside and suggested, "Stewart, to be effective, sometimes ya have to rise above principle."

Then again, one of the conservative firebrands offered a countervailing opinion. "Doug, you must put principle before politics. Consistency is the key!"

Another over-imbibing colleague belched out at a cocktail party, "Consistency is the hobgoblin of small minds. Hic!"

Doug was humored by some of the liberal Democrats' attempts at schmoozing, probing to see how gullible he was to flattery. "You're not like the other wild-eyed, hair-shirt conservatives around here. You seem very sensible. We can work well together."

It was not entirely entertaining; Doug was disturbed by the lack of harmony within the Republican ranks. During the often stormy caucus meetings, he kept silent and listened attentively to all sides. The only discussion he allowed himself to get into was over how long it would take for the Los Angeles Clippers basketball team to succeed the Sacramento Kings as the dominant team in the Western Division.

In particular, he noticed their caucus chairman, Lon Schmitz, was indecisive, moderate, and too conciliatory to hold the turbulent meetings together. Due to his unwillingness to limit debate, the discussions frequently turned into shouting matches and acrimonious name-calling. Schmitz's caucus chair was in jeopardy and he knew it. Trying to please everyone, he pleased no one, allowing the meetings to deteriorate into little more than bombastic diatribes where big egos were bent and badly bruised. The budget debate elevated the clashes to such a violent level that during one acidic screaming match, much to everyone's surprise, Lon Schmitz resigned in disgust.

The ensuing argument over his replacement was equally heated and troublesome. Finally, Brad Clark, seizing the opportunity, suggested they appoint someone temporarily to chair the caucus until after the budget was resolved. "We need someone who hasn't been deeply involved in one side of the debate or the other." He cast a glance around the conference table, then stopped at Doug. "I think Doug Stewart fits the bill . . . any objections?"

All eyes turned to the freshman legislator. His exalted business reputation, along with the gossip about his great wealth, had grown to ridiculous heights. No doubt, Doug was by now perceived as a campaigning guru, a genius, and a direct-mail wizard. It was also rumored that he was being considered for a high-level cabinet post in the nation's Capitol and that he intended to leave office bound for Washington's greener political pastures, after serving out his first term. A number of heads nodded affirmatively at Brad Clark's request to seat Doug in the caucus chair; however, not all.

"Now, wait a second," offered one of the moderates. "Aren't we rushing into this? In all deference to our new assemblyman's ability, he's only been here a few months. Don't you all think that someone with more experience should fill the job?"

"Oh, I completely agree," smoothly interjected Brad. "But we're only talking about a temporary chairman, nothing permanent. That's why I think Stewart best fits the bill. Don't you all concur? Let's have a show of hands on Stewart filling the job, for the time being."

Hands shot up around the table. A majority seemed to agree Doug Stewart was a good choice . . . a definite majority.

But not Doug Stewart. . . . "Hey guys, I'm the new kid on the block. There're a lot of you who are better qualified for the job." Of course, nobody believed his humble statement. In fact, his self-effacing modesty made him all the more palatable. A good caucus chairman *should* be a little devious.

Eventually, after much cajoling by Brad, Doug said, "Okay, I'll do it . . . but it's only temporary."

There were some smiles and knowing glances; several engaged in subtle rib-jabbing, as well. Brad Clark was more than pleased with his maneuvering, having orchestrated the episode so artfully, even down to Lon's "spontaneous" resignation. He had caught his opposition by surprise and finessed Stewart into a job he knew little about, much less what was in store for him. The portly leader congratulated himself.

Doug took over immediately and with his steady hand at the helm, a semblance of order prevailed. They covered all matters of importance in a short while. As the meeting broke up, the media awaited in the halls outside. They had been tipped that something newsworthy was happening. They clustered around Brad Clark and were told of the change in caucus leadership. He stressed the change was only temporary, but said it in such a fashion that the press saw Lon Schmitz's resignation and Doug's ascendancy in a different light.

The political pundits played it big:

DRAMATIC CHANGE IN REPUBLICAN LEADERSHIP
BUSINESS EXEC TAKES OVER NUMBER-TWO JOB!
ULTRA-CONSERVATIVE HEADS GOP POLITICAL MACHINE

Doug's refusal to hold a press conference and his down-playing of his new role did nothing but heighten the conspiratorial bent of the news. The *San Francisco Times* ran a feature story on the new assemblyman, dredging up anything remotely controversial they could find. Their headline read, "Super-Rich Now in Command?" with the sub-caption, "Multimillionaire takes over fundraising leadership function of the Assembly Republicans."

The body copy was filled with innuendo and half-truths, some of it more than irritating to Doug. He erupted in disgust when he read the article, "Mastermind! Dirty Campaigning!" Grabbing the paper, he stormed about his office and called out, "Lorraine! Find out where Brad Clark is." Lorraine speedily dialed the minority leader's office while Doug fidgeted about the reception area, fuming, swearing softly under his breath.

"Boss, Clark's upstairs in the cafeteria, having a bite to eat."

Instead of waiting for the elevator to reach the second-floor offices, Doug quickly vaulted up the stairway, two steps at a time, to the sixth floor. At ten A.M., the cafeteria was practically empty, with just a few people scattered throughout the large room, drinking coffee, reading the morning papers. In the far corner, next to the windows, sat Clark, polishing off an assortment of doughnuts while conferring with his staff on pending legislation. Brad's large, rotund frame practically obscured the dining chair—ample evidence of doughnuts past.

When he saw Doug's vigorous approach and the newspaper clutched tightly in his hand, he smiled and remarked, "So, I see you've read the morning *Frisco Times*." Turning to the others at the table, he said, "Would you excuse us? We'll finish the briefing later in my office."

The staff quickly got up from their seats, politely nodded to Doug, and left.

"Hope I'm not breaking up anything important."

"Nah, sit down. Rest your bones. Have a doughnut." The rumpled and tousle-haired legislator pushed the plate of remaining gooey, chocolate-covered spheres in Doug's direction.

"No, thanks—I've got something else to chew on." Doug slapped the *San Francisco Times* down hard on the table. "How *dare* they publish garbage like this? Not a word of truth in it."

"Aren't you rich—in fact, a millionaire?" asked Clark.

"Well . . . yes."

"Aren't you the caucus chairman?"

"Temporarily."

"Didn't you run a hard-hitting campaign and send out a ton of negative mail on your opponent?"

"I didn't run squat. I was off fishing the whole time, not even in the country."

"I heard about that," Clark admitted with a wink and a grin. "Brilliant, ab-so-lute-ly brilliant. As far as I'm concerned, that makes you a clever political genius. Only a super-brain could win a campaign and not participate! Why, man, you're the envy of everyone here! For those of us who've been around awhile, campaigning is the armpit of the body politic! Considering you're a conservative Republican and the *Frisco Times* is a liberal rag. . . . You're an old pro, what else did you expect . . . good press?"

Unaccustomed to bad reviews, the attack hurt Doug's pride, having spent years earning the admiration and respect of the business world's media. Favorable articles about Stewart and Associates were commonplace in the trade publications; even the *Wall Street Journal* had published glowing commentary.

"Do you think I should set the record straight with a press release?"

Brad furrowed his brow and shuddered. "You know better than that. Worst thing you could do. That's like responding to 'When did you stop beating your wife?'"

Doug cast him a quizzical look. "What do you mean, beat my wife?"

"Come on, Stewart, stop pulling my leg; you know what I'm talking about. You're hardly new to the world of politics. You know as well as I do that if you respond to a false charge, the charge will be repeated in your denial of it. It's a no-win situation to be in, 'cause every time some poor sucker says he didn't do whatever he's charged with, it brings up the falsehood again." Brad leaned back in his chair and folded his arms across his ample belly. "Wise guys like us don't respond to 'beat your wife' charges." He grinned and winked at Doug again.

Doug sat slumped in his chair, discouraged by the inequity of it all and not fully understanding what Brad was talking about. "Well, what can I do? I don't intend to put up with this."

"You know the first lesson in politics: Don't try to piddle on the shoes of the man who owns the microphone or, in this case, the newspaper. Secondly, don't expect your opposition to toot your horn." Brad reached over and delicately picked up one of the doughnuts between his pudgy fingers and bit a huge chunk out of it, consuming the entire sticky morsel in two bites.

When he'd wiped his fingers clean and had another gulp of coffee, he resumed the dissertation. "Doug, those of us on the inside know there are only three ways our reputations can be made; what we can communicate about ourselves, what the media prints or broadcasts about us and, last but certainly not least, what our opposition says we are. There ain't no others."

"That sounds like two out of the three are on the other side," Stewart grumbled.

"Bright man . . . but not all the media is as heavily biased as the *Frisco Times*. If we work at it and don't get defensive, most reporters will try to be somewhat objective, in spite of their natural portside bent. Let's face it—when we're elected, the press looks upon us as live meat, ready to be slaughtered if we show signs of weakness. Nobody forced us into the legislature."

"Speak for yourself," Doug quickly responded. "I am a product of my dear, departed wife's fertile imagination. For the sake of her memory, I intend to finish out this term, then it's sayonara, adios, auf wiedersehen, and good-bye."

"Sure, uh-huh," winked Brad, not buying a word of it. "I've heard that's your intent. There are few secrets around this place. Now, if you would like, I can give you a suggestion as to how you can get back at the *San Francisco Times*—while you're still here, of course."

Doug's interest picked up and he eagerly declared, "I'm all ears."

"The ultimate pain to all liberals is a majority of conservatives in the legislature," joked Brad, "and since they seem to be in fear of your wealth, why don't you make them sweat a bit?"

"And just how can I do that?"

The minority leader asked Doug if he would be willing to take over the upcoming fundraiser, now that Lon Schmitz had resigned. Ticket sales for the event, scheduled for the following month, were doing poorly.

Clark's enthusiasm was obvious. "You're our present caucus chairman; go out and raise us a few bucks and help us elect more Republicans."

Doug took a few minutes to think over the request. He really wasn't that busy and the extra work would keep him occupied. He certainly had plenty of experience, helping raise money for United Way, the Red Cross, and his church. "Why not?" he said. "If that's my job, I guess I'll have to do it."

Clark beamed broadly and winked at Doug, yet again. "Good for you!"

"Brad, is there something wrong with your right eye?"

"Uh, no, why do you ask?"

"Just wondered."

As soon as Doug left the cafeteria, Mike Buffington strode over from the elevator. "How did it go?"

"I got him to do the fundraiser but we really have to watch him. Without a doubt, Stewart is either the shrewdest operative I've ever met, or the most naive. He plays the innocent freshman to a tee. If I didn't know better, I'd swear he was dumber than a board on the day-to-day working of politics."

"He can't fool you, Boss."

"No," grinned the Republican leader. "But he sure tries hard."

SEVEN

★ ★ ★

IN THE PAST, AND AT Nadine's insistence, Doug had endured more political money raisers than he cared to remember. He viewed them as gatherings put on by masochists who were intent on punishing the attendees. Unappetizing food was too often followed by a gloom-and-doom speech, bemoaning the latest Democrat boondoggles.

First off, this event was going to be enjoyable—a fun . . . raiser. Making his plans for an entertaining evening gave Doug a great sense of satisfaction, and in spite of the stabs of grief he felt each time he thought of Nadine always by his side at such events, he found himself plunging into the endeavor with enthusiasm. He insisted that there be no political speeches, that the dinner must be the best fare available and the music . . . danceable.

He took full advantage of his multiple contacts within the business community for assistance. He had granted many favors for his clients and they willingly reciprocated. Stewart and Associates had been an easy touch for community and humanitarian projects in the past, and now he was calling in the chips. Being extremely well-liked, his giving nature and willingness to help others had made Doug many friends in all walks of life, including the entertainment industry.

The "Who's Who" of the business world comprised the finance committee Doug put together. Assembled in his corporate boardroom, major CEO's gathered to help their newly-elected friend, each taking responsibility to sell tables of tickets with ten patrons per table. They decided on a price of five hundred dollars per person and for anyone choosing to attend the exclusive reception to meet the Hollywood celebrities Doug had recruited to add the right amount of glamour and glitz, the cost jumped to a thousand dollars.

Calling on his many contacts in the film community, Doug Stewart was determined to deliver up an event packed with big-name stars . . . present and past. Academy Award-winner Lola Russell accepted, as did the bosomy, blonde sex symbol of yesteryear, Mitzi "Boom Boom" Mayberry. Three top recording artists said they'd be honored to show up, as did Tina Swift, current film heartthrob. Rex Upholt, the most famous of Western tough guys, would come with his sidekick, Kathy, and Bullet, his equally famous palomino. Sir Ronald Westland, England's Shakespearean luminary, also agreed to make an appearance. Russ Limburg, the nationally popular and hilariously funny talk-show host, consented to be the master of ceremonies.

When word of the celebrities got out, along with the mushrooming advance ticket sales, phone calls started to pour in from U.S. senators and congressmen wanting to attend. Doug agreed . . . at half-price. There were no complimentary tickets for his big fundraiser, except for those reserved for the stars and California's own Republican assemblymen. There were no free rides; even the press had to pay.

To the delight of his fellow legislators, each was assigned to a table with a celebrity, and supplied with a list of the table guests and their financial assets. Doug made sure there were well-heeled business people at every elbow. He averted another caucus squabble by having the single assemblymen draw straws for the privilege of being seated with the alluring starlet, Tina Swift. The older members did the same for the honor of joining Mitzi "Boom Boom" Mayberry.

Doug made sure every detail was carefully covered, so barring one of California's unpredictable earthquakes, he had no doubt the gala would be a smashing success.

★ ★ ★

AND IT WAS. . . .

Indeed, the festive occasion was not only a "fun-raiser," but a noteworthy money-maker. Exceeding by far any prior Assembly GOP event, they cleared more than six hundred and fifty thousand dollars. The morning after, it was definitely the talk throughout the Capitol halls.

The press also took notice, especially the *San Francisco Times*. Galled at having to pay to be admitted, bile flowed in the reportage of the affair. The headline read:

SPECIAL-INTEREST FAT CATS FUND REPUBLICAN BASH!

The column itself was even more vitriolic:

Megabuck millionaires gathered to back Republican fund-raiser, spearheaded by super-affluent new caucus chairman, Assemblyman Douglas Stewart. The privileged rich crammed a king's ransom into the campaign coffers of the Republican legislators . . . blah, blah, blah. . . .

Some other print media took a different slant. The *Sacramento Advocate* called Doug Stewart "the rising star in the Republican ranks. . . . " The *Fresno Mercury* read, "A switch . . . Hollywood glamour turns out for the Republicans!"

Most of the newspaper reports made comment on the outstanding job done by the newly-elected statesman, Doug Stewart, and what fresh air he was breathing into the Republican's caucus operation. True to form, they made sure the Democrats had an opportunity to get in their two cents' worth, which they did . . . unmercifully.

"This clearly shows the real difference between the Republicans and ourselves," said Willie Green, Speaker of the assembly. "We Democrats represent the poor and they are the party of the fat cats." The liberal leader of their caucus, Jesse Boggs, was even more outspoken. "The common man has cause to fear exploitation from the likes of Douglas Stewart. His ties to special interests is evident. If his kind ever gets control, they would undo all the good we've built for the average working people—the aged, students, minorities, the handicapped, the widows and orphans, the welfare mothers and the underprivileged children of the state. Did I mention the forests, the oceans, and the very air we breathe?"

Appalled and angry, Doug tossed the papers down on Brad Clark's desk. "Jesse didn't leave out a thing, did he?"

"No, he usually doesn't," the silver-haired minority leader observed, with a grin. "Ol' Jesse is pretty good at covering all the class-warfare bases."

"Wasn't their last big fundraiser a success?"

"Sure was. The assembly Demos reported raising better than half a mil."

"That's almost as much as we raised!"

"Yep," Brad agreed, smiling. "But, there's a difference. They put the bite on the unions, the public employees, and enlightened human interest associations."

"What's an enlightened human interest association?"

"A special interest that gives generously to the Democrats," responded Clark.

"There's a difference?"

"To them, there is. You must never forget, Sacramento is the justification capitol of California, and justifying the feathering of their proletariat nests isn't the sole property of the Democrats. You saw it liberally applied by Republicans as some found reason to vote for the budget bill."

Doug cocked his head, then asked, "Didn't I see *you* vote for the budget bill?"

Brad haughtily proclaimed, "Doug, one of the cardinal rules of politics is . . . pay no attention to what we *do*, only to what we *say*." Changing the subject quickly, he pointed to the daily journals strewn across his desk. "You should be delighted at all the good press you're getting. It usually takes years for a new assembly member to get the media's attention. You've done it in less than three months, and statewide coverage, to boot."

"This is good press?"

"For a conservative Republican, it is. They make you look like King Kong. Some of our guys would kill for press like that. The political hard-core love it, the liberals hate it, and everyone in between thinks you're a somebody." Brad picked up one of the papers and scanned an article about the fundraiser. Smiling from ear to ear, the portly leader put the paper down and looked directly into Doug's eyes. "Yep, you're now an official eight-hundred-pound political gorilla and . . . the new permanent caucus chairman."

★ ★ ★

DOUG FIRED THE ENTIRE senior caucus staff, keeping only a few of the secretaries. "Poor 'P to BS factors'—low productivity versus high bull stuff," he explained to the press. He had surprised four of the staff playing bridge at two o'clock in the afternoon.

"Late lunch," they claimed, as Doug unexpectedly entered the caucus offices, shocking one and all.

"To your misfortune," he said to the startled card players. "I came in at noon and the place was deserted. Clean out your desks; you're fired!" The prior chairman, Lon Schmitz, never visited the staff's quarters, always holding the meetings in his capitol office. Work habits changed rapidly under Stewart's direction.

Doug was still a hands-on employer with his personnel, until he found their "P factor." Then, if they were competent, they would be given great latitude, along with their responsibilities. If they were found to be incompetent, he sent them packing.

During the first few months of serving in office, Doug learned that everyday practices were very different under the state capitol's dome. He discovered that legislators often exempted themselves from laws they imposed on the general populous. Sacking employees took nothing more than firing them on the spot; working them late hours without additional compensation was commonplace.

Equal-opportunity laws didn't apply either. A legislator could hire as he pleased—black or white, male or female. Matter of fact, Doug found an inordinate number of women seeking the opportunity to work at any job under his direction. Every day, his office seemed crowded with females of all ages seeking employment.

"What gives?" he asked Lorraine. "Aren't there any men after these positions?"

She gave him a sly smile and asked, "Don't you get it?"

"Get what?"

"Boss, you're the biggest catch in Sacramento . . . maybe in the state."

"You must be kidding! I'm an almost fifty-year-old grandfather with a newly acquired extra inch or two adding to my waistline."

"You're also an attractive and popular state official, sophisticated, filthy rich, and a widower. All of that makes you exceedingly handsome—at least as good-looking as Robert Redford with the build of Sylvester Stallone. It's been well-documented that the two most powerful aphrodisiacs for single women over thirty are power and money."

"Lorraine, you gotta be joking!" Doug was truly shocked by his secretary's candid remarks. It never dawned on him that he could be perceived as a prize catch. Now that he thought about it, maybe that's why so many women had been stopping him in the halls, asking inane questions and batting their eyes.

"Boss, you should hear the gossip during coffee breaks in the cafeteria. Seems my job is considered California's premier location for shooting love-arrows in your direction, for an unmarried woman or even married, for that matter. You'd be embarrassed by some of the questions I'm asked."

"Guess I've been pretty blind, not to mention preoccupied," admitted the flustered assemblyman. "Maybe you'd better pick out some happily married gals from your church and I'll handle the guys."

The burst of added attention was becoming an anathema to Doug Stewart, who was suddenly thrust into so much limelight that he was no longer able to be his own very private person. Everywhere he went, somebody or some group wanted to talk to him or have him appear as a featured speaker. The invitations poured into his district office. Every service club wanted him on their program, Republican volunteer organizations pleaded with him to address their meetings, and the local media was demanding his time. He couldn't believe the number of parades each city put on. There was a parade celebrating every holiday and one city even had a Mule Day Parade where Doug was expected to ride a jackass down Main Street as Grand Marshal. Each one sent delegates to his office encouraging his participation, showing great disappointment if he declined.

Doug tried to comply with most requests for the first month or so, but flying back and forth from the capitol to his district and trying to stay awake during dull committee hearings was exhausting. Having learned to say no, he sent his district aide in his stead, who seemed to thrive on each opportunity to promote his boss. At any rate, he had no intention of running for reelection, so there was no reason to wear himself out.

Doug thought the attention would abate during the summer recess, but when he found a TV camera crew and commentator camped outside his Sacramento apartment complex, waiting to do an interview, that did it.

As soon as he entered his office, he buzzed for his secretary. "Lorraine, we've finished interviewing for the caucus staff and I'm satisfied we have a good team to start with. I'm haggard and dragging and need a change of scenery. I'm going to disappear for a few days. Think I'll take the bird over to Reno and take in a show or maybe fly down the coast to Baja for some fresh air. I've already called Executive Air; the plane is gassed and waiting."

"There are several people outside who want to see you. What should I tell them?"

"Tell 'em I'll be back in a few days but don't suggest where I'm going." With that, Doug ducked out the office side door into the hallway. The private elevator reserved for the legislature was just around the corner and, fortunately, no one saw him take it to the basement, where the members parked their cars. Doug hadn't made up his mind where he was going until he turned on the car radio to a station advertising that one of his favorites, Anne Murray, was singing at Harrah's in Reno.

He checked with FAA and found clear weather projected for the next few days. Estimating his time of flight and his ETA, he filed a flight plan, checked the aircraft thoroughly, started the powerful Lycoming engine, and called the tower for taxi instructions.

"Centurion seven, seven niner foxtrot, cleared to runway three zero." Doug pushed the throttle forward slightly and began his taxi. The air traffic was slight and after the run-up and magneto check, he informed the tower he was ready to go. As the monotone instructions of the tower operator gave him his clearance and Doug slowly advanced the throttle to the wall, the powerful engine surged to life, pushing him firmly back into the seat . . . it was a good feeling.

As the plane lifted off the ground, he retracted the landing gear and trimmed the plane for the climb. Banking according to tower instructions, Doug switched over to Sacramento Air Traffic Control until he reached the foothills; then Oakland Traffic Control took over. The Cessna 210 quickly reached cruising altitude and Doug began to "true out" the airship for level flight.

Suddenly, there was a nerve-racking shudder, causing the controls to shake in Doug's hands. He had recently replaced the old propeller with a new one, but something was desperately wrong; the vibration was increasing dramatically.

As Doug immediately pulled back on the throttle, the shuddering decreased; correspondingly, so did the altitude. He promptly went through the proper emergency procedures and set the plane's attitude for maximum glide. Doug considered tuning the radio to 121.5 and calling, "Mayday! Mayday!" but thought better of it. He had just passed over the airport in the small mountain town of Placerville and seeing no aircraft in the pattern, figured he should be able to land there without difficulty.

With no power, he would have to plan his descent just right and hold to tight turns above the runway. Circling down quickly due to the loss of lift, he tried to estimate how to play the wind. The airfield was on top of a wide ridge; any miscalculations on final approach could put him into the side of a mountain.

Switching to the local frequency, he called, "Placerville intercom, this is Centurion seven, seven niner foxtrot. I have a dead engine; I'm circling down from seven thousand feet. Which is your active runway and what is the wind?"

No answer. He repeated the request several times . . . again nobody answered. He was on his own.

EIGHT

★ ★ ★

DOUG COULD TELL BY the drift of the aircraft, banking above the landing strip, that the prevailing wind was coming from the west. He muttered aloud, "Better cut short my downwind leg or I'll drift too far to the east." He dropped the left wing and set up for the final approach. "So far so goo . . . Where did *he* come from?"

Cutting in from below left was another plane. The pilot was not following the prescribed right approach pattern; now directly in front of him was a small Cessna 152, also intent on landing. Doug's approach speed was much faster than the small two-seater's and if both kept their present course, a crash was inevitable.

The pilot of the small Cessna was obviously not tuned in to the intercom channel and was oblivious to any other plane in the pattern. Doug pushed the stick forward and picked up airspeed as he approached the tail of the smaller craft. At the last moment, he dove under the 152, swiftly emerging in front of the startled pilot who, firewalling the throttle, banked away.

In order to attain sufficient speed to glide under the smaller aircraft, Doug had used no flaps, leaving little doubt he would overshoot the runway unless drastic measures were taken. He hadn't enough altitude to circle back and try again; it was now or never. Pulling up the nose, pushing hard on the left rudder, and turning the wheel violently to the right, he side-slipped the Centurion earthward.

The stall button squawked ominously as he kept the plane on the naked edge of falling from the sky. It dropped like a rock and one second before hitting, Doug flared the craft and hit hard close to the end of the runway. With all his strength, he reared back in his seat, pulled the wheel hard to his chest, and jammed on the brakes, spinning the plane to a sudden halt. He came to rest just inches from the ledge's dramatic drop-off.

Doug sat there for a moment, catching his breath, his face bathed in sweat. Slowly, he climbed out of the plane and leaned against the cowling, then looked toward heaven and whispered sincerely, "Thank You, Lord!"

Off in the distance, the Cessna 152 touched down and taxied toward the Centurion. Cutting the motor, the pilot angrily jumped out and came strutting at him, shouting epithets every step of the way. Thrusting his face within inches of Doug's, he snarled, "What were you trying to do, you craz—"

Doug balled up his fist and hit him flush in the middle of the tirade, knocking him flat on his back. Defiantly, Doug stood over him, hoping he would get up so he could bash the errant airman again. But the prostrate, red-faced pilot did nothing but raise himself on his elbow and examine his bloody nose to see if it was broken. Doug bent over him and calmly said, "Next time, Ace, listen to your radio."

★ ★ ★

DOUG FINISHED THE CALL to Executive Air, arranging for a crew to repair, then return his 210 to the Sacramento hangar. Next, he phoned for a cab and was dropped off downtown at a car rental agency. "So . . . this is Hangtown!" He had heard about the old gold-rush village of Placerville for some years, but he never had much time to explore the towns of California's Mother Lode. He liked Placerville. . . he liked it a lot. Nestled in the foothills, the small city was the gateway to the Sierras, South Tahoe, and the magnificent ski and gambling resorts around the lake. To the west, it was less than an hour's drive to the flatlands and Sacramento.

Old brick buildings lined narrow Main Street and, unlike some of the Mother Lode towns, it didn't have the appearance of a tourist trap, dotted with art galleries, novelty shops, boutiques, and fast-food eateries. Most of the storefronts displayed real merchandise and serviced the citizens who lived and worked in the area.

The hardware store, with its plank-board flooring and very high ceiling was crammed with everything from wooden bins of nails to the very latest dinnerware. The tallest building along Main was the three-story refurbished Cary Hotel, erected in 1857 and still receiving boarders.

Doug spent the remainder of the afternoon poking around the old town. It was tucked in a narrow pass, surrounded by steep hill-sides, covered with digger pine and cedars. Victorian homes in good repair dotted the landscape. Placerville didn't appear to be a wealthy town, but it manifested a certain pride, evidenced by a friendly and inviting atmosphere.

Doug checked into the Cary Hotel for the night, enjoyed a leisurely supper, and took in a movie at the antiquated Empire Theater. It was like stepping back into his childhood. The following morning, he slept late, had a hearty breakfast, and decided to walk the full length of Main Street and take in the sights.

Doug felt out of place, clad in his tailored slacks, button-down shirt, and dress shoes, while almost every man on the street seemed to be wearing Western apparel—jeans and cowboy boots. Even the women appeared to favor the same. On impulse, he stepped into D & E Western Boot and Apparel to have a look.

A bright-eyed Indian lady wearing a red checkered blouse and blue Wranglers asked if she could be of help. "No, thanks—just looking around." Then, moments later, a pair of sharp Tony Lamas caught his eye. Turning to the young clerk, he asked, "Mind if I try these on? They happen to be my size."

"Why sure, try on anything you like!"

Doug took off one of his Gucci shoes and pulled on one boot; it was surprisingly comfortable. He tried on the other and walked over to the mirror. He looked as out of place as a dude in a John Wayne movie. He removed the horn-rimmed glasses . . . that helped, but just a little. Doug went through several stacks of Levi's until he found the right cut and size. "Is there a place around here I can try these on?"

"You bet!" she answered. "There's a dressing room right over there, behind the hats."

Struggling a bit, Doug slipped into the stiff jeans and laughed to himself. *Nadine would have a fit!* For some inexplicable reason, she hated any and all jeans and wouldn't allow them in Doug's closet. *Well . . . that was then.* A sharp pain accompanied the realization that he could now wear anything he wanted.

Poking his head between the dressing room curtains, he called to the Indian salesgirl, "Would you please pick out a plain shirt — one with stud buttons, size forty?" Quickly, she brought over three Roper shirts and hung them up on the curtain rod. He tried the blue check with a maroon stripe and pearl snap buttons. Standing before the mirror in admiration, he mumbled, "Not bad . . . not bad at all." Then he hooked his thumbs into the belt loops of the new Levi's and rocked back and forth on his heels, trying to imitate the classic John Wayne stance. As he studied his reflection, he said outloud, "Uh-huh, howda ya like that, Pilgrim!" Doug liked it fine.

After selecting a wide hand-tooled belt with a large brass buckle, he tried on several hats and settled for a white straw Stetson. Although he was somewhat satisfied, something was still not quite right. *Okay, Stewart, let's go for it.* He took off the hat and got rid of his hairpiece, shoving it deep inside the pocket of his discarded dress trousers. With the Stetson back on his head, adjusted forward at a slight angle, Doug said, "That does it!" The transformation was complete; the change in his appearance was more than dramatic. It was drastic.

The clerk was slackjawed, and said, "Sir, I can't believe you're the same person." Then noticing his balding head, she giggled as she added, "Somebody scalp you? You look so different."

Doug laughed with her, as he reached for his wallet. "How much do I owe you?"

Trying to recover her composure, she asked, "Will that be cash or charge?"

"Cash." Doug didn't want to sign a credit voucher; she might recognize the name. The new cowboy was fascinated with the idea of being "a different person." He liked it a lot.

★ ★ ★

THE RENTED FOUR-BY-FOUR Chevy was perfect for the mountainous roads of Durango County. Traveling the back byways, Doug found the Sierra foothills packed with interesting places and new things to see. Excellent small wineries abounded, hidden among the rolling hills of vineyards; Lava Cap, Boeger, and Granite Springs had wines comparable to the best that France or Napa Valley could offer.

Doug then drove by small horse and cattle ranches, lumber mills, apple and pear orchards and dozens of Christmas tree farms on the high ridges. Thick stands of oak and pine filled the draws and steep mountainsides.

Descending the grade of Highway 49 to the middle fork of the American River, he entered Coloma—the site of Sutter's Mill, where the state's gold was first discovered. There he purchased an armload of books about the forty-niners, registered at the old Vineyard Inn, and settled in for the night.

The 1849 gold strike had brought thousands of enterprising people to California, including Doug's ancestors. He stayed awake 'til two in the morning, fascinated by the rich history of the Mother Lode country. One booklet, *How to Find Gold*, especially grabbed his attention—so much so that early the following day, he was induced to buy a gold pan, shovel, and pick and return to the American River. With the instructions fresh at hand, he began panning for the metallic substance that has intrigued man from the beginning of history.

He soon found sluicing for gold to be hard work, particularly in the hot California sun. Sweating profusely, his horn-rimmed glasses kept falling into the water. He took off his shirt and boots and set to work earnestly, shoveling sand and rocks into the pan. Later in the afternoon, when he found color, excitement filled his chest. There was no mistaking it—small specks of bright yellow against the black iron sand, probably no more than ten cents' worth. But to Doug, finding any amount of gold was ample pay for the day's endeavor.

Early the next morning—Sunday—Doug took off again. Still sticking to the out-of-the-way roads, he caught sight of a small Baptist church along Pleasant Valley Road, where cars and pickups were pulling into the parking area. He did likewise and experienced his first communion and church service in months. He wasn't the only one wearing denims, which reminded him once again of Nadine and how dumbstruck she would be to see him now. It felt good to be back in God's house. It felt lonely to be there without Nadine.

Whenever home, he tried to frequent the church in San Gabriel . . . but it wasn't the same. A new minister had taken over who was a bit more contemporary than Doug liked. Now, the kids were grown, living in distant places, and besides—the surroundings reminded him painfully of Nadine's memorial. Consequently, his attendance had been slipping. Though his fellow hometown parishioners were friendly, they were now too inclined to engage him in political talk.

All in all, it had been a relaxing extended weekend, in spite of the airplane failure. *No. . . . It has been a GREAT weekend . . . sore, sunburned back and all.*

Doug felt marvelous for the first time in ages, comfortable in the mountainous area, far more than in the flatland environment around Sacramento. He liked the elbow room and the solitude the foothills offered. The deep forests, deer grazing by the edge of the fields, the dark olive-tinted oaks beside pastures of golden poppies and purple lupine all seemed in perfect balance. He even liked the heat, some-how cleaner and dryer than on the valley floor. "What a neat place to live," he remarked out loud. "And all this within an hour's drive of the capitol and only twelve minutes by air."

Unconsciously, he began noticing realty signs posted on ranch property for sale.

★ ★ ★

THEY WERE BACK IN SESSION; summer recess was over with just one month left to finish legislative business. The calendar of work to be completed was lengthy. Prior procrastination by the legislators was brutally evident by the wealth of bills yet to be heard. Every year it was the same thing—spewing out laws and resolutions at the last minute, without proper review or attention to debate. Members were wandering all over the assembly floor, carrying on unrelated conversations, while others presented their legislation, seeming to pay little attention to the proceedings. "Ronald Reagan was right!" remarked Doug. "The two things people should never watch is the making of sausage and the passage of bills."

Doug's pet hate was the Consent Calendar, a process by which so-called noncontroversial issues were voted on without debate. With just one vote, a legislator could be recorded as voting on a myriad of legislation, often forty and fifty bills at a time.

"If I ran my business that way, I'd go broke in no time," Doug once remarked. He figured that if a bill was worth passage, it was worth discussion and explanation to the elected body. "If not, then kill the turkey and stop wasting precious time gumming up the law books with minutia."

He began to abstain and refused to vote on the Consent Calendar. As long as he was here, he wanted to know what he was voting for. He soon acquired a record of having missed the most votes in the assembly. He couldn't care less, since he had no inten-tion of running again for another term.

As the session dragged on into the night, Doug sat in his chair and listened to the rapid explanations of the bills and an occasional inquiry or debate from one of his colleagues. His mind kept wandering to the past weekend, to the gold country and the marvelous time he had poking around the creek tributaries to the American River searching for the yellow dust. From his pocket, he brought out a small vial and held it up to the light.

His seatmate, Assemblyman Harry Kaloogian, looked over and asked, "Doug, whatcha got there?"

"It's my poke of gold," Doug answered, and grinned. "Panned for it myself."

"No kidding! Let me see!" After careful examination, he said, "I don't see a thing."

"Hold it close to the light."

"Oh, yeah, there it is. Not much, is it?"

"Finding any amount of that precious metal is like trying to find productive people," responded Doug.

"What do you mean by that?" asked the assemblyman.

Doug looked warmly at the young man who was one of the conservative leaders, dubbed by the media as one of the uncompromising Young Turks. "Well, Harry, when you sluice for gold, you have to put a lot of rocks and dirt in the pan. Some of the stones are large and look pretty heavy; you think they'll never wash out when you start to agitate the pan in the flowing water. But sure enough, they flush out while the tiny, heavy pieces of gold settle to the bottom." Doug stopped when he saw the puzzled look in Harry's eyes.

"I don't get it," said Harry.

"Pressure," stated Doug. "The rotating motion combined with the swirling water creates pressure that the rocks and debris can't withstand. Only the heavy gold can take the agitation. It's the same with people. Those who can handle pressure stay in the pan and those who can't . . . wash out. Without some conflict and confrontation, it's hard to tell the real from the phony, the productive from the unproductive."

Harry smiled. "That's pretty heady stuff you're laying on me." The young legislator turned in his seat and looked across the assembly floor at Jesse Boggs. The Democrat leader's microphone was raised and he was about to present a bill. Harry raised his mike as well, signaling the body that he wished to speak on the legislation also. "Well, back to the real world," he sighed, as he rose to debate the bill.

★ ★ ★

THE DELEGATION FROM Pasadena's Chamber of Commerce was in town on Friday, obligating Doug to meet with them. They were clearly pleased with his elevation to the assembly's leadership, getting a vicarious kick knowing that "their man" was one of the capitol heavies. Doug found it curious that each of the visitors claimed to have voted for him, especially since he knew for a fact that most of them were on a first-name basis with Austin Chitmour.

Doug arranged lunch for the Chamber at the Hyatt Hotel and asked the minority leader to address them. Brad Clark spoke eloquently—in particular, over their wisdom in electing such a good man as Douglas Stewart.

As soon as the Pasadena visitors had departed for the airport, Doug ran to his waiting four-wheel drive and sped off to Wal-Mart. He needed more Levi's and his new prescription for contact lenses was ready. His glasses, with the heavy horn rims, were definitely not meant for gold-panning. When he discovered that he could change the color of his eyes from gray to a deep blue, Doug thought, *Why not? Then the metamorphosis of Doug Stewart from city slicker to cowboy will be complete.*

He headed for the hills of the Mother Lode.

NINE

★ ★ ★

LEIF ANDERSON LOOKED out of the expansive window overlooking exclusive Rancho Murieta golf course. Holding his drink aloft, he saluted the golfers practicing their swings, waiting to tee off on the first hole. "Hope they have a better game than I did."

Brad White smiled at the land developer and said, "What are you complaining about? Collectively, you took at least fifty bucks off of our foursome."

"Yeah," added the lanky Sam Hartage, "you put your hand in my pocket for at least half of that."

"You guys played so lousy, I shoulda' won twice that amount," joked Anderson.

Brad watched as the jocular jabs at Leif's golfing ability came thick and fast from the assembled players. Having just finished their eighteen holes, they were relaxing with drinks . . . on Leif. In spite of his advanced years, the elderly Swede was a scratch golfer and even though he gave extra strokes to his golfing companions, he inevitably won. He was tough to beat; his competitiveness—in business, politics, and pleasure—was legendary. Anderson Land Development Company was the largest homebuilder in the state. Its low-cost housing could be found from San Diego to the Bay Area.

Sam Hartage was the major stockholder and president of Big Burger, one of the nation's largest fast-food giants. Also part of the foursome was Cliff Hardcastle, an insurance executive and present chairman of the Republican state central committee, the party's official state organization.

Dressed in business attire, four more people worked their way into the busy lounge. Brad Clark stood up and waved them over to the table. "Stoney! Marcia! Over here." They all shook hands and joked warmly with one another, obviously old friends. The new arrivals were campaign strategist Stoney March; pollster Mervin Meadows; Slim Stacy, the direct-mail fundraiser; and Marcia Conley, senate Republican minority leader.

Stoney looked around the crowded bar. "Are we going to meet in here?"

"No," answered Brad. "We've reserved a more private spot off the dining room. We can eat later. Why don't you guys order a drink and we can get down to business."

Carrying their drinks, they hustled out of the noisy lounge to the dining area, where a full wall of windows offered a spectacular view of the eighteenth putting green. The approach was lined with magnificent live oaks. Rich, green manicured fairways contrasted with the dry summer golden grass of the bordering rough. Three players stood waiting on the green while a fourth struggled gamely to extricate himself from the bunker.

"Brad, remind you of anyone you know?" chided Cliff Hardcastle.

The assembly minority leader cast him a wry grin, not needing to be reminded that he'd taken three strokes to get out of the trap on seventeen. The par five hole alone had cost him ten bucks.

"All right, enough of golf," said Brad. "Let's get down to the business at hand."

As they took their seats, the light banter came to a stop and the discussion began in earnest. Over the years, they had met like this many times before to hash over issues, candidates, and financing. No novices, all were experienced, pragmatic politicos without illusions as to the business in which they were so deeply enmeshed.

Both Leif and Sam Hartage had served as state finance chairmen and had personally contributed generously to the party. Marcia Conley, beautiful and vivacious, was the first woman to attain leadership in the Senate. Beneath her wealth of flowing chestnut-brown hair lay one of the shrewdest political minds in the country.

Governor Edmond Edmonds, newly elected Democrat, had just started his first term. Since Californians traditionally gave their governors two terms in office, the percentages were in his favor of winning reelection three years hence. Democrat numbers were up and registered donkeys outnumbered pachyderms by a three-to-two margin.

Both houses of the state legislature had been controlled by the Democrats for thirteen years. They had been on a roll, passing one new regulatory program after another. State taxes had risen, the economy was tightening, and businesses were getting nervous, starting to look elsewhere for a more favorable climate.

There was no disagreement that California was becoming too expensive and too difficult a state in which to expand or start a new enterprise. Leif Anderson, chairing the meeting, looked over to Mervin Meadows and asked, "Merv, what do the numbers tell us? Do we have a shot at winning the governorship in three more years? What would it take?"

Meadows rummaged through the latest book of polling data before he answered. "It'll take a real turnaround in public attitude. The governor's portrayed himself as a caring friend of the work force and the image has taken hold. Surveys show that few voters relate his administration with the downturn in employment. They think Edmond's a conservative FDR . . . that's Friend of Democrats and Republicans."

Stoney agreed. "That old codger will be a very hard one to beat."

Hartage, cursing, disgustedly threw his pencil down on the table. "Well, what are you saying, Merv? Must we wait until a miracle occurs before we have a chance of electing a Republican governor?"

"I don't like the numbers either," droned Meadows. "But we gotta face facts. For a statewide office, the Democrats eat our lunch. They've done a great snow job in sunny California."

"Any good news at all in the survey data?" asked Cliff.

"Some, but not enough to get excited about," answered Meadows. "A little dissatisfaction is showing up in the job picture. Business folks are grumbling, but that's nothing new. The majority of the voters have the crazy idea that Edmonds is basically independent of either party and above partisan politics."

"That's stupid," spat out Hartage.

"That's the voter," added Slim Stacy.

"Come on, Merv, isn't there anything in that survey we can use?" asked Hardcastle.

"Well, the property tax issue breaks heavily our way—but trouble is, the public doesn't know it. They think one party is just as interested in property tax relief as the other."

"You're joking," stated an incredulous Hartage.

"See for yourself," said Meadows, as he pushed the voluminous survey in his direction.

Sam poured over the figures and whistled. "Eighty-one percent! That's a heavy number."

"Now," smirked the pollster, "look on the next page and see how the Demo numbers compare with Republicans on the same issue."

Sam turned the page and stared at the numbers; then, plainly aggravated, he shoved the survey away. "We better do something fast to take advantage of this taxation issue before the Democrats do." Several shrugged their shoulders, while others nodded their heads.

The group of eight constituted the brain trust of the Republican Party and four of them formed the guts of the executive committee. It was up to them to decide policy. Years earlier, they had taken charge of a party in disarray, the Democrats having decimated the Republican ranks in the prior reapportionments, gerrymandering them almost into oblivion. It had been a hard, uphill climb building the Republicans back into a viable power.

Although their chance of winning the governorship was slim, they were close to winning a majority in the assembly. With effective use of the mail by Slim Stacy and selective targeting of winnable districts by the Republican leadership, they were only a few votes shy. Gaining control in the Senate was considered a lost cause; the upper house was filled with comfortably seated Republicans who would rather get along than combat their Democrat brethren. Senator Marcia Conley was different, for behind her beautiful, calm exterior beat the heart of a shrewd, ambitious combatant. Long range, she was believed by some to be destined to become the first woman governor of the Golden State.

The problem at hand was how to pick up a few more seats in the coming year, so the Republicans had to find good people they could try to elect. Systematically, the eight conferees went over the list of potential candidates—those who actually contemplated filing for office. Among them were city councilmen, mayors, county supervisors, Republican activists, and business leaders . . . good ones looking mighty thin.

"Boy, this is the pits!" swore Hartage, after reviewing the list. "You'd think we could find more credible candidates in this state, those we can elect and also raise money around."

"Trouble is," lamented Slim Stacy, "we need a good candidate to attract money . . . and money to attract a good candidate. It's a chicken-egg scenario, and I know what comes first . . . scratch! If we had lots of feed, we'd be up to our bazoos in good candidates."

"That's not all," tossed in Leif. "It's somewhat important they have some name identity. You can't beat anybody with a nobody."

"Give me enough money and I'll elect a crooked snake," said Marsh.

"We have, and you did," chided Hartage. "Remember that senator from Modesto?"

"How can I forget him? He's still here!"

"What we need are candidates who, at the very least, have a modicum of credibility—and the contacts to raise big bucks, of course!"

"And," Leif added, with a laugh, "doesn't get goosey and panic under attack."

"That's a tall order," replied Marcia. "I can't think of even a few who would fit that description, male or female."

"I can," quickly interjected a beaming Brad Clark. "In fact, we just elected one who fits the bill perfectly. He's now our new caucus chairman. I was going to talk to you about having him join our group."

"Isn't he a bit politically green for this bunch?" inquired Marcia.

"Greener than spring grass, but wising up in a hurry," replied Brad. "But, speaking of green, well . . . "

"What?" asked Leif.

"Money. He's capable of raising big, big bucks. If that's not clear enough, he's personally up to his Adam's apple in federal green."

Every face broke into a wide grin, all resembling Cheshire cats, as Leif asked, "When are we going to meet this dear boy, this . . . answer to our prayers?"

★ ★ ★

As he turned onto Bucks Bar Road toward Grizzly Flat, Doug realized he hadn't felt so free in ages, far removed from the limelight and pressures of the city. Searching Durango County for the perfect hideaway, his thoughts led to James Hilton's classic novel, *Lost Horizon*. Maybe he could find his Shangri-La, as well.

Doug probed deep into the forest on the gravel side roads, covering every narrow byway that could accommodate his Ford Bronco. Weatherworn and partially hidden by overgrowth, he spotted a "For Sale by Owner" placard. Crudely written below on a splintered piece of plywood, was, "Fair price—Used gold mine."

Doug muttered, "Used gold mine? This, I've got to see."

The deeply rutted, weed-choked lane led far back into the trees, causing Doug to wonder if it were passable even with a four-wheel drive vehicle. On impulse, he turned onto the rarely used path and drove slowly through the berry vines, scrub oak, and towering pines. Once past the thick stand of trees, the road began winding its way down toward the middle fork of the Consumes River; then rounding a sharp bend, it leveled out. He found himself on a large, flat bench covered with sage and manzanita, a sizable clearing by the side of the mountain.

There, tucked up against the steep slope, was a large, wooden slatted cabin nestled under some magnificent old oaks. It seemed in fair shape but sorely in need of paint. A sagging, faded red barn with slats missing from its sides was fifty yards beyond. A chicken coup adjoined the old barn, its tangled, rusty wire surrounding an empty pen. A well-worn path led to a slightly askew outhouse directly behind the cabin. There was a wide galvanized tool shed near the mine's entrance, behind a sizable pile of tailings dumped in front.

The property looked deserted until Doug noticed a very low-pressure sprinkler watering a small green garden on the sunny south side of the dwelling. He parked the Bronco up next to the cabin and was about to get out, when a large barking Rottweiler came furiously charging from the direction of the mine shaft.

Doug honked the horn, partially rolled down the window, and called out, "Anybody here?" He tried again . . . still no answer, only the intimidating growl of the dog as it circled the car, leaving no doubt the animal would chew him into small chunks if he got the chance. "Forget this place," he said, as he reached for the ignition key.

"Princess! Come to Papa, sweetheart!" Begrudgingly, the dog left the side of the car and trotted toward her master's voice.

Princess! Doug thought indignantly. *What a misnomer for a bruisin' bowser like that; better named Blood, Fang, or Assassin.*

Doug finally spotted the dog's owner, coming out from behind the pile of hard-rock tailings. He was a small, wiry old man with dust and sweat covering his gray-bearded face. His badly tattered overalls were held up by one strap at half-mast and ready to drop from his thin shoulder at the first shrug. A filthy, sweat-stained straw Stetson sat tightly on his head, forcing his white hair in every direction. A friendly, toothless smile wreathed his wrinkled face as he approached the vehicle and spoke to the dog. "Sit, Princess, and stay!" She ignored him completely, and following on her master's heel, growled menacingly at Doug, still in his car.

"What kin I do fer ya, stranger?"

Doug rolled the window down a bit more but continued to keep an eye on the Rottweiler. "Good afternoon, sir. I saw your sign up the road. Is this property still for sale?"

"Shore is," the miner happily exclaimed. "Git on out of the rig and I'll show ya around."

Doug cast a quizzical glance in the dog's direction. "Is it safe?"

Appearing surprised, he looked at Doug and then at his growling dog. "Princess?" Why, she's just a pussycat. Worst thing she'd do is lick ya to death."

Doug cautiously stepped out of the driver's side, ready to leap back in at any suspicious move from the huge canine. As the old miner stepped forward and extended his hand to introduce himself . . . so did the dog. Poking her nose forward, she sniffed around Doug's bare leg. When the bowser's cold damp schnozzle touched his calf, he jumped a foot in the air. "Yipes!"

"Now, now, Princess; leave the man alone. He don't intend no harm." After several more sniffs below Doug's cut-off Levi's, she finally edged away, satisfied enough to move to the shade of the house and lie down.

More than an hour later, their tour of the property was complete. The old man's name was Amos Wacker. He had owned the property for fifty-two years, and now his advanced age had forced him to stop mining. He said it was time to move to Spokane to live near his son.

Not wanting to reveal his real identity, Doug introduced himself as Hank Kaplowski, a name from out of his past in Vietnam.

Hank had been Doug's best friend, his closest companion throughout officer's training and during months of battle. They got to know each other well, sharing their lives. The long and often dull hours between the action were given over to extended conversations covering detailed stories of home and past experiences. The most intimate insights into the heart of a friend could sometimes be found in the drama of a foxhole, under fire. Hank had been an orphan, living in a foster home before being adopted by the Kaplowskis. Their home was in the industrial south side of Chicago, within smelling distance of the stockyards. Hank had confided that his dream was to become a rancher, own horses in Wyoming, and live in the back country where he'd be far away from the railroad yards and factories of his youth.

Tragically, Hank was killed during the last days of the Vietnam conflict. Doug was sure that Hank would have liked this place — and that he wouldn't mind him borrowing his name.

Doug had paced off the lengthy distance, down the flat from the cabin and mine to where the road sloped upward. It was plenty long enough to land a fully-loaded Cessna 210. Amos said the wind came up the canyon in the morning hours, but was still during the late afternoon, then moved downward in the evening . . . no cross winds to contend with. Doug looked at the altimeter on his watch to check the approximate elevation. It was twenty-seven hundred feet above sea level. All he would need to do to build a runway was bring in a DC-10 Cat to level the road, then spread the crushed mine tailings over the strip.

There would be no complaints about aircraft noise, since the nearest neighbor was miles away. The property on three sides was in the hands of the Bureau of Land Management, assuring no chance of anyone moving close by. The miner's acreage stretched L-shaped around the mountain, then along the path to the county gravel road. With slight modification, the galvanized tool shed could be easily converted into a suitable hangar for the Cessna.

Many of the comfortable amenities of civilization were missing; no indoor plumbing, no water, and no electricity provided by public utilities. The water to the cabin was spring-fed and stored in a large tank on the slopes above, with pressure from the gravity flow providing a steady enough surge for a cold shower. In the winter, the wood stove in the kitchen would supply adequate heat for warmth and hot water.

Although there were no telephones or TV, a small gas-run generator furnished enough electricity to service both the house and the mine.

Amos Wacker brought out early records of the mine, showing that at one time, the hard rock had produced sufficient gold to employ as many as fifteen people. In existence since the 1850's, it had never been a major discovery and had been closed down on several occasions. A series of prospectors had tried to eke out a living from the stubborn, unyielding rock, each one looking for the bonanza vein rumored to be hidden there. Over the last century, the main shaft had been explored deep into the side of the mountain, with side shafts probing in all directions, some connecting, some dead-ending. A literal maze of tunnels was cut out of the stone in search of the illusive gold.

"It's down there, all right," sighed the wizened, silver-headed miner. "There's a vein of gold a yard wide somewhere in the side of that mountain. I'm jest too old and tired to find it."

Doug made Amos a cash offer, which was readily accepted. Thus, Hank Kaplowski—alias Doug Stewart—became the happy owner of a rustic mountain retreat named the Lucky Adele Gold Mine.

TEN

IT WAS HOTTER THAN BLAZES and Doug was sweating profusely as he laid the PVC tubing in neat rows over the top of the cabin. His days of having to suffer cold showers would soon be over. By diverting some of the gravity flow water into a lattice of black PVC, the sun would be allowed to heat the water moving through the pipes.

He got the idea from an issue of *Popular Mechanics* he'd found in the cabin. With the magazine close at hand, Doug was vigorously hacksawing and gluing his way to having his own homemade, solar heating system. So intent was he on the job that he neither heard nor saw the horse and rider trot up to the porch steps.

"Mr. Kaplowski, that you up there?"

The shout of the female voice startled him, causing him to drop the can, spilling the sticky goo all over his hands and Levi's. "Dang it . . . that's my last can of PVC glue." Then remembering his manners, he yelled, "Yeah, I'm Kaplowski; be right down." Butt-hitching his way to the roof's edge, he peered over to see an attractive redhead sitting jauntily on the horse, with one long leg casually hooked over the saddle horn.

Flashing a big, warm, pearly-toothed smile, she said, "I'm Jamie Hagerty, your neighbor. Mind if I get down so we could talk a spell?" Without waiting for his reply, she agilely slid to the ground. "I see you've been pretty busy around the old place. Even a landing strip!"

Doug scrambled down the ladder and turned to greet his unexpected guest. He was surprised by her size. Jamie Hagerty was big, freckle-faced, and well-endowed, literally busting out of her blue denim work shirt. Standing almost as tall as he, she thrust out her right hand and gripped his with a strength to match his own. "Mighty glad to meet you. What's your first name?" It was almost a demand.

"Er . . . Hank . . . call me Hank." Somewhat taken aback by her forcefulness, he asked, "And what is your first name again?"

"Jamie . . . Jamie Hagerty. I'm Grady Hagerty's daughter."

Jamie, he thought, while observing her. *Jamie's a moniker for a wee lass. This gal should be named Brunhilda, or Bertha.*

She appeared impatient over his silence and, in a voice accustomed to command, all but ordered him to the porch. "Let's sit over there in the shade; it's hotter'n Hades out here in the sun." Without a pause, she added, "Could you get me a glass of water? It was a mighty warm ride over here an' I'm thirsty enough to drink the river dry."

Doug took off his Stetson and wiped his sweaty brow. "Sure, let me clean up a bit and I'll get you a drink." He disappeared into the cabin thinking, *Boy, that's a large stack of officious pulchritude. Wonder if she was ever in the marines?* Remembering the contents of the ice cooler, he called out from inside, "Care for a beer instead?"

She called back, "I only drink Mexican beer . . . Corona with lime. If you don't have any, water will do just fine."

Doug appeared back on the porch with a glass of water and a Coors Light for himself. "Sure you won't have a Coors?"

"I don't drink their beer. The whole Coors family are Reagan-lovin' Republicans."

"Suit yourself," answered Doug, as he handed her the glass of cold spring water. Slowly, he took an extra long swig and smacked his lips with Republican relish. "What can I do for you, Mrs. Hagerty?"

"MISS Hagerty!" she shot back, with a touch of defiance. "I'm not married." Changing her attitude dramatically, she asked, "How about you, Hank?"

Amused by her forthrightness, he stammered, "Uh, no . . . I'm not married."

"Do you dance?"

"Uh . . . do I dance?"

"Some of the folks from around here are into line dancing. Most Saturday nights we go stompin' at the Tex-Okie Bar and Bowling over in Mount Aukum. We need more boots on the hardwood floor. Interested?"

Doug smiled and was direct. "Is that the reason you're here — to ask me to go dancing?"

Her face reddened as she snapped, "No, it isn't. I just thought I'd be neighborly is all."

"Well, what can I do for you, Jamie?"

She came straight to the point, regaining her composure in the process. "Are you aware that Durango County plans to build a garbage dump next to this property?"

Doug frowned, "No, I'm not, but I think you better tell me all about it."

For fifteen minutes, he listened to her prolonged and jumbled opinions about why the county should not build a new dump anywhere in the vicinity. To more quickly get to the heart of the matter, he decided to play the devil's advocate, asking contrary questions. She was becoming frustrated with him and he could see her temper rise with each new query. The one thing she clearly made apparent was that the county road leading to his property would be jammed with trash trucks and pickups, all discarding their rubble.

Garbage dumps were an unpleasant but necessary fact of life. Doug sure wasn't pleased with the idea of having one close by, but he wasn't about to tell others what they could or could not do with their own property. He wondered if this Jamie Hagerty was one of those environmental wackos who opposed all dump sites in general and this one, in particular. She certainly was a Democrat; the caustic comment about the Coors family confirmed that. However, she got his attention when she said the existing site off Plymouth Road was less than half-full and that the subject of a new landfill came up, literally, overnight.

Doug's curiosity was now aroused. "Have the supervisors had any public hearings about the matter?"

"Just one," she answered, "and most of us didn't find out about it until it was over. The notice of the event appeared just hours before the meeting of the board of supervisors. There will be one more tonight, at the county courthouse in Diamond Springs, where we've heard they intend to finalize the deal and vote on the land purchase. We're tryin' to round up folks to attend and see if we can build some opposition. Maybe we can get them to put off the vote 'til we can find out more about it."

Having shown no sign of interest in attending the meeting, she interpreted Doug's body language, along with contrary points he'd raised, as indifference. "Well, I'm sorry. I thought you might want to be at the hearing." Jamie had a look of hopelessness in her eyes, the dejection of fighting a losing cause. The worry had softened her demeanor considerably, leading Doug to reevaluate his opinion; maybe she wasn't as tough as she pretended to be. Her bossy attitude masked a very pretty woman—a lot of her, but in all the right places.

She looked so discouraged, he had to ask, "Having trouble getting people to attend?"

She nodded, handing him the empty glass. Without thinking, he found himself saying, "What the heck, I guess I can make it!"

"You can?" Her face brightened and a pleasant glow replaced the downcast look of just seconds ago. She shook his hand vigorously as if to confirm his commitment. Then with a quick good-bye, she left . . . before Doug could change his mind.

"Why did I do that?" he mumbled, as he watched Jamie Hagerty ride away.

★ ★ ★

THE COURTHOUSE CHAMBERS were barely half-full when Doug arrived. Up front, next to the public podium, Jamie Hagerty and friends were adamantly expressing themselves to a bespectacled, stoic gentleman who appeared completely disinterested in what they were saying.

Four of the five supervisors were in their seats on the dais, gabbing and joking with one another. The door adjoining the chamber suddenly burst open and a heavy set, silver-haired, elderly cowboy type strutted into the room, his Stetson pulled down firmly on his head and square jaw thrust forward. The Honorable Boone E. Bates dropped heavily into the chairman's green leather seat, pushed back his hat, threw up the microphone, and commanded, "Let's get this here meetin' goin'. Call the roll!"

Doug immediately thought of the marines and boot camp, a drill instructor calling raw recruits to attention. The gathering clicked its heels in obeisance with an unspoken, "Yes, sir!"

In his raspy, gruff voice, he called to the clerk, "Bring on the first witness." The spectacled man with whom Jamie had been arguing came forth with reams of paper and maps tucked under his arm. He introduced himself as the county's public works engineer, whose entire dry testimony was in favor of the new disposal site.

For the next two hours, a parade of county employees, geologists, landfill experts, and garbage truck drivers gave their biased opinions as to why the proposed dump was needed. Boone E. Bates didn't get around to the opposing side until late in the evening, by which time, everyone was hot, tired, and extremely agitated. Several of the supervisors were yawning and looking at their watches; another was alternately picking at his nails and teeth.

When the opposition presented their case, Supervisor Bates lost no opportunity to repeatedly interrupt each presentation, nit-picking at every salient point. Whenever possible, he tried to portray them as do-gooder environmentalists, extremists without a reasonable cause.

The hearing was a classic railroad job, a dog-and-pony show for the local press. The supervisors' minds were made up and all they were doing was suffering through the opposing remarks, doing the democratic thing, waiting for a suitable time to cast their aye votes. Doug had just spent months listening to testimony given before Democrat-dominated assembly committees, watching the state's best political railroad in operation. With class, they trotted out the doggies and the ponies, their hand-picked witnesses, to manipulate the socks off the press and the public. This Durango five had no class; in fact, the chairman was arrogant, like a king holding court over his fiefdom.

As the so-called hearing was coming to a close, a weary Chairman Bates asked if there were any more to testify before the supervisors took a vote. Doug called out respectfully, from the back of the room. "Mr. Chairman, may I ask a question or two? I'm a landowner. I promise to be brief."

Bates frowned and looked over the top of his reading glasses and before he could object, Doug was halfway down the aisle, saying, "Thank you, Mr. Chairman."

Boone E. Bates had never seen the man who was now standing at the podium. The aged supervisor prided himself for knowing every major landowner in the county. This was a new face, a newcomer. Probably one of those many flatlanders who had moved into the area from San Francisco.

"Be concise," admonished the chairman. "Give your name and who you represent."

"Thank you, Supervisor Bates . . . and gentlemen. My name is Hank Kaplowski. I own property bordering the county road, leading to the proposed dump site. I have just two questions. I listened carefully to the presentation and would like to know why the environmental report left out commentary about the wetlands?" The lethargic audience snapped to attention, including the press.

The board of supervisors sat upright in their chairs and asked, almost in unison, "What wetlands?"

Turning to the planning commissioner, Bates sputtered, "Horace, there's no wetlands . . . is there?"

Looking shocked, the head of planning declared, "There's no wetlands!"

"I beg to differ," smoothly responded Doug. "As I stated, the county road accesses the landfill through my property. Having an abiding interest in ornithology, one of the reasons I purchased the land is because it's a flyway for migratory water fowl. A marvelous small marsh is on the property bordering the road. It is fairly certain the subspecies of the endangered gooneybill fubthrusher inhabits the area in the spring. It may even lay its pretty little bluespeckled eggs there. A very sensitive bird, it tends to leave the nest and desert its young when disturbed by the noises of civilization. Garbage trucks are pretty loud, aren't they?"

Boone E. Bates grew crimson. "I can't see why some bird should affect our vote tonight on the purchase of the property. We can look into that matter later. What's your second question?"

Doug smiled. "Can the County of Durango, and each of you, afford the litigation that will certainly follow any precipitous action you might take tonight? Friends of the fubthrusher are legion and powerful. A lawsuit will most certainly be forthcoming unless this is checked out thoroughly."

"They can't sue us, personally!" snarled Bates.

Condescendingly, Doug smiled again. "It would be wise if your legal counsel checked out the suit filed against the county commissioners in Tallahassee, Florida. Although they won the case on appeal, it cost each of them a bundle in legal fees. Perhaps it might be prudent to remember the old axiom, 'Act in haste, be sued in leisure.'"

The supervisors on either side of Boone leaned over and whispered excitedly as he slumped down in his chair. Doug enjoyed picturing the steam rising in his ears and smoke pouring from his nostrils. Boone E. Bates was not accustomed to losing ground; nor was putting the vote over 'til another day within his agenda. It would take weeks to get an update on the environmental impact study.

But . . . he had no other choice. His colleagues were apoplectic over the thought of being personally sued over an environmental issue. Banging down the gavel, Boone biliously spat out, "This item will be put over for three weeks!" He brought the gavel down again, and said, "This here meetin's adjourned."

Immediately, one of the local reporters cornered Doug with a barrage of questions. As Hank Kaplowski, he played the part of a concerned Durango County resident, just doing his duty.

Jamie Hagerty waited for the newsman to finish his notes, then edged up to Doug and playfully nudged her elbow into his ribs. "A few of us are going to listen to some live music, and celebrate. Come on along, Hank." Wrinkling up her freckled nose, she teased, "I'll even buy you a Coors."

ELEVEN

★ ★ ★

THESE EGGS ARE JUST RIGHT, sweetheart; the yellow's soft and the whites ain't wigglin'. Sourdough's burnt to a crisp . . . just the way I like it."

"Thanks, Dad." Lovingly, Jamie looked across the table at her aged father. He had said the same words a thousand times before, more a family ritual than a true assessment of how the eggs were prepared. She hoped she would hear it a thousand times more, but realistically, she knew her father's time was growing short. The wounds of World War II, compounded by disease, had first driven him to crutches and finally to the confines of a wheelchair. Helplessly she watched his gnarled right hand reach for the buttered toast, clumsily fumbling to pick it up. The once powerful man was now crippled with arthritis which constantly racked his body with pain.

The barely controllable torment pinched his face whenever he diligently tried to help himself, noticeably getting worse, even though he tried to hide the suffering from her. She needed no proof that Grady Hagerty was a brave man, aside from the evidence proudly displayed on the wall. Her father had been decorated for his heroism by the president, himself.

Hanging above the fireplace mantle were Jamie's three favorite photographs. One of them depicted Franklin D. Roosevelt honoring her father in the Oval Office of the White House. The second—

a simple oak frame—contained the nation's highest award, the blue, star-studded Congressional Medal of Honor. The third picture was of Jamie's mother and father, adoringly holding their first and only baby.

Abigail Hagerty died when Jamie was only twelve, leaving her to take over the household chores. As her father became more incapable of handling the multiple responsibilities of running a good-sized cattle operation, Jamie ably pitched in, performing the duties with an efficiency that surprised everyone. While in high school, she had little time for social activities; the same was true during the business courses she attended in community college. Managing the lumber business and sawmill, the Circle-H ranch hands, and tending to the needs of her father used up all her energy and time. There was nothing left to spare.

Young men had found Jamie very attractive, but her dominant personality could be awesome and intimidating. One young buck caustically insinuated, "Her female wiles are in sad repair." However, her authoritarian demeanor was not; it stood her in good stead managing lumberjacks and cowboys, but mostly served as a cold shower to the ardor of the opposite sex.

Her aggressive, take-charge behavior had "de-machoed" many a male. Jamie had to face the fact that managing the sizable Hagerty property and the rough-and-tumble men they hired definitely had its romantic downside. No marriage proposals came her way. Caring for her invalid father fulfilled some of her womanly instincts as dreams of a wedding dimmed considerably. At forty-two years of age, Jamie was terribly set in her ways.

The Hagertys, like many Irish, were Democrats, and had always contributed heavily to the party. Grady's personal contact with FDR ingrained forever his desire to promote the so-called Party of Democracy. He still considered President Roosevelt the statesman who led the country out of the Great Depression and, without question, considered him to be the most exceptional American since George Washington.

Grady raised his daughter in the Hagerty tradition—to love Democrats and hate Republicans. Whenever the subject of his own wealth was raised and friends pointed out the enormous taxes he paid, he'd always say the same thing: "I don't mind payin' more than my share; why should others? It's a great country, worth dyin' for."

Within the last decade, Hagerty's confidence in the Democrat party was somewhat shaken by the assault made on timber and cattle interests. The more liberal members of the party weren't to his liking and the environmental crowd was the major recipient of his ire. The Hagertys leased land from the Bureau of Land Management for grazing their cattle and their lumber mill was constantly bidding to harvest government-owned timber. The environmentalist attempts to paint both interests as despoilers of the earth placed an irritating bone of contention in Grady's political throat.

When the rabid extremists became a voice in establishing the Democrat platform, he was moved to action. "Jamie, we gotta do somethin' about those kooks who are gettin' into the bowels of our party. I'm going to see about gettin' you an appointment to the state central committee."

Jamie willingly complied, since she shared the concerns of her father and, shortly after the appointment came through, it didn't take her long to become a vocal antagonist to the liberal agenda. Knowing firsthand the cattle and timber side of the coin and at the same time, arguing as a Democrat, made Jamie all the more difficult to combat. Her aggressiveness, the power of her family's money, and her articulate opposition to environmentalism established her as a spokesman for many other rural county Democrats. Jamie Hagerty became a force to deal with in the Democrats' ranks.

"Jamie, hon, would you burn some more of that toast?" her father asked politely. "And would ya put a little more butter on it . . . real butter? Not that low-fat imitation stuff." Grady made a wry face and scowled to make his point.

"You've had two eggs, three slices of bacon, and fried potatoes. That's enough fat for the whole day." As she began to clear away his dishes, she added, "Salad for lunch and soup for dinner. Still want some more toast?"

"No, forget it," grumbled her father. "By the way, lassie, what happened last night at the supervisors' meeting? Is old Bates goin' to get his new garbage dump?"

Jamie's face immediately brightened and, uncharacteristically, became as excited as a child with a new toy. "Dad, you won't believe what happened! Old Boonie Bates got put down good by that new neighbor of ours. Man, is that Hank Kaplowski a piece of gold."

She launched into a colorful, enthusiastic, down-to-the-last-detail description of the hearing. "Up until the last minute, we were really getting our cans kicked. Then, like a knight in shining armor, up walks Hank to the podium, all humble-like. Two minutes later, he had Boonie frothin' at the mouth over a nonexistent bird. A gooneybill fubthrusher! Can you beat that?"

Grady laughed at his animated daughter. It had been a long while since he'd seen her so bright-eyed and so flushed with excitement, as she continued to bubble forth.

"We went over to the Tex-Okie for a little celebration and that's when I found out the endangered bird was nothing more than a fowl ball for Boonie." Jamie slapped her thigh and continued, while giggling uncontrollably. "Get it, Dad? *Fowl* ball? Hank said it will take the EPAers at least two weeks to look for a wet spot on the property, much less a marshy area. Hank stopped the Bates' locomotive long enough so we can delve into the matter."

"Who's this Hank Ka-hoop-ski?"

"Hank Kaplowski, Dad!" She spelled it out, "K-A-P-L-O-W-S-K-I."

"Polish?"

"He sure ain't Irish."

"Catholic?"

"Aw, Dad, we didn't talk about religion—especially in the Tex-Okie. But I did find out he was an officer in Vietnam, served with the First Marine Division. I asked him what he got out of being a marine and all he said was, 'A Purple Heart and a college education.'"

I think he's a mining engineer, 'cause he has mining property in the Tehachapis in southern California—travels there a lot."

"Is he good-lookin'?"

Jamie blushed red. "I didn't notice." She turned to finish loading the dishwasher.

"Don't you fib to me, Daughter. I ain't seen you blush like that since you was a little girl."

Jamie turned all the redder. "Well, if you can call a balding fifty-year-old man handsome, I guess he fits the bill. He's no Yul Brynner, but for Durango County, I guess he'll do. Come on, Dad, quit teasin'. He's just a nice neighbor."

Grady temporarily forgot his aches and pains, so pleased was he to see the sparkle in his daughter's eyes. He relished the pleasure he was getting out of joshing with her. He suddenly frowned and feigned seriousness. "This Hank a Republican or a Democrat?"

"Don't know," she answered. "But he sure don't act like any Republican I know. He's gotta be a Democrat."

With a twinkle in his eye, her father asked impishly, "Jamie, my girl, what do you like best about him?" Smiling, she dried her hands and flung the towel over her shoulder. "Well, he won't let me lead when we dance."

★ ★ ★

"Sean, would you come into my office, please?" Shortly, Sean MacGruder, Doug's efficient administrative aide, came bustling in.

"Yes, Mr. Stewart?"

"Sean, there's something I'd like you to look into." Doug handed his cursory notes and explained the information he had collected on the proposed dump site. "Check into it, will you, and give it high priority. I smell a rat."

Sean quickly scanned the notes and asked, "How soon do you need this?"

"A couple of weeks and I'm afraid you'll be somewhat handicapped. I can't go into details, but you'll have to keep this office totally out of the picture. I want no Stewart fingerprints on any material you can dig up."

Sean arched his eyebrows and, without comment, disappeared through the door. He knew better than to ask why the information was necessary.

Doug leaned back in his chair, relaxed, and thought about the previous night. He'd had fun . . . lots of it. He had enjoyed derailing Boone E. Bates. The supervisor was in too much of a hurry trying to jam the appropriation through the board . . . meaning something was fishy about the entire deal. If nothing came of MacGruder's inquiries, he'd not bother showing up at the next meeting, which would surely please the supervisors. In truth, he hoped his hunch was right and something really was amiss. The arrogance of Bates was appalling and letting the air out of that pompous buffoon would be highly enjoyable.

Doug was also looking forward to seeing Jamie and her friends again. He hadn't expected to have such a good time at the Tex-Okie. His attempt at line dancing was clumsy at first, but he soon got the hang of it. The live musical strains of Nevada John's Wailing Waddies was so loud, it drowned out the noise of the bowlers in the adjoining alleys. The four-piece band had a great beat and what they lacked in melody, they made up for in clamor.

Doug was pleasantly surprised at how light Jamie was on her feet. For such a good-sized woman, she moved with a flowing grace. While Nadine had the figure of a fashion model, svelte and angular, she was more difficult to lead than a recalcitrant mule.

As the evening wore on, Doug got accustomed to hearing Jamie's friends address her affectionately as "Big Red." Now that they had become better acquainted, he realized he'd been wrong about her name. "Brunhilda" or "Bertha" didn't fit at all; "Big Red" didn't either. "Bright Eyes" certainly did. Her green eyes sparkled when she talked, and that's what Doug chose to call her . . . much to her pleasure and surprise.

Having closed the Tex-Okie at two o'clock, Doug didn't get back to the cabin until after three, just a few hours before he had to be on his way back to the capitol. At first light, he taxied the Centurion onto the gravel strip, pushed in the throttle, and headed out—a downhill power glide all the way. Within an hour and a half, he was in his office, ready for the conference scheduled by the minority leader. Brad Clark was insistent that they get together with some very important people he wanted Doug to meet. Doug hoped he could stay awake.

TWELVE

★ ★ ★

EXACTLY NINE O'CLOCK . . . that was the time he was told the conference would begin. Exactly? That, in itself, was worth a laugh; for nothing he'd encountered in the assembly ever started on time. Procrastination was the rule and late committee starts were the order of the day. As Doug sipped his coffee and kept an eye on the clock, he read the memo. The meeting had been changed to the Assembly Conference Room to accommodate a larger gathering. Maybe this morning was different.

Doug walked in at precisely nine o'clock and appeared to be the last to arrive. Everyone seated around the large conference table rose as he entered and he was effusively introduced by Brad Clark to each person present . . . one at a time.

Doug was acquainted with a few of those present—Mike Buffington, Brad Clark's political aide, and Senator Marcia Conley. The others . . . he recognized their names as the heaviest hitters in the Republican ranks—Leif Anderson, Sam Hartage, Cliff Hardcastle, pollster Mervin Meadows, direct-mail fundraiser Slim Stacy, and Stoney Marsh, the well-known party mechanic. The entire brain trust of the state central committee was present.

Something is up. Something really BIG is up! suddenly crossed Doug's mind. *Some young chicken's about to be plucked and I'm the only tender political bird in the room.* Any doubt vanished as Brad Clark seated him between himself and Marcia Conley, the senate's minority leader, at the head of the conference table. Every eye was fixed upon him and every face wore a Mona Lisa-like smile. Brad Clark turned to him and said, "Doug, you're probably wondering why we're all here."

Wide-eyed, no longer sleepy, Doug joked, "Gin rummy? You need another table for bridge?"

Over the nervous laughter, Brad said, "No, Doug, something a little more important. But we do have some cards to play and today's game is called 'Change the State Leadership.'"

Without waiting for a response from Doug, Clark went into a long-winded scenario about what the Republicans had to do to take over the state's helm. They needed an issue on which the party's membership could hang their collective political hats, one that would put the Democrats on the defensive. Polling data clearly defined "too much government" as a major concern, and that reducing the bureaucracy claimed better than 80 percent public support among the voters.

Since California could put the issue directly before the voter by way of a ballot initiative, they had a chance to capture the leadership. Brad explained the plan to gather the necessary signatures to qualify a "Cut the Bureaucracy" measure in time for a November election. The liberals and the governor were sure to oppose it, even though it was bipartisan to the core. Brad ended his presentation by saying, "Well, Doug, what do you think?"

All attention was again focused on the new assemblyman. "Why are you all looking at me? It sounds good, like a winner, but why tell me? I'm still the new guy in town, the new kid on the block. I don't even know where all the capitol restrooms are."

Quietly, but commanding attention, Leif Anderson spoke. "We know you have much to learn, Mr. Stewart; however, your background in economics and knowledge of the over-regulatory nature of the present state government make you the perfect person to spearhead the initiative drive. You would be quite credible as its director. Your personal reputation is unassailable and the press knows who you are."

Slim Stacy added his two cents' worth before Doug could open his mouth. "Your signature on a letter to high financial donors would be very helpful. You've shown a great ability to raise big bucks. Your Hollywood contacts are terrific too; they'd add a new dimension to GOP fundraising."

Enthusiastically, Senator Marcia Conley jumped into the dialogue. "Leif's right; your background before you got into politics makes you an excellent choice for this kind of project—successful businessman plus being a decorated Vietnam vet. And don't forget the volunteer work you've done for the Red Cross and United Way is well-known among the right people. You're a USC grad, not to mention the fact that you were on the Trojan football team. All that helps."

Marcia's closing comment got to Doug. "All I did for SC football was provide a live blocking dummy for the first team and a cushion to collect splinters from the bench. To the coach, I was 'Hey you!' He never even knew my name."

"You can believe us, Assemblyman Stewart," interjected the Republican state chairman, "the contributors who count already know your name."

Brad motioned to the seated participants. "All of us here are in agreement; you are the best choice to head up the initiative drive. If we could find somebody better, we would."

"Man, if I'm the best, then our party is in *real trouble*. Ladies and gentlemen, I'm deeply complimented, but I don't have the time. I still have my business to oversee in Los Angeles and property elsewhere that demands my full attention. I honestly haven't a moment to spare."

"Would you consider the job if it didn't take up too much of your time? Let's say, no more than two hours a week?" asked Stoney Marsh.

"Yeah, Doug," piped up Brad, "what do you say about that?"

"Who's kidding who?" laughed Doug. "There's no way that could be the case. The caucus fundraiser alone took up practically all my time."

"Doug, I'll make you a deal," offered Brad. "Accept the title of honorary chairman and if it requires more than two hours a week, your resignation will be automatically accepted, no arguments. How's that for a solid offer?"

"How in the world can you expect me to accomplish anything in just two hours each week?"

Stoney Marsh jumped into the conversation. "We'll see that you have an executive director to do the busywork of handling the press, radio interviews, et cetera. Slim will handle all the mail and Leif will help you set up the finance committee. Marcia and Brad will handle the live TV and I'll oversee the whole operation. All you have to do is approve the initial mail copy, read from a teleprompter for some quick weekly TV commercials, and look handsome. That should take less than an hour and a half; you'll easily have thirty minutes to spare to keep up with what's going on."

Flabbergasted, Doug sat back in his chair.

"Come on, Doug . . . do it," pleaded Brad. Marcia gave him an imploring look and the rest added their collective encouragement.

Doug was more than complimented by the outpouring of kind words and with a firm look at each one, he finally relented. "Okay . . . I'll do it, but with two undebatable conditions. First, everyone must clearly understand that one-tenth of a second over the two hours and I'm gone. Secondly, I want another legislator to share the load. If my seatmate, Harry Kaloogian, is willing, he'd be a great co-chairman. I'm very high on that young man. He's been a big help to me, handling the caucus staff."

Brad Clark nodded. "I think that can be arranged; you're right, Harry would be an excellent choice. Well then, do we have a deal?"

"It's a deal—but I think you're making a big mistake, choosing me. Since you intend to do all the work and give me all the credit, how can I refuse?"

As Doug walked back to his office, he pondered the events of the past several months and how Nadine's little scheme had so dramatically changed his life. He hated to admit that he was beginning to enjoy his tenure in public office—at least, in part. The new endeavor he'd accepted would be challenging. The legislative work was becoming more intriguing, having been assigned to the powerful revenue and taxation committee, a subject he knew a great deal about. The Sacramento scene was a fascinating study on the inner workings of government. The caucus chairmanship showed great promise, especially since bringing Harry Kaloogian on board as vice chair. The eager young man had all the makings of a fine executive; both he and Harry believed they had a real opportunity to make changes desperately needed for California.

With all of this, he still had time on his hands. The legislature convened every Monday afternoon and adjourned on Thursday mornings. Most members rushed back to their districts, where quite a few seemed to campaign all year long. Doug found that flying down to Los Angeles every third week for Thursday and Friday meetings took care of the political needs and what little was necessary to manage his business interests could be handled by phone or fax. The rest of the time, he was able to spend in the backwoods environment which had completely captured his enthusiasm. Digging and probing around in the web of the Lucky Adele's mine tunnels, scratching for gold, added a hint of danger to his long weekends, but proved to be a pleasurable pastime.

Jamie talked him into occasionally joining Grizzly Flat's Foot Stompers, a small local group devoted to line dancing. On Thursday nights they got into their best boots and jeans and met at the Hagerty ranch, where the barn was a perfect place for practice. Looking forward to Saturday nights, when they pounded the floor at the Tex-Okie, became a natural part of Doug's new life which he was also enjoying immensely.

★ ★ ★

BRAD CLARK LEFT INSTRUCTIONS they were not to be disturbed and now they were sequestered in his inner office.

"Think we got the hook into him?" asked Cliff Hardcastle.

"Clean down to the gullet," said Brad. "Stewart swallowed it up to the bobber. I'm pleased as punch he accepted and surprised it wasn't as hard as I thought. You know, there's a rumor he just might not run next year, which would be a heck of a loss to our long-range plans. I'm hoping this initiative will be the vehicle to get him involved and keep him around. By the way, a word of caution to all of you. He very well could back out if those time restraints aren't abided by or if he feels we're trying to use him. When he gets a good look at all the press and TV forthcoming, he might not think he's up to the job; he could bail out. Believe me, he's no way the typical, media-lovin' politician, but a very private person."

Glancing about the room, Clark added, "Help yourselves to coffee. Anybody want a Coke?"

Brad opened his closet door, displaying the small refrigerator and shelves, fully stocked with glasses and a wide assortment of beverages. He pulled out two cold Cokes.

Meadows and Marsh poured themselves coffee from the carafe. Quickly guzzling down the lukewarm brew, Stoney Marsh tore up a napkin and fashioned a pile of spitballs. He placed the empty cup on the table and began tossing the damp missiles from across the room.

Leif Anderson accepted the Coke, chuckling. "When are we going to spring it on Stewart that we orchestrated this whole thing to get him on board so we could hit up his rich friends?"

Brad winced and his eyes darted in all directions. "Not so loud! You know that has to be the best-kept secret in the capitol."

Sam Hartage picked a comfortable chair by the coffee table and poured himself a cup. "This Stewart is a phenomena, probably the most egoless man I've ever met—particularly in one of the two most ego-ridden businesses in America."

"What's the other?" inquired Marcia.

"Hollywood, movie-making!" joked Marsh. "In Hollywood, they pretend to be great; in Sacramento, they're convinced they are."

"Present company included?" snidely asked Marcia.

Marsh rolled his eyes and tossed another wad at the cup, wisely choosing not to answer her.

Brad saw it was time to change the subject. "Doug's extremely likable and very bright. He doesn't know much about the guts of Sacramento politics, but he's a whiz at raising big bucks. He's a hard worker, faithfully attends committee meetings, and asks intelligent questions. It's easy to see why he's done so well in business." Brad took a deep breath, adding, "I wish I had more like him around here."

"Do you think he might change his mind, stick it out, and stay in the assembly?" asked Meadows, while reaching for the coffee carafe.

"I can't answer that; he's not like the rest of us. I recently found out he didn't want to come here in the first place," replied Brad. "He doesn't think he's Moses, ordained by God to lead us out of the sea of red tape. He has yet to introduce a bill and is smart enough to realize that any worthwhile legislation, cutting back on the bureaucracy, would die in Democrat-controlled committee. That's one of the reasons I thought he might like to head up the campaign. With this initiative, we can make major changes. It's my guess Doug Stewart will be gone at the end of next year; he'll quit if he feels he's not effective. The only hope we have is to convince him he's really an important cog in being able to pass the 'Cut the Bureaucracy' proposition."

Meadows concurred, "Hope you're right. Hey! What's this thing in my coffee cup?"

"Sorry," Stoney apologized, grinning. "Errant missile."

"Marcia, I have a hard question for you," stated Leif Anderson. "I know you are toying with the idea of running for the corner office. If you thought there was a chance of elevating Stewart to be the next Republican candidate for governor, would you be pushing him out front now?"

Before she could answer Leif's pointed question, Stoney Marsh sarcastically interjected, "Are you kidding? Marcia and I would boil him in oil if we thought for a minute that could occur. We've already discussed it and fat chance of it ever happening. I talked to Carlos Saracino; you know, he ran his primary campaign. Carlos told me Stewart's wife was the driving force, not her husband. Nadine Stewart snookered him into the election against his will. He said the idea of Doug Stewart making a career out of politics is a joke, a gasser, a leg-slapper. In other words, it ain't gonna happen. Stewart looks upon government as a canker sore on the butt of business and has shown no desire to be a head canker. If any of us thought he had any further ambitions, even a remote possibility, our proposal to Stewart would not have taken place."

Marcia added, "It's an old political maxim; never build up your future opposition unless you're controlling the stool he's standing on."

Leif turned to Stoney, knowing full well Marcia had hired him as consultant for her run for governorship. "Well, I guess that's clear enough."

"In two years' time, if I think Marcia has a shot at defeating Edmonds, I'd say let's go for it." With that, he launched another soggy ball at the cup. "Bingo!"

Leif raised one eyebrow. "But under any scenario, this group will make the final decision. Agreed, Marcia?"

The senate minority leader smiled and nodded her head. There was an almost imperceptible glint in her eye.

★ ★ ★

DOUG WAS SURPRISED AT how quickly the "Cut the Bureaucracy" campaign got under way and, so far, they had kept their end of the bargain. Filming the television ads took only an hour or so and the copy took less than three minutes to read and approve. All calls about the initiative drive coming into his office were automatically referred to Laurie Noble. Doug had nothing more to do than answer questions from his colleagues. More often than not, his comments were short and sweet. "I don't know . . . ask Stoney Marsh." Or, he might say, "Call Laurie Noble; she handles all the details."

It seemed he couldn't turn on the TV without seeing his face or hearing his voice on the radio. There were glowing commentaries about the issue from a host of celebrities. They spoke on behalf of qualifying the measure for the ballot, now called Proposition One Hundred. Doug's horn-rimmed glasses became the symbol of the campaign and the slogan, "Look to the future, cut bureaucracy with Proposition One Hundred." Corny as it was, it seemed to be catching on.

★ ★ ★

THE MOST SHARP, NEGATIVE verbiage consisted of the angry words from Jamie. She unloaded her opinion as she instructed Hank on a new dance step. "Hank, have you heard what those Republicans are up to? Now, first take a step to the right and cross over. They're actually trying to cut money to our schools with this Proposition One Hundred!"

"Over to the right? Like this? Got to admit, 'Bright Eyes,' property taxes are pretty high."

Ignoring Hank's remark, she continued on. "Know who's heading it up? That rich, country club assemblyman from San Marino. Now, twist on your right heel like this. I hear he's a real pro at dirty political tricks and filthy rich to boot. You can bet your bottom dollars Proposition One Hundred will line his pockets further if it passes. Okay, now hop to the left and point your right toe this way."

"I've read that he's a pretty good guy," countered her smiling companion. "Point my toe like this?"

"Ha!" she huffed. "Read it where . . . in the *Wall Street Journal*? Hank Kaplowski, you don't know anymore about dancing than you do about politics. No, not like that . . . like this—and wiggle your hips. All you have to do is take a close look at that dandy's perfectly styled hair and thousand-dollar suits to tell he can't be trusted. Good, now you got it."

"I think he's sorta good-lookin'," teased Hank.

Jamie wrinkled up her face in disgust and stopped dancing. "That initiative scares me as much as that ultra-conservative Neanderthal who's pushing it. Last night at the meeting of the Durango Democrats, we decided to get busy and put on a voter registration drive. By the way, Hank, have you registered since you've moved here?"

The question set him back for a moment. "Uh, er . . . well, no, not yet. But don't worry, I'll get around to it." Then wiggling his hips, he asked, "Is this the right move?"

Jamie looked sternly at him. "You want to vote, don't you? You don't want to see our public schools closed for lack of funds, do you?"

He assured her with a wide grin and wiggled his backside again. "Of course not, Jamie. Calm down. I'll definitely be voting if the initiative measure gets on the ballot—and I'll learn this routine if you stop talkin' politics."

"Good!" she laughed.

"Good, you've stopped talking politics—or good, you like the way I wiggle my fanny?"

"Politics," she answered, and giggled. "After watching you pulsate your posterior, I'm going to take that step out of the routine."

"What?" Hank said in feigned surprise. "I *got* that move from *Elvis.*"

THIRTEEN

★ ★ ★

SEAN MacGRUDER STRODE confidently into the posh, oak-paneled office, smiled at his boss, and with a flourish, placed a thick manila folder on Doug's desk.

"What do we have here?"

"Take a look; it's the research you asked me to dig up on the proposed Durango County landfill."

After a cursory review of the synopsis, Doug let out a low whistle and eagerly looked up at his assistant. "Good job, Mac. Is there a hearing still scheduled for tomorrow night?"

MacGruder nodded. "I thought Robin Hood lived in Sherwood Forest; now I discover it's Durango County."

Doug continued to browse the documents. "I see what you mean. But it appears ol' Boone E. Bates takes from the taxpayers of the county and gives to his rich relatives."

"Precisely!" MacGruder said. He laughed. "And he's not even very subtle about it. I did a title search on the land they want purchased for the new dump and it's owned by a conglomerate named Nev-Cal Realty and Land Development. It's presided over by some guy named Sawville, but I suspect it's owned in large part by Boonie's second cousins."

"Why do you believe that?"

"Just a hunch," countered MacGruder. "When I was digging around the county records, I overheard several of the office help joking about their Uncle Boonie. I got a cold reception to begin with and when I started to ask abut Nev-Cal Realty, it really got frigid. Didn't take me long to put two and two together. For starters, I went through newspaper archives and dug up as much history as I could find on one Boone E. Bates and his relatives. To condense it all, that old coot has kin plugged in everywhere."

"How many relatives are we talking about?" asked Doug.

"Only two brothers but there was a whole covey of sisters — eight, to be exact. He also has a passel of uncles and aunts who begat bountifully. Seems like all of 'em married in their teens and each of them went amorously to work propagating Durango County. And it seems every last one of 'em work within the local government. Bates has got to be the state champion, the premier advocate of hiring within the confines of one's own genes."

"So, old Boonie's kinfolk are scattered all through the county hierarchy, huh?"

"Yep!" replied Sean, "In every nook and cranny. Up until last year, even the sheriff was a Bates relative."

"Any family back-scratching that we can prove?"

"Nothing solid, as yet," answered Sean. "But given a little time, I'll find the source of the stench. The whole operation smells like a fish dock in the noonday sun. As an example, the county's garbage collection contract is held by his brother-in-law. I need to check to see if there were any competitive bids. State law requires it."

"Anything else?"

"Yeah, the existing disposal site isn't even close to being filled and — surprise, surprise — the county planning commissioner is his first cousin."

"Merle Hempton?"

"Yes, that's his name. Merle's the oldest boy of Boonie's youngest sister."

"How long has Bates been on the county board of supervisors?"

MacGruder thumbed through his notes. "Ever since the county split off from El Dorado County close to thirty years ago. Nobody has dared run against him — at least, not in the last few elections."

"Any other kin on the board?"

"One. Harry Rollins. I think he's the youngest boy of Abel and Opal Rollins. Opal is the third daughter of Daymond Bates, Boonie's older brother. The other three supervisors aren't related; at least, I don't think they are."

"Gets confusing, doesn't it?" said Doug.

"Confusing? Look at this." Sean unfolded a chart showing the Bates family tree. It looked like the wiring schematic of a computer board. "It took me forever to dig through all of the newspaper articles and birth records to computerize the data. Then I got a list of county employees, synchronized the names, and did a match with the relatives. Durango is saturated with them, from top to bottom."

"Somewhere in that pile of nepotism, you must have gotten a whiff of corruption," said Doug.

"You got that right! Appropriately, there's plenty at the new garbage dump." Sean reached into the pile of papers, pulled out a ledger sheet, and handed it to his employer. "Look at this."

Doug studied the document briefly and smiled devilishly. "Good work, Sean."

"Boss, if I may ask, why is this office so interested in the affairs of Durango County?"

"Oh, I have some friends who live in the area and they asked me to look into it. They didn't want their local assemblyman, Saul Benson, to know about it. He seems to be tied into the Bates' operation."

"Second cousin, twice removed."

"Really?"

"Really. They're under every county rock; even the Grand Jury's foreman, Melvin Morgan, is his first cousin."

"No wonder Bates is so arrogant."

"Boss, do you want some of us to cover the meeting tomorrow night? The landfill is on the agenda."

The question startled Doug and he said abruptly, "No! . . . No, thank you. I don't want our office within a thousand miles of that meeting. Understand?"

At Doug's emphatic response, Sean shrugged and replied, "Sure thing. Whatever you say."

"Good. Thanks again, Sean. You've done an excellent job; however, this ends the matter."

Confused somewhat by Doug's behavior and his curt dismissal of the subject, MacGruder quickly excused himself and left the room.

After an hour or so of carefully studying the documents, Doug had a clear grasp of the significance of Sean's research. "Gotcha cornered, you old crook!" As he placed the file folder in his briefcase and snapped it shut, he said to the empty room, "Good work, Sean, as usual, but . . . I have no intention of you or anyone else seeing Hank Kaplowski do his civic duty."

THE SUN HAD YET TO CLEAR the eastern horizon as Hank walked into Mae's Country Kitchen Café. The aroma of bacon sizzling on the grill and biscuits baking excited his senses as soon as he opened the door. Platters of eggs with green pepper and onion hash browns, stacks of buttermilk pancakes, and pitchers of hot maple syrup were being served up to the usual morning patrons. He was ravenous, looking forward to his first cup of coffee and one of those platters for himself.

Ever since his move to the foothills, he had come to appreciate a hearty breakfast, unlike the former light meal he had each morning in L.A. A far cry from cereal, nonfat milk, and a cup of fruit, Hank placed his order for king-size biscuits covered with creamy sausage gravy and a half-dozen slices of crispy bacon. The heavy exertion required to care for the Lucky Adele was justification enough.

Mae's Café was set back in the trees on Pleasant Valley Road, miles from any population center but ideal for the working people who lived in the nearby foothills. It was the predawn coffee hangout for painters, carpenters, repairmen, and ranchers on their way to work and was also the favorite breakfast retreat and meeting place for the anti-Boonie, anti-landfill crowd.

Crammed in around several tables that were crowded together in the small back room of the restaurant, they were hotly discussing the night's hearing. There were some new faces in the group and Hank wondered if a Bates relative could be hidden in the bunch.

"We thought you might like to see these." Jamie slipped several articles clipped from the *Placerville Mountain Democrat* and the *Mount Aukum Herald* across the table to Hank. They were highly complimentary of Kaplowski's derailing of Bates' motion to purchase the new landfill property. Hank laughed at the captions: "Local Man Saves Endangered Species?" "B.E. Bates Foiled by Local Miner," and "The Gooneybill Fubthrusher?"

The stories proved that Hank had succeeded in creating confusion and that the Environmental Protection Agency customarily took a great deal of time turning in their revised reports. Tonight, their findings would be made public.

"Hank," commented one of the locals, "you're gettin' to be quite a local celebrity. The press did a lot of research trying to find out what a gooneybill what's-its-name looks like."

"Yeah," added another. "When they couldn't find the bird in any ornithology books, they figured you were pulling old Boonie's leg in order to put off the vote. Glad to see they thought it was hilarious, you trifling with the old coot and his clones. Seems like he's been gettin' under everybody's skin these days."

Linda, the waitress, said, "From what I hear, Boonie's chomping at the bit to get a piece of you tonight."

"You can bet on it, particularly 'cause the press will be there, en masse," added a worried Jamie. "Hank, what are we going to do for an encore?"

"What are we going to do? I've been down south lately. I've had little time to look into much of anything. What's the matter? Haven't you guys come up with any information?"

They all looked at each other. "We didn't come up with much," shrugged one of them. "A couple of us went down to the county offices and tried to do some digging, but all we got was the run-around by the clerks. How about you?"

"Well, I have a friend, a private investigator," said Hank. "He picked up a few tidbits that might be of some use. I'll bring 'em up tonight." The evidence was not complete. He might have to bluff a little to fill in the gaps.

Dejected, Jamie crinkled her nose. "A few tidbits, that's all? Doesn't look good, does it? We're no better off than we were three weeks ago."

Hank stretched his arms behind his neck, yawned, took off his Stetson, and scratched his balding head, "Maybe . . . and maybe not. Maybe I can pull another endangered bird out of my hat."

Attitudes noticeably perked up, with the exception of a middle-aged, gray-haired lady seated at one end of the table. "What do you mean by that, Mr. Kaplowski?"

"Just a figure of speech," he offhandedly replied. The gathering resolved little and was deteriorating into a general bull session. Hank saw it was becoming unproductive and depressing, so he pushed back his chair and stood up. "Well, time to go. See y'all tonight." Moving toward the cash register, he called to the waitress, "Linda, would you please bring me my bill?"

Filing out the door, several of the men slapped Hank on the shoulder and wished him well. A few of the women shook his hand. The middle-aged, gray-haired stranger left by herself.

"Bright Eyes" grabbed his arm and held on tight.

★　★　★

THE FIRST SNOW WAS FALLING, covering the mountainous land-scape with a thin coat of wet white. The merchants of Diamond Springs had already brought out the Christmas decorations and draped their stores with colored lights and tinsel, even though

Thanksgiving was still more than a week away. Carols blared from hidden loudspeakers, announcing the holiday season. The gently falling snow and twinkling lights made the rustic county seat look postcard-pretty.

Doug felt a flash of nostalgia and loneliness rush through him as he realized this would be the first holy season without Nadine and the children gathering around their tree, at home in San Marino. The girls had invited him to visit, but they lived in opposite directions—Marianne in Hawaii and Diana in New Hampshire with their husbands and children. Wally was going to stay in Massachusetts with his fiancé's family. This year, with new responsibilities, he had decided to spend Christmas by himself. It was a lonely thought. *Oh well, plenty to keep me busy around the cabin and the goings on in Durango County,* which brought him back to the business at hand . . . facing off against Supervisor Bates.

The council chamber was so packed when Hank arrived, he had trouble squeezing through the crowd to the front of the room. He couldn't help but notice the nasty stares from one side of the aisle, and the smiles of encouragement from the other. There appeared to be no undecided spectators in the audience.

Chairman Boone E. Bates was already in his chair, impatiently waiting for two of the other supervisors to take their seats. Both were working the audience, as consummate politicians are prone to do, shaking hands, joking with constituents and, unlike the chairman, thoroughly enjoying themselves. Bates' mood had turned decidedly sour upon spotting Hank in attendance. He dramatically raised the gavel and brought it down hard. "This here meetin' will come to order!"

Immediate silence ensued, then shuffling and whispering, as those still standing vied for the few unoccupied seats that were left, or lobbied for the best spaces against the wall.

"Let's git down to brass tacks!" Boone shouted into the microphone and through the loudspeaker system came an ear piercing, electronic shriek, painfully deafening the audience. "Fix that blasted thing!" he wailed, but while hastily trying to cover the mike, he knocked it off the dais, sending it clattering to the floor.

Several panicked clerks bumped into each other in their rush to turn down the volume on the audio equipment. As one of them retrieved the mike and handed it to Bates, he angrily ripped it from his hand. "Gimme that!"

The crowd was chattering and laughing at the Laurel-and-Hardy antics taking place. Trying once more to commence the meeting, Boone spoke into the dead microphone. Crimson-faced, he threw it down, rose from his chair, and yelled at the top of his lungs, "Everybody shut up! Call the first speaker, er . . . witness, which is the EPA folks." Bates glowered at the audience, then said, "That is, after I make a few remarks."

Staring daggers and pointing a bony finger at Hank, he spat out with venom, "We were lied to, last meeting, by that fellow sittin' over there. He claimed there was an endangered bird on his property. . . . Warn't none! He said there was a wetland marsh. . . . Warn't none!" Shaking his forefinger vigorously, he sputtered, "That man's a LIAR!" Content with his graphic exposé, he smirked at his adversary and settled back in his seat, amid scattered applause from his supporters. "Now, let's hear the first witness!"

Merle Hempton came forward and read from the EPA's report to the county, confirming they found no visible wetlands on the Kaplowski property, nor evidence of any bird by the name of gooneybill fubthrusher.

"See!" Boonie growled at the reporters. "There ain't no such bird. You were had!"

The parade of witnesses on hand gave much the same testimony as at the prior hearing. At their conclusion, a gloating Bates looked over the throng, fastened his eyes on Hank, and challenged, "Now, does anyone else have anything to say before we take the vote?"

Hank slowly rose to his feet and dryly responded, "Now that you mention it, Mr. Chairman, I have a few words to say about another

SPLIT TICKET

endangered bird, only this one is a vulture—a buzzard, and old one, to boot."

One of the other supervisors leaned forward in his chair. "We have no more time for your foolishness, Mr. Kaplowski."

"Yes, Supervisor Rollins, I agree. Your mama's name is Opal, isn't it, and I believe she's Boone's sister? You're Boone's first cousin, aren't you?"

"What of it?" he snarled.

Turning to the seated planning commissioner, Hank asked, "You're his first cousin too, aren't you, Merle?"

Merle looked to Boone helplessly. "So what?" caustically snapped Bates.

Hank took off his Stetson and wiped his brow with his sleeve, then pulled out the papers he'd stuffed in the crown. Taking his time, he thumbed through the pages and, with a flair, flapped one noisily toward the supervisors. "Another one of your close kin holds the contract for all of our county's trash disposal needs, right? Please tell us how many competitive bids were submitted. State law requires certain standards. Were they met?"

"Our assemblyman said we did everything right!" retorted Bates.

"You mean cousin Saul Benson?" Hank whipped around suddenly and faced the audience. "Let's see a show of hands of those who are related to Boone and work for the county."

Quite a few hands popped up, then quickly were withdrawn.

"Merle!" Boonie screamed. "Take your dang-fool hand outa the air."

The anti-landfill members broke into hoots and hollers, several collapsing over in uncontrollable laughter.

Bates was apoplectic, violently banging the gavel, vainly attempting to control the raucous gathering.

Hank waited a few minutes before intervening. "Let's all calm down. Come on, folks . . . let's get back to order." When the hilarity finally dwindled to nothing more than an occasional titter, Hank

125

again reached into his hat and produced another document. As the murmuring rose from the crowd, now fully engrossed in the drama, he turned back to face the supervisors. "You want to purchase the land from Nev-Cal Realty . . . correct?"

Nervously, Bates answered, "Yes . . . so what!"

Unfolding the paper slowly, in a precise, clipped tone, Hank continued. "Please tell us which of your relatives own Nev-Cal, or would you like me to read off their names to the audience and press?"

Hank's voice rose, in anger. "Come clean, Mr. Bates; what is your personal financial connection to this rip-off of the county voters?" Then with spirited indignation, he demanded, "Well, who are they? Know this, Mr. Bates—this nepotistic plundering of Durango County is coming to a halt!"

Completely captivated by Hank's oratory, the room erupted into massive applause and shouts of agreement. "Go get 'em, Hank! Give the old so-and-so what for!"

Encompassed by hate and rage, saliva bubbling at the corners of his mouth, Boone E. Bates staggered to his feet. Shaking his fist, screaming vulgar epithets to "Kaplowski," he suddenly arched his back as though punched in the kidneys by a vicious blow. To everyone's shock, he shuddered, then collapsed in a heap behind the dais, disappearing from sight.

"Oh, dear God!" shouted one of his frightened colleagues, as they rushed to their fallen leader's side.

Fifteen minutes later, with an oxygen mask pressed to Boone's face and an attendant pushing rhythmically on his chest, the ashen-faced supervisor was hastily loaded into an ambulance. The crowd milled around in the falling snow, oblivious to the cold, stunned by the shadow of death passing so close overhead. Several jumped as the siren began its fearful sound, startled by its blaring wail. They watched silently as the red flashing light sped away, fading into the frigid night.

No one thought to adjourn the meeting.

FOURTEEN

★ ★ ★

HELLO. YOU IN THERE, HANK? It's me . . . Jamie!" Her voice sounded strange, bouncing off the granite. The tunnel walls seemed to crush in, making her feel borderline claustrophobic. *I've got to get out!* Then, as the desire to see Hank overpowered her fears, she gamely took a few more hesitant steps into the dimly lighted mine shaft and, with voice quaking, called again. "Hank! Are you down there?"

"Ouch!" she groaned as she bumped her head on an overhead beam. "Nuts to this!" Cursing the fact that he had no phone and that she had to four-wheel it through mudflats, to find him not here was frustrating.

Angrily turning in the narrow passageway, she stubbed her toe on a railroad tie supporting the ore cart rail. "Dang it! That smarts!" Limping badly, she gimped her way out, breathing a sigh of relief when she finally reached the mine's exit. As she looked back into the dark hole, she shuddered. "How could anybody actually enjoy hacking away in that . . . that place!"

Brushing off her Levi's and down jacket, Jamie headed across the partially frozen muddy expanse to the cabin. "I'll leave him a note. Good grief, that man is making me *talk* to myself!" Perfunctorily rapping on the door, she entered quickly into the warmth and began rummaging for paper and pen.

"What do you think you're doing, young lady?"

Shaken by the tone of Hank's question, she stammered, "I didn't think you were here and I have something important to . . . "

"Well, come on outside; we can discuss it on the porch." He edged around Jamie, moving her toward the door.

"Can't we stay in here? It's freezing outside."

"Rather not; I need some fresh air." The attitude of his body language made it abundantly clear he didn't want her inside.

Talk about a private person! she thought as she slipped out the door.

Once outside on the porch, he changed radically from harsh to warm. "Glad to see you, 'Bright Eyes' . . . what's up?"

Although Hank had heard her calling to him and he'd yelled back, his voice was muffled by the smallness of the spur where he was working. Backing out as quickly as the narrowness would allow, he moved swiftly into the main shaft and scurried up to the mine's entrance just in time to see Jamie push open the cabin door.

Panic gripped him. *What if she saw them?* . . . the research papers scattered across the unmade bed, the assembly seal and letterhead in full view. The tie and Louis Raphael wool suit hung neatly on a hanger in the open closet and his hairpiece was draped over the post at the foot of the bed. Hank broke into a sweat dashing up to the cabin, hoping, even praying, he could get there before Jamie's eyes had time to adjust to the dark interior. From what he could tell as he burst through the door, he'd made it. While he hustled her outside, he thought, *Next time I'd better be careful and keep the cabin locked.*

Hugging herself to keep from shivering, she blurted out, "Well, Kaplowski, those good-for-nothing supervisors threw us another curve."

"What now? I thought Boonie was in the hospital, still suffering from the stroke."

"He is. Tubes sticking out all over him. Boonie's not the problem; the trouble's coming from Supervisor Harry Rollins."

"Boone's cousin?"

"Uh-huh. Harry's taken over the chair. He called a quickie meeting and the four of them voted to call a special election to put the purchase of the landfill property to a vote of the people."

"A vote of the people? A county referendum?"

"That's right. They're calling it the 'Keep Our County Clean' Referendum. That sleazy bunch has already set the date of the election. They must think they have the votes, that it'll pass."

"What date did they set it for?"

"First Monday in March. That's only a couple of months away. Can't we go back inside? I'm freezing my patootie off."

"Give me a sec to tidy up. The place is a mess."

"Okay, but please make it snappy. I'm about to turn into an icicle."

Hank ducked into the house, shut the door, and began a frantic search for any evidence of Doug Stewart. He closed the closet door and crammed the strewn papers under the sheets. After a fast once-over, he hollered, "You can come in now." Just as Jamie was entering, he remembered . . . *the toupee! Rats, I forgot the wig!* There it was, looking like a possum sitting on a fence post. He edged between Jamie and the bed, blocking her view. "Go on over by the stove and warm yourself."

Jamie shivered, "Ah, yes!"

Hank inched backward to the bed, snatched up the hairpiece, and stuffed it under his jacket. "Jamie, I'll be back in a minute." Excusing himself, he went outside to the outhouse, where he wedged the wig up into the wooden rafters. He waited a respectable moment before joining Jamie in the cabin. "Now, tell me all about this referendum we have to defeat."

Jamie laid out the details, not at all optimistic with her conclusions. "Where in the world are we going to get the money? It'll take thousands and thousands of dollars to defeat this turkey. My dad will contribute a big chunk, but it's peanuts compared to what the Bates clan will be able to come up with. There's not much of an economic base to raise big bucks in this county and really too few of us are directly affected by the dump."

"How about the local business community?"

"Not many are willing to buck up against Boonie and his crowd. Most of their livers are colored lily white."

"How about the environmentalists? Don't you think they might help?"

"They hate my . . . let's just say they aren't too fond of the Hagertys. They believe we despoil Mother Nature with our cows and lumber trucks."

"Who's heading up the referendum?"

Jamie sounded depressed. "No big surprise; they got our very own assemblyman, Saul Benson. He brings name, big donations, and the county Democrats to their side." Stepping up close to Hank, she reached out and grabbed his lapels, then tilting her head to the side and with pleading eyes, asked softly, "Hank, would you help us? We need your advice . . . please?"

He started to say no, but seeing the whipped-puppy look on Jamie's face, he found himself saying, "Well . . . okay, maybe a little, but I won't have much time to spare. I have to be in southern California a lot over the next few months."

"You will?" She threw both of her strong arms about his neck and squeezed him tight, then planted a wet kiss on his bald pate. As quickly as she grabbed him, she let him go. "Hank, you're a dream!" Looking about the room she asked, "Your bathroom?"

"Around the back . . . outside . . . the little building with a quarter-moon cut in the door."

Jamie wrinkled up her nose distastefully, shivered at the thought, and went out into the cold. Hank followed her through the door and waited by the mud-spattered Hagerty pickup. When she returned and climbed inside the truck, over the clanking of the diesel engine, she smiled broadly. "Thank you, Hank, for taking this on. I'll do everything I can to help."

"I'm counting on it, Jamie. As I said, my time is limited."

She waved good-bye and rolled up the window, then lowered it an inch and moved close to the glass. "Oh, by the way, Hank—I think you have a possum hiding in your outhouse rafters."

★　★　★

IT'S A GOOD THING I'M NOT a woman. With my propensity to say yes, my reputation would be in question. Doug Stewart's political plate was full—in fact, overflowing. He had accepted the responsibilities of caucus chairmanship without fully realizing the complexities of the job. Not only was he responsible for fundraising for incumbent assembly Republicans, he had to coordinate with the senate Republicans, as well. That, by itself was a monumental undertaking. But having accepted the post as chairman of the "Cut the Bureaucracy" initiative, "Hank's" recent weak moment with Jamie was ridiculous. How did I get myself so involved?

The legislature had convened in January and it seemed that every lobbyist in the state was trying to see him. Doug found it more productive to have lunch in his office, for whenever he ventured out for a meal, several politicians would inevitably drop by his table and request an appointment. Also demanding his time was the proliferation of constituents visiting the capitol, who, more often than not, would show up unexpectedly. Most were content to talk with members of his staff, but whenever a Chamber of Commerce or a delegation of city councilmen arrived, they usually weren't satisfied until they saw Doug himself.

His recent prominence in leadership made him a sought-after guest by every statewide association visiting Sacramento. If Doug wanted to, he could be out every night, attending this reception or that testimonial dinner. He tried it for awhile but after a few weeks, gave it up.

Most legislators reveled in all the attention they received and tanned their egos in the sunny glow of adulation beamed constantly upon them . . . not Doug. It didn't take him long to realize that much of it was a waste of time and energy, that schmooze events were for the schmoozees, schmoozors, and the schmoozable.

Having committed himself to a ton of work, Doug found himself contemplating the startling possibility of seeking another term. Brad Clark had convincingly argued that his reelection would be a cake walk, with only token opposition.

"You gotta do it, Doug," Brad pleaded. "You can hold the fifty-fourth assembly seat with ease. Besides, we need you to run the caucus. If you're still set on getting out, retire next year—but please, stick around and help me gain control of the assembly."

Brad took a deep breath, bit into a granola bar, and sipped his coffee before continuing. "Stewart, leaving the legislature at this juncture would also do damage to the initiative drive. You've done a beautiful job managing the Proposition One Hundred effort; there's no doubt enough signatures will be gathered to qualify for the November ballot. The polls show you're becoming a very popular and exciting figure to the property owner . . . Democrats too. Your leaving office at this time would be terribly disappointing to a tremendous number of people."

"I've been giving it a lot of thought."

"Good! Promise me you'll seriously consider it a priority. Roll it around real good in that wise cranium of yours."

Doug grinned affectionately at the worried minority leader sitting beside him. He couldn't help but admire and even like the portly, ruffled leader, coffee-stained tie and all.

"Okay, Brad; I'll rattle it around real good and give it my best shot." For some unexplainable reason, he didn't feel comfortable telling Brad he was close to making the decision to stay another term, but . . . not for the reasons Brad Clark put forth.

Doug Stewart had little desire to go back to the encompassing routine were he to return to L.A. For the time being, he had lost all interest in the day-to-day machinations of Stewart and Associates. Chairing occasional meetings of the corporation's board of directors was the only responsibility he wished to retain. He no longer cared to reside in the crowded urban area, tripping over the memories of last year's tragedy.

The latest chapters of Doug's life were fulfilling what would otherwise be a vain existence. He felt like he'd been born anew with the arrival of Henry "Hank" Kaplowski. Playing the part of a Mother Lode miner one day and a rather sophisticated political leader the next tickled his fancy, adding a rush of excitement, an invigorating touch of danger and drama.

Doug Hank Stewart Kaplowski, he mused, *you're having the time of your life keeping all these balls in the air.* The sobering thought of returning to the former life of a CEO was momentarily out of the question.

Through the intercom on Brad's desk, the monotone voice of the assembly sergeant at arms was calling the legislator to the floor. Clark clumsily rose from the couch and stretched. "Well, time to go to war. A new year has begun; time to protect the people from the vagrancies and vicissitudes of the viscoelastic nature of bureaucracy."

"Like us?"

"No!" Brad answered in mock indignation. "You and I are statesmen; all the others are the problem."

FIFTEEN

★ ★ ★

As soon as Jamie spotted Hank walking into the campaign headquarters, she rushed up, bubbling over with enthusiasm. Although her face was wreathed in joy, her tone of voice sounded like she was scolding a lost puppy. "Henry Kaplowski, where have you been? I've driven over that muddy road a dozen times looking for you, worried something bad had happened." She grabbed him and gave him a big hug, holding on a little longer than necessary.

Somewhat startled but pleased by her embrace, he blushed. "Hey, I'm all right. Remember, Jamie, I told you that every so often, I'd have business to attend to down south."

"I know, I know . . . but we all missed you. All kinds of good things have been happening." Holding onto his arm, she led him toward her small corner office. "I've got tons of great information to show you."

Hank dug in his heels, pulling Jamie to a stop. "Not so fast; I'm starved. Let's go to Mae's and get something to eat. I think she serves breakfast 'til noon."

Jamie was clearly disappointed. "But Hank, I've got some things you have to see."

"Show me after breakfast. My eyes don't focus on an empty stomach. I left L.A. early this morning and haven't had anything except a bag of peanuts and a can of tomato juice."

Changing her tone, she tugged on his sleeve and coaxed

enticingly, "Please, Hank, I'm dying to show you a few things. Those peanuts will hold you for a bit; your stomach can wait."

Hank took a good, long look at her and stepped back in surprise, grinning ear to ear. "Jamie, you're wearin' a dress! Going to a wedding or a funeral?" He had never seen her in anything but her denims and cowboy boots.

"Neither!" she snapped. "Go stuff your face. Get your danged breakfast!" Turning on her heel, she whipped into her office and slammed the door.

"What's wrong with her?" Hank stood for a moment transfixed on the spot, amused yet befuddled . . . but still hungry. "I can figure this out better at Mae's . . . on a full stomach."

Less than an hour later, he poked his head through Jamie's office door. "Am I still welcome?"

Without looking up, she replied, "Sure, come on in."

Tossing her a verbal olive branch, he said, "The dress looks nice."

Jamie raised her eyes and gave him the coldest, blankest stare he had ever seen, then calmly said, "Sit down, Hank. I've got lots to show you."

While lowering himself into the chair next to her desk, Hank displayed the warmest, friendliest smile he could conjure up. "Whatcha got to show me, 'Good-Lookin'?"

"Compliments will get you nowhere, Bucko; it's too late for damage control."

What did she mean by that? Nadine had also confused him more than once with similar behavior. He discovered the best course of action was to shut up and change the course of the conversation.

"Jamie, what do you want to show me?"

Begrudgingly, mumbling under her breath, she began searching through the pile of papers on her desk. She'd been anxiously waiting to show him the new literature that arrived just that morning, not to mention the pile of favorable press clippings they'd accumulated.

Jamie put his sojourn to Mae's out of her mind. "Well, all kinds of good things have happened since you've been gone. One of the newspapers has been digging up the number of Boone's relatives who work for the county, and have they found a gold mine! In almost every issue, they expose a new Bates nugget—like who heads this department or who is being paid to serve on that commission. They've also been sticking their collective noses into Nev-Cal Realty, much to the embarrassment of the entire Bates clan."

Aha, thought Hank, watching Jamie's demeanor improve. He could see she was having a hard time containing her enthusiasm; the campaign's progress was obviously agreeing with her. *She even looks prettier, more slimmed down, effervescent, full of vinegar and zeal.*

Jamie's green eyes began to sparkle, as she ran-on about the referendum. "Can you guess who's getting the credit for uncovering the corruption?"

"I haven't the foggiest! . . . You?"

"No—you! That's who!" beamed Jamie. "Hank Kaplowski is becoming a household name in Durango County." Reaching over, she punched him playfully on the arm, "Hank, everybody's talking about what you did at the board of supervisors meeting. Your masterful exposure of the Bates clan hit a sensitive cord with lots of people. For years, Boonie's been intimidating citizens and getting away with it. People are overjoyed that the old goat finally got his comeuppance."

Again, Jamie rummaged through the stacks of papers, some sliding to the floor. She produced several front-page newspaper articles relating to the last board meeting, and pointed vigorously to the yellow highlights where Hank's name was prominently marked.

"All of us are taking advantage of your popularity. Wait 'til you see *this!*" She handed him a full-color brochure, and her smile grew wide. "What do you think? The printer sent it over this morning." Illustrated on the cover was a square-jawed, ruggedly handsome cowboy standing on a mountain ridge, gazing far off into a panoramic sunset. The caption read, "Join Hank Kaplowski in the fight against corruption in Durango County."

Hank laughed. "Is that fine-lookin' guy supposed to be me?"

Visibly disappointed, she shot back, "Don't you think it looks like you? I can't believe you're not pleased! I worked for days trying to capture the spirit of your character and the substance of our campaign. We've had nothing but compliments from the girls in the office."

Diplomatically backtracking, Hank apologetically stammered, "Ah, well . . . I think it's quite . . . um . . . it's, ah . . . attractive." Then he added modestly, "I just don't think I look that good and I'm amazed; you're really quite an artist."

Jamie allowed herself a small smile and said under her breath, "You're better lookin' than you think, Bucko."

She proceeded with a long, detailed explanation of what had occurred in his absence. Her father not only contributed, but enthusiastically went to work raising substantial dollars from his many business contacts and pals. "Dad has been giving and giving for years and he had a lot of chips to call in. What's more, he enjoyed doing it."

Looking about the busy office, Hank inquired, "Have you had much help?"

"Oh, yes, more than we could actually use. A lot of gals volunteered to man the headquarters, lick stamps, handle the phones, and help the guys deliver literature door-to-door. We have a real grassroots effort going."

Taking a deep breath, Jamie continued. "The local press has done more than cooperate, editorializing extensively on behalf of the NO vote. Can you beat that?" She was bubbling with increased excitement as she added, "And, have you heard that Assemblyman Benson backed out? Boy, that shocked all of us, knowing the family connection and all. None of us can figure why."

Hank could. Weeks ago, he made sure the word got out around the capitol that Saul Benson, in his vociferous support of the

Durango County referendum, had made himself vulnerable in the forthcoming fall election. Doug Stewart placed Benson's name near the top of a phony priority list of defeatable Democrats, then leaked the information to a liberal member of the press. Saul Benson's withdrawal from the landfill referendum drive came just a week later. Hank pretended surprise. "I'll be darned; that's really good news. Saul got out, did he?"

"Yep. With his withdrawal, and with my encouragement at the last county committee meeting, the local Democrat structure bailed out too." Jamie's face was radiant. "Looks like we have a chance, a real horse race."

"Sorry I haven't been more help," offered Hank, "but business interests in the south kept me tied up longer than expected."

When they had first met months ago, Hank told Jamie his mining claims in the Tehachapi Mountains required his presence during weekdays, sometimes many days at a time. *She'd positively keel over if she knew I've been less than sixty miles away, tending to Republican business and running a massive "Cut the Bureaucracy" initiative.*

She accepted his apologies with a wave of her hand. "We've struggled along quite well without you, Henry Kaplowski. But, one thing that came to light really concerned me. While checking the precinct lists, I found out you hadn't registered to vote yet. I panicked—in fact, almost went into orbit—when I couldn't find your name on the rolls. The deadline to register was just a day away and I didn't know how to contact you. I was terrified someone would find out. We'd look pretty stupid if the opposition discovered the great Hank Kaplowski, the titular leader of our drive, didn't even care enough to vote."

Hank gulped. "You're right! I forgot all about it. Rats, I sure hope nobody else finds out."

"Don't worry; they won't," Jamie confidently remarked. "I knew you must have forgotten, so I took the liberty of registering you by mail."

"You *what?*" Hank was dumbstruck. "Jamie, that's against the law!"

"Oh, so what? It's no big deal. I copied your signature from the fundraising letter you signed for us. I think I did a good job, fudging your manly scribble, if I say so myself. I gave your proper address. You're sure not going to cast a ballot anywhere else in the state, so what's the problem? I've honestly done nothing morally wrong; just a practical solution to a potentially sticky situation. Don't you agree? Anyway, nobody else has to know, right?"

Doug weakly nodded, although he felt boxed, cornered and with a sense of *déjà vu*. His mind raced back to Nadine. Once again, his alternatives were nil. If he tried to alter what Jamie had done, she could be put under arrest. He was faced with no choice but to play along 'til election day, then not vote! He had gotten away with it before, so why not again? And as Jamie assured him, who'd find out?

Suddenly, another revolting thought hit him, boiling to the forefront, adding more perspiration to his already sweating brow. *She wouldn't, she couldn't . . . oh, yes, she would!*

"Jamie," he said softly, his voice barely above a whisper. "In what party am I registered?"

"Why, Hank, what a question! I registered you as a Democrat . . . what else? Isn't that what you've always been?

★ ★ ★

THE HEADLINES OF THE *Mount Aukum Herald* read, "Kaplowski Wowski," imaginatively announcing the overwhelming victory. The new dump site referendum was defeated by better than a two-to-one margin. Jamie was ecstatic and responding to inquiries by the press, gave Hank all of the credit for their success. "We were whipped puppies before that man came along and joined our effort. He gave us hope, leadership, and the will to win." Everyone at the victory party cheered and began chanting over and over, "Hank . . . Hank . . . Hank Kaplowski!"

The celebration at Tex-Okie Bar and Bowling lasted into the wee hours. Hank and Jamie danced until their feet hurt, then retired to the big corner booth where the rest of the gang were boisterously singing along with the band.

Jamie Hagerty looked longingly across the table at Hank, who was deeply engrossed in a conversation with Norman Moore, the new sheriff of Durango County. Norm "Bulldog" Moore was a close friend of the Hagertys from grade-school days. "Bulldog" was a high-school football hero and considered by many to be the finest fullback the Durango Panthers ever had. His popularity was sufficient to overcome his opponent, endorsed by the Bates faction.

Norm was the closest thing Jamie ever had to a boyfriend, having occasionally dated him in school. Although a Democrat and a good ol' boy, he never lit her fire or came close to arousing the emotions she was now experiencing whenever she thought of Hank. Jamie didn't know how to cope with the infatuation, the ardor surging through her body.

She resisted the temptation to grab Hank and kiss him 'til he fought her off. She was positive that he didn't feel the same way . . . and it hurt. She knew he liked her, maybe even a lot, but he treated her more like a good friend, a buddy, a conversational pal than an object of desire. Jamie felt woefully short in her stock of female wiles. She knew how to arm-wrestle and cut up with the boys, but understanding how to capture the affections of a man was a lesson she had never cared to learn . . . until now.

★ ★ ★

TWO DAYS FOLLOWING the referendum election, the *Diamond Springs News* reported, "Supervisor Boone E. Bates passed away at Placerville General Hospital." The story chronicled his years of public service and included many comments of local sentiment. The article concluded with the county's procedure for filling the vacancy created by Bates' demise. The county charter required that a vacancy on the board be filled by appointment, selected by the remaining supervisors.

One week later, the headlines read: "Stormy Session of County Supervisors." The text went on to say:

> The first meeting after the death of Boone E. Bates turned into a name-calling vitriolic donnybrook. The large crowd of local citizens, led by Jamie Hagerty and Sheriff Norm Moore, threatened the board with recall if their selection to fill the vacant seat had any connection with the Bates clan. After much acrimonious debate, the supervisors, on a three-to-one vote, offered the job to the popular Hank Kaplowski. Mr. Kaplowski wasn't in attendance due to business in southern California, but Jamie Hagerty, speaking on his behalf, gladly accepted for him.

★ ★ ★

DOUG AND HARRY KALOOGIAN were actively engaged in conversation, somewhat ignoring the presentation being given by the Republican caucus staff. One of the researchers was dryly reviewing assembly district data when Doug was nearly jarred out of his chair by an observation made by Steve Gilliard, the caucus' chief consultant. "I thought we had a good prospect against Saul Benson, but I found out he's a Democrat. Name's Kadowski or something like that. He's just been appointed to fill the supervisorial vacancy in Durango County. Very popular guy. Betcha we'll have to watch out for him down the road."

Taking a deep breath to keep his voice steady, Doug asked, "Uh . . . *who* did you say?"

"Kapzowski or Kuwuski; he's Polish extraction for sure, with a name like that. He was appointed to the Durango board by the other supervisors."

"When did all this happen?" asked the aghast chairman, slumping limp into his chair.

"When did what happen?" asked Gilliard.

"The Durango board meeting!"

"Last night. It was all over the news. Great TV coverage of the fight."

"What fight?" gulped Doug.

"Where've you been?" laughed Harry Kaloogian. "I saw it on the late news. A couple of brawls broke out after the vote; they got it all on camera."

"Yeah," Gilliard added, with a laugh. "In the main event, some big, good-lookin' red-headed gal took a roundhouse swing at a discordant supervisor. Knocked him fanny-over-teakettle."

"What was the vote?" asked Doug.

"I don't know," responded the consultant. "All I know is Kapwowski, Kakowski, or whatever his name is, got the job. I think it had to be three-to-one. But for sure, that's a dynamite redhead in his corner." He winked, knowingly. "I bet she's . . ."

"Watch your mouth," Doug barked, astonished by his own anger.

Gilliard was shaken by his employer's unexpected response. "Sorry about that, Boss. I just meant that she's obviously a lot of woman." Staring strangely at Doug, he asked, "Do you know the lady?"

Doug cleared his throat, "I, uh, no . . . no, never heard of her." Dabbing at the beads of sweat on his forehead, he allowed a few more legislative districts to be discussed before he spoke up. "Harry, would you take over the meeting? I have another appointment; can't get out of it."

"Sure, no problem."

With a hasty good-bye, he left without a word to anyone about where he was going.

An hour later, Doug touched the Centurion down on his mountain landing strip, quickly changed clothes, and hopped into his Bronco. Spinning and spitting gravel, he headed for the Hagerty ranch.

"There's no way I'm going to be trapped into serving on that hick county board of supervisors. There's not a chance that conniving, redheaded wench can talk me into doing it. I got bamboozled by one woman, rest her soul; I'm too old and too smart to be taken advantage of again! Once is enough!" He stopped speaking aloud, intent on having every line, every vituperative adjective well in mind.

SIXTEEN

★ ★ ★

HEY, DOUG, WAIT UP!" Stewart looked behind him to see Brad Clark puffing laboriously down the south capitol path. Walking at any pace exceeding a mosey was not the overweight minority leader's strong suit. Copiously sweating from the effort to catch up, he mopped his brow, wheezing, "Your staff told me I could find you out here in the park. Whatcha doing way out here?"

"Smelling the roses, Brad, just smelling the roses. It's sure pretty here in the spring with the roses and azaleas in full bloom. Have you ever noticed what a marvelous rose garden we have on the capitol grounds? Take a whiff; smells great, doesn't it?"

Doug turned and pointed to the expansive planting of hybrid teas, florabundas, and grandifloras in colorful, full bloom. "See that deep red one? That's named after President Lincoln. I think the white one next to it with the pink center is called French Lace. Magnificent array, don't you think?"

Taking no notice, Brad yawned. "Yeah! Magnificent. Well, Doug, old boy—you did it!" He clasped Doug's shoulder with his massive hand and shook it approvingly. "Never has state initiative qualified with such ease. My office was just notified of the good news and I had to congratulate you on a job well done."

"Thank Kaloogian; Harry did most of the work."

"You're the one who selected him," retorted Brad. "Doug,

there's no question about it; you have the Midas touch. Everything you lay your hands on seems to prosper and turn to gold. Frankly, my good friend, I'm jealous."

"Hah!" Then Doug let out a loud, sarcastic horselaugh, startling his large companion. "Brad, if you only knew! But thanks for the compliment, anyway." Seeing the baffled look spread over his friend's face at his sudden outburst, he composed himself and quickly returned to the subject.

"Winning the initiative come fall won't be that simple. The public employee unions will be out en masse, fighting us tooth and toenail. Getting the signatures to qualify it for the ballot was one thing. Getting the majority to vote for it is another—especially when millions will be spent against us."

"Yeah, I know, I know," agreed Clark. "But that's the downside. On the upside, we'll frame the issue, establishing the perimeters of the debate. No matter how you cut it, our opponents will have to argue against cutting the bureaucracy—not an easy chore. Mark my words—we'll pick up a few assembly seats on this issue, maybe a couple in the senate."

"Hope you're right."

"Doug, I've gotta go. Be seeing you tonight at the celebration party, right?"

"Afraid not. I have a previous engagement I can't miss."

"You goin' back to your district to see constituents?"

"Yeah, something like that. I have to fly out pretty soon."

"Taking care of the voters back home is always first priority."

"Sure thing . . . back home . . . first priority." They shook hands and parted. Doug stayed for awhile longer while Brad lumbered past the trout pond, up the south steps, and disappeared into the capitol. *Yeah, I'm going to see constituents—those in the Fourth Supervisorial District of Durango County.*

Tonight would be his third Thursday meeting of the board of supervisors where, once a week, they met to vote on current issues affecting the county. Several items on the agenda would require his opposition—leftovers from the Boone E. Bates regime.

Strolling along the garden walkways, he mumbled aloud, "I sure don't have the Midas touch in Durango County. Everything I've done there has turned to horsepucky." Doug thought back to his visit to Jamie's, where he'd had every intention of turning down the job . . . flat! He'd decided to disappear from public view, hoping the citizens of Durango County would forget that Hank Kaplowski ever existed. He knew turning down the appointment would be a bitter pill for Jamie to swallow, but so what! She was the culprit who'd accepted on Hank's behalf and should be the one to tell the press that Hank Kaplowski couldn't serve and wouldn't serve, period! End of discussion!

Jamie was fully to blame, having led the push for his appointment. That buxomly redhead knew perfectly well that he didn't encourage her to seek the seat on his behalf. In fact, they never even discussed the matter. She mistakenly assumed he would jump at the chance to fill the vacancy on the board. If he had to, if absolutely necessary, he would tell her who he really was.

Jamie, I'm Doug Stewart, Republican caucus chairman! That would shock her! Disastrous as the confession might be, he would do it if he had to, no matter the chance that learning his real identity, she could freak out. On the other hand, to do so publicly would expose her falsification of the voter registration rolls. Twice, in two years, he had been snookered by women. Feeling miserable, he'd groaned, "What a mess and what a tangled web women weave!" Well, he'd had enough!

★ ★ ★

HE CLEARLY RECALLED banging hard on her front door, firmly and authoritatively, a no-nonsense knock. What happened after that was not so clear. He remembered Jamie opening the door and standing on the step above him, throwing her arms around his neck and as she'd done once before, burying his head in her chest while showering his head with kisses. Before he could extricate himself from her impassioned embrace, someone grabbed his arm in a vice-like grip and began pumping his hand vigorously.

It was the sheriff, Norm Moore. At that moment, the very last person on earth that Doug wanted to see was the "Bulldog" of Durango County. What could he say to Jamie now, with him here? Tell 'em both the truth? "Bulldog" Moore had a reputation as a stickler for enforcing the letter of the law. It was rumored he once gave a traffic ticket to his own mother-in-law.

Doug could just imagine himself foolishly saying, "By the way, 'Bulldog', uh, Sheriff, your old classmate and I have been breaking the law—forging documents, falsely registering, impersonating a dead Vietnam officer, and making fools out of supporters like you. Isn't that hilarious? You don't mind, do you, now that I'm your supervisor?" Doug suspected Sheriff Moore would slap them both in jail and let 'em rot.

Doug would never forget standing dumbstruck, while Jamie and Norm waxed on ecstatically over their imagined good fortune. She was an erupting volcano of fired-up enthusiasm. "Hank, not only have we gotten rid of the landfill issue, but we've placed you in Boonie's seat. Now, there's no limit to the good we can do!"

Sheriff Moore, without letting Doug get in a word, launched into a liturgy of problems demanding prompt attention within the sheriff's department. Any improvements he tried to make had been opposed by the supervisors on a three-to-two vote. "Now, with you on board, old buddy, we can return some semblance of law and order to the county."

Jamie added, "And, Mr. Kaplowski, you can't believe how intimidating your impending presence on the board seems to be. We've already had two department-head resignations. The Bates clan are in retreat, going back under their rocks."

"Good riddance too!" came a voice from the kitchen doorway. Grady Hagerty, with obvious difficulty, maneuvered his wheelchair into the den.

"Let me help you, sir." Sheriff Moore bolted across the floor to help, but Grady would have no part of it.

Waving him off, he said, "I can handle it myself, young man." With pain clearly written in his eyes, he slowly, agonizingly, moved the wheelchair across to where the three were standing. Offering his weathered hand to Hank, he broke into a warm smile. "Good work, Kaplowski. Your appointment made it worth all the time and effort."

"And the pain," added his daughter as she placed her arm about her father's shoulders and hugged him. With tears glistening in her eyes, she said, "Dad put in many long hours on the phone. You know, my father was the real hero in defeating the referendum. We never could have generated such wide public interest without the dollars he raised."

"Naw," modestly denied the crusty old rancher. "It's this here Kaplowski that deserves all the credit. I'm proud of you, son. It takes a good Democrat like you to get things done." Turning his wheelchair, Grady gradually moved himself over to the fireplace. "Come over here, boys, I want to show you something." Pointing to the photo of himself with President Roosevelt, he said, "There was the Democrat to end all Democrats. Best leader there ever was. If it wasn't for him, we coulda lost the free world to the Japs and the Nazis."

Grabbing Doug's arm and looking from one to the other, he continued, "You boys are cut from the same cloth. Neither of you were behind the door when guts were handed out." With sincerity and close to tears, Grady finished. "You're good Democrats and good Americans. I'm proud to know both of you."

Everything after that was anticlimactic, comfortably prosaic, as Jamie held on to Doug's arm. "Come on in to the kitchen. We just finished supper and were about to have some rhubarb pie topped off with vanilla ice cream. Have you eaten yet? There's plenty of meatloaf left over. I can rustle up something in a jiffy."

Doug finally had an opening to say, "No," . . . and he did. "But I think I'd like a piece of that pie."

★ ★ ★

"THAT WAS THE ONLY NO I said all evening—in fact, for months!" Angrily kicking a discarded aluminum can beside the rose garden, Doug cast his eyes upward and prayed, "Lord, some fix I've got myself into, deceiving with white lies that have turned into whoppers. It'd be a miracle if You let me out of this mess, undetected. Do You suppose I can keep up this charade until next year when my term expires? I haven't meant to hurt anyone and, so far, I don't think I have. Please get me out of this political pickle. And, oh, yes. . . . Please forgive this poor sinner, will You, Lord? I've sinned against You in thought, word, and deed and I'm in dire need of Your forgiveness. I ask this in the name of Your Son, my Savior. Amen."

As Doug hurried up the granite steps to the capitol office, he muttered, "Chances are, sooner or later, somebody's going to fry my deserving hide."

SEVENTEEN

★ ★ ★

WALLY SORTED THROUGH the beautifully wrapped gifts displayed beneath Doug Stewart's huge Christmas tree. He picked one up, put it to his ear, and shook it.

"Son, can't you wait until tomorrow morning?" teased his father.

Wally smiled sheepishly and carefully put it back.

"He hasn't changed much since we were kids," piped up Marianne, the elder sister. "Remember, Dad, Mom was always on his case for being too curious." Quickly, she turned her attention to the two-year-old reaching for one of the ornaments and sharply reprimanded, "Luke, don't touch!" She hoisted the squirming child into her arms, scolding him playfully. "You're just like your Uncle Wally."

"Anybody for eggnog?" called Diana's husband from the kitchen. "How about you, Dad?"

"Sure, Cleve, I'd love one, but make it light."

Doug sat comfortably on one end of the living room sofa, listening to the holiday carols playing softly in the background, enjoying Christmas Eve. The heartwarming lyrics of one of his childhood favorites filled the room. "Away in the manger, no crib for a bed, the little Lord Jesus lay down . . ." was interrupted by the cry of Diana's firstborn on the other end of the couch. Doug bent over and picked up the tiny baby, gently cradling her in his arms. Rocking her back and forth, he cooed, "There, there, Krissy—Grandpapa will take care of you. Uh, oh!"

"Diana!" he cried out to his youngest daughter. "Krissy needs you." Gratefully, he handed the damp and whimpering infant to her mother.

As Doug leaned back comfortably, watching Diana expertly change the diaper on the wiggling baby girl, a warm, wonderful glow enveloped him. He silently counted his blessings, the two grandchildren and one more on the way, and having his entire brood home for the holidays. It had cost him a pretty penny to fly them all home from such faraway places, but he had no intention of spending Christmas alone . . . no matter the distance. Wally asked if it was okay to bring along his fiancé. No problem. If necessary, Doug would have purchased the airline company to gather them all for the celebration of Christ's birthday.

"Well, Dad, you've had a very eventful year, haven't you?" remarked Cleve as he handed the eggnog to his father-in-law.

"Yeah, Dad," added Wally. "From what the neighbors tell me, you're rarely home. Being a big-time politician must agree with you."

"It's not too bad and, yes, it's been a busy year." Doug looked with affection, at his family, all seated about the spacious room. If they had an inkling as to what their father had gone through during the last twelve months, they could rightly question his sanity. Busy wasn't the word for it . . . insane, wild, unbelievable, zany, would be more precise.

So far, he had kept all the balls in the air, juggling precariously between the capitol and Durango County. It hadn't always been easy; on several occasions, he met people in Diamond Springs who he knew worked in the capitol. Somehow, they didn't connect the balding, country boy Hank Kaplowski to the urbane, bespectacled Assemblyman Doug Stewart. At board meetings, to further the distinction and mask his identity, he began wearing loud, more colorful cowboy shirts and a black leather sheep-lined vest.

Purposely, Doug wore a hat less often, allowing his balding head to shine like a billiard ball under the light. Slowly at first, then more pronounced as weeks passed, he began dropping his "g's" and talkin' more like one of the local hometown cowboys. Since the supervisors met on Thursday nights and the state legislature adjourned at noon on the same day, little conflict existed between county board meetings and his assembly duties. Most weekday visits with Durango constituents were out of the question, except on Monday mornings and an occasional Friday or Saturday. Fortunately, he was able to hire an intelligent secretary and a part-time administrative aide to handle the day-by-day supervisorial chores.

By the end of the first month, everything was going surprisingly well, with only a minor glitch or two. In particular, the county treasurer needed to pay Hank, requesting his Social Security number and asking him to complete a W-2 form. He had no choice but to turn down the salary, offering a lame excuse that he really didn't think he should take the money. Little did he figure that the treasurer would make a big deal out of it.

Touting the new supervisor's concern for the county's fiscal plight, the well-meaning treasurer embellished Doug's generosity to the press. "I guess Kaplowski wants to set a good example for the other supervisors, since the county's budget exceeded revenues." Hank's renouncing his county pay made more headlines. The foothill newspapers thought it was great copy and gushed out their admiration for the new man's obvious dedication to fiscal responsibility. It must have been a slow news day because the wire services picked up the story and ran it statewide.

In reaction to the broad publicity gained by Hank's magnanimous gesture, the other supervisors felt it necessary to substantially cut their own pay in order to follow his heroic example. Hank found himself more of a hero than ever. As one supervisor wryly commented, "They believe Kaplowski could walk across Lake Tahoe without getting the soles of his feet wet."

Fear of Kaplowski had its salutary impact upon the local officialdom. Bates' kin began a mass exodus out of county government and with them, a substantial reduction in county costs. Living under the threat of the ax, remaining department heads found inventive ways to cut their budgets and were pleasantly surprised to receive merit pay increases, compliments of an ordinance instigated by the new supervisor.

Delighted by the results of their efforts to economize, a surge of enthusiasm swept through Durango employees to get lean and mean, while offering better services to the public. Contracts with suppliers were reviewed and renegotiated, bureaucratic red tape was cut, the building permit process was made less cumbersome and more timely. Personnel worked overtime to satisfy constituent needs and the influx of new construction which had sprung up with the healthier business climate.

It became a frenzy to see which public official could be the most efficient, spending the least amount of tax dollars. By autumn, the deficit turned into a sizable surplus and the supervisors delighted the residents by declaring that a property tax cut was in order. In other California mountain counties, supervisors began to take notice and some tried to emulate Durango's success. They called it, "Cleaning Up the Bureaucracy with the Polish Brush."

Several of their regional papers asked to interview Hank but, in all cases, he refused, giving the other supervisors all the credit. Protestations to the contrary, the denials did nothing more than whet the appetites of reporters and encourage them to write about the county that was out in front, bucking the trend.

Doug was finding it harder and harder to stay incognito and low key. Though he sat quietly through the board meetings, his fellow supervisors asked his opinion about every matter. His reticence continued to make him all the more appealing, a wise sage in the minds of the media and the general public.

Durango's supervisorial sessions were becoming social events, attended every Thursday by whomever could arrive early enough to find a seat in the small council chambers. Jamie Hagerty sat up front in the first row. She had painted another portrait of Hank, a heroic, bigger-than-life oil, steely-eyed, rock-jawed, and ultra-masculine.

Full-color reproductions were made, selling for five bucks apiece, with the proceeds going to Durango's Democrat campaign account.

Every so often Hank was asked to autograph one of the posters and once, in a lapse of sanity, he signed the name, *Doug Stewart.* Even that inadvertent slip earned him points, not to mention a big laugh as he crossed out the signature and boldly wrote, *Hank Kaplowski.*

In addition to Durango County, Proposition 100—the "Cut the Bureaucracy" initiative—was capturing the attention of every county in the state. Strong emotions boiled forth on both sides of the issue. Demonstrations and vituperative confrontations were a daily occurrence on college campuses and on the steps of city halls. Some state employees chained themselves to municipal flagpoles, teachers took part in a one-day hunger strike, and talk-show hosts filled the airwaves with acrimonious callers; many featured the debate daily. Vast amounts of money flowed on both sides. Billboards, for and against, seemed to scream from every street corner. Every other TV spot was of Doug Stewart, extolling the virtues of Proposition 100, or a contrary ad denouncing the measure.

As Doug was obligated to dedicate more time to the campaign— time he didn't have—ballot Proposition 100 soon became identified as the "Stewart Initiative." The subject became so controversial that the networks offered free time for a debate, if qualified spokesmen could be lined up. The governor jumped at the opportunity, since the polls showed it losing 60 percent to 35 percent, with only 5 percent undecided.

Edmonds decided that he should be the one to offer the negative side of the debate—that is, if Doug Stewart would argue for the issue. The governor's political advisors were sure it was a win-win situation, since Edmonds was a polished professional and would surely devour the freshman assemblyman.

But Doug's keen mind coupled with his detailed knowledge of the subject matter turned the governor into a shouting, then sputtering, boob. Overnight, Stewart became the hero of the conservative Republicans and Edmonds lost a lot of his luster.

Instead of losing overwhelmingly, as the polls had predicted, Proposition 100 failed by only a very thin margin. Doug's verbal manhandling of the governor was given full credit for putting the initiative into such a competitive position. Without question, Assemblyman Stewart was now the most popular and well-known conservative in California.

Stewart and Kaloogian raised more than two million dollars to promote Proposition 100, while the opposition spent three times that amount. Doug hated to lose, especially to opponents who had no trouble distorting the truth and using gutterball tactics in the process. They insinuated that the passage of Proposition 100 would create massive environmental problems, destroy the public school system, and severely affect the elderly's ability to enjoy their retirement years.

Doug was especially irritated by the personal attacks, both on himself and some of his former clients—in particular, the slick TV spots with his face superimposed over oil fields and posh homes in San Marino. The silky voice of the commentator asked, "Do you have any idea how much this millionaire will gain by the passage of Proposition One Hundred? Plenty!"

The ads then pictured clients of Stewart and Associates, inferring a monetary connection where his firm would financially benefit were Proposition 100 to pass. They played heavily on public fears, even suggesting the loss of thousands of jobs. "They had a point! A lot of bureaucrats WOULD have been out looking for real jobs." The Proposition 100 campaign had given Doug a deep insight as to how low public employee unions would stoop to protect the status quo.

He and Nadine's family had worked long and hard to achieve success, creating jobs for thousands of others while providing quality products and services to thousands more. Being made the villain by union bureaucrats got under his skin—an irritation he was not likely to forget. Come January when the legislature was back in session, Doug and Harry Kaloogian would be able to continue their plans in the fight for regulatory reform.

Not everything turned out poorly on election night. Stewart overwhelmed his opponent in the Fifty-fourth Assembly District, easily winning re-election. The Democrats had nominated a portside professor from one of the area's community colleges; a day after the election, nobody could remember his name.

All Republican assembly members were re-elected to office; plus, one more was added to their ranks, assuring that Brad Clark retained his minority leadership position. Senator Marcia Conley wasn't as lucky. The Republicans lost a key senate district, aggravating enough of the incumbents to bring about Marcia's replacement as their leader. Her loss of the post put a large dent in her aspirations for higher office.

★ ★ ★

ON ALL COUNTS, IT HAD BEEN a wild-and-woolly ride, a memorable year. But now, time to relax, put politics on the back burner, enjoy the Christmas week with his family together, and look forward to Southern Cal beating the perennial Big Ten powerhouse—Northwestern—in the Rose Bowl.

"Care for another eggnog, Dad?"

"No thanks, Marianne; it's time I hit the sack. Gotta save up my energy for tomorrow morning. Will you look at all those presents?"

Christmas mornings past were special occasions. He wondered if the family could recapture the joy without Nadine. Coffee and juice and an assortment of toasted breads were available for snacks as soon as the family arose. Everyone gathered comfortably about the living room as Doug read scriptural passages about the birth of Christ.

Opening the Bible to the Gospel of Matthew, Doug read, "Behold, a virgin shall conceive and bear a son . . ." Afterwards,

Doug or one of the boys alternated playing Santa, handing out the presents one by one. Everyone waited for each gift to be opened and after the oh's and ah's, kisses, hugs, thank you's, and snapshots taken, another present would be selected from under the tree and the same process would begin all over again. About noon, the last gift would be opened, with both sorrow and delight that the ritual was over for another year. Torn wrappings would be collected and shortly thereafter, a delicious brunch would be served.

As Doug undressed in the bedroom, he wondered if tomorrow would be the same. Then quickly, he answered his own question. "How could it be without Nadine?" Loneliness suddenly engulfed him. "Oh, sweetheart, how I desperately wish you were here." He crawled underneath the covers and turned out the lights. He found it difficult to sleep. It had been a long time since he had slept in that bed. Many memories still lived in that room, now speedily, vividly, turning over in his brain.

In the dark, he could almost feel Nadine resting beside him. Sleep didn't come easily. Reaching over to the other side of the bed, he then grabbed Nadine's pillow and tucked it under his head, positive that it still held her fragrance. Rolling over, he partially buried his face into its soft form, whispering, "Honey, you sure got me into a royal fix, but it hasn't been all that bad. I hope you approve of the job I'm doing."

Holding tightly to the pillow, sleep finally came.

★　★　★

JAMIE STOOD BY THE LARGE bay window and watched the snow gently falling, the large wet flakes covering the mountainsides with a thin haze of white, adhering only moments to the pines and oak before slowly melting. Her thoughts were miles away from the winter scene as she was abruptly brought back to the present. "Jamie, think it's cold enough to stick? It'd sure be nice to have a white Christmas."

"I don't think so, Pa," she sighed dejectedly. "It's not very cold outside; it will probably be a muddy Christmas rather than a merry one."

Grady was saddened by the tone in his daughter's voice. Usually, the holiday season was a happy time around the Hagerty home, but this year, Jamie seemed subdued—even morose. Then, without notice, she became combative, appearing to resent the festivities. He thought he knew what was going on with her, but he wasn't sure. "What's the matter, honey? Somethin' bothering you? Anything your pa can do to fix it?"

She turned from the window and gave him a warm, loving smile. "No, Dad, there's not much anyone can do."

"It's that Kaplowski guy, isn't it?" questioned her father.

Her lips pressed together firmly and her body tensed before she burst forth with an uninterrupted discourse. "Did you know he took off for southern California for the whole holiday season? Said he had friends to see. Can you beat that? What does he think he has right here? Enemies? We were invited to two parties on New Year's Eve and I made plans for us to go to that big shindig over in Mount Aukum. We were getting really good, dancing together. And since my old things hang on me like sacks on a post, I went all the way into Folsom to buy a new outfit for the evening."

Jamie took a deep breath and gestured toward the Christmas tree. "See over there? I have three presents for him. Since he has no kin close by, I'd hoped he'd spend tomorrow with us. I planned to cook a turkey and . . ." Tears dampened her eyes and her voice began to crack. "Do you suppose he had a gift for me? Probably not. He didn't even wish me a Merry Christmas and a Happy . . . Oh, Daddy, sometimes I wonder if he knows I even exist!" Turning again toward the window to hide the flood of tears, she hopelessly whispered, "Look at me, I'm falling apart. A forty-year-old acting like a schoolgirl."

Grady wheeled his chair closer his daughter. "Honey, he could have some very important business to attend to. Hank seems to be a real nice person and I'm sure he likes you a lot. He probably just forgot."

"Forgot Christmas? Hardly! Forget me? You bet!"

"Could he be seeing family?" asked her father. "Was he ever married? Maybe he has some grown kids."

Jamie, frustrated, faced her father. "Daddy, I haven't a clue. I know Hank's not married now and he's been really mum about his personal life. It's obvious, he doesn't want to share much with me. I think he may have been married, but I'm only guessing." Drying her eyes, she said, "One thing is for sure—he's not letting me in on much of his past."

"Don't you think you better find out more about this guy before you get yourself in too deep?"

Jamie stood still, looking at her father for a few moments, thinking about the advice. She wiped her nose, and nodded her head.

EIGHTEEN

★ ★ ★

WAYNE FAT, FRANK FAT'S eldest son, stuck out his hand and gripped Doug's firmly. "Good evening, Mr. Stewart. A few of your guests have already arrived." Doug glanced at the narrow stairway leading to the small private dining quarters upstairs, a room where a more sizable chunk of the state's political business was transacted over a bowl of won ton soup than over factual data at the capitol. A few short blocks from the legislative halls, Frank Fat's Restaurant had, for generations, been the favorite dining spot for California politicians and lobbyists.

The "who's who" of the movers and shakers could usually be found there at noon or in the evening, clustered around the bar booths. They feasted on excellent Chinese fare, savoring Fat's specially prepared New York steak and consuming, or serving up, the latest fare of gossip. It was a fitting place for the implementation of what Doug had in mind.

The day, so far, had been a political shocker. Coming as a complete surprise at a hastily called press conference in the governor's office, his press secretary announced the immediate retirement of Governor Edmond Edmonds. Subsequently, the reins of power would be turned over to the Lieutenant Governor Malcolm McKlatchy.

The action taken was due to the governor's pressing need for heart bypass surgery. His physician gave a detailed report on the severity of the operation and, on account of the governor's age, the need for a lengthy recovery. The secretary said that since the legislature was in full session and another tumultuous budget hassle was in progress, California's need of an active governor at the helm was of great importance.

When the media asked why Edmonds didn't just temporarily step aside and return to office when recuperated, he explained that a re-election bid was out of the question and the governor's retirement from politics was permanent.

No hydrogen bomb dropped into the Democrat ranks could have been more devastating. Edmonds was the glue that held them together, the moderating agent between the more radical leftists and the traditional blue-collar, pro-labor Democrats. Malcolm McKlatchy, however, epitomized Eric Hoffer's portrayal of the true believer—the committed ideologue who expresses an ideology without remotely comprehending the underlying premises.

However intellectually vacant he happened to be, McKlatchy was still one of the champions of the leftist camp. He was an extreme radical while a student at Berkeley, and later became an assemblyman from San Francisco, then deputy director of the welfare department. There wasn't a new governmental program McKlatchy didn't like or a businessman he didn't suspect of exploiting employees. The mere mention of Malcolm McKlatchy as governor invariably sent shivers through California's business community.

Only minutes after the announcement of the governor's retirement, Doug picked up the phone and personally called a number of key people from all corners of the state, asking each to meet with him that evening for dinner at Frank Fat's.

He spent the rest of the day making phone calls to all parts of the nation, including several to Washington D.C. Harry Kaloogian was high on Doug's list, in order to discuss the multiple implications of Edmonds' resignation. By late afternoon, he'd contacted his Los Angeles business office with instructions to sell blocks of preferred stock in two major oil conglomerates and a portion of his federal treasury bonds. The funds were to be transferred to his personal account.

At five minutes before seven, he left the capitol for the short walk to Fat's. So totally preoccupied with his thoughts was he that Doug didn't notice the friendly waves of two passing lobbyists or the sweltering heat of July's early evening. His first notice of the 104-degree temperature was when the restaurant's cool air conditioning hit him in the face, bringing his attention to his drenched shirt and the sweat on his brow.

Doug returned Wayne Fat's greeting and headed straight for the stairs, followed close on his heels by two of his invited guests, Carlos Saracino and Arnie Kleinberg.

"Hey, Doug, come on over," called out Sam Hartage from the small bar across the room. Everyone turned to greet him and after a few cordial handshakes, Doug announced, "Everybody get your liquid refreshments now because when we've all had our fill of Fat's great cuisine, the waiters understand their services will no longer be needed."

The long dining table set up in the center of the room was already being laden with a wide assortment of Fat's famous Chinese dishes. No further encouragement was necessary as they eagerly sat down and began helping themselves to the delectable creations. Although the meal was worthy of slowly savoring each bite, they ate quickly and in near silence, anxious for their discussion to begin.

With the table cleared and fresh tea and coffee served, Doug rose and caught everybody's attention. "You all know the reason I called you to Sacramento. I spoke to each of you about the need for immediate action, following the announcement from the governor's office this morning. So, you all know that I'm contemplating running for the office and we need to talk about it. I assume some agreement in the possibility of my seeking the governorship, or you wouldn't be here."

"We think it's a very interesting idea, Doug," said Leif Anderson, "but none of us can figure out why you, of all people, are serious about it."

"Yeah," agreed Sam Hartage, "we all thought you couldn't wait for the first chance to bail out of the assembly, much less run for governor."

"Well, I do want to get out of politics, but not right away." With a grin, he joked, "You've got to admit, running for the governorship gets me out of the assembly. If I lose, I'm out anyway—and if I win, I intend to serve just one term. What I intend to do . . . if I'm elected . . . will infuriate many people. I doubt if the populous would elect me for a second term."

"Come on, Doug, tell us the real reason," interjected Leif, still the titular head of the state central committee's kitchen cabinet.

"To put it bluntly, if I win, I'll have a real opportunity to fire a lot of bureaucrats, cut this bureaucracy in half, and stop the exodus of business from our state." Doug paused to make sure they got his message, then continued with some harshness in his voice. "The public employee unions really got under my skin last year, with their outright lies and the half-truths they spread about Proposition One Hundred. It was appalling, underhanded, and deceitful. Those people are killing California; you're well aware that the mass exodus of business has already started. Only an optimistic fool would try to set up a new enterprise here."

"There's another reason, and it's personal. My parents came from the lower end of middle-class America. My dad felt he was lucky to have a job, much less acquire any wealth. I'm a product of moral, hardworking people who taught me the American dream can come true if you're willing to work at it. I believed them . . . and they were right. I've worked hard to get where I am."

"When Edmonds and the rest of the anti-Proposition One Hundred crowd made me the bad guy because I've been successful, it really gave me a pain where a pill can't reach. Being an ex-marine, I don't take kindly to personal attacks. I intend to make them regret defeating the initiative."

There was no mistaking the determination on Doug's face, nor any doubt of his sincerity as he added, "Today I've set aside two million dollars out of my personal accounts to seek this office; if necessary, I will add to it. Friends and associates have committed to match that amount and have promised to raise more." Turning to Carlos Saracino, he said, "Carlos has accepted the job as my campaign manager and Arnie will do my polling."

Looking to his right, Doug addressed Leif Anderson and Sam Hartage. "Are you two still committed to helping Senator Conley if she decides to run?" Both were taken aback by Doug's direct question and shifted uneasily in their seats before Leif answered. "We were, up until the time she lost the minority leadership, which put a different light on her chances. But with Edmonds' resignation, it's probably up in the air."

"Is she still thinking about it?"

"Probably," answered Hartage. "She has the bit in her teeth, especially now that Edmonds is no longer in the picture. She called me this morning, in fact."

"We've seen her campaign financial reports," stated Saracino. "She's still in debt from her last campaign."

"We know," groaned Anderson. "Sam and I have been approached to help her clean it up. Not an easy job for a newly deposed leader."

Doug faced them again. "Marcia hasn't made her desire for the governorship public knowledge . . . as yet. I'd like both of you to reason with her, explain the difficulties she'll face if she decides to run against me."

"Is that the reason you asked us here?" gruffly inquired Anderson. "I thought you were interested in our advice."

"I am. Your counsel is important. But at this point, I'm not the recipient of your wisdom. Marcia is. You two would be key players, if she attempts to run. Without you, she hasn't a ghost of a chance; you know it and she knows it. And remember, if she tries, she won't be able to match me dollar for dollar, nor will she have the same level of name identity going into the race. My stats are much better than hers; I already have a twenty-point lead on her. If you don't believe me, ask Arnie."

"No kidding, Arnie?" asked Leif.

Arnie's sarcasm oozed. "Don't you know that already; you too broke to do any polling? We've been in the field for four months, long before Edmonds planned to hang it up. Doug's state I.D. is fabulous; Marcia's is so-so."

"So what are you telling us?" angrily asked Hartage. "We haven't a chance with Marcia?"

Doug could see that Arnie's caustic remarks had hit a raw nerve. "No, nothing of the kind. Carlos, tell them your suggestion."

Carlos calmly offered the following. "We want you to encourage her to seek the vacated lieutenant governor's office, while Doug goes for the top of the ticket. In four years, she'll be the obvious successor when Doug declines to seek the second term."

"Who knows," interrupted Doug. "If I can accomplish what needs to be done any sooner, I'll retire early and let her automatically step into the governorship; then she can run as the incumbent."

Doug now had their interest. Hartage looked skeptically over at Anderson, as he inquired, "Would you run as a team, make sure her campaign had proper financing?"

"Yes, I would—that is, if she's totally cooperative and isn't biting at my heels. I know Marcia won't like playing second fiddle, but if she puts on her charming face and works to win, I'll do all I can to help."

Harry Kaloogian had been listening attentively and watching every expression. Finally, he spoke up. "Doug and Marcia would make a dream team. She'd become the state's first woman lieutenant governor. And Doug's being too pessimistic about the public's response to what his administration would try to accomplish. If he cuts the bureaucracy back to size, tax relief is a distinct possibility, not to mention stopping the outflow of business from the state. A Stewart administration could be the most popular ever. Marcia could coast into office four years from now."

Leif got up from his chair and motioned to Hartage to do likewise. "We'll think about it and let you know."

"No," said Doug firmly. "You'll tell me right now. Walk out that door and you're clearly on the other side. Stay, and you're a major part of the team."

Leif looked baffled by such a stark ultimatum. "You know, Doug, there are others with whom we have to discuss this."

"Not really. Brad Clark gave me his support this morning and Slim Stacy would be delighted to do my mail, since Marcia still owes him a bundle from her last campaign. Hardcastle, our state chairman, is supposed to be neutral in primaries, even though we know better. But he wouldn't be much help anyway. The only dissidents would be Marcia and her campaign manager, Stoney Marsh, who I doubt would see the matter clearly with you still on her side. If you two commit to support me, you'll be helping her see the real predicament she'd be in."

"Can't you even give us a day?" asked Leif.

"No, I'm sorry, I cannot. I intend to announce tomorrow and it's important to know exactly where the kitchen cabinet will be, the majority on my side or a split. I have to know if you'll be with us or against us."

"You say Brad is with you . . . and Slim Stacy too?"

"That's right. In writing."

"Why isn't Brad here?"

"My idea. He was willing but nervous. I thought it better to handle the meeting without him."

"What part do you have in mind for us?" asked Hartage.

"I want you on my executive advisory board," countered Doug convincingly. "I'll count heavily on your advice. You've always wanted a Republican governor who listens to you. I intend to give you one . . . me!"

"Can Leif and I go over in the corner and at least confer for a minute?"

"No!" laughed Doug. "What's to confer about? Both of you are CEO's. Daily you make quick decisions based on your knowledge of the subject matter presented to you. I'm sure you've already considered the difficulties associated with trying to elect Marcia governor, even without having to oppose me in the primary. With me in the mix, the decision is obvious . . . so please make it." Smiling warmly at both of them, he asked, "So what is it . . . yes or no?"

A wide grin cut across Leif Anderson's leathery tanned face. "I haven't been handled like this since I was a pup. By golly, maybe that's what we need . . . hard-nosed leadership!" With that, he extended his hand. "I doubt if Marcia will like it."

"She'll come around," said Hartage, as he also reached out to shake Doug's hand. "She's a reasonable person, especially when we point out the advantages."

★ ★ ★

"YOU DID WHAT! I CAN'T believe my ears! You want me to step aside for a wet-behind-the-ears assemblyman? Have you lost your minds?" Marcia Conley stormed across the floor in her capitol office and shook her fist under Hartage's nose. "You two get your butts right over to Stewart's office and tell him the deal's off. You promised me your support for the governorship, not that rich twit from the assembly. DO . . . YOU . . . HEAR . . . ME?"

"Oh, yes," coolly responded Leif Anderson. "It'd be difficult for anyone in the capitol not to hear you." With that, he walked over and closed her office door. "Calm down, Marcia. I'm about to give you four million reasons why you haven't a chance of beating Stewart in a primary. First off, he already has that much in the bank and more to come. Have you forgotten, you're still a hundred thousand in debt? Secondly, I won't raise you a dime. I didn't earn my way up by making kamikaze business decisions, so I know a bad deal when I see one — and also, a good one. Your running for lieutenant governor would be a wise move."

Were Senator Conley's eyes twin laser beams, they would have burned two holes through Anderson's forehead. She hadn't listened to a word they had to say. "Get out of my office, you traitors; I'll win the race without you. OUT, GET OUT!" Quite literally, she pushed them both toward the door.

★ ★ ★

LORRAINE, DOUG'S SECRETARY, poked her head into his office. Seeing her boss was on the phone, she entered quietly so as not to disturb him. She placed a memo on top of his desk, which read, *Senator Conley is on line two.* Doug quickly terminated his call and pushed the button. "Marcia, how are you?"

Her tone of voice was sickeningly sweet. "Doug, how wonderful of you to consider me for your running mate. I was positively delighted when I heard you intended to run for governor and simply overwhelmed when Leif told me I was your first choice. Is it true?"

Doug felt his throat tighten and he tried to swallow, tasting the syrupy venom seeping through the phone line. "Yes, Marcia, that's pretty much what we talked about. I hope you're interested. Everyone thinks you would make a great running mate. Do you accept?"

"Why, of course, dear boy. I'm sure you'll be able to buy the election . . . for both of us."

NINETEEN

★ ★ ★

IN COMPLETE DISGUST, Jamie exploded and flung the paper down on the table. "Blast it! That's really bad news for Democrats!"

"What's bad news?"

"Look here!" The hot-headed Hagerty shoved the newspaper across to Hank and sputtered, "See who's running for governor on the Republican ticket! It's that highbrow, got-rocks conservative from southern California. He announced yesterday in Sacramento. With McKlatchy as our candidate, that prissy right-winger has a chance of becoming our next governor."

"The same guy that spearheaded the Proposition One Hundred initiative?"

"Yeah, that's him. From what I hear at our headquarters in Placerville, Doug Stewart is the dirtiest campaigner in the state and richer than Rockefeller. He'll be a tough one to beat."

Hank looked over at his other breakfast companions and winked. "Why, Jamie, I've heard tell a passel of voters think he's pretty handsome and intelligent too."

"Slipperier than an eel, is what I'd say," replied Jamie emphatically. "We were talkin' about him the other day at the Democrat county central committee meeting. We were all wondering what Republican mucky-muck would take on McKlatchy. When Stewart's name came up, we agreed he'd be a great opponent."

"Why's that?" asked Hank, somewhat surprised by her answer.

"Simple. We figured Edmonds could have handled him easily. Stewart's too conservative, when matched up against him. Edmonds would have eaten him alive."

"I wouldn't be too sure of that," piped in Sheriff Moore. "I saw the two of 'em debate the Proposition One Hundred issue. Edmonds didn't do so good that night. Stewart boxed his ears off."

Jamie waved off his remark. "That was just a fluke. Anyway, the whole matter is hardly relevant, since Edmonds is out of the picture now. Stewart looks like a moderate against McKlatchy."

"Frankly," said Hank, eyes twinkling, "I think Steward, or is it Sewart? . . . I think he's a good-lookin' dude for a Republican."

"You've gotta be kidding!" An incredulous smirk spread across Jamie's face as she glanced about the table. "Does anyone here really think that over-coiffured twit's good-lookin'?" With everyone laughing at her partisan exuberance, she proudly proclaimed, "Hey, guys, the Democrats have plenty of good-lookin' men in office . . . like . . . like, like Hank sittin' right here!"

Hank laughed as loud as the rest. "Okay, 'Bright Eyes.' You wanted to have breakfast so we can do some talkin'. So, what's up?"

"Hank, we don't want to be pushy, but we'd like you to consider running for another term. We're afraid of what will happen if you're not on the board."

Hank moved his plate away and leaned back in his chair, obviously irritated by the request. "I thought you all understood that I have no intention of servin' another term. This one is it," he emphasized. "I promised to serve out Boonie's remaining time in office, no more."

The sheriff eagerly spoke up. "Hank, since you've been in office, things have really improved. With the board backing me up, the bad guys are leavin' the county for better pickin's."

Hank knew that to be true. "Bulldog" Moore, no longer fearing the collective wrath of Durango's supervisors, vocal do-gooders, or the local branch of the ACLU, had been vigorously enforcing the law. He was hassling the bums, drunks, and deadbeats, putting them to work cleaning up county roads, fighting fires, and making little rocks out of big ones. With great fanfare, he busted two marijuana farms and was locking up anyone caught with drugs, no matter who their family happened to be. The message was getting across that Durango County was an unhealthy environment for crime.

"I appreciate what you're sayin', Norm, but there's bound to be others to take my place, now that Boone is gone. I want to work my mine, plus I have other properties down south that take up too much of my time." Trying to avoid the looks of disappointment, he added, "Look, I'll try to do the best I can for the remainder of the term, but please, respect my wishes, won't you?"

Begrudging heads nodded . . . all except Jamie's.

★ ★ ★

JAMIE SAT IN THE UNCOMFORTABLE folding chair on the floor of the Ambassador's Auditorium, listening to Governor McKlatchy drone on about the plight of the current budget. Once more, it was 10 percent higher than the prior year and again revenues weren't adequate to pay the bills. The newly appointed governor was an uninspired speaker. He had switched subjects several times and was now tediously babbling about the destruction of the environment by the enemies of nature . . . the business community.

Jamie was not impressed with the man or his message. When he mentioned the lumber industry in negative terms, she burned with hostility. The summer weather didn't help her temperament; it was blistering hot, a real southern California scorcher. Though the air conditioning was at full blast, it afforded little comfort to the packed, perspiring audience. With most collars unbuttoned and clothing wrinkled and damp, attendees were removing their shoes and fanning themselves with program schedules or brochures.

In itself, the convention was fairly incendiary due to the resignation of their beloved Governor Edmonds. His replacement, former Lieutenant Governor McKlatchy, had bumbled badly from the very first day of his administration, alienating not only the leadership of both houses of the legislature, but his own leftist friends as well. Three other Democrats had subsequently announced intentions to seek their party's nomination for the governorship—Alfonso Rodriguez, the mayor of Los Angeles; Ellen Knox, San Francisco's outspoken councilwoman; and Damon Darling Hollywood Western star and past-president of the Screen Actors Guild.

Of the lot, Jamie favored Damon Darling. His image as a rugged outdoorsman suited her best and from what she knew of his political views, they seemed to match hers—at least, better than the rest. The other three were cut from the same mold . . . all liberal, all captives of the environmental crowd, all big-city oriented. All the candidates were attending the convention, each hosting elaborate receptions for the state central committee members. They took turns visiting the separate caucuses, soliciting support. There were the feminists, the black caucus, the gays, the environmentalists, labor. Even the rural counties formed their own group, nicknamed the CCC.

The Cow County Caucus had swollen to include most of the small, rural political entities in the state; thirty-four of the fifty-nine counties were represented. The CCC came to be regarded as a voice for the old-line, New Deal Democrat. Although a minor force in the overall ranks, it was the most disapproving of the party's direction. Jamie was the foremost organizer and first chairperson. Since its inception, no one had the votes to replace her nor the fortitude to try.

They interviewed three of the candidates—McKlatchy, Rodriguez, and Knox. All laid big eggs, attempting to placate the CCC on the environmental issue, smothering them with words that had no meaning, each vying to garner support without alienating some other segment of the party. They all were sensitive to and deeply concerned and, of course, all their statements repeated the same monotonous, "My staff and I are committed to a solution." All three were trying to be consensus candidates. As one of the ranchers put it, "They were testing the political waters with their pinkies."

After each had delivered their spiels of verbosity, the hard questions came thick and fast. "How can you say you're sympathetic to the workers in the mountain counties when you supported the administration's position to restrict lumbering on all forest land, both public and private?"

And from the cattlemen, "Will you or will you not support the present system of allowing grazing rights in the national forests?" The valley farmers pressed, "We need more water. Will you immediately take a public stand in support of more dams on our rivers? We don't want future promises." One elderly rancher who was losing a number of sheep to cougars, asked succinctly, "What do ya city fellers think a mountain lion is, a predator or a pussycat?"

Typically their answers didn't vary much. "Yes, perhaps, but then again," and "I'll give it my full attention, once I'm elected," or "Absolutely, I'll look into that."

"Once I'm elected, once I'm elected," spat out one of the rural delegates. "If I hear that once more, I'll scream! Why don't they have the guts to tell us what they really believe? I swear, those three must take a poll to see if it's okay to go to the bathroom."

Finally, the candidate of Jamie's choice, Damon Darling, appeared before their caucus. He was everything she hoped he'd be—tall with a deep, weathered maturity etched in his handsome, tanned face. She loved the abundance of steel-gray hair protruding from under his light tan Stetson. For their group, he was perfectly attired in a simple beige suit with a silver-tipped string tie, instead of the usual neckwear. His pale blue shirt, dark brown Tony Lama boots, and flashing smile completed the dashing picture.

Darling immediately set about introducing himself and shaking hands with everyone present, another good sign . . . until he shook Jamie's. His grip was non-existent, like clasping a cold, damp, under-inflated balloon—squishy and boneless. Damon Darling's cologne was overpowering, like he had bathed in a vat of cheap French perfume. But, the latter observations were quickly forgiven as soon as he began to speak. His address was powerful, to the point, and impressive. He stressed the importance of the home and family and the need to return to the bedrock values put forth during the New Deal and the Kennedy Administration.

The Cow County delegates loved it, giving him a standing ovation. Jamie was flushed with excitement as they talked together afterward. Now she had a candidate to take on that Los Angeles Republican Stewart—a Democrat who reflected the moral ethics of her father. Her euphoria was growing, until he reached around and grabbed a fistful of her behind.

★ ★ ★

"DOUG, I CAN'T BELIEVE how well the campaign is going." Harry Kaloogian placed his feet on the desk, aimed the TV remote, and flicked to a different channel. "NBC News did a fair job, playing up our release of the polling data. They said it matches up with the most recent Field Poll, which gives us a commanding lead. Chances are, by filing time, you won't have anyone of substance opposing you for the nomination." Harry smiled from ear to ear. "How about them apples?" Once more, he changed stations. "Oops! There's your charmin' self again, now on channel eleven."

Doug appeared on the screen, walking along the beach at sunset, with his coat casually carried over one shoulder. The soothing voice-over eloquently stated the Republican candidate's many exemplary qualifications.

"Good-looking shot, Doug. Corny, done lots of times before, but effective."

"Got my shoes soaked, doing retakes. I asked Carlos if I could do it barefoot, but he said no dice. Ruined a good pair of loafers," joked Doug. "Saracino insisted on that corny stuff. Says he has to humanize me to the voter. I figured he's the manager and should know . . ." He stopped short upon hearing the silvery toned broadcaster. "And now to the headquarters of Damon Darling, one of the Democrat hopefuls. Lisa Ann has the story . . . Lisa?"

A pretty, cheery-faced blonde appeared in the telecast, clutching a microphone. "I'm here at the campaign headquarters of Damon Darling, hoping to get confirmation or denial of the rumor that a seventeen-year-old by the name of Clarita Johnson has filed a paternity suit against the former Western star. If this is true, Mr. Darling could be charged with statutory rape, since Miss Johnson is underage. This recent charge comes on the heels of a sexual harassment claim made by two of Darling's former campaign volunteers."

Kaloogian turned off the TV. "Hey," let out Doug. "Turn that back on. I know someone who might vote for that old lecher." Harry flicked the TV back on, but by this time, the newsman was reporting a drowning.

"Still want it on?"

"No, turn it off. Looks like the actor turned politician is drowning too. In fact, it seems as though the whole bunch of 'em are riding the rapids down the river of no return. I've never seen such vicious infighting." With a devilish leer in his eye, Doug remarked, "Hope it continues."

"It will . . . until the primary's over. Then they'll band together like an orgy of snakes and develop mass amnesia about the rotten things they've said about each other."

"With all that backbiting, how can they bury the hatchet?"

"Believe me, they will," claimed Kaloogian. "Right in the middle of our backs. They might still dislike each other, but they hate us — and woe to the Republican who forgets that. Nothing unifies liberal Democrats more than the thought of a conservative in office."

"Not all of 'em are that bad. I know a few pretty nice people registered as Democrats." Doug couldn't help but smile with some affection as he thought of Jamie, her father, Sheriff Moore, and a number of the others he'd gotten to know. Trouble is, they were living in the past.

Then he remembered Jamie voicing possible interest in backing the actor. He wondered what she'd do, now that her choice for governor was charged with offending volunteers and impregnating a minor. She must be hopping mad at these latest revelations and completely frustrated with the viciousness amongst the other

Democrat gubernatorial candidates. He couldn't wait 'til "Hank" could tease her about the situation.

Harry Kaloogian took his feet down from the desk, stood up and stretched his blocky, muscular frame. "Let's go get something to eat; I'm starved. We've been working on your schedule long enough; I need some brain food." Yawning loudly, he asked "What time is it, anyway?"

Doug looked at his Rolex. "Son las cinco para las once."

"Very good!" exclaimed Kaloogian. "Five minutes to eleven. Practicing to capture the Latino vote? I see you're going to give Rodriguez a run for his money if he's the Democrat's choice."

"Being from San Diego," Doug flippantly replied, "I thought you'd get the message that I'm in the mood for Mexican food. Comprende?"

★ ★ ★

JAMIE WAS SICK WITH DISGUST as she put down the phone. "That Hollywood phony's nothing but a pile of rat-droppin's." Her personal encounter with Damon Darling's roving reach had tarnished his dazzling image a little, but not enough to switch her support to any of the other, unacceptable candidates. However, this was the proverbial backbreaking straw, requiring reconsideration of the other three possibilities.

Which one to back . . . the mayor of Los Angeles? Alfonso Rodriguez was an ethnic radical, constantly harping that California was stolen from Mexico and how the state needed "closer political ties" with its southern comrades. Included in his platform when he ran for mayor was an absurd idea that the Spanish language be mandated in all grades of public and private schools, clearly suggesting that it be the state's primary language. Rodriguez was a class-warfare soldier who rejected the nation as a melting pot, where all nationalities became one . . . Americans. Jamie was convinced he was a sure loser if, by some chance, he got the party's nomination.

These thoughts of Rodriguez upset her stomach, leading her to the kitchen for something soothing, maybe milk and dry toast. Upon opening the refrigerator, she looked longingly at the jar of chunky peanut butter . . . it had been months. She snatched the nonfat milk carton from the shelf, quickly closed the door, and poured half a glass. While nibbling on a slice of unbuttered rye, she pondered the other choices.

Ellen Knox? Her sexual preferences were questionable, unpopular. As last year's Grand Marshal of San Francisco's Gay Pride Parade, Knox left no doubt where she stood on the issue, and her dogmatic advocacy of every and all feminist causes was another concern. Jamie believed women weren't getting a fair shake in the marketplace and she knew that Ellen Knox avidly supported same work, same pay legislation. But, military women in the front-line trenches and sexual quotas in hiring? No way! The last thing the Hagerty logging operation needed was a mandated number of female lumberjacks forced on them. Ellen Knox would drive more male voters to the Republicans and would lose by a larger margin than the Los Angeles mayor.

Still feeling queasy, Jamie returned to the refrigerator and reached for the forbidden peanut butter jar. She scooped out a teaspoonful of the chunky peanuts and spread a thick layer on a large stalk of celery, then eagerly enjoyed every crunchy bite. "Ah, that feels better; just a little more should do it." Admitting to being a peanut butter fanatic, she helped herself to another spoonful, allowing the fat-laden morsels to melt in her mouth.

Screwing the top back on the jar, she gave it an extra twist, murmuring, "That's all for you, Jamie Hagerty." There was one more candidate to consider—but the thought of McKlatchy, the newly appointed governor, as her only remaining choice only made her yearn for the peanut butter again. Clenching her jaw muscles, she repeated her original opinion of him, "I have no intention of supporting that weak-kneed, tree-hugging friend of the slug!"

Jamie nervously paced about the kitchen, setting her brain to work, tossing names about in her head, weighing each one against the other, then matching them up against Douglas Stewart. As each new name was examined, then emasculated and discarded, she felt her anxiety building. *I wonder if I'm the only one who feels this frustrated.*

Trying to relax her over-stressed brain cells, Jamie stretched out on the living room sofa, hands clasped behind her head. Like a bolt from the blue, she thought of a proverb vaguely remembered from childhood. She rushed into the den for the family Bible, where thumbing through the pages of the concordance, she found the word *counsel* and turned to Proverbs 11:14. "Where there is no counsel, the people fall. But in the multitude of counselors there is safety." Jamie concentrated on the passage, then reached for the phone.

For the next three hours, she contacted the entire leadership of the Cow County Caucus, insisting on a conference call for the following day. Time was extremely important; in just two days, the filing date for the governor's race would close. Between now and then, they had better come up with a decent candidate, or the Democrats were doomed to lose the next election. Her phone calls confirmed that she wasn't the only one worried and turned off by the present crop of nominees.

JAMIE READIED THE GELDING, swung hurriedly into the saddle, and headed down the steep trail, making her way through the canyons and up over the ridges. She descended through the oaks and stands of digger pine until she reached the Consumes River, where she dug her heels into the side of the horse to cross the shallow water. Working around the tangle of wild berry vines, she forced the gelding into a rapid climb up the sharp slope to the flat above. Once on Hank's landing strip, she galloped the lathered horse to the cabin door. "Hank! Are you in there?"

She trotted the horse over to the mine entrance and called once more. Noticing the generator was silent and no light appeared from the tunnel, she glanced over toward the hangar and saw that the door was slightly ajar. "Doggone it, Hank," she shouted. Jamie leapt out of the saddle, ran over, and found the plane was gone. She was both downhearted and angry, trudging back to the cabin, dropping hard onto the steps. Two times she had made the ride that day. The note she had left was still tucked under the door. In total exasperation, she cried out, "Where are you, Kaplowski? Dang it, where the devil are you? I've got to talk to you!" Jamie broke into frustrated tears, balled up her fists, and stomped the ground.

She waited until the sun was about to set before being convinced he wouldn't be back before nightfall. Wearily, she pulled herself into the saddle, taking note that the light was fading fast. She needed to get going, hoping to cross the river before it became too dark to see. Tomorrow, at daybreak, she would drive over, take the long way around in the four-by-four truck, and wait for him. Jamie was anxious to get his opinion about the Cow County Caucus discussion and the conclusions they reached. Time was of the essence.

TWENTY

★ ★ ★

IN HIS SACRAMENTO APARTMENT, Doug was vigorously brushing his teeth when he heard the phone ring. He quickly rinsed out his mouth and hurried to answer it. *It's only six-thirty; wonder who's calling this time of the morning?*

"Hello, Doug Stewart here."

"Good morning and congratulations, old buddy; this is Harry. Didn't wake you up, did I?"

"No, Harry, I'm wide awake, just about to get dressed."

"Good news, Doug. Last night I checked with the secretary of state's office and no one—at least, no one of substance—has filed to run against you in the primary. So, Stewart, up until the general election, it should be a cake walk! Great news, huh?"

Doug couldn't help but grin at Kaloogian's perennial exuberance. Even this early in the morning, he was enthusiastic to a fault.

"Yeah, that is good news, Harry. How about the Democrats; anyone else get into the race?"

"Oh, sure, the peace-and-freedom crowd filed a candidate. So did the greenies—you know, the beetle-bimbos."

"That last one's a laugh. You would think McKlatchy would be their choice; he's done everything the tree-huggers have ever wanted."

"Not everything. As soon as he became governor, he allowed a bill to go through that he could've vetoed; it allowed some redwoods to be harvested near a spotted owl habitat. Really upset the feather freaks."

"Think they'll campaign against him?"

"Nah. Just filing a candidate will make McKlatchy wet his undies and promise 'em the world . . . if they won't work too hard at turning out their troops."

"Anybody else file?"

"Nobody of importance. Just some county supervisor from the foothills with a Polish name."

Dead silence.

"Doug, are you still on the line?"

"Uh, yeah, I'm still here," stuttered Doug. "Uh . . . is he . . . is uh . . . his name Kaplowski?"

"Yeah, that's it. Do you know the guy?"

★ ★ ★

"Stop crying, Jamie, it's not the end of the world." Doug hated to see a woman cry—any woman, but especially, one close to him. From early childhood, bawling upset him terribly, probably because his mother was a weeper of the first order. She sobbed when she was unhappy, fairly happy, overjoyed, and ecstatic. She wailed and whimpered when frustrated, shocked, disappointed, or angry. She wept at his grade-school, high-school, and college graduations. She would even tear up over reading the obituaries . . . of strangers.

Surprisingly, she didn't wet an eye during most of his wedding ceremony. She didn't approve of another female taking her boy away, but once the "I do's" were over, she monsooned the church. The floor of the maternity ward was drenched when each of her grandchildren were born. Nobody could outweep Mama.

Nadine, on the other hand, was a calculated crier, knowing just when to cry and how many teardrops were necessary to get what she wanted. It rarely failed; streaked mascara had a powerful impact upon Doug. Today was no exception.

"I tried to get ahold of you." Jamie angrily sobbed. "Did you leave me a phone number that I could have called? NO! Or an address where you were staying? NO! You just take off in that plane of yours with no thought of anyone else. What happens when I finally see you? You bawl me out, yell at me, and treat me like I've committed a major crime! All I've ever wanted was to please you." Jamie shuddered as she buried her head in the sofa pillows to keep her sobs from waking her father, sleeping in the adjoining room.

Hank sat down beside her and tried to comfort her by patting her gently on the shoulder. "I'm sorry, 'Bright Eyes,' I didn't mean to be so gruff, but I went into shock when I found out what you did."

She looked up from the pillow. "You have no idea all of the work and anguish I've gone through these last few days, and on your behalf! Filing your papers for the office of governor was no easy task. Since then, I've been flooded with requests from everywhere for information about you, but all I could do was guess how you would stand on some of the issues."

Jamie sobbed on, "When I bragged about the great job you've done as our supervisor, I was surprised how many knew about it already, mainly the elected officials from other rural counties. Naturally, in the cities, they've never heard of you or didn't know much. Now that I think about it, neither do I."

Dabbing her eyes, she continued, "Hank, I really hardly know a thing about you, personally. I guess I should have checked with you before I jumped the gun. Honestly, I still can't believe you're not pleased. You can't imagine how much confidence everyone has in you!" Jamie's crying began anew. "But you're not pleased! You seem actually furious about what we've done . . . why? Tell me . . . you haven't done anything illegal, have you? You haven't *killed* anybody or anything like that?"

Her lower lip began to tremble. "It never occurred to me that you could have done something you're ashamed of. But the way you yelled at me, now I'm not so sure." Blowing her nose with a tissue, she sat upright and asked quite formally, "Well, Mr. Kaplowski, have you ever been in prison or maybe arrested?"

Hank had to choke back a laugh. The deadly seriousness on her tear-streaked face warned him that even a slight grin would have been life-threatening. Matching her sober vein, he resolutely replied, "No, Jamie, not even a serious traffic ticket blots the Kaplowski name."

The tears stopped suddenly as she snapped her head back. "Have you ever been married?"

He hesitated before he answered. "Yes, I have. I'm a widower. My wife died several years ago."

"Have you been married more than once?"

"No. Just one gal; she stuck with me for better than twenty-five years."

"Did you love her a lot?"

Jamie was getting a little too personal for Hank's tastes, but he was trying to be forthright. "Yes, I did. In fact, I loved her a great deal. Her death was a real blow."

"What about . . . do you have any children?"

She was getting too close for comfort, so he offered up a sad-hearted smile. "No, unfortunately, the Hank Kaplowskis had no children."

Although his answer seemed to please her somewhat, she continued to press on. "Please be completely honest with me, Hank; are there any skeletons in the Kaplowski closet?"

"Only that the Kaplowskis have an aversion to running for political office. Hank Kaplowski won't run for governor and nothing will make Hank Kaplowski change Hank Kaplowski's mind. To put it succinctly, Hank Kaplowski won'tski runski . . . get it?"

Jamie stuck out her lower lip. "Well, what shall we do?"

"Withdraw my name from the race; that's it, period."

"Can't," she replied. "Once your name is on the ballot, it's there to stay. Besides, don't you think trying to pull out would raise major questions?"

"You are right, it might." Hank was visibly concerned, hemmed in by the insane predicament. "Jamie, you sure boxed things up for me."

"You didn't complain when I registered you by mail or when I helped you get the supervisorial slot. How could I know you'd feel this way, that you wouldn't be glad so many of us country folks want you as our governor? I thought it was the right thing to do; in fact, I still think so. I'm just sorry you're such a spoilsport about the whole thing."

"Spoilsport? You have the nerve to call me a spoilsport? You have no idea how torn up I am. I haven't got time for a statewide campaign. I have a million other things I'd rather do than run for governor."

"Like what?"

"Fish!" he angrily shouted. "Go hunting! Kill something!"

Jamie began to cry again. "Oh, darn it, Hank, you're right. I've really messed up. Don't worry, I'll confess that it was my idea and that you knew nothing about it. I'll probably g . . . g . . . go to jail!" By this time, she was sobbing uncontrollably.

"Oh, for Pete's sake, Jamie, calm down. As I said, it's not the end of the world. You won't have to go to jail."

Jamie turned and buried her head in his shoulder, "Oh, Hank, what'll we do?"

"Let me think about it." Dislodging himself from her grasp, he got up and began to pace, taking long strides across the room.

"The best course is to do nothing. We will just do nothing. That's what candidates did in the early eighteenth century. They thought it was beneath the dignity of the office and personally demeaning to solicit votes. They offered themselves as candidates, but left all the campaigning to their supporters. Did you know that Abe Lincoln didn't even attend the convention that nominated him for president?"

"That's weird . . . but nice. What'll you say when the media asks why you aren't campaigning?"

"We'll just tell them I'm from the old school, that it's too undignified to hawk votes. They'll think I'm demented and in a short
while, they'll forget I even exist."

"Do you think it will work?" Jamie dried her eyes again as he
returned to his place on the sofa.

"Outside of you going to jail, do you have a better idea?"

"Now that you mention it . . . no."

Hank put his arms around her and gave her a hug. It felt good
holding her close. She shifted her head slightly and kissed him on
the neck; that felt better still.

★ ★ ★

IT WAS JUST AS HANK HAD predicted. Once the initial curiosity of
his entry into the gubernatorial thicket had died down, and the
media found out he was a candidate raising no funds who didn't
intend to campaign, they forgot he existed . . . except for one inves-
tigative reporter with the Associated Press. D.B. Willis' inquiry into
the political campaign tactics of early Americans made for fascinating reading, especially when compared to the four Democrats
actively campaigning for governor. They were ripping each other
apart, lobbing grenades at one another. When they weren't attack-
ing Doug Stewart, they were cannibalizing their own.

The Associated Press article detailed how some candidates for
major office in the past century usually took the high road, often
to the point of mentioning the better attributes of their opponents.
Although they might debate the key issues of the day, the negative
shots were left to the press and their ardent supporters. It seemed
these major officeseekers of yesteryear generally tried to behave as
gentlemen and not be so uncouth as to actually ask for votes, leaving the solicitation of ballots to others. D.B. Willis was fascinated
to discover the candidate for California's governorship who was, in
fact, following this outmoded course—a countrified supervisor by
the name of Kaplowski.

Willis' story was eagerly picked up by newspapers across the state and soon thereafter, a flood of requests for more data on the Kaplowski campaign flowed into his supervisorial office. Hank wasn't around to see the influx of mail, so Molly, his secretary, called the red-headed Hagerty for advice.

"Jamie, I really don't think I should answer all these letters that came in Friday's mail. They're requesting information on the boss and have nothing to do with county business. You know, I'm under strict orders not to handle any matters not related to Durango County. Mr. Kaplowski isn't expected back for several weeks, and he hasn't called in for three or four days. What should I do? This stuff is all political."

Jamie contemplated telling her to throw the letters out, but reconsidered after she realized it might cause more trouble. "Hold on to them, Molly; I'll be right down to pick 'em up." By the time she arrived at the county building, Monday's mail had been delivered; two large bags were stuffed to capacity. The letters were not only requests for reference material, but offers to organize Kaplowski volunteers in other parts of the state. Many of the envelopes contained financial contributions, several with sizable amounts.

"Molly, don't bother to tell Hank about this; I'll take care of it next time I see him. Okay? He's so busy, no need to burden him with minor stuff. Give me a call if any more come in, will you?"

"All right." She hesitated a few seconds. "But, you'll tell him . . . won't you?"

"Believe me, Molly, I'll be very happy to." Then, under her breath, she whispered, "Right after I win him the nomination."

★ ★ ★

DOUG WAS EXHAUSTED, never realizing before how enormous an area California covered until he'd campaigned into its far corners. It was a relief to take several days off to relax in his Palm Springs condo, play a few rounds of golf with Harry Kaloogian, and get ready for the last hectic month of campaigning. They'd traveled the last few days by plane over densely wooded mountains and sparsely settled valleys. Starting from a breakfast speech in Crescent City to lunch with city fathers in Susanville, they traveled down the east side of the Sierras, skimming over thirteen-thousand-foot peaks for a dinner in Bishop.

The following morning, a brunch was scheduled below sea level in Death Valley; then it was across barren deserts to attend a press conference in San Diego. Doug now looked upon California as many states crammed into one, each section quite different from another. The one he was in resembled much of the Rockies—vast deserts reaching out from the base of high alpine peaks—a mix of cactus-covered Arizona and mountainous Montana.

The northern coastal regions with dense rainforests and towering redwoods were not unlike western Oregon and much of Idaho. The central valleys of flat farmlands stretched hundreds of miles, reminiscent of Illinois and Kansas, and the Pacific Coast's eight hundred miles of scenic shoreline . . . nothing else like it anywhere in America. Strictly California, Doug felt that he had covered every inch of the Golden State and talked to every editorial board from the *L.A. Times* to the *Hayfork News*.

Stewart's campaign staff was overjoyed at the reception he and his message were receiving and the endorsements flowing his way. His chance of winning the primary nomination and the following general election looked very good and what's more, the polls confirmed it. The Stewart campaign was helped immeasurably by the hysterical hyperbole of the Democrats, picking away at each other.

Doug was nervous about the AP article on Kaplowski, but since nothing seemed to come of it, he put it aside. Only one more month and the March primary election would be over. Then he could concentrate on beating Governor McKlatchy, the obvious leading candidate among the Democrats. The other three contenders were rapidly falling by the wayside, each tending to self-destruct before the public's eyes.

Ellen Knox came out of the closet; Damon Darling's bedroom escapades got him in trouble with the law; and Alfonso Rodriguez was caught hiring illegals, most of them distant relatives he'd helped smuggle across the border. Only McKlatchy had kept his laundry clean.

Within a few months, he would be able to ditch the supervisor's job and sell the Lucky Adele Mine property. As a gubernatorial candidate, he wouldn't have time to fool around in Durango County anymore and one day soon, Hank Kaplowski would have had to disappear. Doug intentionally left Hank's supervisorial duties unattended for weeks at a time, figuring before long, people wouldn't mind his leaving.

Jamie Hagerty, however, tugged mightily at his conscience. He had left her flat out on her own, after their last lamentable discussion. She was undoubtedly bearing the brunt of criticism, which must have emerged with his recent vanishing act. Having to answer questions about his lack of campaigning for the Democrat nomination could be sticky. *But, so what? It was her dumb idea, anyway. Let her defend her own stupid actions.*

★　★　★

DOUG WAS TOO TIRED to think about anything but getting out of his suit and climbing into bed. A few rounds of golf and quietly lazing about the pool would be in order for the next couple of days. Hank Kaplowski's bid for high office was a forgotten issue.

Jamie's impulsive, infectious laughter skipped into his mind. *How can I stay angry with her?*

TWENTY-ONE

★ ★ ★

"SOMEBODY GET THOSE PHONES!" shouted Jamie Hagerty. It was hard to be heard above the noise of the crowded Kaplowski campaign office. She tried again, this time a little louder but more specific. "Charlie, Mary, would you answer the phones, please!" Jamie rolled her eyes at the ceiling. "Organized pandemonium—that's what this gubernatorial race is!"

"The call on line five is for you, Jamie," yelled Charlie from the back of the room.

"Tell them to hold and I'll be right with them." For the past three weeks, Jamie felt she had a telephone permanently attached to her head. What had started out as a test to determine the popularity of a Hank Kaplowski for Governor campaign had turned into a mushrooming explosion, geometric in growth.

Jamie, in response to the mail requests, had done nothing more than send out details of Hank's accomplishments in Durango County, plus a few paragraphs explaining where she thought he stood on other issues and skimpy information about his personal background. She included a copy of the ruggedly handsome portrait she had painted of him and a reprint of D.B. Willis' Associated Press article. The mail package was informal, direct, and to the point, lacking the glossy sophistication of most campaign pieces.

It said nothing negative about his opponents and promised nothing if elected. In its utter simplicity, it called upon the

Democrat citizenry to return to the family values once voiced by their party—vigorous individualism, pride, belief in God, and personal responsibility. Jamie paraphrased John F. Kennedy's famous statement and added it to the bottom of the last page. "Ask not what California can do for you, but what you can do for California."

The material struck a responsive cord in many Democrats, especially those who had become disenchanted with the constant leftward drift of their leaders. Many blue-collar workers found it harder and harder to maintain loyalty to a party that advocated such massive governmental intrusion in their lives. They were leaning more to the Republican position but felt disloyal by doing so. When they learned about the Kaplowski campaign, it gave them an out— a way to stay within the Democrat ranks.

The Kaplowski literature, easily reproduced by copy machine, was soon tacked-up on bulletin boards in union halls and warehouses across the state. Every rural county had Kaplowski for Governor signs along roadways and Our Hank portraits displayed in store windows. It was rapidly becoming a grassroots effort, par excellence . . . in the non-metropolitan areas. In the large population centers of Los Angeles, San Diego, Orange County, and the San Francisco Bay areas, they were just beginning to hear the rumblings from the hinterlands. "Hank Kaplowski? Yeah, I've heard of him. Doesn't he play second base for the Chicago Cubs?"

★ ★ ★

SENATOR SAL BALQUIST, chairman, called the Democrats' caucus to order. Looking over the gathering seated around the large senate conference table, he counted noses, those who were committee chairmen in both legislative houses. "Where's Rick and Hershal? The Speaker doesn't want to discuss the issue until we are all present." Sal motioned to one of the senators. "Victor, get the sergeant-at-arms to hustle 'em up. We have some very important matters to talk about and we don't want to go over it twice." Victor got up and hastened out.

The gray-haired Balquist was not in a good mood, nor were the majority of the other senators and assemblymen in attendance. Most sat sullenly quiet in the comfortable leather arm chairs, sipping coffee and selecting breakfast rolls from the large tray passed around the immense walnut table. The assembled group represented the Democrat leadership of both houses. In low tones, Willie Green, the assembly Speaker, was conferring with John Burns, senate pro-tem, and Jesse Boggs, the Democratic caucus chairman. Through the large, double oak doors, the absent legislators quickly entered the room, apologizing for their tardiness while looking for empty seats.

Balquist gruffly asked them to sit down and listen carefully to what the Speaker had to say. Willie Green laboriously pushed back his chair, as if in pain, and rose to speak. His thin, small frame leaned nervously from side to side as he cleared his throat. Usually neat in appearance, he looked as though he hadn't slept for a week. His tie was twisted, suit wrinkled, and his sparse blond hair was matted to his head so as to seem unaccustomed to comb or brush.

Clearing his throat again, he hesitatingly began, "You all know that another problem has developed in the gubernatorial race . . . we're here for damage control." An ugly grumble sprung up from the table; rumors were flying fast and furious that Governor McKlatchy may be forced to resign. Everyone started talking at once about the prevailing gossip.

"Calm down," admonished the Speaker, "it's not as bad as you've all heard. I've spent the last two days running it all down and I brought the photos to show you." Once more, the noise level rose as each one felt compelled to offer an opinion.

"Where are they, Willie, let's see 'em!"

Speaker Green opened a clasped manila envelope and passed out several copies. Low whistles and groans came forth immediately. "What a dumb klutz!" disgustedly said one. "Why in the world did he do anything so stupid!" barked another.

"The guv doesn't photograph too well from that angle, does he?" guffawed one of the senators.

"You can say that again," giggled another. "His bod looks like a pear held up by two toothpicks."

"Yeah, but did you ever see such rosy cheeks?"

"Hey," roared another, "I got a great idea for a bumper sticker— 'Mooned by McKlatchy!'"

"Knock it off, guys," angrily barked Jesse Boggs. "We're all going to have to bear the consequences of the governor's indiscretion and protect him best we can."

"I can barely believe you're asking us to bear the brunt of his bare behind," wisecracked another assemblyman.

Several of the legislators were beside themselves, holding their sides in mirth, tears rolling down their faces. The Speaker, however, was red-faced over their ribald buffoonery. Willie Green saw nothing hilarious in the titular head of their party addressing a nudist colony in the buff, especially when some enterprising cameraman was present. No matter that the event took place a number of years ago, when McKlatchy was a freshman in the assembly; his present opponents for governor would make a very big deal out of it.

Willie had already been informed that the sensationalist weekly, *The National Tattletale*, had gained access to the photos and were on the verge of releasing them in their next issue—a panoramic, full-color exposé of the governor's portly, nude frame, complete with a superimposed fig leaf to obfuscate the obvious. The cover shot of the pulp tabloid was to be the south side of McKlatchy's pearly white, pear-shaped posterior pointing north. When caught by the camera, he was addressing the attentive, totally suntanned throng, oblivious to what was occurring behind his behind.

Willie knew that the day after the *Tattletale* hit the stands, McKlatchy's lead in the polls would drop 10 percent—maybe more. What really concerned both the Speaker and the pro-tem was the ripple effect it would have on the rest of the Democrats in office. They were holding onto a narrow edge in both the senate and the assembly and something like this could reflect badly on incumbents, especially if McKlatchy won the nomination.

"As you know," droned on Willie, "our majority could evaporate in just one election. Most of you in this room have endorsed McKlatchy, and some of our colleagues in marginal districts were counting on riding back into office on his coattails."

"Coattails!" sarcastically snapped Victor. "The silly bugger isn't even wearing a pair of boxer shorts!"

Willie threw him a dirty look and continued. "We Democrats are reasonably sure that Doug Stewart will win the Republican nomination and will be quite formidable. We had pinned our hopes on the incumbent governor to stay our ship of state. However, that hope is disappearing fast, unless we can figure a way out of this present mess." He cast a glance around the room, waiting for a response.

As none was forthcoming, the pro-tem spoke up. "All of our other gubernatorial candidates have shown some vulnerability. Our only hope is to discredit Stewart, discover some hidden skeletons in his closet. In the meanwhile, the job at hand is to play down the governor's past indiscretion and engage in damage control. In other words . . . NO MORE JOKES!"

"What does the governor have to say about all this?" asked the senate majority whip.

Willie looked at his watch. "Well, in a couple of minutes you can ask him. John and I have invited him to this meeting to explain his actions. I hope you'll all give him the courtesy his office requires."

"Oh, come off it, Willie . . . courtesy? The clown's taken us all down the tubes with what he's done. He would do us all a favor by dropping dead."

Just then, both doors to the conference room suddenly burst open and security guards rolled into the room. Huddled in their midst was the governor. The entire body was surrounded by a pack of hungry, bloodthirsty members of the media, shouting questions, jabbing microphones in McKlatchy's direction, and shoving TV cameras between the guards who were trying to protect the harried governor. Chaos reigned until several sergeants-at-arms slammed the large doors after the last remaining reporter, amid their strong objections.

As the racket from the media outside the conference room was beginning to subside, Senator John Burns was trying to quell the equally loud clamor inside. "Ladies and gentlemen, please! Let's have some level of decorum. Quiet! Do you hear me? SHUT UP!" Finally, the noise level toned down sufficiently to introduce the governor.

The Honorable Malcolm McKlatchy strode to the head of the table, expanded his chest and with a defiant look, began to speak. "Thank you, Mr. Speaker and Senator Burns, for calling us all together for this special meeting of the leadership. I appreciate the opportunity to share the truth before you read it in print or see it on TV."

The governor paused, lifted his chin, and with a quivering lower lip, continued. "A number of years ago, I was honored by an invitation to address the Moon Festival of the Bay Area Buff Bathers. Every August during the full moon, they gather on the east shore of Lake Pardee to experience the benevolence of Mother Earth and to honor the celestial lantern of the night. It is a joyous time, a summer solstice under the stars where one can be unencumbered by the constraints of intolerance . . . "

"Or skivvies!" one of the legislators humorously interjected.

"Or narrow-minded bigotry!" snapped back the angry governor.

"You tell 'em, Governor Moonbuns!" cracked an assemblyman.

Once more, the room was in an uproar, laughter and nasty cracks flowing from all directions.

"Calm down, everybody!" reprimanded John Burns. "Show some respect." He glared daggers at the boisterous, smirking solons, before the guffaws and giggles slowly died down. Haughtily, Burns addressed McKlatchy. "All right, Governor, you may continue. There won't be any more interruptions."

Malcolm McKlatchy wiped his sweaty brow and, with a tremble, resumed. "I am not ashamed of what I did. I wanted to establish a meaningful relationship with others who had equal concern about our fragile planet. I wanted to participate fully in a summer solstice, to meditate with others of like mind, develop a oneness, commune with the serenity of our delicate environment. I needed to abandon repressed feelings and uptight, unnatural inhibitions that had invaded my space. I yearned for a pristine experience, to be in synergy with those of like mind and body, to remove all artificial barriers between me and fragile nature."

"Does that include trousers, Malcolm?" Once more, gales of laughter broke out.

"I don't have to take this!" shouted the frustrated governor. "Not from fellow Democrats, I don't!"

Several of the more liberal members rose to defend him, while the more moderately bent continued to give him the raspberries. "Hey, Malcolm, are you going to spread that fragile tripe to the 'fragile' longshoremen?"

"Yeah, Malcolm, going to tell that to the 'fragile' teamsters?" disgustedly spoke another.

The governor's face turned from red to purple. Sputtering, he wheeled around and faced the Speaker. "I thought you said we would have a fair discussion, but I see now your word means nothing." With that, he moved rapidly to the door and bolted out into the waiting arms of the media, followed fast on his heels by his few supporters and security guards.

John Burns once more settled down the remaining members, then shrugging his shoulders, said, "As you can all see, we have a massive problem."

"Not as massive as Malcolm's backside," joked the whip.

"Oh, yes, it is," retorted the highly irritated pro-tem. "We stand to lose all the committee chairmanships, including the committee on reapportionment. If the Republicans gain control, they'll gerrymander us into oblivion, just like we've tried to do to them. We can't afford to have the top of the ticket as weak as it is." Burns looked around the room at the startled faces. The magnitude of their dilemma started to sink in.

The whip turned to Willie Green and with consternation, asked, "Is it really that bad, Willie?

"Worse," answered the Speaker. "In a head-to-head survey, we asked a large sampling of voters who they would vote for if the election were held right now. McKlatchy was holding a slight lead over Stewart, but Stewart was killing our other three by a two-to-one margin. The survey also showed that the number-one issue was America's need to return to basic values. You know, God and all that stuff."

Green continued, "I can guarantee that speaking in the buff to a bunch of moon-worshippers won't cut it with Mr. and Mrs. Joe Sixpack either. When this episode hits the news, Malcolm McKlatchy will be the laughingstock of the nation, especially if he attempts to defend it. What's worse, it's too late for us to find another candidate; the date for filing papers is long gone."

"Maybe we can back a write-in candidate," offered one of the senators.

"Fat chance. A write-in for governor is a joke," stated the Speaker.

"Wait a second," jumped in a Cow County senator. "There's another guy who's filed for the office. A supervisor by the name of Kaplowski from the foothills in Durango County. I've heard some pretty good things about him. His signs are all over my district."

John Burns lit up slightly. "What's so good about him?"

"Well, he's the only public official I know of who's lowered the cost of county government and been responsible for giving a healthy tax cut to his constituency."

Willie Green's ears perked up as well. "A tax cut?"

"Yep, and a healthy one at that."

Willie Green and John Burns made eye contact. John spoke first. "Mr. Speaker, let's you and me get to work. You dig up as much dirt as you can on Stewart and I'll look into this Kaplowski character. Maybe we'll come up with something." Burns slapped Willie's shoulder playfully, almost knocking the Speaker down. "Let's get with it. We're not dead yet, not until the polls close. Maybe this Kaplowski will be just the answer we need. It's a long time between now and November."

TWENTY-TWO

★ ★ ★

As THE LEAR JET'S right wing dropped, it started a lazy bank into the downwind pattern of the Eureka Murry Field. Doug was surprised by the unrestricted view of the shoreline. Usually in early September, a thick layer of clouds habitually pressed up against the coastal mountains, requiring an instrument approach to the airport. Not today. The overcast was gone, swept clean by the strong offshore breeze. It was a beautiful day. The wind was kicking up whitecaps on the waves below, adding sparkle to the sea, while fishing boats crisscrossed the water, cutting white trails in the deep blue bay.

Doug looked at his watch. He was right on time for his appointment with the lumber industry's representatives. Their luncheon meeting was to take place at the Ingomar Club in the historic Carson mansion, a beautifully restored Victorian overlooking Eureka's harbor. He liked the small north coast fishing and lumber community, and admired its citizenry.

The town had pride. The citizens of Eureka had obviously taken great care with their old Victorian residences, not allowing them to fall into disrepair. Street after street in the old section of town displayed brightly painted, century-old homes. Their front yards were laden with multicolored geraniums and the neatly manicured lawns were surrounded by low, white picket fences.

Doug had visited the area many times, while flycasting for steelhead and salmon in the nearby Klamath, Smith, and Mad Rivers.

Those were far better times. The northernmost coast of California had become a depressed area, devoid of new jobs, holding tight to the ones it had. Its inhabitants had been severely affected by the diminishing ocean fishery and the timber region's loss to excessive environmental concern.

The spotted owl was not their favorite local bird. Unemployment was high and the population was declining. The young people were being forced to leave in order to find jobs elsewhere, while the elderly were trapped, skimping to get by.

Carlos Saracino, Doug's pragmatic campaign manager, suggested they meet with the area's remaining business leaders. Though predominantly Democrat in the past, the current economic malaise led Carlos to believe the residents would now be more receptive to a Republican governor—especially since Governor McKlatchy, an outspoken ally of the radical environmentalists, was the odds-on-favorite to win his party's nomination.

Up to the present, most of Stewart's campaigning had been in the metropolitan centers where the largest concentration of votes were located. Saracino was convinced, for all intents and purposes, that Doug was sure to win the Republican primary balloting. He had an insurmountable lead over several underfunded, lackluster opponents; none had the necessary capital to effectively challenge the Stewart machine. "Now is the time to look ahead to the fall election, cut into McKlatchy's Democrat base, go for the jugular," is how he put it.

The jet proceeded to final approach, landing gear and flaps down, gliding rapidly toward the landing strip. Doug ceased thinking about the bygone days of flycasting for a fighting steelhead, while Carlos rearranged some survey data. Before placing it into his briefcase, he ceremoniously picked out one sheet and handed it to his boss. "Here ya go, future governor; look at this piece of delightful news."

Doug studied the material carefully, a synopsis of the latest public opinion poll. On a weekly basis their expert pollster, Arnie

Kleinberg, tracked the changes in voter attitudes. It was expensive but enabled the campaign management to stay up-to-date on the ever-changing public attitudes. Carlos was always on top of what news pushed the voters' collective hot buttons. Doug whistled when he read the latest statistics on McKlatchy. "Boy, the governor is dropping like an anvil."

"Yeah . . . for now," replied Carlos. "But, in two months' time, the average Democrat will forgive and forget. By the time the primary election rolls around, he'll still win big since he has no real competition. The office of governor carries a lot of weight—too much smack to be waylaid by something as trivial as going bare-butt to a nudist convention. None of his opponents has either the cash or the credibility to exploit McKlatchy's weaknesses. Besides, the kooks and kinks in his party will not only think nothing of it but will applaud him for his progressive posture."

"You're kidding!"

"Nope, not a bit. One San Francisco newspaper has already editorialized about it, complimenting McKlatchy on his skinny dippin' speech. They said it made him all the more sensitive to the masses wishing to be 'empowered.'"

"Empowered? Just what is that supposed to mean?"

"You got me; I'm no lib," Saracino said, adding a snicker or two. "All I know is that if he's their nominee, that little episode will make you the next governor. Our surveys show a resentment building within a sizable segment of the Democrat ranks on the environmental issue. McKlatchy is 'King Ecology' and very unpopular with some of the blue-collar vote, especially those in construction. That's one of the reasons we're here in Eureka, to fan the flames of discontent."

Doug looked over the survey data once more. "I don't see any stats on Kaplowski."

"Who?"

"Kaplowski, that supervisor from Durango County."

"Oh, him!" Carlos rummaged through his papers. "Let me see; I've got it right here, someplace. Oh, yes, here it is." He held up the data sheet. "As you can see, he doesn't even show up on the radar screen."

"What do you mean?" laughed Doug. "He's doubled his impact."

"Yeah, from two percent to four . . . big deal! His campaign people must be smokin' pot to even think he has a ghost of a chance."

"That bad, huh?"

"That bad." Carlos braced himself as the jet rolled to a stop.

As soon as the pilot opened the door, they hustled out and greeted the waiting contingent of Stewart supporters, gathered together as a welcoming committee. Time was short but with warm, hasty handshakes all around, they quickly loaded into minivans and headed along the pine-bordered highway toward town. Something caught Doug's attention, flashing by the corner of his eye, causing him to swiftly whip his head around . . . a campaign sign tacked to a tree.

There . . . another one. This time easier to see, it hung over a barbed-wire fence. Within a quarter of a mile, three more. Feeling more than uneasy, he slumped down in the seat . . . in big, bold letters, the posters read, KAPLOWSKI FOR GOVERNOR.

"Carlos, did you see that?"

"See what?"

"Those Kaplowski for Governor signs. I thought you said he had nothing going for him."

"He doesn't. Those are probably the only signs in the state. Don't let it bother you. The survey figures don't lie."

"Well, Hot Shot . . . what about that!" Doug pointed a finger to the side of the road. There, in full color, was Jamie's painting of Hank Kaplowski's likeness, with motto, "A real man to match our mountains."

Doug sputtered, "Doesn't that bother you?"

"Sure does," quipped Saracino. "Stealing such an old, corny cliché for their slogan . . . very tacky."

★ ★ ★

SENATOR JOHN BURNS WAITED impatiently in the reception area of the assembly Speaker's office, tapping his foot, shuffling the papers in his hands. His agitated behavior did not go unnoticed by the attractive receptionist. "Senator, would you care for a cup of coffee while you wait?"

Ignoring her offer, he gruffly asked, "Does Willie know I'm out here?"

The pretty young lady smiled sweetly, showing dimples and an even row of white teeth, "I believe so, sir; I told his executive secretary you were here."

"That's not good enough," he commanded. "Stick a note under Willie's nose and tell him I'm waiting."

"Yes, sir, right away, sir." She nervously jumped up from behind the desk and vanished into the inner offices, smart enough to know it was job-threatening not to immediately obey the commands of the senate's pro-tem. She also knew the same fate could await her if she walked, unannounced, into the Speaker's office. Laws pertaining to hiring and firing, overtime pay, and employee rights were applicable on the outside only. Inside the capitol walls, the rules were different. All personnel worked under the arbitrary whim of the legislature.

Any legislator could send a staff member packing at a moment's notice, for any reason, no matter how minor. If they didn't like the way an employee parted his hair or the way he laughed, it was, "Good-bye, out of here."

One newlywed, though extremely efficient, got sacked just for getting pregnant. Work overtime? Sixty or seventy hours a week with no additional pay? Just standard procedure. Complain to your union? What union? The only alternative to a capricious boss was to quit.

The young receptionist stepped lively to the secretary's desk. She was aware that Willie was in conference with several colleagues and wished not to be bothered. She had no intention of being the one to disturb his space; that was up to Martha, the Speaker's diplomatic executive secretary.

"Martha, Senator Burns is about to wear a hole in the reception-room carpet with his pacing about. He wants you to tell the Speaker he's here; he says it's important."

Moments later, Martha hurried into the reception area with an apologetic expression written across her matronly face. "Oh, Senator, we're so sorry to keep you waiting. I just slipped another note to the Speaker and he said he would be with you in less than a minute." With a smile that would sweeten the bitterest of sentiments, she invited, "Please Senator, come inside and wait in my office."

Burns followed after her into the inner sanctum. The offices were the epitome of nineteenth-century decor—heavy antique furniture, polished walnut paneling, ornate brocade draperies, and a massive Bierstadt landscape adorning the west wall. The rooms reeked of wealth—in large part, due to the multimillion-dollar restoration project in the seventies and eighties.

In order to meet newly-mandated earthquake codes, the old capitol building was literally restructured from the inside out, duplicating every architectural detail of the past, from inlaid floors to its domed rotunda. While the rest of the legislators took care of business in offices in one of the latter-day additions, the Speaker of the assembly and the senate pro-tem wallowed in the richness of California's past opulence.

They had no sooner arrived than the Speaker and several assemblymen exited his quarters—laughing, joking, shaking hands, and slapping each other on the back. Willie jovially bid them all good-bye and immediately waved to the pro-tem. "Come on in, John. Sorry to keep you waiting."

"No problem, Willie."

Speaker Green walked over to the seating area of his large, luxurious office and slumped down in one of the huge high-backed chairs. He motioned Burns to the richly upholstered sofa. "Take a seat, John; rest your bones." After a moment's pause, "How're things with you? What can I do for you?"

Taking no time for small talk, Burns tossed several pieces of material on the antique cherrywood coffee table. "Here's the literature being handed out by the Kaplowski people. Pretty simple stuff, nothing fancy. As you can see, the printed material is as plain as you can get, but that full-color illustration is quite a grabber; nice piece of artwork of the candidate."

Willie picked it up, held it at arm's length, then put on his glasses for a better look. "Rugged, good-looking dude, even though he's bald," observed Willie. "Quite a contrast to that slick fashion plate the Republicans are pushing."

"Yeah," agreed Burns. "Hairy versus hairless."

"What else did you find out about the guy? Did you talk to him?"

"No, he wasn't there; however, I did meet with the people running his headquarters and the gal in charge of his campaign." John grinned widely, "You might remember her. She's very active in the state central committee. Name's Hagerty. She's that well-built red-head from one of the Cow Counties. You should remember her, Willie. She's the one who gave the environmentalists fits at the last state convention. Her father is the Hagerty that gives megabucks to the party."

Willie Green frowned and chewed on the temple of his glasses before his eyes widened. "Oh, *yeah!*"

Burns looked over to the cabinet in the opposite corner. "Got any suds in there?"

Without answering, Willie got up and went over to the hand-carved credenza that concealed a small refrigerator. He extracted a can, popped the tab, and handed it to Burns. "Where was Kaplowski . . . out campaigning?"

"I assume so, but I didn't specifically ask. I can tell you one thing; that headquarters was unbelievably busy. Volunteers were everywhere, phones ringing constantly, gals opening bags of mail, people rushing in and out . . . a real grassroots operation. I was impressed."

"How much money do they have?"

"Very little. Most of it nickels and dimes. The only heavy contributor is old man Hagerty. He's dumped in ten thousand. But they haven't even sent out a fundraising letter. Can you believe it? The only money they have received has been strictly *pro bono*. The volunteers are sold on Kaplowski; they think he's King Wenceslaus."

"Wasn't he a Czech?"

"Who?"

"Wenceslaus."

"Who gives a rat's butt? You know what I mean—the Polack. They're convinced he's the most qualified candidate in the race. I spoke to a number of the locals, including the sheriff. He says Kaplowski's tough on crime and a strong leader. The county treasurer says that he's responsible for lowering the tax rate while improving county services. I didn't believe it, but he showed me the facts to prove it."

"Did you find out anything negative?"

"Yes and no." The senator scratched his head and searched through the papers on the table. Finding the Willis newspaper piece, he handed it to the Speaker. "Take a look at this. I don't know how to take his crazy idea about not campaigning."

Willie scanned the article without grasping the point. "What crazy idea?"

"Jamie Hagerty told me and that Willis' Associated Press write-up is true. Kaplowski won't campaign. He honestly believes hustling up votes is demeaning to a candidate and that promoting the office seeker is the responsibility of those who support him. He thinks it's undignified to ask for votes."

Willie Green cocked one eyebrow. "I've never heard of anything so ridiculous."

"Neither had I . . . but it seems to make sense to his supporters. They claim it adds dignity to politics, particularly at a time when that trait is sadly lacking." A cynical smirk crossed Burns' face as he pointed to the AP article. "Willie, when was the last time you heard anything about a politician trying to restore dignity to political campaigning?"

"Dignified candidates never finish better than second place, especially ones that won't press the flesh and kiss the kids."

"Now, wait a second, Willie. We've had some candidates who would have been better off if they'd kept their mouths shut and never exposed their ideas to the public. Ellen Knox would still be a viable candidate for governor if she hadn't blabbed about her sexual preferences."

"Yeah, you're right," laughed Willie. "McKlatchy would be, as well . . . if he hadn't exposed more than his ideas. Who knows? Maybe Kaplowski isn't so crazy after all."

Burns took the last swig, crushed the can, and arched the empty container toward a nearby wastepaper basket. "Slam dunk . . . score two points. Willie, what if we hire a topflight consultant, turn loose a few bucks for a survey, and real quick test-market this Kaplowski character. We might be in for a pleasant surprise."

Still on his feet, Willie walked to the window overlooking the spacious capitol grounds. Suddenly, he turned and exclaimed, "I don't know; we could be pouring money down a rat hole. What do we really know about this guy? Are there any goblins in his closet? For all we know, he might be a Polish transvestite. Maybe he has a credit card to Nevada's Mustang Ranch. Or, worse yet, maybe he doesn't even like girls."

"I can't answer any of that, but what are we going to lose by sending in a team of pros to his campaign? If anything negative shows up, we can always back out. A little cash spent on that Polish sausage just might make for a great political breakfast."

Willie gave him a sidelong look. "Okay, John, 'fess up. Who do you have in mind?"

The pro-tem grinned. "Willie, you read me like an open book. All the decent mechanics in California are already tied up; what's left are the dregs. But I checked with the party's national office in Washington, and guess what? They recommended Byron Burke. He was handling a Vermont senate race that just folded . . . he's now available."

Willie let out a low whistle between his teeth. "That's a stroke of luck; Byron's first-cabin."

"You got that right. We couldn't do better."

"We should contact him right away."

"I'm way ahead of you," Burns answered, smiling. "I've already gotten in touch with him. He said the timing is good, that he was tired of freezing his buns off in the northeast, and that he would love to winter in California . . . for a price."

Willie's brow furrowed at the mention of money. Byron wasn't available for peanuts or prestige; it took big bucks to hire him. He was credited with successfully managing several eastern states in the election of the nation's presidential team. "Okay, John, how much?"

"Five a week. If Kaplowski wins the primary, a bonus of ten. And then we renegotiate for the general election. Not bad, huh?"

"You're right; that's not bad at all." Burns waited while the Speaker thought it over. "Let's see, that'd be only fifty thousand for the next two months if Kaplowski wins . . . not bad. Byron must really be sick of the east coast." Willie's excitement over the prospect of Burke coming west was evident as he two-stepped across the room. "Let's do it! I'll come up with half of it and you raise the other twenty-five. Go ahead, John, send for him. It's worth the gamble."

"What gamble?" sarcastically queried the pro-tem. "We are on the verge of losing control of the state legislature, turning over to the Republicans billions of dollars to spend as they see fit. What's a paltry million or two in campaign expenses when we're talking about controlling sixty-five billion? We're talking real power . . . raw power."

Willie stopped his dancing about the floor; the seriousness of Burns' demeanor bathed him in a shower of cold reality. With their present crop of candidates for governor, all Democrat incumbents stood a real chance of being babies thrown out with the gubernatorial bathwater. A political drenching loomed dead-ahead, with Democrats losing control of the legislature in the process. Willie shuddered at the thought. *Kaplowski, you don't have any idea how important you are.*

TWENTY-THREE

★ ★ ★

JAMIE LOOKED UP from her desk and didn't like what she saw. It was Hank weaving his way through the crowded headquarters, returning cursory, clenched-teeth smiles to those who greeted him. Over the noise in the room, she could hear his boots hit the floor with authority as he marched, more than walked, toward her office. Closing the door, he rested his back against it and motioned to the activity outside. Acrimoniously, he asked, "What, pray tell, is all of this? Are you running someone for governor?"

His biting sarcasm was not appreciated. Jamie was in no mood for snide remarks. Petulantly, she said, "Don't you give me any lip, Kaplowski. Where on God's green earth have you been?" She erupted from her chair, knocking it over backward. "I haven't heard from you in weeks. Your secretary called me and asked what she should do with all of the political mail you were getting. All I did was take it off her hands and answer inquiries."

Jamie continued, "I sent out a brief outline on your background, a picture of you, and a copy of Willis' AP article. I included a letter saying that was all they could expect, that they were on their own and if they wanted you for governor, they'd have to take the ball and run with it. Don't blame me for what they've done. It was your idea in the first place . . . remember?"

Hank was taken aback by her straightforward explanation, and he couldn't deny there was some truth in it. He was indeed the one who dreamed up mentioning that stuff about the old-time approach to campaigning. As he started to say something, Jamie rolled over him with a continuing flood of querulous commentary. "Ever since the press reported the news of McKlatchy baring his buttocks, we've been inundated with requests for information about you. What do you expect me to do? Forget about people who care; let one of those four clowns win?"

Jamie's eyes began to well up as she poured out her anger and resentment. After weeks of pent-up frustration, she finally had the opportunity to vent her emotions and Hank was not sympathetic in the least. In fact, he seemed completely ungrateful.

Hank's face began to redden and he couldn't keep the sharpness out of his raised voice. "I thought we had a clear understanding. You promised me you wouldn't do anything. I told you, emphatically, I didn't want to seek the gubernatorial office. How could I have been more direct? Answer me . . . how could I?"

Hank expected her to become docile and defensive as he saw tears streaming down her face, but instead she continued on the offensive and self-righteousness seeped from her every pore. "What exactly would you have me do, return all the letters unanswered? Send the contributions back? Tell them to vote for one of the fools on the ticket?"

Jamie whipped out a Kleenex and blew her nose . . . hard. Suddenly, her demeanor changed from indignant to conciliatory. Her voice softened, but the tears continued to flow. "Hank, a whole bunch of us think you would be a great governor, a long sight better than any of the other Democrats. You can't blame us for hoping you'll change your mind. You're bright, honest, and certainly as qualified as those yahoos who are seeking the office. A lot of people are counting on your winning the nomination . . . now, more than ever!"

Hank stiffened. "What do you mean by that?"

"Your candidacy has attracted some attention in high places; like last week, John Burns stopped by and asked a ton of questions." She blotted her wet cheeks.

Hank felt his knees go weak. "John Burns, the senate's pro-tem?"
"Yes, and that's not all. . . ."

Before she could finish, the door banged open, pushing Hank
aside. An effervescent, balding, babyfaced balloon burst into the
room, clutching faxes in his fat hand. "Hey, Jamie, look at this. Oh,
excuse me . . . Hey! You're Kaplowski!" Thrusting the messages
under his left arm, he stuck out his right hand and grabbed Hank's
with an eager grip. "Man, am I glad to finally meet you."

Jamie introduced them to each other, "Hank, I'd like you to
meet Byron Burke. The pro-tem sent him over to check us out and
give a helping hand."

Doug immediately recognized him. For years, he had been a
regular guest on Washington D.C.'s political gossip program,
"Inside the Beltway." Hardly a week went by that some national TV
pundit didn't ask for Burke's astute opinion on the affairs of the
nation. Unfortunately, he remembered him too well from the days
when Nadine insisted on watching that program every week. No
one got under her conservative skin like Byron Burke.

Burke epitomized the slick, liberal, professional Democrat.
And worse, he was the architect of many a conservative's defeat.
*What is such a big-time, Eastern hot-shot like Burke doing in
Diamond Springs? What did Jamie mean when she said he's here to
give us a helping hand?*

Burke's conversation faded from Doug's consciousness, way into
the background, as his mind churned. *Oh, what a tangled web we
weave, when first we practice to deceive. Practice? Who's practicing?
I'm just an innocent bystander who's been trampled by the fickle feet
of fate!*

Never in his wildest nightmare could Doug imagine being
involved in such a mess. In a simple desire to please, he had
allowed a tiny, harmless fib to grow into a whopper of a lie—in all
probability, to the detriment of many others. He and Jamie could
be prosecuted and jailed. The entire Republican Party would be
the laughingstock of the country; tens of thousands of his GOP

contributors would be embarrassed. His children would be mortified and disgraced and his business reputation ruined. Outside of that, what else mattered?

Doug couldn't help but wonder how the inside of Folsom Prison looked. *Shall I confess and repent? Too late!* He was in too deep for sackcloth and ashes; the only course open was to bluff through it and hope no one would catch on. One thing was certain; Hank Kaplowski had to lose the primary election! But with his hapless luck, he'd probably win. Staying away, out of the local limelight, had only made matters worse. Maybe the wisest move would be to stick around and sabotage the campaign from within.

And the first thing he had to do was discourage Byron Burke's participation. At last, Hank interrupted. "Did Jamie bother to tell you I don't want to be governor?"

"Yes, she did," Burke enthusiastically answered. "She also told me you had no intention of campaigning. Admirable, very admirable. It's time we had more people running for office who think that way. It makes it much easier on the campaign manager, especially in statewide races. No offense, but candidates sometimes get in the way."

Hank stuck out his jaw and said firmly, "I won't raise money, not a dime."

"Don't expect you to." Condescendingly, Byron put his hand on Hank's shoulder and gave a little squeeze. "Others have offered to help. Basically, this will be a grassroots effort."

"I won't even return phone calls."

"No problem; Jamie and I will handle all the important ones."

Defiantly folding his arms across his chest and raising his chin, Hank looked Burke straight in the eye. "I won't give a single speech . . . not one."

"No problem—ties right in with your theme of having the citizenry promote you. However, we will request that you make just one appearance and say a few words."

"When's that?"

"When you accept the nomination."

★ ★ ★

THE SENATE WAS IN SESSION, casting votes on the daily file of legislation. Over the loudspeaker located outside of the back entrance to the chambers came the monotone utterances of the desk clerk, reading the next bill to come before the body. His voice could barely be heard over the chatter of the lobbyists loitering about the third-floor hallway, each waiting to see how their bills fared.

Byron Burke handed his card to the sergeant at arms and asked that it be delivered to the pro-tem. Without a word, he took the card and disappeared into the lounge behind the chambers. Moments later, John Burns bustled out through the door, motioning Burke to follow. Several lobbyists tried to get a word in with the senator, but he summarily brushed them off. "Some other time, not now."

In order to keep up with the fast-paced Burns, Byron Burke had to dog-trot after him, around corners, through the crowded halls, and into the senator's outer office. A group of visiting dignitaries from Burns' hometown was waiting to see him. With a quick smile and rapid handshakes, he apologetically waded through the delegation and into his private office, shutting the door behind him.

Byron was sweating from the exertion; moving at a speed above a slow shuffle was a new experience for him. Removing a cork from a bottle of vintage Zinfandel constituted the sum total of Burke's normal daily exercise. "Senator, do you motor down the halls like that all the time?"

Burns ignored the question and sat down behind his desk, then signaled the portly campaign manager to do likewise in the chair beside him. "Well, what do you think of him?"

"What *him* are you talking about?"

Burns glowered at the flippant easterner; he was in no mood for jokes. Prior to being on the assembly floor, he had spent several hours in the governor's office and was unnerved by the experience. Looking daggers at the consultant, he barked, "Byron, knock off the crud and answer my question. I don't have all day to piddle around."

Burke changed his attitude immediately. "Something bugging you, Senator?"

"You got that right." The irritated Burns wadded up a ball of paper and threw it across the room. "I just spent the morning with old bare-butt McKlatchy. He has convinced himself that there's no need for damage control concerning his buck-naked romp with that birthday suit brigade at Lake Pardee. He thinks it's a trivial matter and will be easily forgotten. His staff is intimidated and won't level with him; nor will those idiots who are running his election drive."

The senator continued, "McKlatchy's living in La-La Land and his advisors must be smoking something. The polling data clearly shows that he will lose twenty-five percent of the Democratic vote even if he were running against the most repulsive Republican imaginable. The other seventy-five percent say they'll vote, but in varying degrees of holding their noses while doing so. Against Stewart, he's history . . . and maybe the rest of us will grace the pages of posterity, as well."

"That bad, huh?"

"Worse. He ain't going to get any better." Burns took a deep breath and sighed. "You've heard that old political dodge about the three kinds of people in elected office?"

Not wanting to interrupt the pro-tem's chain of thought, Byron said, "I think so . . . but remind me."

"One type of legislator makes things happen, one watches things happen, and the other asks, 'What happened?'" Burns screwed up his face in disgust. "McKlatchy doesn't remotely fit into *any* of those categories. That brain-dead dunce doesn't know what happened when it happens to him. We've got to look someplace else for our party's candidate. Now, tell me what you think of Kaplowski."

"Didn't learn much about him because there's not much to learn. He's led a fairly dull life. He didn't attend college. However, he was smart enough to get a marine commission. Served in Vietnam, has two Purple Hearts and a Silver Medal. He was married, wife died a few years ago, and they had no children. After he was discharged, he went into mining. Owns gold-bearing property in the southern Tehachapi Mountains and works a small claim in Durango County. He drinks Coors beer and likes to line dance. It seems he's spent most of his adult life underground, hard-rock mining for gold. That's about it . . . he's duller than a flat river rock. Also, he really isn't interested in being governor."

"Then why did he file?"

"You got me. I would guess it was Jamie Hagerty's idea. She thinks he's terrific, but so do a lot of others. Telling a derogatory Polish joke in Durango County will get you a fist in the snotlocker. The folks up there worship that hayseed."

"Think he's worthy of our support?" inquired Burns.

"Actually, I do—and for the weirdest reason, unlike any of the races I've ever managed."

"Why's that?"

"Because he's a big blob of political putty, just right for being molded into just about anything we want. More often than not, the biggest pain in the keester is the candidate himself or his wife. I would love to run a campaign where I'd never have to deal with either. From my viewpoint, Kaplowski may be the perfect gubernatorial candidate—the dark horse of the century. With five aspirants in the race, we could win it with less than twenty-five percent of the vote. With the rural counties solidly behind him and a few percentage points from the metropolitan areas, we could win it all. There's just one hitch."

"What's that?" asked the extremely interested pro-tem.

"Money. We'll need lots of bread to crack the urban Democrat."

"How much?"

"A million, maybe two."

Senator Burns leaned back in his leather swivel chair, placed one foot against the edge of his desk, and rocked back and forth. "You sure we can do it for that amount?"

"Give or take a few hundred thousand."

Burns stopped rocking and gave Burke a long stare. "Go do it. Willie and I will raise the money. Now, get outa here; I've got work to do."

TWENTY-FOUR

★ ★ ★

"CARLOS, DO YOU HAVE a minute?" Saracino looked up from his word processor to see two heads poking through the doorway to his office. One belonged to Mark Cutting, the other to Wendall Timmerman. Both were bright young staffers temporarily borrowed from the Republican caucus to work on the Stewart crusade for governor.

Carlos really didn't have time to see anyone. The last month of any statewide campaign is hectic at best and chaotic as usual. During the closing weeks, time was all-important—especially to management. Although he had little time to spare for the two energetic campaign workers, he waved them in. Both, he thought, were destined to play important roles in future state politics—either as key assistants, or possibly as candidates themselves.

They had been assigned jobs as speechwriters, collecting salient facts onto three-by-five cards for Stewart's perusal. Their most immediate responsibility was to construct a speech to address the annual state convention of the California Republican Associates, the most powerful conservative volunteer organization in California. The campaign management team decided that the CRA talk could set the theme for November's general election by aggressively taking the offensive early and establishing the parameters for upcoming debates.

Since major media people would be in attendance, it was a perfect time to launch a new attack against the present administration. Carlos was now sorry he had given such an important job to political neophytes; yet, he felt to take the job away from them would be poor judgment. With a little bit of senior advice, last-minute rewriting, and consultation with Stewart, he believed they could make it work.

Without looking up from his computer, Saracino said, "Come on in, boys; I can give you a few minutes."

"Thanks, Boss," they said in unison.

Flopping down on the couch across from Carlos' desk, Mark Cutting aggressively took the lead. "Mr. Saracino, we have a problem."

Carlos hated that word "we," as in "we" have a problem. *He* had no problem; *they* had a problem. Obviously, the boys had come to a point where they needed to share their quandary and pick his superior brain. So, he sighed, "What problem do we have?"

"Well," nervously responded Wendall, "it has to do with religion."

Carlos raised his eyebrows in surprise. "Religion?"

"Yeah," answered Mark, chewing on the end of his pencil. "Mr. Stewart's a religious man and so are most of the folks in the CRA. From what I hear, the group is chock full of devout Christians. We need to know how many times we should use 'God' in the speech, or should we even use that word at all?"

Wendall quickly expanded on their predicament. "Okay, so we know the CRA crowd is fairly religious, but we also know the convention will be well-attended by the liberal media, most of whom take any reference to God as a sign of rabid, fundamental conservatism. So, do we play the religious card for the sake of the audience, or do we focus in on the press, concentrating on a much bigger constituency?"

Carlos gave them a telling smile, acknowledging that they had come to the right person. Who better to solve this question than one of the most astute, sought-after campaign consultants in the nation?

"Gentlemen, you can do both. Now, go back to your offices and bring me the recent survey data you've been working with." Both disappeared and quickly returned with the polling results.

With an attitude of wisdom surpassing all neophyte understanding, Carlos began. "Turn to the page that gives you the demographic data on those with religious convictions. I believe it's toward the back of the book."

Wendall eagerly leafed through the computer pages until he found the right one. "Okay, I've got it."

Carlos asked, "How many people in the survey say they believe in a divine being?"

"Seventy-eight percent."

"How many are agnostics?"

"Twelve percent."

"Atheists?"

"Eight percent," Wendall replied.

"How many go to church regularly?" Carlos continued.

"The numbers are about fifteen percent."

"What does that tell you?" Carlos asked, and grinned.

Both of the young staffers looked at each other with blank expressions. Mark finally said, "Okay, we give up. What does that tell us?"

"It's all percentages," the sage consultant offered. "The CRA audience is important, but they constitute just a fraction of the voting populous. The press and their readership are, by far, the more important."

Waxing eloquent, he continued, "What is printed or seen on TV will be broadcast to the public in numbers surpassing the CRA members by a thousandfold. Of course, if only CRAers were in attendance, it would be a far different story; we could preach to the choir. But, since the event will be heavily covered by the press, the religious group becomes of secondary importance. The first rule is to always play to the largest voting segment."

Saracino paused to see if the message was sinking in. It was. Both young men were enraptured, as though the words emanated from

Mecca. "The second rule is to figure how many might be pushed out of shape if God were mentioned and balance it off against those who would be pleased, were He to be given a plug. It boils down to the churchgoing Christians versus the atheists. What are those numbers again?"

"Fifteen percent Christian churchgoers against eight percent atheists."

"That's approximately a two-to-one margin. Good odds."

Wendall's brow furrowed. "Shouldn't we use the seventy-eight percent who say they believe in God?"

"Nope," smirked Saracino. "The fact that seventy-eight percent say they believe in God is nice, but it means little. Only a small percentage of that seventy-eight percent go to a Bible class or regularly read the Bible. Just because they *say* they believe in the Almighty really doesn't cut much mustard; it's the devout that are turned on by the mention of God. As for the seventy-eight percent, since most don't care enough to attend church regularly or at all, they don't really care one way or another if God is mentioned."

"If that's the case," asked Mark, "why bother?" He grimaced, as he considered the options.

Carlos gave him a warm, fatherly smile. "It's good politics to know how to use God, especially among the true believers. The Demos rarely mess with or mention the Almighty; thus, to a certain segment of the devout population, it gives us a bit of an edge. As you well know, elections are won or lost by small margins. But, even under those circumstances, it's important to know where you can put God in a speech. As an example, never mention His name in conjunction with any issue."

Wendall looked confused. "What do you mean by that?"

"It's threatening to the audience and makes the speaker judgmental and seem 'holier than thou.' Most of the people in that seventy-eight percent have their own comfortable image of what God is and a politician foolish enough to mention God's laws usually steps on somebody's private toes. Keep in mind, we're not in the foot-stompin' business."

Carlos leaned back in his swivel chair, put his hands behind his head, and gazed at the ceiling. "Remember, boys, we're not in the salvation-and-revival business; our job is to get as many votes as we can. Electioneering isn't for educating, soul-saving, or for leading the pilgrims out of the wilderness, but for properly relating our candidate to the public's present whims. Getting God into the equation usually messes things up to the masses."

Both of the young men were awed and somewhat appalled by what they were hearing . . . pure political gospel from Saint Carlos.

"So, then, what are the standards we must go by?" asked Mark. "What constitutes truth?"

"It's that polling data in Wendall's lap," yawned Saracino. "That book establishes what truth is all about. What's important to us? . . . The percentages! They tell us what the voter thinks and feels right now. To us, all else is of secondary importance."

"Isn't that the way the other side operates?" asked Mark.

"Sure, it is," replied Carlos, "and the winner is the one who correctly interprets the data."

"Well, then," asked Wendall, "are you telling us we're better off not mentioning God at all?"

"No siree!" emphatically stated Carlos. "We are Republicans; we've got to mention the Old Boy . . . but only in the closing of the address. The candidate should look very somber, ask for divine guidance, and pray that God will bless what we're doing; but again, not be specific."

"Our candidate makes no bones about being a Christian," said Mark. "Shouldn't we mention Jesus in some fashion?"

"No, too risky," answered Carlos. "The word God is sort of a generic term that very few take offense to. However, the name Jesus riles up some folks; unless, of course, it's used as a swear word. When using God in the right context, even atheists don't complain too much. Christ or Jesus, though . . . that's another matter."

"Isn't that a little cynical?" asked Mark.

"Of course, it is!" Carlos admitted with a laugh. "But so is the business of politics. Gentlemen, we're in the manipulation business

—not pure and simple but impure and complex. Our job is to elect Republicans and, to do so, we must abide by the rules."

"What rules?" asked Mark.

"They're in the book on Wendall's lap."

"Polling data?"

"What else?" smirked Carlos. "Tell me one thing that is more important."

The side door separating his campaign office from Doug Stewart's suddenly jerked open. Doug stood in the doorway with an icy hardness engraved on his face. "You ask what's more important? How about moral values and ethics?" Turning to the young men, he commanded, "You two, into my office." Both hastily complied.

Closing the door as soon as they'd scurried past, Doug faced his chief consultant. "Mr. Saracino, you left the intercom open between our offices. I couldn't help but overhear your erudite lesson on contemporary political ethics; or, should I call it Cynicism One-oh-one? Most enlightening, but dramatically different from my own."

Seeing that he had Carlos' full attention, Doug went on. "Polling data might tell us what the majority of people are thinking now—at this moment—but it can't decide how you or I should behave, or where we will be in the hereafter. There's a detailed book on that subject, divinely inspired by that 'Old Boy' you so glibly referred to."

As Doug partially opened the door to his office, he curtly added, "Carlos, you're in serious need of a moral attitude adjustment. In the meantime, I'll take over the task of advising the boys what we shall say to the CRA, and you constrain your activities to the daily mechanics of this campaign."

Awaiting no response from the slack-jawed Saracino, Doug withdrew to his office and communicated to Mark Cutting and Wendall Timmerman his own thoughts regarding the origin of truth.

TWENTY-FIVE

★ ★ ★

Exhausted from late-night campaigning in the San Francisco Bay area, Doug Stewart sluggishly opened the door of his Sacramento apartment, bent down, and picked up the morning newspaper. He armed himself with a bowl of Wheaties, a banana, and a carton of nonfat milk and shuffled from the refrigerator to the kitchen table. Ignoring the front-page news, Doug removed the sports section and searched for the results of last night's basketball game. *Ah, here we go—Sacramento Kings 102, Seattle Supersonics 99. Hmmm, close game.*

A column about the possibility of a Major League franchise coming to the capitol area caught his attention. Out of the corner of his eye, while reaching for the bowl of Wheaties, he noticed the front page of the paper. The headlines screamed:

DEMOCRAT LEADERS ABANDON GOVERNOR MCKLATCHY
FOR UNKNOWN COUNTY SUPERVISOR!

Doug knocked over the milk carton while grabbing frantically for the paper. He read:

Speaker Green and Senate Pro-tem John Burns regretfully announced their withdrawal from Governor McKlatchy's reelection campaign. Speaking for both of them, Senator Burns said,

"We're sorry we have to leave our old and dear friend, Malcolm McKlatchy, but our first duty is to the state and to our constituents. The Speaker and I are confident that our best hope for the continuation of our Democrat agenda lies under the direction of Hank Kaplowski."

Burns then proceeded to give the many reasons for their surprising switch, one of which was Kaplowski's promise to continue the programs recently implemented by the Democratic Party. Kaplowski couldn't be reached to comment on his good fortune.

Doug crumpled the newspaper and threw it on the floor. "You bet, I couldn't be reached."

As Hank Kaplowski, he had tried to gum up the campaign; but with skill that had to be admired, Byron Burke, his adept campaign manager, had circumvented his every act. First off, he'd moved Kaplowski's campaign strategy headquarters out of Diamond Springs to downtown Sacramento. Doug was convinced that the best policy for Hank was to stay out of sight—especially in Sacramento, where he could possibly be recognized.

★ ★ ★

FOR ALL INTENTS AND PURPOSES, Hank Kaplowski had disappeared from the face of the earth. *How can they elect an invisible candidate? Impossible! It has to be impossible.* Glancing once more at the headlines, he shook his head. *Ha! I thought it was out of the question to be elected to the assembly, but here I am!*

He was now wide awake . . . and sweating. *Only two more weeks and the primary election will be over. There's no way I can be the nominee of both parties . . . period!*

Doug made a pot of coffee and began to pace about the apartment. Then, bolting toward the Zenith console, he switched on channel 13's A.M. news. Capitol commentator Stan Patkins was announcing the recent turn of events, declaring how the switch added new vitality and flair to the Democrat's primary race.

The camera cut to several party legislators who, likewise, were deserting McKlatchy's sinking gubernatorial ship. "Kasluwski's our man! We've been watching Hank for a long time and have always been impressed with his ethics and down-home morals."

Doug bellowed at the television, "Watching for a long time? Give me a break; you clowns don't even know how to pronounce Hank's name!"

He was glued to the screen as a commercial flashed on. There was Sheriff "Bulldog" Moore, leaning against a Durango County patrol car, waxing on about the law enforcement credentials of Hank Kaplowski. "Yes, sir, folks, Hank gave me the tools to clean up crime in our county. Let's give him the chance to help the other sheriffs do the same."

Then, there appeared Jamie's heroic-looking illustration, depicting Hank as strong and virile, a bigger-than-life Western patriot. The voice-over stated, "The man to match our mountains." It was an extremely effective TV spot, better than any of the other highly professional ads for the other gubernatorial candidates . . . even better than the slick commercials currently running for Doug Stewart.

Stan came back on the screen and, with a toothy smile, announced, "We're fortunate to have Mr. Kaplowski's campaign manager here in the studio. This special report is being fed through the network to our sister stations around the state." Seated next to Stan Patkins was a smiling, relaxed Byron Burke.

"Mr. Burke, you are, without question, one of the most astute political consultants in the nation. Why is a man of your reputation handling the campaign of a little-known Cow County supervisor?"

"The nation's changing, Stan, and so is California politics. I want to be in the forefront of this dynamic movement."

Before Stan could pose another question, Byron casually leaned forward, placed his elbows comfortably on the table, and in a matter-of-fact manner said, "As you know, we Democrats have historically been the working man's party and, I'm sorry to say, we've gotten away from that. Unfortunately, we now have the reputation of being the party of the bureaucrat, and I must admit, we deserve that label . . . at least partially."

Changing his delivery from relaxed to firm conviction, Burke shook his fist and spoke very seriously. "Those days are gone, Stan. We're going back to our Democratic roots and Hank's the one to lead us there."

The surprised commentator asked, "Do you think he is of that caliber? The stuff that . . ."

"Absolutely," he broke in. "As I see Kaplowski, he has the down-home quality of Harry Truman and the brains of FDR."

"Really! That's quite a statement. What's this I hear about him not campaigning?"

"Hank honestly believes that it's the voters' responsibility to advance the credentials of their candidate. He thinks it's demeaning to the office of governor to plead and beg for votes, or make false promises that can't be kept. He has only promised to keep in tact all the good social programs the Democrats have put into place. He has an amazing record as county supervisor . . ." Doug reached out and turned the TV off.

"When did Hank ever say that? Campaign managers, auggggh!" He needed another cup of coffee.

Doug was shaken out of his blue funk by the jangling of the phone. Cursing under his breath, he picked it up and gruffly said, "Stewart, here."

An excited familiar voice greeted his ear. "Hey, Doug, Harry Kaloogian. In case you haven't heard, there's been some really great news."

"What's that?"

"Some hayseed supervisor just captured the support of the Democrat's leadership. Can you believe it?" Kaloogian had trouble holding back his gleeful laughter. Doug could hear him breaking up as he continued, "Green and Burns have actually deserted our skinny dippin' guv for some rural rube. The Dems must be in real trouble, trying to pull off a stunt like that."

"Harry, do you think Kaplowski has a ghost of a chance?"

"Who knows? Things are so screwed up on their side of the aisle that anything could happen at this stage of the game. I'm reasonably sure their primary turnout will be low. The average Democrat is pretty disgusted and will probably sit out the election. I'd bet their turnout will be less than forty percent."

"And a low turnout might help who? McKlatchy?"

Mark thought for a moment before answering. "Maybe . . . maybe Kaplowski, but probably not. The Demo bigwigs switching loyalties knocks everything cockeyed. If Kaplowski comes up with mega-megabucks, it could be a Polish celebration. But more likely it'll be like a Polish wake."

Doug's knees felt like jelly. "Uh . . . thanks, Harry, thanks for the information. See ya later." Clumsily, he hung up the phone and wandered back into the kitchen. The very thought that Hank had a slim chance of winning made him sick to his stomach. If it happened, his goose was fricasseed, stewed, deep-fried, and barbecued.

Pouring himself a cup of coffee, he sat down at the kitchen table to finish his breakfast. The bowl of cereal was limp and soggy; the banana was turning brown. *That's how I feel . . . limp and soggy.* He rose and poured the milky, mushy mess down the garbage disposal and again filled the cereal bowl, then reached for the milk. Empty. Taking too big a gulp of hot coffee, he burned his mouth.

"Ya know," he mused out loud sorrowfully, "some days start off better than others."

* * *

"WHADAYA MEAN, YOU CAN'T find him? Get out there and hustle; Kaplowski couldn't have disappeared." John Burns rocked back and forth in his red leather chair, unmistakably agitated by the pronouncement from Byron Burke.

"We've done everything but call out the police," testily replied Byron. "We've scouted out his mine, searched every bar and grill in

Durango County, and checked the morgue. I tell you, John, Kaplowski's nowhere to be found. We've even staked out one of our staffers at his cabin doorstep, with orders to bring him into headquarters when and if he ever shows up. So far, no luck."

"This is ridiculous! He's got to show up soon," pitched in the pro-tem. "The election's only a week away and the press is getting very antsy. They're beginning to question if Hank Kaplowski really exists. Danged few capitol reporters have ever seen him."

"Well, let's hope he makes an appearance real fast," soothed Byron. "We still have an outside chance if we can properly expose him to the media. The polls show we've made up a lot of ground, but nowhere enough. To be honest, it doesn't look great; we don't have the cash to push him over the top."

"Or the candidate, it appears," sneered Burns. "What's your best guess; think we're going to lose?"

"Frankly, yes. That's what the pollsters are telling us. But they also say that with a little bit more money and some cooperation from the candidate, it's still possible. We've made great gains, but we started from too far back. Our ads have been excellent. Some of the best I've ever put together."

"Yeah!" laughed the pro-tem. "I like the one where the county auditor talks about how 'Hank carved the lard outa county budgets.' That corny stuff goes over like gangbusters."

"Too little, too late," dejectedly mumbled Burke.

"Okay, Byron, who do you think will win it?"

"McKlatchy." The consultant cocked his head and gave Burns a sidelong look, "How 'bout you and Willie Green? Won't the governor rain on both of you for deserting him like that?"

"Ah, who cares what Malcolm thinks," John Burns glumly answered. "He's history anyway. Doug Stewart will clean his clock, come November. We'll be lucky to hold the majority in either of the two houses."

"That bad?"

"Yep . . . that bad."

SPLIT TICKET

IN THE DIM GLOW OF THE setting sun, Jamie wearily swung down from the mare and tied the reins to the railpost in front of the barn. She loosened the cinch, hefted the saddle off, and hung it over the rail. Removing the bridle, she slipped a halter over the animal's head and led her inside to the stall, where she tied the lead rope securely. After lugging all the gear to the tack room and spreading the damp blanket over the saddle to dry, she grabbed a brush in one hand and a flake of alfalfa in the other.

When Jamie had fed the hay to the hungry animal and brushed her down, she rested her forehead against the horse's neck. "Well, ol' girl, we've made that trip over to the mine a time or two, haven't we?" As Jamie ran her hands over the smooth, shiny back, two tears trickled down her face. "Where is he, gal? He's been gone for weeks."

Jamie realized her terrible mistake, forcing Hank into politics. In her misdirected enthusiasm, she had driven a wedge between them, resulting in strained relations every time they were together. She could actually see the anxiety, the uneasiness manifested in his every move. No longer were they good pals, laughing and joking, enjoying each other's company. He hadn't called her "Bright Eyes" in quite awhile.

It had been a long time—months—since they had danced the night away at the Tex-Okie Bar and Bowling. Angrily biting her lower lip, the red-headed firebrand cursed and cried out loud, "It's all my fault."

In frustration, she threw the brush hard against the barn wall, startling the horse, inducing the wide-eyed mare to rear back and pull against the halter rope. "Whoa, gal, didn't mean to get you in an uproar. One of us is enough."

Sighing deeply, she faced the fact that she was hopelessly, desperately in love with Hank Kaplowski. For the first time in her life, she was mooning about like a lovesick, teary-eyed school girl. *And him, does he care one whit? By now, he probably hates my guts. Jamie Hagerty, you got it bad . . . really bad!*

★ ★ ★

THE GNAWING AT DOUG'S insides wouldn't go away. He should be feeling fairly comfortable about the way things were going, but that constant hint of uneasiness was evident. His Republican primary election was a slam dunk. In the Democrat's primary, Hank Kaplowski wasn't making an appreciable impact with the voters, and in a matter of days, it would all be over. He'd be relatively free from the deception and the fear of being found out.

Gubernatorial candidate Kaplowski would be forgotten; Supervisor Kaplowski would resign from his supervisorial seat and quietly disappear into oblivion. He would sell the Lucky Adele property and Hank would be nothing more than a fond memory to some and a pain in the rump to others. *Why doesn't this ideal scenario bring me more satisfaction?*

Try as he might, Doug could not put a stop to the pleasant pictures flashing past his mind's eye—line dancing at the Tex-Okie Bar, the hilariously successful struggle to oust Boonie Bates, and many memories of enjoyable times in Durango County. All had one thing in common . . . that volatile, female package of fiery-haired trouble . . . one Jamie Hagerty.

He sensed a burning in his chest as he thought about her. *She does have a beautiful smile, and those green eyes absolutely brighten up the day. And now that I think about it, she's lost a lot of weight since I first met her; she sure curves in all the right places.*

Doug was grinning as he basked in a warm glow. Then suddenly, gloom enveloped him. Upon Hank's demise and Doug's election, Jamie would become nothing more than a heart-tugging remembrance.

The chances seemed quite real that he would become the next governor of California. Even if he were to lose the election, he could no longer afford the luxury of a double life, could no longer risk being discovered. His business reputation would be ruined and he could well be the laughingstock of the nation. No, Jamie Hagerty had to be relegated to the bygone days of treasured memories . . . a friend he could never hope to see again.

How come that makes me feel so empty . . . so downright miserable?

TWENTY-SIX

★ ★ ★

DOUG CURIOUSLY WATCHED the TV screen as the sharply dressed reporter was interviewing one of the many supporters crowding the spacious ballroom floor of the Beverly Hilton Hotel. It was election night, and the polling places were just about to close. Doug asked, "Brad, who are all those people?"

The Republican minority leader laughed. "Well, Mr. Nominee, most of them are groupies, drinking your free booze and rubbing elbows with the political stars they expect to see here tonight."

"Volunteers who worked in the campaign, huh?"

"Nah, only a few of them." Brad Clark looked at his watch. "The real workers are still out there in the precincts, almost finished with the job of turning out the last of the Republicans, the ones committed to vote for you. Those downstairs are mostly popinjays, flitting around the edges, wanting to be seen with the 'who's who' of California politics."

Harry Kaloogian, phone in one hand, notebook in the other, called out excitedly from the far side of the hotel suite. "Hey guys, the absentee ballots are being counted and it looks like we're blowing 'em away!" The Stewart campaign eagerly awaited the registrar of voters' early tally of those who voted by mail; the figures released right after the polls closed. Although Doug's opposition had put forth a feeble attempt to capture that vote, Saracino had already made sure that base was well-covered.

"What's the tally?" someone asked.

232

"Better than ten-to-one," yelled Kaloogian.

"Everybody! Listen to this!" Brad Clark turned up the volume so everyone could hear above the racket in the crowded suite. CBS's gray-haired pundit was ready to name the projected winners in some of the races. "Our exit polls from up and down the state conclude that Douglas Stewart has easily won the Republican nomination for governor. On the Democrat side . . . "

Brad Clark turned down the volume and let out an uproarious shout, obscuring the TV screen. "Doug, you did it!"

Everybody crowded around the candidate, expressing their joyful salutations; all three of his children were alongside, beaming with pride. Close friends and associates were excitedly shaking his hand, hugging him and toasting his good fortune. Doug cast a sideways glance at the TV, trying to see how his "other half" was faring. To no avail; more well-wishers came pouring into the room and Doug became engulfed, trapped in the euphoria of victory.

Champagne corks were popping everywhere. Although there were gallons of it, Doug hadn't touched a drop. For him, the waiting was just half-over. He was waiting for the other victory he had to see take place, the victory embodied in a defeat—a loss that had to occur. From what he could tell, the Democrats' absentee ballot results were looking okay. McKlatchy had a clear lead, Rodriguez was second, and Knox was running third. Kaplowski had yet to be mentioned. So far, so good.

Carlos worked his way through the crowd. "Time to go down to the main ballroom, Doug, for your acceptance speech."

Doug rummaged through his pockets, looking for his notes, a few thoughts scribbled on three-by-five cards. Statewide television coverage awaited him downstairs while he tried to remain calm, still searching. He breathed a deep sigh of relief when he found them buried deep in his inner coat pocket. *No long-winded dissertations, Stewart,* he vowed to himself. *Keep it short, sweet, and political. Thank those who helped, promise a tough, aggressive campaign for the fall election, then shut up.*

The hallway was packed with more well-wishers; Doug and his

family literally had to elbow their way through the crowd to the elevator. Downstairs, it was twice as bad. Some of the Stewart supporters had been hitting the free champagne pretty heavily and swarmed around him as soon as they arrived at the mezzanine level. In their eagerness to congratulate their nominee, they completely impeded progress. "Give it to 'em, Doug!"

Another shouted, "Atta boy, Stewart! McKlatchy or that guy Kaplowski don't have a chance against you!" It took both diplomacy and muscle for Doug's sons-in-law to clear the way to the ballroom floor. Even though pandemonium broke out when he was spotted entering the room, his mind wasn't entirely focused on the present joyous festivities. A ball the size of a grapefruit was growing in his stomach. *What did that guy mean, "Kaplowski hasn't a chance?"*

Doug mumbled his way through the acceptance speech and during the interviews that followed with ABC and CNN, the grapefruit grew to the size of a basketball when one of the newsmen asked, "Assemblyman Stewart, you've been campaigning aggressively against Governor McKlatchy, assuming he'd be the Democrat's nominee. But now there seems to be an outside chance that the dark-horse candidate, Hank Kaplowski, might pull the upset of the century. Have you made any contingency plans, a special strategy perhaps, if he is their man?"

"Uh, er, no . . . uh yes. I've thought about it, but uh . . . just a little. Actually, no, not much at all. I didn't think I had, uh . . . I didn't think he had much of a chance." Doug felt red in the face. Frustration was rising uncontrollably in his chest. All his plans would go up in smoke if Hank was the nominee. He would be trapped, cornered like a blind gopher on a sunny day. His throat was dry, like he had swallowed the Mojave sand dunes. He managed to ask, "Are you guys predicting that Ka-Kaplowski could po-possibly win?"

The reporter grinned decisively, vicariously enjoying Doug's flustered stuttering at the mere mention of Kaplowski's name. Stewart had been unflappable during the entire primary campaign.

His cool, analytical dissection of McKlatchy's administration had been duly observed and admired by the media. The scuttlebutt was that he had ice in his veins. However, his present weird behavior, this hesitant stammering, were such unexpected departures from Stewart's usual smooth demeanor that the sharks couldn't help but smell blood . . . and they pounced.

"Assemblyman Stewart, you seem to be inordinately disturbed over the possibility of facing Kaplowski in the general election. Does his conservative manner of electioneering create a particular problem for you?"

Angry with himself and his own stupidity, Doug impulsively reacted. "Let me tell you, that dumb Pole won't be around long if I have anything to say about it."

Seizing the moment, taking full advantage of Doug's ill temper, the ABC commentator fired back, "Why, Mr. Stewart, that sounds like a racist threat. Are you afraid of Kaplowski?"

Suddenly realizing his thoughtless blunder, Doug forced a smile. "No, of course not. I'm sure he'll be a worthy opponent. I wish him well." Then waving back at a cadre of supporters, he turned to the reporters and said, "Will you please excuse me now? I have a lot of people I need to thank." Without further comment, Doug quickly mixed with his waiting fans.

"The normally reserved Douglas Stewart showed obvious irritation over the possible nomination of . . ." The broadcaster's well-modulated tones faded as Doug hurriedly worked his way through the noisy crowd, shaking hands and smiling broadly, until he reached the back exit behind the stage area. Quickly slipping through the door, he ran up several flights of stairs two steps at a time, reaching the third floor. He entered the hallway at a dead run and rushed to the nearest elevator where, out of breath, he impatiently paced.

Fortunately, only two people were on the elevator—an amorous young couple more interested in smooching than taking note of the harried gubernatorial candidate. In their passion, the lovers leaned against all the floor buttons, stopping the lift at every level. It seemed to take forever to get to the penthouse suite. When they finally made it to the top, Doug raced down the maze of hall-ways to his suite.

He was relieved to see the rooms were empty, that everybody was still downstairs celebrating. Half-filled glasses of pop, platters of cheese and crackers, and empty plastic champagne glasses crowded every surface. The three television sets were still on, blaring away. NBC was covering the latest Democrat results, showing McKlatchy still leading, but by a narrower margin over the other hopefuls. Occupying the commentators was the sudden appearance of Kaplowski as a major contender. The ABC affiliate in Sacramento had sent a camera crew to the Kaplowski campaign headquarters in Diamond Springs, where a young correspondent was interviewing Jamie Hagerty with Byron Burke at her side.

The pretty interviewer was bubbling over with excitement. "I can see you are all thrilled at the way this election is going," gushed the neophyte announcer. "Who would have thought you guys could be in such a tight race with Governor McKlatchy. Tell me, do you think you have a chance of winning?"

"Yes, we are thrilled," exclaimed a worried-looking Jamie. "Hank is a great man and will make a fabulous governor. Right now, we're still behind, but the last ballots to be counted will be the Cow Counties. We're sure that by midnight, Hank will be out ahead and by morning, victorious."

The youthful commentator clearly noticed Jamie's optimistic words didn't match her anxious expression. "You look concerned, not too happy about how things are going. Is there something you can share with us?"

Jamie compulsively blurted out, "Well, there *is* something bothering us. We haven't seen or heard from Hank in better than two weeks. I'm afraid something might have happened to him." Suddenly, she was angry, "You know, there are a lot of people who don't like what Hank stands for."

"Who?" asked the startled interviewer.

"Who!" exclaimed the irritated redhead. "Didn't you hear that mean, low-down threat from that no-good Republican, Stewart? I get worried sick over people like him! That slick urban dude has a reputation of being the dirtiest campaigner in the state. I'd put nothing past him!"

The wide-eyed reporter appeared incredulous. "Are you saying that Kaplowski has been missing for two weeks and you're somehow afraid of Doug Stewart?"

Byron Burke immediately jumped into the conversation, casting a cool influence over Jamie's heated words. Smoothly, he purred. "No, no, no. We're certainly not afraid of anybody; nor are we worried. I've been in constant contact with our candidate. I'm sure he will be arriving here at headquarters later this evening and we're not the least bit intimidated by Doug Stewart's intemperate remarks. We'll fix his political wagon come November."

The interview ended as the latest numbers from Los Angeles County appeared on the screen. Doug couldn't believe his ears. The news anchor team was explaining that Kaplowski had narrowed the lead, having picked up surprising strength among southern California's organized labor. "The Teamsters and the powerful United Auto Workers have jointly announced their endorsements of Kaplowski, thanks to the efforts of the senate pro-tem and the assembly Speaker."

Doug was in a daze as the numbers for the other offices were being analyzed. He held his head in both hands, agonizing, rocking back and forth. "What if I win? Good Lord, I *can't* be the nominee of both parties!"

Just then a TV commentator came on the screen with a news update. "CBS has just learned that Hank Kaplowski hasn't been seen for several weeks and according to an undisclosed source, there is some concern over his safety. We will keep you updated on any late developments as we try to confirm the possible disappearance of Mr. Kaplowski."

"Great! . . . that's just great!" he groaned outloud. "Now, I'm a missing person. If anybody starts rummaging around in my cabin looking for me, I'm a dead duck!"

"Who's a dead duck?" Doug whipped around and saw his son standing behind him with a bewildered look on his face. "What's the matter, Dad? You look positively sick."

"I am, Wally. I think I better get out of here."

Wally couldn't help but notice the green pallor on his father's face. "Good idea, Pop. Want me to drive you home?"

"No thanks, Son. I have my car in the parking garage. I think I can make it alone, but do me a favor; stay here and represent me. Tell anyone who asks that I had some key people waiting to see me, and if they ask who or where, tell them you don't know. Okay?"

"Sure, Pop," answered his concerned son. Doug gave him a bear hug and left the room. Walking swiftly to the service elevator, he descended to the underground garage unnoticed. In a mood bordering on panic, he slipped behind the wheel of his Mercedes and headed directly for the Burbank airport, where his 210 Centurion was, as previously ordered, fueled and waiting. The night was clear; no need to file a flight plan. As he taxied to the active runway, Doug mused, "Firewalling it, I could make it to Mexico in less than two hours."

★　★　★

JAMIE'S FEARS MOUNTED AS the night wore on; it was close to midnight, and no Hank Kaplowski. The media had now turned the "no show" candidate into a state and national incident, suggesting all sorts of weird scenarios as to the cause of Hank's disappearance. Foul play was receiving the most credibility. One rumor had him abducted by Mexican militants, while a crank phoned in a message that he was being held hostage by a group calling themselves the Lesbian Task Force.

Late-night talk-show hosts were having a field day. Renaldo Gueverra, the nation's most popular gab-show emcee, quickly found three lawyers and two political consultants to "analyze" the disappearance. The consensus was two for dead, one for drunk, and two who refused conjecture.

Even Byron Burke was losing his cool, having several times snapped at the probing media when they repeatedly asked about the whereabouts of his candidate. Byron had never met a politico who had shunned the limelight like this—especially on election night.

Late as it was, more and more media crowded into the small headquarters. The Kaplowski campaign was big news, especially since the national networks had noticed the unique phenomenon taking place in quirky California. A country boy county supervisor was moving closer and closer to defeating a powerful incumbent Democrat. "Who is this guy, and how did he do it without campaigning? Impossible!"

Many of the well-known political pundits were saying it couldn't be done, but the numbers were proving to the contrary. By one in the morning, Kaplowski's vote count had moved ahead of all the lesser candidates and was pulling even with Governor McKlatchy. By two o'clock, he inched into the lead. Wild pandemonium broke out in the small town of Diamond Springs. Their boy Hank was winning the Democratic nomination . . . big-time!

It seemed that much of California had been swept up, energized, and tuned in to the excitement of a back-country miner beating out California's bare-it-all governor. They liked Hank's humble demeanor and his message of strong family values, cutting taxes, and jailing criminals. Millions of citizens were still awake, glued to their TV sets, fascinated by the neck-and-neck contest unfolding before their sleepy eyes. The mystery of Kaplowski's apparent disappearance added enough drama to outdo any soap opera!

Not everyone was enthralled by it all. Jamie was exhausted, emotionally spent. Bone-tired, she went into her small office and closed the door, knowing Hank wasn't going to show up. In fact, she no longer cared if he was even nominated and was secretly hoping he would lose. Maybe then, they could recapture the normal lives they'd led before all this election mess. Maybe Hank would like her again, hold her close when they danced, have breakfast at Mae's Country Kitchen. And maybe someday, he could forgive her . . . *but not if he wins the nomination. You cooked your own goose, Hagerty. Your big mouth has lost you the sweetest man you've ever known.* She cradled her tired head down in her folded arms on the desk and quietly cried herself to sleep.

By 3:15 A.M. it was about all over. Hank Kaplowski led by a wide enough margin that a disgruntled Governor McKlatchy conceded defeat. Rodriguez and Knox had given up hours ago, as had all but a few members of the media, their hope of ever seeing Kaplowski having dwindled.

At the first glimmer of daylight, one of the few remaining newsmen looked at his watch and announced to his CNN cohort that it was long past time to leave. As they wearily dragged their equipment toward the door, a slightly familiar looking Western-clad stranger came sauntering in. "Where's the party?" he asked.

"Kaplowski!" bellowed the correspondent. "Where the hell have you been?" Quickly turning to his groggy colleague, he shouted, "Charlie! Set up the camera and wake up the boys in the remote truck. We've got a live feed to the East!"

Jamie jerked awake at all of the commotion and dazedly staggered into the room. "Hank!" Without another thought, she rushed to him head-on and threw herself into his arms, kissing him flush on the lips, knocking his Stetson to the floor. Unmindful of the CNN reporter or that her passionate embrace had been broadcast nationwide, Jamie stood back and asked what everyone else wanted to know. "Where on earth have you been!"

Reaching down to retrieve his hat, Hank nonchalantly responded, "Oh, I've been lookin' over some mining property in north-central Nevada. I'd have been here sooner, but my Bronco broke down. Had to thumb a ride into Elko to catch the bus from there. Sorry to be so late. By the way, how'd we do?"

The CNN commentator burst out laughing. "How'd you do! Why man, you won the Democratic primary!"

Other reporters who'd been having breakfast down the street were filing in. Soon a small crowd had formed around Hank. Flashbulbs were popping and normally laid-back newshounds were excitedly asking questions.

"Mr. Kaplowski, are you serious? You really didn't know you had won?"

Doug played the rustic miner to perfection. "Nope, 'fraid there wasn't a radio on the bus, and Nevada folks don't care much for California politics. Anyway, all they have on their radio stations are Randy Travis and Reba."

Doug's eyes scanned the sparse group and stopped on a familiar face. *Uh-oh . . . trouble!* One of the reporters he knew from the Sacramento scene was present. The guy from the Capitol Press Corps kept eyeing him suspiciously and eventually asked, "Kaplowski, don't I know you from somewhere else?"

Doug ducked the question and warmly smiled, inquiring in response. "You look familiar to me too. Didja happen to cover this year's National Gold Miner's Convention? I never miss it. Last one was in Elko, Nevada. Sure was a doozie; 'bout half of the guys got a little snockered."

"No, I didn't cover that," answered the sleepy reporter.

"How about the Bishop Gold Digger's Ball? It's held every year in conjunction with their Mule Days Parade. Big event; anybody who's somebody is there. Could we have met in Bishop?"

"Hardly," responded the bored writer.

"Do any time in 'Nam? I was there with the marines."

"No, I was in Berkeley, attending the university."

Hank raised one eyebrow and lowered his voice menacingly, "You weren't one of them hippie demonstrators, were ya?"

The reporter didn't answer, but he lowered his eyes and looked away as Hank continued to glower at him. Doug Stewart would never do anything so brash as to stare down a reporter.

Hank good-naturedly answered a few more questions before holding up his hand, "Mind if I talk to ya'll later today? I'm goin' to go home and get some sleep, then I gotta figure out how to get my

Bronco outa Nevada." He ignored the rapid-fire questions coming his way by calling out to Jamie. "Gal, can you give me a ride home?"

"Sure, Hank, be glad to." Pushing their way through the crowd that had gathered, both walked slowly past the well-wishers outside to her Ford pickup. As the engine roared into action, the sun had just crept over the eastern mountains. A thin strip of gray clouds hugged the horizon, edged in brilliant red.

Doug closed his eyes; he was dead tired, although his mind was racing over the events of the past twenty-four hours. He had headed the plane for Mexico but by the time he'd neared the border, he had devised a plan of action—a risky one, but with any luck, it would work. Aware that Hank had won the nomination, it entailed getting back to Durango County. His scheme could be dangerous, but worthy of the attempt.

Banking the plane 180 degrees, Doug had flown north, circling above his airstrip at the Lucky Adele until there was barely enough light to land. He rapidly changed into some of Hank's rumpled clothes and dusty cowboy boots, then drove his Bronco into town where he parked it behind Grump's Seed and Feed.

Doug walked down the street to the campaign headquarters where he'd counted on a few newspaper reporters still being on hand, but he'd hoped for no TV cameras. Jamie had been an unexpected help, smearing his unshaven face with lipstick, improving immeasurably the disguise. With the Stetson cocked on the back of his balding head, the dirty jeans and boots, red kerchief around his neck, and lipstick camouflaging part of his face, Doug was close to positive that no one would believe that he and Hank were the same man.

So far, so good.

Jamie didn't speak for the first few miles. She kept her eyes straight ahead, not wanting to look at him. Finally, she said, barely above a whisper, "I'm sorry, Hank. I'm truly sorry you won."

Doug was surprised. "What are you talking about, Jamie? I thought winning was all-important to you."

"I thought it was . . . until I discovered it would cost me the most important thing in my life."

"You're one confusing lady," he said. "Just what is now so important?"

"You."

Doug was at a loss for words. In the morning light, he could see the wet streaks on her face and more tears about to spill from her eyes. He was keenly disturbed by her presence, torn between wanting to cuss her out for the predicament she had gotten them into and the overpowering desire to hold and comfort her. He let out a sigh of relief when, at last, they pulled up to the cabin. Immediately, he jumped out and closed the door, mumbling a perfunctory good-bye.

Jamie rolled down her window and softly called to him. "Hank, would you come around here, please?"

He circled the pickup to the open window and leaned his elbows on the sill. "I honestly don't know what to say, Jamie."

"Hank, can you ever forgive me for the mess I got you into? I'd go to jail tomorrow if I thought it would make it any better and you could care about me again."

He reached through the window and gently cupped her face in his hands. Leaning down, he kissed her tear-stained cheeks. Tenderly, he kissed her several times, then firmly on her soft, willing mouth.

"Good-bye, 'Bright Eyes.'"

Without another word, he strode off toward the cabin, not once looking back.

TWENTY-SEVEN

★ ★ ★

DOUG HAD TO BE very thorough. Wearing rubber gloves, he wiped clean all of the utensils and dishes in the cupboard. The wood stove, the old linoleum tabletop, the lightbulbs in the sockets, the windows, door frames, any smooth surface that could hold a fingerprint—all had to be free of any sign.

On hands and knees, he looked behind the dresser and on the floor of the closet for any loose scraps of paper that could tie the place to Doug Stewart. He even rummaged around in the burn barrel, making sure every item had been completely destroyed. It took most of the day to painstakingly go over everything, getting rid of evidence that could implicate him or reveal his true identity.

Doug went so far as to inspect every inch of the tool shed, the hangar, and the outhouse. Everything but the mine shaft, which would soon be in rubble, was given a meticulous going over.

All items that might be traced to Stewart or raise an eyebrow of suspicion were loaded into the Centurion—ashtrays, wearing apparel, bric-a-brac, and tools. Most of his work clothes and Western attire, he left hanging in the closet . . . but not until he'd gone through each pocket and wiped off the big brass buckle on his tooled belt. Nothing was left to chance.

Now for the note. Doug took a grease pencil and a large hunk of cardboard to print the message:

Howdy. Do not enter the mine. I am blasting out a pocket way
down deep. Could be dangerous! Be up soon.

—Hank

With great care, Doug arranged the cabin to look as though he
were still nearby. He left dirty breakfast dishes soaking in the sink, a
mug of half-consumed coffee, clothing strewn about, a fire burning
in the cookstove, and the cabin door ajar.

Donning coveralls, he went to the tool shed and picked up one
of the boxes of dynamite and carried it into the mine. It took him
several hours to set the charges, carefully placing the sticks where
they would do the most damage. At the moment, Doug was grateful for his familiarity with explosives, acquired while serving as a
demolition technician in Vietnam.

Doug wanted to collapse the mine in such a fashion that excavation would be next to impossible. The Lucky Adele underground
was a honeycomb of passageways, a myriad of small tunnels at
multiple levels. He needed to make it a massive cave-in, one shaft
collapsing on another. The rescuers had to feel that looking for his
body would be a hopeless task.

After double-checking his work, Doug set the timing device for
the explosion to occur in one hour, then worked his way to the surface. Nailing the cardboard warning sign on a post next to the tunnel's entrance, he patiently waited by the aircraft. Catching him
off-guard, the explosion was much louder than he anticipated.

From the mouth of the Lucky Adele came a rush of dust and
smoke billowing skyward, bringing to mind a long-buried giant, violently coughing forth grit and debris. The ground shook noticeably
as the underground tunnels collapsed, one passageway caving in on
another. The earth grumbled for more than a minute before sub-
siding.

Doug felt pleased with himself. *They'll never unearth that pile
of rock.*

* * *

MORTON MILLS FELT HIS horse move uneasily beneath him as they both heard the sound of the explosion, followed shortly by the powerful roar of an aircraft taking off under full power. Looking up, the Bureau of Land Management ranger saw the plane zoom overhead, then circle once and fly away. Curiously, he asked outloud, "Old hoss, what was that thunderin' noise all about and didya see that plane circling up there?"

Ranger Mills was a new pilot, having earned his wings just a few months earlier. Aircraft of all kinds fascinated him, especially those as powerful as the Cessna Centurion. He took out his notebook, jotted down the plane's N number, and put it back in his shirt pocket, soon forgetting about it. He had a lot of hard work to do, clearing the forest trails under his supervision before the influx of summer hikers.

* * *

TWO DAYS LATER, in his legislative office, Doug read the morning headlines:

KAPLOWSKI FEARED DEAD!
DEMOCRAT'S NOMINEE KILLED IN MINING ACCIDENT

The article described how Hank Kaplowski failed to show up at a scheduled press conference the day following his astonishing defeat of Governor McKlatchy. Several members of his campaign entourage went looking for him at his mountain home and discovered a disastrous explosion had taken place at his nearby Lucky Adele Mine. Evidently, the main shaft had collapsed and, based upon the warning message found at the scene, there was speculation that the new nominee could be buried under tons of rubble.

Ah, good job, Doug thought. Continuing, he read that mining engineers with heavy equipment were working day and night searching, but there was little optimism of finding Hank Kaplowski alive, according to Durango County Sheriff Norm Moore.

He was sure Hank's accidental death would cause some pain and remorse to a number of people, "Bulldog" Moore for one. Jamie would take it hard and, in truth, Doug was already feeling a loss. The thought of never seeing "Bright Eyes" again was far more painful than he had imagined. The sensation of her last touch lingered on his lips and he could still see her beautiful auburn hair in the early morning light, the tears glistening in her lovely green eyes.

The phone buzzed, ending his reverie. Lorraine said, "Mr. Stewart, Assemblyman Kaloogian is out here pacing about. He wants to know if you have a moment to see him?"

"By all means; send him in."

The ever-exuberant young man burst in, waving the headline story above his head. "Doug! Have you seen this? Man, if this doesn't shake up the Democrats' cookie jar!" Plopping himself down in a sumptuous leather chair and speaking rapid-fire, he said, "Got any coffee? Been a doozy of a morning. You know what the Dems have to do if Kapowski's bought the farm, don't you?"

"Kaplowski, not Kapowski; there's an 'l' in it."

"Well, it's all 'wowski' to me. If he's really dead, it'll throw the libs into a feeding frenzy."

"How so?"

"How so? Just a sec."

Kaloogian jumped up from the couch and opened the door to the executive secretary's office. "Lorraine, would you please get me a cup of coffee, cream and sugar? Thank you."

Without appearing to take a breath, Harry continued to fire away. "If what's-his-ski is dead, it'll be a very bad omen for the voters 'cause they'll be completely left out of the picture. Since there's no new election, the Democrat state central committee appointees will have to pick a successor. Their party's voters won't have a choice. The ultra-libs own that body—lock, stock, and hatchet."

Jubilantly, Kaloogian continued, "It will be a war! We'll have a lot of fun watching the feminists, gays, and environmental wackos choose the worst of three evils. I hear that after the blood fest, it will probably wind up being McKlatchy. If so, the November election could be a breeze, a cake walk for us, a stroll down Lover's Lane."

Harry lazily stretched his arms over the back of the couch, crossed his legs, and flashed a toothy smile. "Well, how do you like them sweet patooties, Governor?" As Doug was about to answer, Lorraine entered with a tray of coffee and donuts.

"Ah, sustenance!" The hungry assemblyman scooped up a gooey maple bar and stuffed half of it in his mouth while moving across the room to turn on the television. "Let's see if the ten o'clock break has anything new on digging out Kaplowski."

Sure enough, CBS's channel 13 had a remote crew at the mine site and was interviewing Durango County's sheriff. The TV commentator asked, "Sheriff Moore, do you hold out any hope of finding Hank Kaplowski alive?"

"I'm afraid not," replied the solemn officer. "We're about to give up the excavation. You see, the total collapse of the main tunnel and the subsequent cave-ins of the many old side-tunnel walls caused extensive damage. We don't even know which direction to dig. By now, if Hank was in there, he'd be out of air."

"What about that? Are you sure he's even in the mine?"

"All I can say is, the evidence points to that fact. Hank left a note saying he was goin' down into the mine to set off some charges. The cabin looked to be recently occupied. There are, of course, unanswered questions such as, where's his airplane? The hangar door was locked and the Cessna was gone . . . so was his Ford Bronco."

"Quite a mystery," stated the commentator. "Could they be under repair?"

"Could be," answered the sheriff. "Sooner or later, we'll find them both." "Bulldog" looked toward the camera. "If any of your viewers have information as to the whereabouts of a beat-up 1991 tan Ford Bronco, license plate MBU247, please call the sheriff's office in Durango County."

As CBS switched to the weather forecast, Kaloogian turned to his colleague. "Doug, think he's still alive?"

"Nope; he'll probably never be heard from again."

"I agree," quipped the gregarious assemblyman. "He's probably deader than McKlatchy's dream of being governor." Reaching for another donut, Harry headed for the door. "Gotta go. I'm late for the public health and welfare committee."

Doug watched his good friend bound out of his office. Harry never did anything without displaying a confrontational exuberance; he couldn't even walk at a normal pace. Doug leaned back in his chair, wishing there were more like him around the capitol.

He contemplated "Bulldog" Moore's remarks about the plane and the car; neither comment was too bothersome to Doug. Having kept the Centurion in the hangar at all times under lock and key, no one had actually seen it close-up—not even Jamie—so there'd be no tracing it. As for the Bronco, he'd paid for it in cash at a used car lot in Placerville, under Hank's name. Undoubtedly, it was still parked behind the feed store in Diamond Springs.

The missing car, along with the disappearance of the aircraft, might cause some concern if Hank were still alive. But time would resolve that problem, since Hank Kaplowski would never be seen again . . . alive or dead.

TWENTY-EIGHT

★ ★ ★

No way did she believe it, when Sheriff Moore told Jamie Hagerty the tragic news.

"Hank may be dead? Impossible!" But when the anguished look upon Norm's face told her the truth of the matter, Jamie quivered involuntarily and staggered backward; had he not grabbed for her, she would have collapsed on the floor. Supporting her around the waist, he helped her to the nearby sofa. She sat stock-still, trying to recover some composure. There were no tears, just a stunned silence as she struggled helplessly with the emotions welling up within her after hearing the shocking news.

Barely audible, she whispered, "Tell me what happened."

With great patience, Norm explained what he knew of the accident. Jamie thought for awhile before unsteadily rising to her feet. "Norm, there's got to be some chance he may still be alive."

He didn't need to answer; the pained expression on his face spoke volumes.

Jamie, though trembling, made it to the front door. "Take me out to the mine, Norm. I've got to see for myself."

Her teardrops were evident as he drove the rut-filled road approaching the mine. There were no wailing or uncontrolled fits of sobbing—just an occasional sniffle and dabbing at her wet eyes. Few words were spoken, a question here and there was followed by a terse response. Norm and Jamie were too deep in sorrow to discuss the heartrending matter in greater detail.

The Lucky Adele Mine was crawling with members of the media. As soon as the camera crew spotted the sheriff's vehicle, they rushed forward, filming as they came. As Norm Moore opened the car door, the reporters were already shouting out their questions, poking microphones in his face.

"Giving up, Sheriff?" asked the ABC-TV unit. "We've been told the rescue guys have decided that any further attempts to dig for Kaplowski would be futile, a waste of time. Can you comment?"

The question shocked Jamie, but she saw that the reporter's information was obviously true. The excavation equipment operators were packing up, getting ready to leave. In panic, she cried out, "Norm, what are they doing? Where in blazes are they going?"

He had to grasp her by the arm and hold tight. "It's no use, Jamie. The way things look, they have to dig for weeks to get even a part of the mine uncovered. There's no chance Hank's still alive. A lone tunnel collapsing is one thing . . . but the whole mine caving in is another." Moore let his words penetrate before he relaxed his grip. She didn't struggle or move at all. She just leaned against her old friend and quietly sobbed, tears of grief spilling down her face. "Please, Norm, tell me this is a nightmare; tell me I'm gonna wake up."

While he comforted her, the cameras were running, filming it all, panning close to capture Jamie's every mournful expression, every heartbreaking sob . . . her obvious agony made for hot copy.

★　★　★

IN ORDER TO EASE JAMIE'S anguish and at the same time settle a point of curiosity, Sheriff Moore asked the excavators to continue digging for a few more days. "See if you can find out why the blast was so destructive and the damage so extensive." The engineers speculated that there might have been hidden gasses or ignitable dust set off by the initial explosion.

Other theories bandied about were that Hank may have miscalculated the amount of dynamite needed; or, that it could have been nothing more than a chain reaction, compounded by the collapsing of one tunnel after another. It was anyone's guess as to what really happened . . . all raw conjecture at best. The only conclusion agreed upon was that Hank Kaplowski's bones were at the bottom of the rubble.

Guessing wasn't good enough for "Bulldog" Moore. He wanted to know for sure, hoping a deeper excavation might shed some light on the investigation. Another day or two of digging could reveal some pertinent facts.

The task was continually complicated by the host of press people getting in the way. Helicopters hovered overhead while reporters kept asking the same incessant questions. Television and radio stations were pleading for interviews and someone representing the Democrat leadership was calling the sheriff every hour, trying to ascertain if Kaplowski was really dead.

The working crew of hard-hats were under strict orders not to talk to the media; any and all information regarding the search for Kaplowski's body had to be channeled through Moore's office. Although the sheriff thought it would take more than a few days before he could give the press any pertinent information, surprisingly, it didn't take that long.

Buck Presley, the crew foreman, uncovered some startling evidence—new information that would thoroughly muddy the present conjecture. To avoid alerting the ever-present media, Buck hightailed it to the sheriff's office to relay the facts. A few reporters, suspecting something was up, followed and their curiosity was further heightened when Presley pulled into the county officials' parking lot. They crowded around him as he entered the building, posing questions, blocking his way. But looking straight ahead, the foreman said nothing as he continued to push his way forward. He didn't speak a word until he'd entered the sheriff's private office and closed the door.

"Whew, ain't they a pain in the keester!" Dropping into the chair beside Moore's desk, Buck squinted both eyes conspiratorially. "Sheriff, I shore got some interestin' news for you."

"Good, what's up?"

"We're pretty sure that more than one charge was set—multiple charges, maybe three or four. Maybe more."

"What? . . . Multiple charges?" Norm suddenly arched both eyebrows. "How do you figure that?"

"Well, Sheriff, as you ordered, we kept on diggin' and further down the main tunnel we found where another new blast occurred."

"So?" asked Moore, chewing on the rubber tip of a lead pencil.

"There's no chance a blast at that point coulda collapsed the rest of the mine. It did a good job of shutting down the main tunnel, but the deeper shafts . . . no way. It now looks like it took a whole slew of dynamite to create that much damage."

"What are you tryin' to tell me?"

"I'm sayin' it looks like someone . . . someone who knew what they were doing . . . was intentionally tryin' to blow up the whole thing."

Sheriff Moore rocked back in his chair and spat out a small bit of rubber eraser . . . genuinely mystified. The first thought to cross his mind was frightening in its implication. *Could Hank have committed suicide?* He was privy to the fact that Kaplowski was avidly against running for governor; Jamie had confided that he had second thoughts and was unhappy about it.

Moore was also aware that Hank had been skipping an inordinate number of the supervisor's meetings, and that he had made it clear that he had no intention of seeking another term. *Come to think of it, the last few times we saw each other, he wasn't his usual jovial self. Could gaining the gubernatorial nomination have driven him to do such a foolish thing, or . . . were there maybe other things bothering Hank that none of us knew about?*

Suicide was a distinct possibility. The disturbing report of multiple charges being planted inside the Lucky Adele certainly could lead a rational person to that conclusion.

The crew chief spoke up. "Looks like he did himself in, don't it?"

The sheriff spoke sharply to Presley. "I'd keep that under my hat, if I were you."

"Whatever you say, Sheriff." Presley removed his cap, scratched his head, and asked, "Want us to keep on diggin'? By next year we might find somethin'."

"That bad?"

"Yep, it appears Kaplowski knew explosives and where to best set the charges. He brought a big part of that mountain down on his head."

"Bulldog" Moore stood up and tossed the chewed pencil in an open drawer. "Okay, you can stop excavating. No need to do anything more. And remember, don't talk to anyone about this."

"Anything you say, Sheriff," gushed Presley. With an almost imperceptible smirk on his lips, he bid the sheriff good-bye and left.

For certain, Norm Moore didn't want Buck Presley's unconfirmed assumptions circulated among the press . . . for there were other possible alternatives that came to mind. Hank was too tough, too determined a man to kill himself. *Maybe Hank isn't buried under all that granite rock, after all. Could be he blew up the mine and flew off somewhere. At least, it would explain why the plane was missing; but it doesn't make sense that the aircraft wasn't registered. Danged confusing.*

Moore pulled a red handkerchief from his back pocket, removed his Stetson, and wiped his brow. "It's too complicated to figure out by myself," he said aloud. "Maybe Jamie has some ideas on the matter."

He picked up the phone and dialed the Hagerty ranch. No answer. *Probably working out in the barn or over at the lumbermill.* Norm sighed heavily, as though the weight of the world rested on his broad shoulders, never having coped with trouble of this mag- nitude. *I'll keep calling her on the cellular while I drive out there.*

As he left his office at a fast pace, he brushed by the reporters. "Sheriff, can we talk to you?" Norm just smiled and kept moving. "Sorry guys. Much to do, little time to do it." He climbed into his patrol car, turned on the ignition, and with relief, sped away. *There's just too many unanswered questions rattlin' around in my brain, and I need some answers before I talk to you yahoos.*

For instance, how did Hank's Bronco get from Elko, Nevada, to the parking lot behind the feed store where a patrol car came across it that morning? Then there was the missing plane and not a clue as to where, or why it was gone. The sheriff checked with the appro- priate state agency and finding there was no record of an aircraft registered to Hank Kaplowski, he had asked the Federal Aviation Authority to investigate further in other states.

So far, nothing had turned up. Of course, he looked into the State Bureau of Mines, attempting to find out where Hank's dig- gings were located in the Tehachapie Mountains. That, too, had drawn a blank. He had to see Jamie. She knew Hank better than anyone and might be able to tie some of the loose threads together.

No sooner had he turned onto Buck's Bar Road, than the dis- patcher called through on the two-way radio. Her voice squawked, "DS–1, DS–1, this is Dispatch. Call in, please. Over."

"Okay, Gracie, this here's DS–1. What do ya want? Over."

"Sheriff, there's somebody here in the office that says he's gotta see you. Says it's real important. Over."

"Who is it, Gracie?"

"Don't know his name, Sheriff, but he appears to be a Bureau of Land Management ranger."

★ ★ ★

"Look at this, Norm. Have you read this?" Jamie was in a snit as she waved the newspaper under his nose. "Hank was no suicide victim; he was too macho to do anything that dumb." Jamie paced nervously about the sheriff's office, incensed over the news reports that Hank had possibly killed himself. Angrily, she cried out, "How could the press print such lies?"

Norm Moore knew how. One Buck Presley had too big a mouth, a boca grande, big flapping lips that right now Norm wanted to smash with his fist.

Pointing to the news story, the feisty green-eyed beauty read:

> A reliable source reported that multiple blasts occurred deep underground and simultaneously near the surface, eliminating the chance that the cave-in was accidental. Kaplowski, being a miner, was very familiar with explosives, ruling out the accidental-death theory. Our reliable source concluded that the incident had to be classified as a suicide.

Jamie crumpled the paper and tossed it toward the wastebasket. "Blasted lies! How dare they sully the memory of such a great guy!" Jamie Hagerty was on a self-imposed guilt trip, feeling personally responsible for Hank's death. All of this could have been avoided, had she left well enough alone. She was facing the fact that her political meddling had been the sole cause of much anguish. Hank was probably tired and wasn't thinking clearly when he entered the mine, probably under too much pressure to think straight. Brimming with tears again, she bawled, "Oh, Norm, it's all my fault!"

"Maybe not, Jamie." Feeling a deep sorrow for his good friend, he couldn't help saying, "There's things you don't know, Jamie— things I'm just now finding out. Hank's death might not have been accidental at all." The worried look on Norm's face added emphasis to his words. "Nope, no accident at all."

Wiping her eyes with her shirt-sleeve, she asked, "What do you mean, might not have been an accident?"

"I mean Hank wasn't the only person at the mine that morning. Somebody else was there."

Norm wondered if he had said too much but Jamie was his life-long friend, very close to Kaplowski, and if anyone had a right to know, she did. Besides, he needed her counsel. The only crimes he had handled to date were chasing small-time marijuana growers out of the surrounding mountains and arresting belligerent drunken drivers. Conducting complicated investigations was beyond the purview of his department and the latest information coming to light made him very nervous and super-cautious.

"Jamie, no one but me knows what I've got so far. If I tell you, you've got to keep it to yourself. A major crime may have been committed and it's now a matter for the law to handle. Your silence is very important."

Jamie nodded, a look of bewilderment on her face.

Norm walked over to the door to his office and made sure no one was lingering about, perhaps listening from the other side. Yesterday, he'd caught a reporter leaning up against his door, ear to the wood. With his voice barely above a whisper, he confided, "Just a few minutes before you came in, I received a report on the identity of the airplane which was spotted leaving Hank's landing strip shortly after the explosion!"

"A plane? Right after the explosion?"

"That's right. A Cessna Centurion took off within minutes of the mine goin' sky high." Gulping, he added, "You'll never guess who was in that powerful aircraft." Before she could ask, Norm nervously blurted out, "It was Douglas Stewart, the Republican nominee for governor."

Jamie staggered back, "You must be joking!"

"No, I'm not . . . look at this." With that, he handed Jamie the communication from the State Department of Transportation, which verified that the ownership of the plane was listed as Stewart and Associates and that its primary pilot was the CEO of the company, Doug Stewart.

Red-faced, Jamie asked, "What was that evil rat doing at Hank's diggin's?"

"Good question. And why didn't he report the explosion? He was there at the time."

Jamie's jaw dropped, "Do you think that he . . . "

"I don't know. All I can say is that, on the surface, it's extremely suspicious, and very bad news for Mister Stew . . . "

The phone rang, interrupting the conjectures. Norm grabbed it quickly and asked curtly, "What do ya want? Oh! Okay, bring it right in." The door opened and a middle-aged uniformed woman hustled into the inner office and handed several faxes to her boss. "Thanks, Gracie." Norm rapidly scanned the printed material, "Ah, hah! What do we have here?"

Handing a fax to Jamie, he pointed excitedly to a paragraph in the middle of the page. "Jamie, get a load of this!"

"What is it?"

"It's background information on Douglas Stewart. Go ahead, read it."

"What part?"

"The fifth paragraph down."

"Uh, the part about his marine service in Vietnam?"

"Yeah, read it carefully."

"Okay. It says Lieutenant D. Stewart, USMC Demolitions Expert . . ." Jamie gasped, dropping the fax from her shaking hands. "You don't think . . . "

"It certainly has entered my mind. The illustrious Republican gubernatorial aspirant knows how to blow things up."

"Do you suppose he . . . ?"

"Don't know yet, but the number-one Republican in the state may well be guilty of murder."

★ ★ ★

KALOOGIAN SWIVELED IN his chair next to Doug's on the noisy assembly floor. "Hey, seatmate, have you heard the latest Polish joke about Hank Kaplowski going Ka-boom-ski?"

"Not very funny, Harry."

"Yeah, I guess you're right—I shouldn't make fun of deceased Democrats, even if they're all brain-dead to start with." Harry grinned, "Sure is weird what's goin' on over on their side of the aisle. Their candidate six feet un . . . no, six *hundred* feet under and, as rumor has it, done in by his own hand."

Kaloogian leaned back in his posh leather chair, looked up to the assembly chamber's ornate ceiling, and philosophically proclaimed, "Now that I meditate upon it, if I were the Democrat's gubernatorial nominee and had to face the awesome Stewart political juggernaut, I'd kill myself too. Do you concur, good buddy?"

Doug sat stone-faced in his chair. Nothing was funny to him. *Maybe when I get out of prison, I'll see some humor in it.* He reached for the file folder on his desk, removing one of the phone messages his secretary had given him. It was from the sheriff of Durango County, requesting that Doug meet with him, along with a deputy from the State Department of Justice.

TWENTY-NINE

★ ★ ★

STANDING SILHOUETTED in his office doorway with one hand on the door frame and the other on her hip was the slimmed-down high-school girl he had dated twenty-five years earlier. For the first time, Norm Moore noticed the dramatic change that had taken place in Jamie's form and manner. Over the past twelve months, she had become much more feminine in her appearance, trimming down perceptively . . . but in manner? She seemed to be tougher than ever, especially since Hank had died.

Jamie exuded all the earmarks of being on a mission, righting the grievous wrong that had been done to Hank Kaplowski. The volatile redhead had convinced herself that Hank was too smart to have accidentally blown himself to smithereens. She insisted that she knew he was too religious and too stubborn to have killed himself. Also, she said she was absolutely positive that Hank was far too courageous to have run away. The only explanation, in Jamie's mind, was that he had been murdered in cold blood.

And . . . there was no question who did it. Douglas Stewart, who else? He had the motive; he had even threatened to get rid of Hank on national television. Obviously, he had the opportunity and the knowledge necessary to blow up the mine. Jamie had already expressed her opinion—that Stewart also possessed a dirty political reputation, making him just the man to execute such a heinous act. The only question remaining for the excitable redhead was how soon would it be before he, Sheriff "Bulldog" Moore, her old friend, would get up the nerve to arrest the Machiavellian fiend. She said she couldn't understand why Norm was taking so much time.

"Well, Sheriff, what have you found out since the last time we talked?" Jamie's voice was sharp and combative, addressing him as "Sheriff," rather than "Norm." The social slight didn't escape his attention.

He had found out a lot, but had no intention of telling his hot-tempered pal a thing. Having made a grievous mistake sharing with her in the first place, he didn't intend to repeat the error. It was all too clear that Jamie's affection for Hank, her rabid animosity toward Republicans in general and Stewart in particular, had clouded her thinking.

If it were up to Jamie, Stewart would within the hour be breathing poison gas at San Quentin Prison or hanging by the neck from the highest point in the capitol rotunda. Norm Moore thought, *Hell might have no wrath like a woman scorned, but hell had not met the likes of Jamie Hagerty when she happens to be on the prod.* Vengeance was the Lord's prerogative; however, Jamie Hagerty was bucking hard to be His earthly agent.

Sheriff Moore thought it best to play dumb and tell her as little as possible, yet giving her no information at all would be another mistake. "Not much, Jamie—little to report, except I did receive a personal phone call from Doug Stewart."

Jamie's mouth dropped open. "He phoned you? How did that come about?"

"I called his office to set up an appointment to see him—accompanied, of course, by a deputy attorney from the Justice Department. Naturally, we wanted to ask him about what he was doing on Hank's property the day of the explosion. To my surprise, Stewart called me back right away. He had a rotten cold, could barely speak above a whisper. Anyway, he asked me what I wanted, so I told him."

"You what?" Jamie's eyes were flashing danger signals. "You asked that over the phone and not in front of witnesses? Norm, have you lost your senses? It's just your word against his! He probably lied like the viper he is."

The sheriff felt the blood rise in his face. He wasn't used to being called stupid. Friend or no friend, this insulting firebrand better show more respect. Slamming his fist down on his desk, he bellowed, "Listen here, Hagerty, you're stickin' your big nose into police business! You've got Doug Stewart convicted and hung without all the evidence being gathered. You're forgettin' that in America, a person's innocent until proven guilty. I asked Stewart if he was at the Kaplowski mine; you want to know what he said . . . well, do you?"

Without waiting for her to repeat her tirade, he continued. "Of course, you do. Stewart said that he was there—admitted it right off. He said he wanted to talk face-to-face with his opponent and get some rules set down between the two of them. He claims he told Hank that he admired his old-fashioned style of conducting a campaign and hoped they both could stick to the issues and avoid dirty campaigning. He said they had a cup of coffee together, agreed to keep it clean, and shook hands. Stewart then got in his plane and took off. Jamie, it sounded like a rational excuse to me."

"How about the explosion? Did he tell you why he didn't report that?"

"He said he heard no explosion, that it must have happened after he flew away."

"That contradicts the BLM ranger, doesn't it?"

"Yes . . . but the BLM guy could be wrong about the timing and the sequence of events."

"Do you honestly believe that?" she sneered. "If so, I own a bridge between Oakland and San Francisco I'd like to sell you."

"Don't get smart with me, Hagerty. You want me to arrest, handcuff, and throw behind bars the most influential Republican in the state? Based on what—your woman's intuition?"

Shaking his finger vigorously, he went on, "Just because your bowels are in turmoil, there's no need for mine to be. I don't have a solid motive, substantial evidence, or a *corpus delicti*—or any body, for that matter. But, just to make sure that we've covered all our bases, I have a bevy of forensic experts from the Department of Justice combing the cabin, the mine . . . even the outhouse. If there's any additional evidence found, I just might consider letting you know. But for now, keep your big female mouth shut; the press should never get wind of this."

He started to sort through the papers on his desk, then caustically requested, "Do me a favor, Jamie—get your pretty behind out of my office; I've got work to do." With his hand, he motioned her out the door.

Jamie stormed from the office with several of Norm's sexist remarks burning a hole in her pride. *Women's intuition, big female mouth, pretty behind . . . I'll show that blind, chauvinist macho-mouth a thing or two!*

★ ★ ★

SOME DAMAGE CONTROL was crucial. Doug knew it was only a matter of time before the news leaked out about his story of visiting with Hank Kaplowski at his cabin. The last thing he needed was panic in his campaign committee. Without mentioning the reason, Doug asked that an emergency meeting be held in his corporate offices in southern California, thinking it best that his legal counsel be present and that he be far removed from Durango County's sheriff.

"Bulldog" Moore seemed to accept Doug's explanation for being at the mine with Kaplowski and allowed him to delay the deposition request until another day. The excuse of ill health and a vicious schedule appeared to temporarily placate the law officer. Doug had to figure out a way to avoid meeting with Sheriff Moore; if anyone could sniff him out, it would be the "Bulldog."

So far, providence had shined down upon him, encountering no soul who could expose his political Jekyll and Hyde—or was it

Hyde and Hyde—identity? The reporter in Diamond Springs "knew him from somewhere." Although Doug had hayseeded his way out of that encounter, he knew he might not be so lucky if there were a next time. He was confident that he had left nothing behind which could connect him to Hank's disappearance. *How then, did Sheriff Moore know about me being there? Did someone see my plane take off? That must be it . . . a witness.* Fortunately, he thought fast enough to come up with a plausible excuse. Doug couldn't deny it; someone had to have heard his powerful, noisy Centurion, seen him circling low over the mine. Whatever the case, he was observed. *And the law knows about it.*

★ ★ ★

ALL INVITED PRINCIPALS showed up as requested for the meeting at his Los Angeles offices. The entire executive staff, management, Assemblyman Kaloogian and the new Republican nominee for lieutenant governor—Senator Marcia Conley. Doug thought it wiser to include Marcia than continue to leave her outside the loop. The former senate minority leader hadn't been too cooperative during the primary; in fact, she had been a royal pain in the keester.

Rumor had it, she was still miffed over not being selected by the powers that be for the governor's slot, especially when the kitchen cabinet and the remaining Republican leadership deserted her for Stewart.

Doug felt Marcia was smart enough to understand they needed each other, particularly now that the primary was over. It was obvious they'd both benefit by running as a team. After discussing it with his management people, the consensus was to bring her in and ask her opinion when making major decisions. Kaloogian was the lone dissenter, saying in a sing-song voice, "You'll be s-o-r-r-y!"

By and large, the meeting went as planned. Everyone agreed that Doug making contact with the Democrat's candidate wasn't a bad idea. In retrospect, they'd have preferred that he not have acted on impulse but checked with them before visiting with Kaplowski, especially considering the tragedy that happened shortly after he left. Leif Anderson remarked that Doug's visit to Kaplowski, without telling anyone, looked peculiar.

Marcia Conley's eyes lit up at his comment, and in saccharine tones she asked, "Doug, when you heard about the accident, did you call the authorities to tell them you had recently been there with Kaplowski?"

"No, Marcia, I didn't. Frankly, I knew the media would find out and possibly construe it in a different light. No one knew we had met, and I felt no logical or moral obligation to report it. Obviously, someone saw my plane or maybe Kaplowski mentioned it to somebody. No matter; the press will probably find out soon enough, and I wanted you to hear it first from me."

"Sticky business," offered Anderson. "Specifically, since the authorities think it might be suicide."

"Well, we'll weather the storm," piped in Carlos Saracino. "Doug hasn't committed any crime by talking to his opponent. In fact, we can put a positive spin on it by telling the press Doug found him very depressed and tried to cheer him up."

"Who'd believe that?" gagged Kaloogian. "Mickey Mouse?"

"Well then, how about—"

Doug interrupted them both. "We're going to play it straight. I was there; we talked, and I left. Since what we discussed is no longer germane, there's no need to go into detail. I doubt if the media would believe it anyway."

"Doug's right." John Rogers spoke up. "Until the body is recovered or, at least, he is officially pronounced dead, Doug's better off saying as little as possible to anybody."

"That's true. Taking the advice of my counsel, I'm going to hole up for awhile, take a little vacation, try to relax, and forget all about this mess."

"Where will you be going, Doug?" inquired Marcia.

"Fishing, Marcia . . . fishing."

★ ★ ★

UNABLE TO CONTAIN HER GLEE, Marcia Conley kicked off her high heels, sending them flying against the wall. "I've got him! At last, I know how to fix that rich, egotistical cur!" She began pacing excitedly about her office. *Who shall I leak this to? Of course, the San Francisco papers; they hate his guts as much as I do.*

There was little doubt in Marcia's mind that, given the chance, she could beat any of the Democrats running for governor. But her golden opportunity was snatched away by Doug Stewart. Years of planning went out the window. If Stewart won in November, she would be relegated to the "nothing" office of lieutenant governor, having to wait too many years to make another try. If Doug was seriously implicated in the death of Kaplowski, he'd surely be forced to give up the race. *And, without a doubt, I would be the obvious choice to replace him.*

It was a win-win situation if Doug Stewart were out of the picture, either by defeat or by indictment. Up until today, she was faced with a dreary political future, all lose-lose. But now, with this juicy new morsel of political dirt to savor, the opportunity to be the first woman governor of California was once more a reality.

Lighting a cigarette and taking a deep drag, she slowly exhaled, fully enjoying the delicious thoughts cruising through her devious political brain. *Did Stewart really go to Mexico to fish? Looks to me like he's fled the country. I've gotta make sure.*

Picking up the phone, she dialed her secretary and asked her to get Doug's Sacramento office on the line. "Hello, this is Senator Marcia Conley. Doug gave me his phone number in Baja, but somehow I've misplaced it. Could you give it to me please? Thank you, I'll wait." Moments later, the young secretary came back on the line with the number. "Thanks again—in fact, thank you very much."

Marcia knew Doug couldn't possibly have arrived in Cabo San Lucas already . . . all the better. She was right; the phone was answered by a woman who couldn't speak English. "Bueno?"

Senator Conley had prepared well for the day when she would run for governor by conscientiously learning to converse in Spanish, the language of so many former Mexican citizens now living in California.

"Soy Senator Conley, un amigo del Señor Stewart. ¿Quién habla?" Marcia asked.

"Señora Lopez a su servicio; soy la cosinera."

"¿Señora Lopez, ha llegado el Señor Stewart?"

"No, Señora, no esperamos que llegara hasta la tarde."

"¿Hablo para decir que hiba llegar cómo a las seis y media?"

"Si, Señora, cómo a las seis y media."

"Bueno, no es muy importante, so a la mejor le hablo al rato. Muchas gracias."

Marcia hung up with a look of absolute satisfaction in her eyes. *So, he's going to be there for sure — expected by late afternoon.* A sardonic grin crossed her face as she unctuously lamented, "Imagine that . . . the Republican candidate for governor has fled the country, secretly absconding to Mexico to escape the investigation into the disappearance of the Democrat's choice for guv. My, my!"

Once more, she dialed her secretary and asked her to get two specific Bay Area reporters on the phone.

★　★　★

DUE TO THE SENSITIVE nature of the investigation and its political implications, the Justice Department took every precaution in making sure no stone was left unturned in their quest for the truth. Their job was complicated by the large number of people involved in the excavation project, not to mention the abundance of media personnel. Identifying all the fingerprints collected was next to impossible, since there had been so many bodies milling about the area. However, when looking for a specific set of prints, the search narrowed significantly.

The investigators gained easy access to Doug Stewart's prints, which were discovered in several places; two of them were incriminating. One thumb print was found on the cardboard sign alerting visitors to stay out of the mine. The other was lifted from a label marking a half-empty box of dynamite, located in the tool shed. Additionally, the lettering on the sign closely resembled handwritten printed memos attributable to Doug Stewart, memos taken from his assembly office. The evidence was mounting that foul play had occurred and it led indirectly to Doug Stewart.

Sheriff Moore found himself between a rock and a hard place. Swearing out a warrant for the arrest of such a prestigious and highly reputable citizen was difficult, especially when all the evidence was still circumstantial. On the other hand, he agreed with Jamie that the Hank Kaplowski they knew personally wouldn't have killed himself; nor was he the sort to run away. Why should he? It didn't make sense.

Hank had risen to a position of major importance as the nominee of his political party, duly chosen by the Democrats from the great Golden State. He was popular—a highly thought of county supervisor—and he certainly had a slew of friends and admirers. What possible reason could he have to give up so much? Clearly, foul play couldn't be ruled out.

Fact was, Doug Stewart did make a veiled threat on TV on election night. Maybe they fought and Hank was killed in the tussle. In order to hide his crime, Stewart could have dumped Hank's body deep into the mine and blown it up, then covered his tracks by tacking up the warning sign. Naturally, he wouldn't expect someone to hear his plane leave and jot down the I.D. number.

But, then again, a small county sheriff couldn't be too careful. Just recently, his department had applied for a state grant, hoping to get funds for a helicopter. He could really keep the pothead marijuana gardeners under control with such equipment. Make a dumb move to arrest a popular assemblyman—possibly the next governor—and the grant would go up in smoke.

The following morning, the issue was taken out of Norm Moore's hands by the featured story in the *San Francisco Times,* amid the pack of reporters outside his front office and Jamie Hagerty pounding on his private door. It was time to fish or cut bait . . . and perhaps, kiss that helicopter good-bye.

THIRTY

★ ★ ★

THE LOOK ON JAMIE'S FACE was one of raw satisfaction, when finally, the sheriff was galvanized into action. With all the information now in his possession, Sheriff Moore approached the Superior Court for the necessary papers to arrest Douglas Stewart. In spite of the suspicion-of-murder charge, Norm had still been hesitant to make such a bold move, but he had no other choice when the media announced that Stewart had fled the country. The local citizens were incensed, instigated into a "let's hang 'em" mood by the Hagertys and Supervisor Kaplowski's Durango friends and supporters.

California's Democrat central committee and the governor were even petitioning the U.S. President to immediately start extradition proceedings. Since Stewart had beat a retreat from American soil, they also demanded that the FBI and the CIA be brought into the case and were clamoring for him to be listed among the nation's "Ten Most Wanted."

Headlines in Los Angeles blared, "Stewart Accused of Murder!" In the Bay Area, "Republican Deep-Sixes Democrat Foe?" In Fresno, the news was worthy enough to replace the projected grape harvest report on the front page.

Liberal columnists called for the Republicans to promptly denounce their nominee and suggested their central committee select another candidate. Sensationalist publications "discovered" witnesses who actually saw Doug Stewart bludgeon Hank Kaplowski to death.

A world-famous medium visited the explosion site and following a prolonged trance, several vigorous trembles, and a short swoon for the cameras, pointed to a specific spot on the mountain and pronounced, "He's buried there — six-hundred-eighty feet straight down."

Four University of California professors of psychiatry, two ACLU lawyers, and a Republican housewife were interviewed on the Renaldo Gueverra talk show. The professors concluded that Stewart was guilty, based upon his verbal manifestations on election night, reflecting repressed inhibitions over being a rich Republican. The ACLU lawyers decided the circumstantial evidence was sufficient to ask for the death penalty, even though they personally were opposed to it.

The Republican housewife didn't say much but offered the opinion that she would like to wait until a jury had heard all the evidence. Her comment invoked disdain from the other panelists, such as, "What do you need, a videotape of the bloody murder to be convinced?"

As the statewide chairman of the Stewart for Governor campaign, Assemblyman Harry Kaloogian tried to calm the troubled waters by widely distributing a press release stating Doug's innocence of any wrongdoing. "Assemblyman Stewart is taking a brief vacation at his beach home in Baja. He is deep-sea fishing for marlin off the coast of Mexico, and cannot presently be reached. We expect to hear from him within the next two days. Anyone wishing further information may contact his legal counsel in Los Angeles."

Instead of calming the waters, Kaloogian's statement did the opposite. "Aha!" screamed the Democrats, almost in unison. "It's true! He's fled the country! If we must go through his lawyer, he's got to have something to hide."

Sheriff Moore's press conference added more fuel to the fire, especially when he let it slip that forensic experts had uncovered further evidence. When the reporters pounced on this vital tidbit,

Norm Moore refused to reveal more information, opening the door for wild speculation.

The television cameras singled out Jamie as the most attractive and vocal person to interview. Her remarks were incendiary, intimating personal knowledge of facts that Sheriff Moore would not divulge. "I find it impossible to believe that Hank had anything in common with that swine, Stewart. They are, or should I say *were*, complete opposites."

Jamie wiped a tear from the corner of her eye, cleared her throat, and with difficulty, continued. "Stewart is a high-falutin' city slicker . . . personified! Hank, on the other hand, was wholesome, down-to-earth, and not afraid of hard work."

"Ms. Hagerty," asked a sympathetic newscaster, "do you think they may have gotten physical—you know, had a fight. Then Stewart dynamited the mine to cover his crime?"

"No, I do not," emphatically stated Jamie. "Hank was a man's man, taller and more muscular than Stewart. That pompous wimp couldn't have bested Hank unless he struck him from behind."

"You don't think . . . "

"Yes, I do," interrupted Jamie. "That underhanded snake has a reputation of playing dirty politics. Who knows how far he'd go to get what he wants; what's the killing of an honest, decent man . . . to him?" She couldn't finish, breaking down in an avalanche of tears.

Exhibiting deep respect, the interviewer turned to the camera and with compassion said, "I guess that says it all. . . . Back to our newsroom."

★ ★ ★

As the yacht rocked gently with the ocean rolls, Doug lay stretched out on the deck, soaking in the warm sun. Fishing had been more than satisfying, after having hooked up a number of times to large marlin. He brought them fighting into the boat, only to quickly release them back into the sea. He and the crew were taking their time returning to San Lucas, following along close to the shore. The day was hot. Doug chose to take it easy and do some skin diving in a small bay that had always been one of his favorite spots, where the water was crystal-clear and the underwater rocks held a wealth of marine life.

Thoroughly relaxed by balmy breezes and the warm saltwater, he was now enjoying a cool drink, a fistful of tortilla chips, and a generous portion of jalapeño sauce. Doug watched his Mexican hands keeping time to the music blaring from a small portable radio.

Suddenly, they were speaking excitedly to each other, casting inquisitive glances in Doug's direction. After a bit, one cautiously approached with a sheepish grin on his face. "Why don't you tell us, Señor, that you keel hem and we are running away?"

Doug raised up on one elbow, "¿Por que? What?"

"El radio say Señor had a fight and keeled some hombre with a machete. They say thee Yankee federales are looking for you, Señor. ¿Es verdad?"

Doug quickly got to his feet, sending the chips flying and spilling bright red salsa all over the deck. Angry over his clumsiness and curious as to why his problem was big enough to make it all the way to a local Mexican station, he apologized for the mess and answered his deck hand. "No, it's not true; I haven't killed anybody." Brushing himself off, Doug called to his captain, "Manuel, get me La Paz on the radio and you better crank up the diesels; we may have to go back to base, pronto."

At dusk, they pulled into the private slip and while the hands secured the vessel, Doug hurried up the path to the beach house. Señora Lopez, his housekeeper, met him at the door, fretfully wringing her hands. She told him the federales had come by looking for him. She was instructed by the authorities to keep her mouth shut and call them if he returned. He thought about phoning them, being acquainted with Angel Paredes, the chief of the local federales. But first, he had to find out what was going on in the States before he spoke with anyone.

It took Doug three calls and a few harsh words with one officious secretary before he got his lawyer on the line. "John, what the blazes is going on?"

"Oh, Doug, thank God you called! Pandemonium is breaking loose up here." Then, in a manner unlike his customary unruffled demeanor, John Rogers told a disjointed story of utter chaos. "Doug, you know I'm a corporate attorney; I'm over my head. You're going to have to hire an experienced criminal attorney. This just isn't my thing. Civil cases are my strong suit, not defending people charged with murder."

John's voice began to rise as he got more agitated, "From what I can tell, they've come up with more evidence, seriously incriminating you. What's more, there's a warrant out for your arrest, uh, for the slaying of Hank Kaplowski. The press says you've skipped out, fled the country, and the governor has demanded speedy extradition proceedings. Compadre, you're in hot soup!"

Doug didn't immediately reply.

The silence was too much for John, so he yelled, "Doug? Do you hear me? Are you there?"

"I hear you, John. I'm just thinking."

"Well, you better think long and hard about getting the best criminal counselor money can buy. My advice is to come back to the States as soon as possible. Your being in Mexico makes you look terribly guilty."

"That bad?"

"Yes, good friend . . . that bad."

Doug dialed another number, getting through right away.

"Harry, this is Doug."

"Doug who?"

Doug had to laugh. Kaloogian never missed an opportunity to lighten things up, as he added, "Gotcha, huh? Hey, Stewart, I've been hoping you'd call."

"Harry, I've only been gone four days. How could it have gotten so terrible so fast?"

"Well, my felonious friend, the very day after you left, the you-know-what hit the proverbial fan. The only explanation is that someone close to us spilled their guts."

"Any idea who it was?" asked Doug.

"The papers offered no names; they just used the old 'reliable source' routine. I have a sneaking hunch it was Marcia."

"Marcia Conley?"

"None other. She's already dropping hints that you should do the noble thing and resign. In tones of humble servitude, she has coyly suggested that she'd be willing to take over the burden of running in your place; that is, of course, if the party so desires. Marcia's more liberal Republican cohorts are calling for an emergency session of our central committee to discuss alternatives . . . whatever that means."

"Think they'll call for my resignation as party nominee?"

"They might. In fact, they will for sure if things get any hotter. That sheriff added fuel to the fire when he got the warrant for your arrest." Harry's voice grew somber. "Doug, what are you going to do? You have to come back and get this mess straightened out."

"Yes, I hear you. John Rogers gave me the same advice, but I'm not about to spend time in prison for something I didn't do. Let me think about it. I'll let you know soon."

"Okay, I'll hold off the heathens as long as I can, but don't count on it getting any better without you being here."

"Good-bye, Harry. I'll keep in touch."

"Yeah, do that."

Doug hung up the phone. He needed time to think, time to sort through his options. He thought about turning tail and making a run for it, but that would merely confirm that he was a murderer and a fugitive. He could go back to Durango County and confess all, thereby making a royal fool out of himself, his party, and his family. He could wait it out in Baja, but in time he would only be extradited and probably held for awhile in a rotten Mexican jail.

Doug could always fly to Costa Rica, catch an airline to Brazil, then on to South Africa or Europe. He had sufficient funds in Switzerland to live out the rest of his life in exile—and that meant enough wealth to hire the legal eagles to fight extradition, maybe even get the case dismissed.

As Doug considered each alternative, his remorse grew and a deep sense of loss enveloped him. Every element of this messed-up situation stemmed from telling a few little white lies. Doug wondered how many little white lies it took to make a big black one. "Only one," he muttered. "My clever little fibs have multiplied into major trouble." They started out small, seeming petty and insignificant, but grew unrestricted into whoppers.

Doug remembered feeling no guilt about using the name of Hank Kaplowski when he bought the Lucky Adele Mine. He perpetuated another lie when he allowed the Kaplowski name to be registered as a Democrat, then continued the lie by not having the name expunged from voter rolls. *This miserable dilemma began when I covered for Nadine and left my name on the Republican ballot. I was an irresponsible idiot for not putting a stop to it right at the beginning. In retrospect, I should have known she was up to something.*

When Doug told the sheriff that he had visited with Kaplowski, he'd concocted a story so full of holes one could drive a loaded logging truck through it, with room to spare. Thinking about it, the list of his prevarications seemed endless, and he had to admit, *Doug Stewart, you are a liar. You've stepped on, run over, and brutalized the truth. You've ignored God's law, in particular—"Thou shalt not bear false witness," one of His Ten Commandments. No wonder you're in such deep trouble.*

Guide me, Lord—what should I do? There was no question about it; Doug needed to clean the slate, pray for forgiveness, and get on with the truth. With a sigh of relief, a smile lit up Doug's features. *No more lies, not one. As it says in Scripture, the truth will set me free.*

Doug dialed one more phone number. The woman answered, "Durango County Sheriff's Office."

"This is Assemblyman Doug Stewart. May I speak to the sheriff?"

He could hear her calling to someone, "Hey, Charlie, there's another nut on the phone, claiming to be Stewart. Wanta handle it?"

A youthful-sounding voice came on the wire. "Hello, this is Deputy Peterson. Sheriff Moore is busy right now. What can I do for ya?"

"Deputy, this is Assemblyman Stewart calling from Mexico, not some demented wacko looking for kicks. Get 'Bulldog' Moore on the phone, will you please?"

"How do I know yer really Stewart?"

"I'll tell you how. Mess up this call and you'll know for sure the next time you don't get your merit pay raise. Now, Deputy, get me the sheriff." There was a prolonged silence as the young man contemplated the message.

Then, in a voice commanding respect, Doug stated, "I'll say it once more, Deputy, get me Norm Moore."

"He's not here right now, sir. He stepped out for a bite to eat. Can I be of any help, sir?"

"Yes, you can. Tell your boss that I will turn myself in the day after tomorrow. I'll fly into the Placerville Airport around two in the afternoon and surrender to the proper authorities. Tell the sheriff to be there, even with the press, if he wants. Understand?"

"Yeah, I gotcha—two o'clock Wednesday," answered the excited officer.

"If the sheriff wants confirmation, he can call Assemblyman Kaloogian or my attorney, John Rogers. Got that?"

"Yeah, you bet! Check with Roger Kalwogian." Deputy Peterson's voice cracked nervously, having raised at least an octave during the conversation.

"Close enough," replied Doug, as he hung up.

"Señor Stewart?" Rosita Lopez stood in the doorway, again wringing her hands and casting furtive glances over her shoulder.

"What is it, Rosita?"

She continued to look toward the room behind her, as she spoke. "The federales are at the front door. They want to talk to you."

"Stall them, Rosita. Ask them to wait; tell them I'm in the shower . . . tell them *anything* . . . but give me a few minutes."

Doug raced to the bathroom and turned the water on full force, then dashed to the closet for his jacket and pants, quickly pulling them on over his swimming trunks. Checking his wallet for cash, he grabbed his flight case and headed out the back way, grumbling to himself, "This is no time to be penned up in a Mexican calaboose."

The fast jog up to the private airstrip on the plateau above and behind his beach house was only a short distance . . . but exhausting and nerve-racking. As he approached the solid corrugated-steel structure housing the valuable Centurion, Doug suddenly stopped to ask . . . *Did the federales think about placing a guard at the hangar? Better find out.*

Stealthily circling the hangar, he peeked around the corner, relieved that no one was in sight. He fumbled fruitlessly through his pockets for the keys to both the plane and the padlock, before remembering where they were—on top of his dresser. *Rats! Gotta go back.* Doug hurriedly retraced his steps, entered through the back door, and slipped down the darkened hallway to his bedroom.

Doug could hear the police talking in the kitchen and was grateful to Rosita for having invited them in. She was offering them refreshments. Their conversation sounded relaxed as they joked with her—that is, all except one. "Señora, does he always take this long to bathe?"

"Sí. Señor Stewart is one very clean gringo."

They all laughed.

Good for you, Rosita! Quick thinking. Doug swiftly retrieved his keys from the top of the dresser and, once more, escaped out the back exit, this time knocking a broom clattering to the stone patio. Doug froze, then listened for a brief moment. Sensing no change in the chatter from the kitchen, he moved to the path and rushed up the slopes to the runway, running as fast as he could in the dark. Doug tried to quietly roll back the large hangar doors, but the screeching cut through the night like fingernails scratching down a blackboard.

Within seconds, angry voices reverberated up the rocky hillside. Confident that starting up the powerful motor would bring them running at a full gallop, Doug yanked open the cockpit door, swung into the left seat, primed the engine, and turned the key. The sturdy Lycoming coughed once, then with a roar that shook the corrugated-steel walls, the three-hundred-ten-horsepower engine surged to life. Doug pushed the throttle forward and exploded from the hangar, hitting the gravel full-bore, leaving a cloud of dust billowing behind.

Doug flipped on the landing lights and firewalled it. With flaps down, 20 percent, he lifted off and pointed the nose skyward. Retracting the landing gear and throttling back from full power to climbing speed, Doug swung the Centurion in a hard left turn, banking back over the beach house. He wanted the federales to see the direction he was heading . . . southeast, over the Sea of Cortez, toward Mexico's mainland.

When out of sight, he lowered the nose into a gentle descent, picking up speed. When barely fifty feet over the water, he slowly banked northward and angled back to the coastline. It was dangerous, flying at such a low altitude, where small rock islands could suddenly loom into view, but necessary to avoid radar surveillance. Maneuvering over and around rocks at close to two hundred miles per hour, though risky, was exhilarating—especially in the dead of night.

The Centurion was topped off with fuel, easily putting Doug within reach of his first destination . . . that is, if Providence would let him survive the night.

THIRTY-ONE

★ ★ ★

THE NATIONAL GUARD F-16 jets didn't pick up his aircraft until
Doug had crossed the high mountain peaks, northwest of Bishop.
The powerful updrafts had pushed the Cessna far above the
Owen's Valley floor, causing the altimeter's indicator to circle like
the second hand on a clock. A thirteen-thousand-foot altitude was
needed to fly through the Sierra passes, an elevation reached with
breathtaking speed.

The jets circled menacingly above as Doug gently banked west-
ward toward Yosemite Valley—a magnificent, massive display of
snow-covered granite cliffs, rugged rock, and windswept pine.
Crossing over Half Dome, a twin-engine 310 Cessna suddenly
appeared alongside, flying wing tip to wing tip. Doug could see the
TV cameraman, holding a zoom-lens Beta Cam, filming his flight.
Then, closer to Placerville's airport, two other aircraft lined up
beside him; a national guard helicopter and a twin-engine Piper
joined the procession.

Doug smiled and waved to his company. *Looks like I'm in for a
humongous reception.* He wasn't mistaken; several other planes
were buzzing about the field, including a Sacramento County
police helicopter. Doug dialed in 122.8 on the transmitter and
called "Placerville Unicom, this is Centurion seven, seven niner
foxtrot. What is your active runway?"

Last year, the first time he attempted to contact Placerville field, no one responded. This time, a strong male voice immediately answered, "Centurion seven, seven niner foxtrot, right-hand pattern, use runway two-three-zero." Then he added, "Mr. Stewart, there's no one else in the approach."

Doug turned downwind and eight hundred feet above the runway, he could easily see that his arrival was a big event. Television mobile unit trucks, groups of onlookers, and police cars were everywhere. The narrow single road leading to the plateau where the small airport was located was jam-packed with cars. Men, women, and kids leaning against the fence were held back by a picket line of national guardsmen. Demonstrators carrying signs and banners milled about, contained by police wearing riot gear.

Doug smartly banked the plane ninety degrees to base leg, then checked to see if his landing gear was down and locked. Banking ninety degrees more, he set up for final approach. Noticing that he was coming in too high and too hot, he methodically throttled back and adjusted the flaps for a steeper, slower descent. The large single-engine craft glided smoothly toward touchdown when, suddenly, several placard-carrying demonstrators ran out onto the runway, directly in its path. Waving their signs, they had obviously misjudged the descent of the heavy plane, assuming it would fly by overhead. Giving the Centurion full-throttle and banking slightly to miss the terrified demonstrators, Doug's heart did double-takes as the propeller and landing gear barely cleared their heads. Fighting for air speed and altitude, the Centurion screamed close over the police posted by the edge of the runway, scattering them in all directions.

Gaining airspeed and control, Doug maneuvered the plane back in the landing pattern and gazed down at the pandemonium below. The demonstrators were being bodily dragged from the runway as the rest of the spectators moved about in general confusion. Doug radioed once more. "Can you keep the runway clear, please? I intend to make another approach."

An agitated voice broke in. "Mr. Stewart, this is Sheriff Moore. Sorry for the mishap; it won't happen again."

Doug smiled, welcoming the sound of Norm Moore's voice. He liked the sheriff a great deal; he was a friendly, affable, decent man. Doug wondered if Norm would see the urbane, well-dressed, bespectacled Douglas Wallace Stewart, or look beneath the hairpiece and glasses to see his good friend, Hank Kaplowski.

Over the past year, Doug had found it necessary to carry two suitcases in the plane—one filled with a wardrobe befitting a rich state legislator, the other containing the mining garb of Kaplowski. Never knowing which he might have to use, he decided it would be most practical to be prepared for any situation. But now, the bag containing Hank's clothing was no longer in the plane, dumped unceremoniously while he was still in Mexico.

He taxied the Cessna to the area designated for transit aircraft and killed the engine. Before the propeller stopped rotating, police were at both doors. Doug unstrapped his seat belt and motioned for the officers to back away so he could get out. Swinging his long legs out, he hopped to the ground, adjusted his horn-rimmed glasses, then faced the window of the plane. In its reflection, he straightened his tie. Turning back to the officers, he grinned while camera flashbulbs popped away. "Do you do this for *all* the pilots who land in Placerville?"

★ ★ ★

NORM MOORE DIDN'T recognize him. In fact, he seemed slightly intimidated by the Stewart image. "Bulldog" Moore was downright apologetic, and appeared chagrined over having to arrest such an important person. Doug wisely hadn't opened his mouth since his initial caustic question after alighting from the plane. It had been previously arranged that his lawyer, John Rogers, would do all the talking to the law, while Assemblyman Kaloogian would handle the press on his behalf.

Both emphasized that it was all a major misunderstanding. Assemblyman Kaloogian called it, "A travesty of justice," and John Rogers declared, "This is the unwarranted arrest of an innocent man."

Jamie Hagerty had a different opinion. Standing under a banner calling for a speedy trial and a conviction, she argued that the Stewart trial must be held in Durango County and that no change of venue should be granted. "If held in any other place, Stewart will buy his way to freedom—especially in Los Angeles County." The redheaded Hagerty was particularly colorful when she declared, "The crime was committed here. The trial should be held here, before a jury selected from here!" Then, as an afterthought, she added, "The execution should be handled here as well. We've got plenty of rope and lots of big oak trees."

The press loved it. Someone handed her a coil of twisted hemp to hold as the TV crews interviewed her, beside the "Welcome to Hangtown" sign, noting Placerville's moniker during the gold rush of the rugged 1800's.

Summarily, Doug was moved through the incarceration process, fingerprinted, given the county's jail outfit to wear, and placed in a separate room apart from the cells containing the other inmates. Doug hated having to strip down and change clothes; removing his expensive garb made him feel naked. Stripped of his urbane camouflage, he felt infinitely more vulnerable. Fortunately, he hadn't come in contact with anyone who might readily recognize him as Hank Kaplowski. Sheriff Moore, the most obvious, was kept busy with the media. Now that he had apprehended the nation's most sought-after fugitive, the sheriff was in great demand.

Stewart's attorney, John Rogers, was the first to visit Doug in the small room provided for Durango County's most illustrious prisoner. Looking around the old dilapidated cell, the lawyer was decidedly disgusted. "Doug, I'm sorry I couldn't arrange to keep you out of here. The county district attorney had a fit when I asked the judge to grant you bail. Only one judge in this flea-bitten Cow County and he didn't have the guts to release you 'til trial. Seems like he's up for reelection this year and isn't willing to take the heat. Looks like you'll be cooped up in this rattrap for awhile."

Rogers looked glumly at his client, then brightened up. "The good news is, I've contacted three of the most famous criminal attorneys in the land, and all of them are willing to defend you . . . for a price, of course."

"Of course," Doug laughed. "They'll condescend to defend me if I split my fortune evenly among the three of them."

John frowned and looked befuddled, "You don't seem to be taking this very seriously. You know something that I don't?"

"Yes, I do. I didn't, literally, *kill* Kaplowski . . . maybe figuratively . . . but not literally."

"What do you mean by that?" asked the confused counselor.

"Nothing you need to know about right now." Doug stretched out on the cot in the corner, put his hands behind his head, and smiled. "Look, John, if worse comes to worst, you can smuggle me in some dynamite and I'll blow my way out of this antiquated dungeon."

"Stop joking around, Doug. This is serious business. You will probably be in this cell throughout the trial. At least, they've quartered you apart from the other prisoners, most of whom are being incarcerated in the holding tank. It's one miserable community cell where all inmates suffer together. From what I gather, this room is normally a holding area for runaways and female juvies and, frankly, it's downright luxurious compared to what your fellow inmates must endure."

Doug got up from the bunk and looked around. Indeed, the room was tiny—less than eight-by-twelve feet. Aside from the steel-framed cot, there was only a stained porcelain wash basin and a seatless commode. The scarred gray-green walls bore scratchings of previous residents and some graffiti still remained. On tiptoes, Doug peered out the small, reinforced thick glass window overlooking the street outside. Placard-carrying demonstrators were walking in a large, elongated circle, chanting "Justice for Kaplowski!" Doug's heart quickened for a moment as he saw Jamie in the midst of them, holding a sign, shouting with the rest.

"John, is there any way we can delay their questioning me? I don't want to talk to anyone for the next several days . . . especially the sheriff. After that, I'll tell them anything they want to know."

"Yes, I think I can handle that," replied the worried counselor. "I'll just tell them that you've been advised by your attorneys to say nothing until we've had ample opportunity to confer." Rogers gazed quizzically at his friend and client. "There's a lot you're not telling me . . . isn't there?"

Doug grinned, and said, "Carloads, John, carloads."

Rogers didn't like Doug's response. "Where have you been the last two days? The news reported you escaped the clutches of the Mexican authorities and flew south toward Mexico's mainland. Where did you go from there?"

While still standing tall to see out the window and watching the milling crowd, he answered, "Arizona. I have some good hunting friends just across the border from Mexico. They have a dirt airstrip on their ranch and I landed there for a couple of days. Marv Glenn and his family run a small cattle operation and do some guiding for hunters in the fall and winter. It's a terrific place for mountain lion and trophy Coes deer. I figured no one would look for me there, so I stayed with them until it was time to fly north."

Turning his attention away from the window, Doug continued, "The Glenn folks are grand people and fantastic hunting guides. They're pretty isolated—tucked back in the hills, east of Douglas. They knew nothing about what was happening to me. I left it that way."

"Well, ol' friend," Rogers caustically countered, "if you expect me to be a part of the team to defend you, I'll have to know everything, sometime before the trial."

"In a couple of days, John, if need be . . . in a couple of days." Doug looked out the window again. The demonstrators were breaking up, moving away down the sidewalk until only one remained. She just stood there, facing the building, defiant, grim-faced, unyielding in her posture, with fiery red hair blowing in the wind.

★   ★   ★

IT HAD BEEN A BUSY NIGHT around the Durango jailhouse. Extra law enforcement had to be brought in to quell the disturbances cropping up all over the county. Three inebriated Kaplowski admirers, having downed too many suds at a local bar, were having a rip-roaring good time trying to organize a lynch party for the purpose of storming the jail. Caught up in the spirit of the moment, a number of Mount Aukum's locals joined in the fun. When one hollered, "I got some rope!" everyone cheered. The jovial raucousness was reported to the sheriff by an unduly excited bar patron.

Sheriff Moore overreacted . . . big-time.

Calling for additional law-enforcement help from the surrounding counties, his precipitous action didn't escape the attention of the media. Special bulletins flashed on the tube, interrupting regular TV programming. "Lynch mobs mobilizing to storm jail in Diamond Springs!" Adding fuel to the fire, it was broadcast that mobile camera units were being rushed to the scene. Upon hearing the news, saloon rowdies from miles around traveled to Diamond Springs to get in on the fun. Within hours, a milling, beer-drinking crowd filled the streets where the frivolous jocularity of three drunks had turned into a national media event.

Fights broke out. One cameraman and two commentators were decked and a mobile unit was overturned and set afire. For several hours, pandemonium reigned . . . to the curiosity and consternation of the national TV audience. By one o'clock in the morning, the Durango jail's holding tank was crammed full and, by two o'clock, the overflow was being trucked to adjoining county facilities. At three o'clock, it was all over. The bars had closed, the media had left, and the man with the rope had gone home. Only then did Doug Stewart find enough peace and quiet to drift off to sleep.

★ ★ ★

"GET A GOOD NIGHT'S REST?" asked a cheerful deputy. He placed the breakfast tray on the corner of the cot, as another officer stood watch by the door. Doug nodded, with a smile. He'd been awake for more than an hour, had already brushed his teeth and washed his face over the small sink in the corner of the cell, and was now lazing back on the bunk.

"We sure had a lot of action around here last night. Seemed like a John Wayne movie, ya know, where the good sheriff saves the villain from the lynch mob." Then, reflecting on what he had just said, he stammered, "Uh . . . no offense intended."

Doug grinned. "No offense taken." He sat up, placed the tray in his lap and tasted the fare of scrambled eggs, greasy potatoes, and dry toast. He was hungry, which moderated somewhat the unappetizing cold eggs and burnt, stale, sourdough bread.

"Eat and enjoy," joked the young officer. "After awhile, we'll be back to take you to the shower, delouse you, and supply ya with a clean set of our special bright orange overalls. Standard procedure around here."

A worried look crossed Doug's face as his mind raced. *Delouse me? Showers? How's my toupee going to hold up under that set of circumstances?* This was a contingency he hadn't planned on. *Being nuder than a jaybird while hot water pounds on my hairpiece? No way!* He couldn't allow that to happen. Hesitatingly, he asked, "Is the shower private?"

"Sure is," guffawed the older officer standing by the door. "Just you and ten other guys. No girls allowed."

Doug paced about the room after they left, deep in thought. *What'll I do? I can't let them bathe me. Not yet. Gotta stall for time . . . but how?* All of a sudden, an idea flashed into his mind. *The door! It's solid metal with just a little peek-through window. Unlike most jail cells where the doors swing outward, this minimum security room has regular doors which open inward. The bunk is metal framed and moveable. Just might work!*

Doug hurriedly ripped off the bedding and pulled the heavy metal bed toward the door. Hoisting it up and standing the bunk on end, he rocked it back and forth until he had it in place. Then, yanking it down, he wedged the cot flush against the door. He ripped strips from the bedding and tied the bottom of the bed frame to the door handle.

Doug figured that by placing minor pressure on the bed, it would be extremely difficult for anyone outside to apply enough weight to enter the room. They'd have to take down the cement wall to get him out. That would take some time—maybe all that Doug needed.

★ ★ ★

TELEVISION VIEWERS WERE tuned in around the state and nation. "Aw, come on out Mr. Stewart. Open the door." The vociferous, frustrated pleading of "Bulldog" Moore could be heard outside the jail.

The camera panned back from the side of the building to the man with the mike. "Since early this morning, California Assemblyman Douglas Stewart, the Republican nominee for governor, has barricaded himself within his cell, defying the local authorities and refusing to come out. Everyone here is at a loss, trying to figure out the reason for his peculiar behavior. We have it on good authority that if Stewart doesn't emerge soon, the authorities will attempt to tear down the walls and take him by force. Back to you, Cleve."

The distinguished gray-haired anchor appeared on the screen. In deep resonant tones dripping with presumed omnipotence, he said, "With our remote unit, we have been able to contact Associate Professor Abdul Nasnab, criminal psychologist from the UCLA campus." The camera lens zoomed in on a poorly dressed, scraggly bearded thirty-year-old. "Professor Nasnab, could you possibly explain to us why Assemblyman Stewart would display such strange behavior?"

"Yes, I believe I can," the professor assured condescendingly, and smirked. "What we are witnessing here is called regressive, repressive-syndrome psychosis, brought on by suppressed guilt formulated during post-natal conditioning by an overly protective nanny. The inevitable result is a maniacal desire to flee a past, reprehensible, anti-humanistic lifestyle."

"What, er . . . is such behavior dangerous?"

"Most certainly. Such actions usually result in attempting suicide or trying to kill again."

"I'm sorry to interrupt our conversation, Professor, but I have just been handed a special bulletin." The distinguished, suave manner evaporated instantly as he excitedly announced, "Well, kiss my wrist! Ladies and gentlemen, Hank Kaplowski has been found . . . and *he's alive!*"

★ ★ ★

JAMIE SAT SHELL-SHOCKED before the television set, waiting with her father to watch a videotaped commentary by Hank Kaplowski. The special bulletin was followed by the news that the taped message had been sent, special delivery, to all the networks and the major print media. "KNBC, Los Angeles, was the first to receive and view this startling message. Our NBC investigators have found that it was filmed at a small TV station in Agua Prieta, Mexico, just south of Douglas, Arizona.

"There appears to be no question that it was made by Hank Kaplowski and there is no doubt that the filming took place within the past week. The station manager finally confirmed that he personally filmed the interview and subsequently reproduced the video you are about to see."

The poorly-lighted picture appeared on the screen, with features blurred but discernible. Jamie could tell immediately by his casual posture and dress that it was her Hank. She let out a small cry and grasped her father's hand as they sat, transfixed, listening to every word.

"Folks, I am not dead. I'm alive and well in Mexico. By the time you receive this video, I'll be long gone to parts unknown. I was hoping y'all would believe I was dead, buried at the bottom of the mine. But that didn't work. When I discovered you were accusing an innocent man of my murder, I had to speak my piece, even though he *is* a Republican.

"First, my name's not Kaplowski. The real Hank Kaplowski was killed in Vietnam. I admired him a great deal and I took his name for reasons I won't disclose. I didn't want to be a county supervisor and I didn't want to be a candidate for governor. I don't like Democrat politics too much because, by and large, I don't like the politicians Democrats elect or the programs they promote.

"I tried not to campaign, but people with axes to grind did too good a job selling me to the voters. So, with a minority of ballots, I won by accident—with no help on my part. I want everyone to know I'm not a criminal. I've committed no crime except parading for awhile under false pretenses. That's no more than a lot of folks do most of the time. I just did it on a grander scale, much to my shame.

"I intend to disappear, so there's no reason to look for me. I can't and won't be found." A sad tone crept into his voice as he was about to close. "There are a few of you I'll miss not seeing again. There's one of you, I'll miss desperately. So long, 'Bright Eyes.'"

Jamie's father held her head to his shoulder and wrapped her shaking, sobbing body in his arms. There was nothing else he could do, no words to stop her crying and soothe her broken heart. Finally, he exclaimed, "Don't worry, honey, we'll find him. I'll spend whatever it takes. Don't fret; we'll find him, for sure."

THIRTY-TWO

★ ★ ★

WITH THE ADVENT OF an inordinately hot summer, raging fires broke out in the hills of Los Angeles, threatening homes and the huge Hollywood sign that symbolized the glitzy city of movie stars. The state's soiled economy took another turn for the worse with major layoffs occurring in the computer and defense industries. To the red-faced embarrassment of the environmentally sensitive, a Greenpeace schooner skipper, high on pot, accidentally rammed into a drilling rig off the coast of Santa Barbara. The oil spill was massive. The environmentalists' response was, "Well, things *do* happen."

Another sensational murder-sex scandal involving several famous cinema personalities occurred in Beverly Hills. These four formidable tragedies created media trauma and became the center of the populous' attention, leaving the missing Hank Kaplowski and temporarily incarcerated Douglas Stewart . . . old news.

The Democrat state central committee convened in San Francisco and selected Governor McKlatchy as their replacement-candidate for governor.

Public sympathy increased immeasurably for Doug Stewart, once he was absolved of the murder. Stewart's lead in the polls became overwhelming. By autumn, the Democrats had done everything but concede defeat; thus, election night was anti-climatic. Exit polls predicted a Stewart landslide, carrying with it a solid Republican majority in both legislative houses.

Surprisingly, the only Republican loss was the lieutenant governor's race. Senator Marcia Conley barely lost to a conservative Democrat, J. Albin Paul, a San Diego businessman who, for all intents and purposes, was abandoned by his party due to his conservative views. J. A. Paul hadn't been given the remotest chance of winning by any of the political pundits.

The majority of the press reported that Conley's loss was a fluke, that the conservative Democrat's victory was considered a political aberration. However, a few astute insiders thought otherwise, especially after watching a flood of negative mail about Marcia Conley appear in the campaign's last two weeks. Well-designed hit-pieces noting wide differences between Stewart and Conley arrived in mailboxes on three successive days before the election. The Democrat, Paul, was shown to be more compatible with Republican Stewart than his own running mate.

The Stewart campaign did nothing to deny it and Conley ignored it, much to her own peril. Much of Paul's financing came from sources in the oil industry, many of them Republican and, coincidentally, several who were clients of Stewart and Associates.

To the shock of many, the newly elected Lieutenant Governor Paul, in a show of bipartisan fervor, promised to work in close cooperation and harmony with Governor Stewart, the new Republican head of state. While the media gave Paul's statement only cursory attention, the liberal Democrats were sullen and the public was pleasantly pleased. To one insider, it was no surprise at all. . . . To Carlos Saracino, it was a matter of organization.

★ ★ ★

GRADY HAGERTY WATCHED as Jamie reached for another chocolate and plopped it into her mouth. She had just finished reading the private investigation report for the second time, and in a sudden display of frustration, she slapped the papers down in her lap.

"No good news?" asked the concerned senior Hagerty.

"Not a thing, Dad. Absolutely nothing we can hang our hats on. Every lead has led us down blind alleys. The investigators are as perplexed as I am."

"How about the fingerprints at the cabin?"

"That," grimaced Jamie, "is the greatest mystery of all. Norm Moore gave me photocopies of all the prints found on the property. There were a total of seven that were unidentified. Our private investigators have contacted everyone who was seen around the mine and the cabin—the TV crews, the excavators, the police . . . everyone.

"Well, after months of work, they finally matched up every print. No unidentified print that could have been Hank's was found. You would think they'd be everywhere around his place—in the mine, at the cabin, but no . . . not one. It makes no sense!"

"I'll say it doesn't! How about his supervisorial office?"

"Clean as a whistle. Hank's secretary is a neatness freak, constantly dusting and polishing. We couldn't find a single discernible fingerprint."

"Bank accounts?"

"He paid everything with cash."

"How about his Bronco and the airplane?"

Jamie sighed. "The old Bronco was purchased in Placerville at a used car lot. Hank paid cash and registered it under the name of Kaplowski. The plane, he kept hangared with the doors locked." Jamie rummaged through the paper wrappings in the near-empty chocolate box, found one remaining almond cluster, and tossed it unceremoniously into her mouth. "I never got a real good look at the plane . . . nor did anyone else."

Grady Hagerty gazed apprehensively upon his despondent daughter. The lapse of time had markedly changed her attitude, behavior, and shape. Gone were the dresses, the makeup, and the sparkle. Back were the faded blue denims, work shirts, and braided hair. The change in her attire and the few extra pounds he could stand, but not the despondency on her pretty face. These days, his

beloved daughter was constantly unhappy. Her normally effervescent personality was becoming a thing of the past, disappearing
with the ghost of Hank Kaplowski.

Grady could see that Jamie's ambitious hope of finding her
loved one was fading into oblivion. Like a knife creating ugly scars
on her portrait of dreams, it cut anew with each piece of bad news.
Grady was beginning to resent the impostor who had disrupted their
lives. That charlatan—that pretender called Hank Kaplowski—had
captured the affections of his only child. Why couldn't he have left
her alone? Why, in his video confession, did he have to end it by
mentioning her?

Hank's parting remark had caused Jamie to hold out a glimmer,
a faint ray of hope, intimating that somehow everything would work
out and they would meet again.

But not Grady. After a year of diligent searching, there was little doubt in his mind that the secret life of Hank Kaplowski was
ominous and dark, filled with criminality, an existence not fit for his
daughter to share. It was time to call off the search—to cut off the
funds and give up chasing the ghost of Hank Kaplowski.

★　★　★

HARRY KALOOGIAN FLOPPED heavily on the soft couch, stretched
his arms wide, and wiggled his behind down into the expensive
leather upholstery. Looking about the governor's private office, he
sighed, "Man, I could get used to this."

Doug laughed heartily. "Maybe someday you will, Harry . . .
give or take a decade or two."

"Nah, Guv, I'll never make it. I have the propensity to open my
yap at the wrong time . . . as I have on numerous occasions. I've left
a trail of quotable quotes that would sink the highest aspirations of
the most noble of politicians . . . namely me, of course."

When the phone on the governor's desk rang, Doug was still
laughing as he picked it up. "Okay, Lorraine, tell them we'll be

there in just a few moments." Turning to his good friend he said, "Well, Harry, it's time we have our first indoctrination meeting with the entire cabinet. They're a good bunch, but greener than grass about how government works. It's time you and I give them their first lesson."

Harry impishly grinned. "So . . . is it time they lost their intellectual virginity?"

"Yep, and better by us than by the bureaucrats."

Regaining their dignity, they opened the double doors to the adjoining chamber and were greeted by polite applause and warm salutations. Doug looked at the eager faces of his cabinet gathered around the spacious, oak-paneled conference room. They were a good lot, far better than he had expected to recruit. It had taken him months to put together a quality cadre of business personnel to run the state government.

Doug had succeeded in convincing many top executives to accept the horrendous jobs as agency heads, leaving behind lucrative private-sector CEO positions in the process. None had held positions in government before and they were eager to help the new governor reverse the downhill direction of the state's bureaucracy. All had agreed that they wanted to help the governor "run government like a business."

Doug knew that the time to bust that balloon was during this first gathering of the cabinet—and it was the reason he'd invited Harry Kaloogian, bubble-buster par excellence. Political experience had taught both of them that government wasn't a business, nor could it even remotely be managed like one. *Government is government . . . a monopoly, police-power, a monolith with its own set of dynamics, rarely subject to the free-market pressures of the business world. What government manages, it manages poorly.*

Doug realized that there were only a few essential services the state could inadequately provide—public protection, roads, water, and disposal of sewage. But beyond that, government spent most of its energy redistributing wealth it didn't earn. Doug had learned the hard way. He said, "We don't run government; we shrink it and keep it small, or it will grow uncontrollably. There are no other choices."

Checking to see that everyone was in attendance, Doug strolled to the head of the long teakwood conference table and asked for everyone's attention. "All right, ladies and gentlemen, time to get down to business."

Everyone sat down.

"For those of you who have never met Assemblyman Harry Kaloogian, I'd like to introduce him. He's the second most powerful member of the assembly, serving as caucus chairman, and is my primary contact with the politics of that body." Doug then watched as Harry circled the table, shaking hands, patting others on the back.

"I have asked Harry to join me in your first indoctrination meeting. Our purpose is to outline the parameters of what I expect from you. We have the momentous job of making major cuts in state government. It won't be easy and we will not be liked . . . but that doesn't matter. We will be here in Sacramento for just four years, but our approximately one thousand four hundred and sixty days will be remembered long after we have gone home."

Turning to Harry, the governor smiled and said, "Mr. Caucus Chairman, tell them about the Death Valley Plan."

"Happy to, Governor." Assuming the air of a professor, Kaloogian began to speak. "Rule number one: Remember, you have no friends in the departments you will manage—only enemies who will kiss up to you. While working diligently to keep their jobs, they will foul up every effort to shrink the department. Your job will be to cut, slash, and trim, and theirs will be to schmooze, survive, and re-bloat."

Eloquently, Harry continued. "By law, you are entitled to appoint a few deputy directors. Make sure that they're junkyard dogs and totally loyal. Select them from outside your agency. The bulk of your staff will be uncivil servants intent on keeping the department intact—individuals who, for all intents and purposes, you cannot fire . . . and they know it."

A hand went up. "How can we cut our departments if we can't let people go?"

Kaloogian responded, "There are two basic ways that can be accomplished. The first is to submit a budget that is substantially less than the previous year's. That will be difficult, but something you must do. Within each of your agencies, the budget will be formulated by career civil servants. We will be bringing in outside help—accounting people—to keep them honest. Hopefully, the new legislature will be tough enough to resist pressure from the public-employee unions and the bleeding-heart media. The second way is to transfer them silly. There's nothing in the laws that prevents this administration from transferring personnel. That's where the Death Valley Plan comes into effect."

Doug chuckled as he interceded with his own thoughts. "We've discovered that the state of California owns land in Death Valley, complete with a sizable number of galvanized Quonset huts already in place. We are in the process of cleaning them up, placing rows of desks in each one, and assigning several of these huts to each department. For instance, some will be used to house the Death Valley Division of the Department of Commerce, while others will be used for the Department of Highways, the Welfare Department, and so forth."

Doug continued, "Should any of you find a worthy recalcitrant bureaucrat in your agency, send him packing to the galvanized sweat spa we've created in the hottest spot in California. It won't take the rest of the bureaucrats long to get the idea."

As the group laughed, one individual offered, "You're kidding, of course."

Both Harry and Doug looked at each other, then took note of the person who made the remark. She would have to be watched.

"Rule number two," continued Kaloogian. "The bureaucracy is in the business of *finding* problems, not solving them. To understand that pearl of wisdom, each of you must grasp what a bureaucrat must do to put food on the table for his kiddies.

"To get ahead, to advance in job opportunities, two things have to happen. Someone above him must retire or die so that he can move up within the system, or the department has to expand, adding new employees below him, thus justifying new management positions. Only through an agency's growth can they rationalize pay raises. That upward monetary movement can't occur by solving problems and eliminating the very reason for the agency's existence. A bureaucracy can only grow by complicating existing problems and finding new ones to attack . . . on our behalf, of course."

Harry banged his fist on the conference table. "Ya'll understand what I'm saying? The bureaucrat justifies his actions by claiming everything is done on behalf of the public good. Thus, to help the public, they must find ways to increase their budgets, hire more employees, and tax the working citizenry. In this manner, the bureau can attack the new difficulties they've just discovered. Do I make my point clear?"

"In other words," stated one of the new cabinet members, "Poppa Bureaucrat can't send junior to Stanford by resolving trouble, but only by inventing or discovering new social inequities."

"You got it," answered Harry. "None of you will find anyone in your department who will admit they're not needed, or essential to the public good. Cut the department and you'll be both perceived and portrayed as a blood-sucking Count Dracula the first moment you try to invoke real change. The liberal press will attack you, and special interests will declare that you are hardhearted and uncaring. Your hallways will be filled with those on the taking end of government, orchestrated to zip around in wheelchairs with forlorn looks upon their faces, bellyaching for their rights to the tax dollar."

Doug looked over the audience, trying to judge their reactions to Harry's pithy comments. Few of them had ever been directly involved in the confrontation they would soon face. Doug knew from experience that competitive business was a cakewalk, a stroll in the park compared to fighting ensconced bureaucrats and their liberal legislative allies. Doug also knew that all of his new cabinet members were extremely competent competitors in the market-place. But . . . he wondered if they could handle the nastiness in store for them in politics. In the following weeks, he would certainly find out.

"Point number three." Kaloogian's expression was still deadly serious, and there was no mistaking that he meant what he was about to say. "You must take pleasure in the pain you will invoke. Understand that you must smile, enjoy, and revel in the incessant complaining you will encounter. If they see any weakness in your resolve, any lack of determination on your parts, they will drive you nuts with their anguished cries and cause you to weaken. If that happens . . . you're out. No hard feelings, but we will get someone to replace you."

The room was silent and the governor got up to speak. "I told you this wouldn't be easy. In your former careers, working harmoniously with your employees was a necessity—the mark of a good employer. Not here. Your job is to downsize a bureaucracy where you can't fire, or hire those you would choose to run the agency.

"You will battle the incumbent bureaucracy daily and, what's more, go face-to-face with the liberal legislators who have created the very bureaucracy you're trying to cut. And many of those lawmakers are still in office. The new Republican majority will be of some help, but most of them aren't used to leadership—at least, not yet. As I've told you before, government isn't a business and you can't run it like one." Glancing over the group once more, Doug asked, "Anyone want out?"

No one moved, but finally, the woman Doug had appointed to head the Health and Welfare Agency sweetly spoke up. "Well, Governor, when do we get our brass knuckles?"

★ ★ ★

"I CAN'T UNDERSTAND what the governor is up to. He's been driving me nuts." Jude Haney, Stewart's appointment secretary, nervously balled up a sheet of paper and threw it toward an overfilled waste-paper basket, missing it completely.

"What's the problem?" asked his assistant.

The harried red-faced executive threw up both his hands in frustration. "I don't know what he wants! I can't seem to deliver. That last list of Democrat women I showed him was a good one; I thought any one would fit the bill. But he just looked at it, quickly scanned the résumés, and curtly said, "This won't do; try again."

"Oh, now I know what you're talking about," claimed his secretary. "He wanted us to dig up some innocuous Cow County female Democrats he could appoint to a few of the agricultural commissions. I assume it's to counter the attacks by the press over our conservative appointments. It's a good idea—a show of bipartisan fervor, you know."

"That's it," Haney said, frowning. "The only problem is, I've run out of the innocuous types. All that's left are some hard-core babes, most of whom hate his Republican guts."

"So go ahead, give the governor some of their names, but warn him that there are some barnburners on the list."

"I haven't the nerve."

"Aw, go ahead. He's not happy with what you've come up with so far. What do you have to lose?"

"My job," moaned Haney. Once more, he went over the file of Democrat résumés. "Here's one he's sure to reject. This broad once tried to get him hung. The only good thing about her is she's not an environmentalist. In fact, she's gone to war against them."

"Put her on the list."

"No way! She was the driving force behind electing Hank Kaplowski. This lady is too much of an activist—nothing but red hair and trouble. It'd be a sorry day if she ever got on one of the governor's commissions."

With a bold stroke of his pen, Haney drew a line through the name of Jamie Hagerty.

THIRTY-THREE

★ ★ ★

SLOWLY AT FIRST, then with increasing speed, California's economy began to turn around. The word was spreading nationally that the anti-business attitude of the Golden State was a thing of the past. Subsequently, new enterprises both large and small started to inquire about setting up shop in California. With knowledge that the state's extreme environmental restrictions were revised and relaxed and the most onerous laws of the regulatory laws repealed, industry began to flood into the state.

Business, income, and personal-property taxes were reduced by the legislature and signed into law. With an invigorated market climate and the proliferation of new jobs, tax revenues soared, allowing public debt to be reduced. Correspondingly, the state's bond ratings improved. California was well on its way to economic recovery.

It wasn't long thereafter that the name, Douglas Stewart, was being circulated about the country as a potential presidential candidate. His picture was featured on the covers of *Business Week*, *Time*, and *Fortune* magazines. Laudatory comments about the governor's superb management of the state administration were commonplace in the national media, especially in the Wall Street publications.

Doug's insistence that he had no further political ambitions fell on deaf ears. No one could believe that such a successful politician would not automatically covet the presidency. Truth be told, scores of people had a vested interest in his political future. His friends, staff personnel, political allies, could already see themselves either laboring in the White House or as weekend guests at Camp David. Even Doug's family added pressure to the cause. Both sons-in-law received job promotions and hints from their employers that they would "deem it an honor" to meet their famous father-in-law. The very fact that "Dad" was perceived as presidential timber was heady stuff for his children, not to mention his close acquaintances.

Doug Stewart continued to ignore the national hype and buried himself in his work, taking little credit for the state's recovery. "I didn't do much of anything, nor did I create one job. All I did was remove barriers to progress. The free market did the rest."

Addressing the prestigious Comstock Club about the state and national economy, Doug attracted full television and press coverage. Since his public addresses were rare and considered to be extremely newsworthy, C-Span, CNN, and NBC were all on hand, prepared to film the entire speech to the packed and attentive group.

Halfway through his address, the governor suddenly hesitated, then faltered. Floundering, he put his hand to his chest and collapsed behind the podium, temporarily shocking the audience into inaction. Finally, three doctors rushed to the dais to attend the crumpled body, while others, regaining their senses, hastily called for an ambulance.

The assemblage milled about in worried, nervous confusion as the sound of sirens signaled the emergency. No sooner had the medics rushed in and placed the oxygen mask on the face of the unconscious body of the governor, than the stretcher was carried quickly from the auditorium into the waiting ambulance. With police escort, the blaring vehicles raced from the scene, leaving the stunned and silent audience filing from the room.

★ ★ ★

BRAD CLARK, NOW THE assembly Speaker, knew that Kaloogian had just returned from visiting Sutter Memorial Hospital where the governor was slowly recuperating. Over the past few years, Clark had developed a great affection and admiration for Doug Stewart— a true friend, a man to be trusted. In the political world where friendships were often a dangerous luxury, he was an exception to the rule, as was Harry Kaloogian, who came close to fitting within that category also. They both felt the same way about Doug and were more than a little anxious over the well-being of their illustrious friend.

Kaloogian showed concern and sadness was in his voice as he replied, "Well, Brad, I guess we should've expected this. Long hours with minimal sleep, no exercise, and a lack of attention to his health has caught up with our good buddy. The doctors say the flu bug bit him badly, laying him low with a high fever and one lung full of pneumonia. He's got tubes sticking out all over him and they've been shooting him full of penicillin."

"That bad, huh?"

"Not good. Believe it or not, I've been worried about Doug's attitude lately. There's not much joy in him. He's definitely not a happy man."

"Really? Aside from his present illness, you'd think he'd be sitting on top of the world. I know a zillion people who would kill to be in his shoes."

"He's not like the rest of us, Brad," solemnly replied the normally jovial legislator. "He's a very private person in a very public world. He doesn't like the job but feels it's his responsibility, like serving in the marines during the war—a tour of duty, so to speak. When this term is up, he'll be gone, out of here . . . that is, if he lives that long."

★ ★ ★

JUDE HANEY NERVOUSLY PACED about his office, chewing on the end of his ballpoint pen. With a desperate look in his eyes, he careened around the door, "Helen, get me all the résumés on file from women who are Democrats from northern California. The governor's requesting to see a new list right away."

"Is he still bedridden at the governor's mansion?"

"Yes, he is, and as mean as a caged cougar . . . so I'm told." Haney dropped heavily into his plush, executive swivel chair, placed his elbows on the desk and his head between his hands, and groaned. "This is such a great-paying job; I wonder what I'll be doing next."

His assistant smiled coyly, speculating whether or not she could step into the juicy position of the governor's appointment secretary, once Haney was let go. Her boss drove her nuts with his incessant whining and complaining; she firmly believed he wasn't qualified to do the work. A great deal of it was dumped in her lap and since she did most of the research anyway, why shouldn't she get the high salary and the credit?

There was no doubt in Helen Kinder's mind that she could more than fill his shoes with ease. *I certainly have the experience and the right contacts. Why not help him along on his way to some new career?*

"I'll make up a list right away." From the file cabinet, she removed all the folders containing the résumés of the Democrats whom she and her boss deemed acceptable for gubernatorial appointments. Then, with a devious afterthought, she reached for the file of unacceptable firebrand Democrats, people summarily rejected and considered too partisan and controversial to be appointed to anything.

"If this doesn't do him in," she gleefully chuckled, "nothing will." Intermingling a few of the controversial résumés in the middle of the stack, she placed them all in a large manila envelope and, for added precaution, she sealed it. Grinning broadly, she handed the packet to her apprehensive superior. "Here, Boss, have a nice day."

★ ★ ★

Much to Helen Kinder's surprise, the appointment secretary was back in the office within two hours. Rushing past her without bothering to say hello, Jude slammed the door to his office, picked up the phone, and made several hurried calls. Looking through the plate glass that separated their offices, she could see that he didn't look too thrilled. "Bet he's looking for new employment," she giggled.

Barely half an hour later, he buzzed her on the intercom. Through the glass, she saw him beckoning, angrily motioning for her to come into his office. There was a strangeness about him, one she hadn't noticed before. She knew she was in for it but felt the gamble was worth it if he got sacked. Haughtily, she entered his office.

"Sit down, Kinder. We have much to talk about. I have pertinent information that will severely affect both of us."

"Wha . . . what do you mean?" she timorously asked.

Jude relaxed and leaned back in his chair, cogitating his reply. "I gave the packet of files to the governor, or I should say, he practically ripped it from my grasp. He wasted no time sorting through the résumés, tossing the rejects on the floor. The guv was still in his bathrobe, looking very pale and sullen; you know, like death warmed over." Jude stopped talking, scowled, then stared long and hard at the uneasy assistant sitting before him.

"Well?" she finally asked.

Jude Haney, clearly agitated, continued the dialogue. "Suddenly, Stewart's eyes got real wide and he seemed pretty excited when he asked me, "What do you think of *this* gal?"'

Leaning forward in his chair, Jude asked between clenched teeth, "Guess whose résumé he forced upon me?"

Helen looked wide-eyed and played dumb. "I don't know . . . who?"

"The devil, you don't!" he shouted. "You salted that bloody packet with some of the most horrendous wenches in the state! I almost fainted when I saw the one he handed me."

"Who was it?"

"Of all people, that red-headed bombshell who led the lynching party . . . Jamie Hagerty!"

Cowering, she asked, "Did he fire you?"

"*Fire* me? He gave me a hug! Danged near lifted me off the floor while smiling ear to ear. He exclaimed that she was just the kind of person he'd been looking for to appoint to the NRC—the Natural Resources Commission. He said Hagerty would fill the bill perfectly since she was a vocal opponent of environmental extremism, yet had impeccable Democrat credentials."

Helen's mouth was agape. "You gotta be kidding!"

"Kidding? Far from it. He told me to contact her immediately and ask her to serve as co-chairperson to the commission!" Haney was bubbling with excitement as he spun around in his swivel chair. Then he stopped abruptly to peer menacingly into Helen's eyes.

"I just got off the phone with her. It took me five minutes to convince her that my call wasn't a joke. With a long explanation and some serious pleading, she finally accepted the appointment. The second call I just made was to the governor, telling him it's a done deal." The appointments secretary beamed. "The guv thanked . . . no, he *heaped praise* upon me and said he was deee-lighted."

"That's weird!"

"What's weird? The praise, or the fact he was delighted?"

"How could he possibly be that happy over appointing a Democrat rabble-rouser like Hagerty?" asked the bewildered assistant.

"I haven't the foggiest . . . nor do I care. I only believe two things. One, my wife and baby will have food on the table for months to come."

Taking note of the devilish glint in her boss' eye, she apprehensively asked, "What's the other?"

"What was the other *what*?"

"You said there were two things you believed for sure."

"Oh, yes. You're right." Jude Haney grinned from ear to ear as he whispered, "Well, would you believe, you're fired?"

★　★　★

THE GOVERNOR'S EXECUTIVE staff had never seen Stewart pay such close attention to a mere gathering of a state commission. Usually, such trivial details were left to the board's employees. Not this time. Even the location of the weekend session was changed to satisfy the chief executive's request. He continued to confuse everyone further when he informed the staff that he planned to attend the second and third days of the meeting.

This was most definitely out of the ordinary. In general, one of the department's deputy directors would be present and sometimes the head of the agency would appear also. Only on the rarest of occasions did the governor show up—and then, only for a cursory moment or two . . . but to stay for two days?

Normally, NRC meetings were held in the capitol, but Governor Stewart became quite philosophical, insisting that the board members should be like "the mountain that goes to Mohammed." He advised they meet the public in the outlying cities and back-country hamlets, mingle with the citizenry, and let them know the Stewart administration "really cares."

There were no arguments when Doug insisted the next NRC session be held in the small city of Eureka, the lumber and fishing center on California's far northern coast. He strongly suggested that the entire entourage stay at the Eureka Inn. His recommendations were immediately approved by the commission board and followed to the letter.

A noticeable change in the governor's attitude was taking place and he was appreciably happier. The perennially dour look was gone and in its place, there was a warm friendliness. To everyone's relief, he was industriously back to work in the capitol, filled

with enthusiasm and vigor, though just a bit edgy. It was obvious
. . . he had something fairly important on his mind.

★ ★ ★

DOUG HAD STAYED IN the Eureka Inn's comfortable presidential
suite many times before when he had fished for steelhead and
salmon with Will Holbrook, his good pal and fishing guide.
Together they had cast many a monofilament line into the great
rivers surrounding Eureka.

The inn suited Doug's plans perfectly. His suite of rooms was on
the top floor, with elevators down the hall and a convenient stairway
leading outside. It wouldn't be too difficult to slip away from his
security late at night. The lounge downstairs had a small dance floor
where, on weekends, a four-piece Western band pounded out cowboy tunes until closing at two in the morning.

He was certain Jamie would show up there sometime late in
the evening and, in all likelihood, alone. She was a real night person who loved Western music and staying up late. Many a night
past, he had to practically drag her from the Tex-Okie Bar and
Bowling so that he could get some sleep. She had a purse full of
pleas and excuses. "Aw, Hank, just one more dance," or "They're
just about to play a medley of Hank Williams hits." She'd try anything to delay the inevitable. Doug smiled as the memory warmed
his insides, filling him with longing.

He had to see Jamie alone, with no one else around, no one
suspecting they'd ever met before. He needed to test her emotional
response, take the risk she wouldn't recognize him right off. And if
she did recognize him, how would she handle it? She had, on more
than one occasion, been testy and said nasty things about Doug
Stewart, calling him the devil incarnate . . . and worse. If she were
vindictive and spiteful, she could undo everything he had accomplished. In a moment, she could destroy him.

Doug was aware of Jamie's tireless search for Hank Kaplowski, evidence that she still cared for him. *But how she'll feel when she discovers that Hank Kaplowski is Doug Stewart was another matter.*

He had taken a big gamble by appointing Jamie to the commission, but he clearly recalled the many times she had griped about the arbitrary pronouncements made by the multitude of environmentalists Governor McKlatchy had placed on the Natural Resources Commission. Jamie's fervent desire was that the commission would someday be more reasonable and tolerant of the lumber and cattle interests.

Doug, once elected, had systematically replaced most of the liberal appointees with people who had "hands on" familiarity with the state's natural resources—cattlemen, farmers, and mining personnel. He knew Jamie would fit in very nicely and that her experience with the problems facing the timber industry would add direction and balance.

Concern over the makeup of the NRC wasn't Doug Stewart's first priority; it was far more personal. He missed Jamie desperately. He had missed her just a little at first. But then, like a rushing river, it dawned on him that life without her was empty, lacking in substance and meaning. Doug was alone. Though his children were devoted to him, they certainly didn't need him any longer. They were personally responsible for their own lives and families to raise. He had no one—nothing but his job and the constant pressures that went along with it. Try as he might, he couldn't erase the memories of his days in the mountains, dancing and laughing, sharing troubles and joy with the red-headed tempest from Durango County.

Jamie's pretty Irish freckled face was constantly appearing in his thoughts, disrupting the course of the state's business, haunting his mind. The reality came slowly but was as dramatic as being hit by a runaway truck. Doug recognized that he was undeniably in love—so much so, that he was willing to take any chance to find

H. L. RICHARDSON

out if she cared as much for him. *Yes, it will be worth the gamble. I have got to know, and there's no better time than tonight.*

★ ★ ★

ONE O'CLOCK IN THE MORNING and no Jamie. Doug had been huddled in a dark corner of the lounge waiting, unhurriedly sipping a drink. He successfully eluded his security detail by taking the side stairs to the first floor, then circling the building to the kitchen entrance. He slipped into the lounge unnoticed. In the murky interior, the waitress didn't seem to recognize him, nor did any of the other patrons sitting nearby. Politics wasn't on their minds . . . or on Doug's.

The music was loud and the lead guitarist was nasally singing, slightly off-key, "Mama, don't let your babies grow up to be cowboys. . . ." Three rhythmically disinterested couples were aimlessly moving abut the dance floor. Friday night was slow, the hotel lounge was half-empty, and a few patrons were already heading for the exit.

Things weren't working out as planned and Doug felt a deep sense of disappointment. *If she were coming, she should be here by now.* At one-thirty, the droopy-eyed waitress asked if he wanted anything else. Doug shook his head, reached into his wallet, and paid the tab.

The band leader called for another short break and subsequently, more customers got up to leave. So did Doug. He headed for the hallway, mumbling to himself, "The best laid plans of mice and governors. . ." Seated near the door were two inebriated men, heatedly arguing over who should pay the bill. As Doug turned his head to view the noisy discussion, he bumped straight into a tall lady entering from the hall.

"Oh, excuse me . . ." There she was, Jamie! Blood rushed to his face and, flustered, he was momentarily dumbstruck—at a loss for words.

310

Her jaw dropped open in awe and embarrassment. "Oh, my, Governor Stewart! I beg your pardon. I should have watched where I was going."

They both stood there, apologizing to each other until Doug asked, "Were you going in?"

"Why . . . yes, I was."

"May I join you? I have a few questions I'd like to ask you."

Jamie nodded, then grinned. "And I have a few for you, Governor. I'm more than curious about why you appointed me to the NRC."

Doug guided her back to the table he had just left, in the dim corner, and they sat down. The winged, high-back leather chair cast a shadow over his face, somewhat hiding his features. Doug thought Jamie looked beautiful and was content to just stare at her and listen quietly as she thanked him for the appointment. Then, as the thought occurred to her, she spoke her piece. "I must be honest with you, Governor—I have a mind of my own and I have a few strong opinions."

"Just a few? I've heard that about you."

"You must know I'm a Democrat."

"I know," Doug admitted, and grinned. "I'd bet you even have a picture of FDR at home, over the fireplace."

Surprised, she laughed delightedly. "How did you know that?"

"My research team is excellent. You'd never believe the things I know about you."

Jamie's Irish curiosity was piqued. Raising an eyebrow, she asked, "Such as?"

"I know, for instance, that you were in love with Hank Kaplowski." He couldn't have shocked her more; his words zapped her like a hot electric wire. A sharp gasp escaped her lips but before she could speak, he added, "And, I know that he was in love with you."

Confused, tears came to her eyes and she started to get up and leave. Doug quickly leaned across the table and grabbed her arm.

Reassuringly, he said, "Please don't go. I'm sorry, I didn't mean to hurt you."

Settling down in the lounge chair once again, she hoarsely whispered, "How did you know about . . . *that?*"

"Hank told me." Doug moved back into the shadows and explained. "When I met with him at the cabin, you were on his mind. He couldn't stop talking about you, said he thought about you all the time . . . couldn't get you out of his dreams."

"He told you all that? The rat! I can't believe it; he never even gave me a glimmer about how he felt!" Jamie fought back the tears and tried to smile. She seemed to be torn between anguish and delight.

"Yep, he told me that and more—acted like a puppy dog in heat," joked Doug. "Actually, he agonized over not knowing whether you loved *him* or not."

"Loved him? I worshipped him," she exploded. "My bones still ache just thinking about him. A lot of good this news does me! He's nowhere to be found. My dad and I have spent almost a hundred thousand dollars looking for that bum. If he truly loved me, he'd have shown up by now."

"Maybe he will . . . if you'll have him."

Jamie sighed deeply. "Anyway I can get him, Governor, anyway I can get him."

"Even if he were a Republican?"

She laughed. "Even that." Shaking her head, she said, "You know, I feel like a heel. For a long time, I thought you were such a bad guy. Matter of fact, I even thought you killed Hank. I hate to admit it . . . but you've been a pretty good governor . . . for a Republican. Our family business is booming, and my dad has gone so far as to say some very nice things about you. And now, this appointment. I want to thank . . ." Suddenly, she sat upright in the chair. "You know where Hank is, don't you?"

"Yes, Jamie, I do."

Overwhelmed with excitement, she sprang forward and reached for his hand. "Where . . ."

The waitress interrupted in a monotone, barely heard over the volume of the music. "We're closin' in ten minutes. What'll ya have, dearie?"

Doug edged forward a bit, out of the shadows, and answered, "The lady will have a Corona with lime. She won't drink anything else . . . and I'll have a Coors Light."

Jamie's green eyes were glued to his face when he said, "How ya doin', 'Bright Eyes'?"

Like a curtain rising, Jamie's eyes opened wide . . . and rolled back in her head. She slumped down in the chair in a dead faint.

"Hey, is she all right?" asked the waitress.

Doug veered sideways to his knees, held Jamie upright, and gently caressed and kissed her tear-stained cheeks. Smiling at the waitress, he assured her, "She's going to be just fine; don't worry a bit. Nothing's wrong with her that a wedding won't fix."

ABOUT THE AUTHOR

★ ★ ★

H. L. RICHARDSON (RET.) is a twenty-two-year veteran of the California State Senate and, although he was born in Indiana, proudly calls the Golden State home. Founder of Gun Owners of California and Gun Owners of America, Richardson has focused his extensive political career on the preservation and protection of our Second Amendment rights.

An active hunter and outdoorsman, Richardson remains involved in state and national politics, and is a popular speaker. He continues to provide colorful media commentary on a host of issues. He has written for numerous national publications, and is the author of two successful humorous political books, *Slightly to the Right* and *What Makes You Think We Read the Bills?* The latter is used as a textbook in political science classes throughout California.

In spite of his significant business, political, and hunting activities, Richardson has deftly combined his love of writing and extensive knowledge of the American West to author a series of Western mysteries for Word—beginning with *The Devil's Eye*.

Richardson and his wife, Barbara, have three children and six grandchildren and reside in the Sacramento area.